TESTED BY TEMPTATION

TRACKING TROUBLE
BOOK 5

LINDSAY BUROKER

ACKNOWLEDGMENTS

Thank you for following along with my Tracking Trouble series. This is the final book in Arwen's and Azerdash's adventures, and I hope you'll enjoy seeing how things come together for them.

Thank you to my editor, Shelley Holloway, my beta readers, Cindy Wilkinson and Sarah Engelke, and my audiobook narrator, Vivienne Leheny. Thank you, as well, to my cover designer G&S Cover Design Studio, LLC.

1

When Arwen arrived at the Coffee Dragon in Fremont, the front door was propped open to take advantage of the warm late-summer morning, and loud voices and raucous laughter wafted out. With her arms full of cookie tins and pie boxes, she braced herself to deal with the crowd.

Boisterous coffee-shop patrons, she reminded herself, were nothing compared to skulking through dark-elven tunnels filled with traps to deal with her kin. Besides, she sensed Val, the Ruin Bringer, and her dragon mate, Lord Zavryd'nokquetal, inside. They would keep trouble from breaking out—and overly friendly shifters from hitting on Arwen.

"You sure this is the place?" her father called through the window from the front seat of his truck. He'd driven her into town but couldn't see the coffee shop, thanks to an illusion that hid it from mundane humans. "All I see is an ice-cream shop and a woo-woo psychic place—and you staring into an alley with your shoulders hunched."

"What you *think* is a wide alley is the coffee shop. And my shoulders aren't hunched. They're at a normal level relative to my ears." Arwen took a deep breath and lowered her shoulders. They probably *were* hunched.

"Then your ears are afflicted with a serious droop."

"Funny, Father."

"As I always aim to be. When do you want me to pick you up?"

"You can run your errands and go home. I should be able to get a ride back."

"From Azerdash?" His eyebrows rose wistfully.

More than once, her father had told Arwen she shouldn't date the powerful half-dragon, especially given all the trouble chasing him, but he also had a row of mechanical equipment lined up in the barn in case Azerdash came by. Father gave Frodo, the tractor that now had a gnomish drivetrain, and the mulcher, now souped up with a magical sentience, loving pats every time he walked by them.

"No, probably from Val," Arwen said. "Azerdash is busy..." *starting a war* were the words that leaped to mind.

She'd already told her father about how Azerdash and his allies were uniting the intelligent beings of the Cosmic Realms to oust the dragons who ruled over their worlds. She *hadn't* told him about the rumors proclaiming that Gemlytha, a half-dark-elven half-dragon comrade that Azerdash cared about, might have been magically resuscitated and that Azerdash was looking for her. And that if he found her... Arwen didn't know. Would he ditch her in favor of the long-time friend he'd wished had been a lover?

She shook her head. "He's away."

Father grunted absently. Unaware of her concerns, he was watching a delivery van run up on a curb as it attempted to park in front of him. He put the truck in reverse to make room. That was a good idea because Arwen sensed a goblin in the driver's seat. A few seconds later, the rear door of the van dropped backward, landing with a *clang* in the street where Father's truck had been.

A lumbering ogre peered out of the back and waved cheerfully at Arwen. The baked goods she sold at the Coffee Dragon on Wednesdays were making her popular with the clientele.

The ogre stepped out carrying a crate that would have been huge for a human but fit easily in his arms. He set it down with a thump on the sidewalk. Black letters on the crate read: Donut-O-Matic, some assembly required.

"Ah," Arwen said. "I think that's for me."

Nin, one of the owners of the shop, had suggested Arwen add deep-fried desserts, including apple fritters, to the offerings she made for the patrons. Arwen had never made donuts for the farmers market—or anywhere else—but she'd found a couple of recipes and was game to try. Though she was spending a lot of time worrying about Azerdash, as well as the repercussions that might come her way for *not* killing Val, as her dark-elven mother had magically programmed her to do... she'd had time lately to harvest and bake. She'd even caught up on all the orders she owed people. For the moment.

One of the goblins ran into the shop, unconcerned by the crowd, including the dragon shape-shifted to human form, shouting, "It's here, it's here!"

Meanwhile, the ogre caressed the side of the crate while smiling toothily at Arwen.

"Human fritters," he said in a heavy accent that suggested he hadn't been a refugee on Earth for that long.

Her father, who *could* see the unloading, and perhaps wondered who the goblin was yelling to in the alley, gaped.

"*Apple* fritters," Arwen corrected the ogre. "They'll be made with delicious heirloom varieties from our farm. The recipes might have been made by humans—with a few tweaks of my own—but there won't be any *human* bits in the fritters."

"*Delicious*," the ogre said without argument as Nin came out the front door.

Arwen didn't know if the ogre had understood her, but it probably didn't matter. She waved to Nin.

"Excellent." Nin's blue-dyed pigtails bounced as she trotted to the crate. "Take it into the kitchen and unbox it, please." She gave the ogre one of the shop's grass-fed-beef sticks for a tip.

The dragon assassin who'd come after Azerdash had sneered at the cellophane-wrapped food—dragons, of course, preferred their meat straight off the bone of their recently slain prey—but the ogre happily accepted it and carried the crate inside.

A couple of Nin's workers also came out, Earth natives with half- or quarter-magical blood, and she waved for them to take the boxes from Arwen's arms. Arwen pointed to more secured in the back of her father's truck. The workers eyed the treats with great interest as they unloaded them. Arwen wondered how many more *tips* Nin would have to provide to sate the staff.

Once the baked items were inside and Arwen's father had driven off, Val stepped out of the shop with her phone in hand. She had probably been talking to Colonel Willard about some new mission, or maybe they were still trying to figure out where the dark elves had gone after the entrances to their tunnels under Mill Creek had disappeared.

Her long blonde braid slung over her shoulder, Val wore her usual jeans, tank top, and duster, and she carried her magical sword in a scabbard on her back, as well as her semi-automatic pistol in a thigh holster. As often as the coffee shop was targeted by bad guys, Val didn't relax, even while sipping a drink and munching a biscotti. Arwen's own bow and quiver were slung across her back. After being attacked by a dragon while delivering pies in Carnation, she'd also learned not to leave her weapons at home.

Val smiled and waved at Arwen, but when her mate strode out behind her, Zavryd clad in a silver-trimmed black elven robe and fluorescent-yellow Crocs that had definitely not been made by elves, he scowled at Arwen.

"*You.*" Zavryd pointed at her.

Surprised, Arwen touched her chest. "Me?"

"Your odious mate has stirred up the entire Cosmic Realms."

"Didn't we decide he's also your relative?" Val asked him. "Created using the genetic material from your uncle Ston?"

"That does not make him less odious, not when he's starting a war, one which I'll soon be called from Earth to participate in. You know I do not fear battle or enforcing the laws of the Cosmic Realms, as is my duty as a Stormforge dragon and the son of the queen, but she has implied that my mate may be expected to join the battle and stand at my side. Even though my mate is a capable warrior for a mongrel half-elf, I worry about her safety. I know she is also conflicted on the matter of who is in the wrong in this brewing confrontation." Apparently finished speaking about Val in the third person, Zavryd turned his squint on her.

Arwen had listened to the words with growing distress. She hadn't guessed that Val would be entangled in Azerdash's war. She'd assumed all the fighting would be done elsewhere, that the dragons, who had no interest in the "vermin-filled wild world" of Earth, would never open a portal here. Why would the queen want Val to join in?

"It's my understanding," Val said dryly, "that your mother wants me to spy on the elves and give you information on troop movements, not stand at your side and battle half-dragons."

"The fighting might come to you if you are involved."

"I suppose that's true. Trouble does like to come to me, no matter where I am."

Arwen stared bleakly at Val. Though Arwen had nothing to do with Azerdash's war efforts, and she hadn't wanted him to get involved to start with, she worried for the first time that they could endanger not only Azerdash but her friends here on Earth. If Val were killed as a spy, what would Arwen do? Val was her friend, one of her *few* friends. And Arwen had been the one to find the legendary galaxy blade that was helping Azerdash rally world leaders to his cause. It would be her fault, at least to some extent.

Zavryd turned his frown down the street toward a black van rolling around a corner and into view. It was armored with magic, but that didn't keep Arwen from sensing the auras of orcs inside. *Many* orcs.

Val groaned. "There's trouble now."

2

THE SIDE OF THE VAN READ: FIONA'S FLOWER DELIVERY. ARWEN HAD been attacked by the orc mercenaries before—multiple times— and couldn't help but wonder if her dark-elven brother, Harlik-van, had hired them again. Since he'd *killed* as many as he'd hired, she wouldn't think these guys would be eager to work for him anymore, but who knew what went through orc brains?

As the van drove closer, Arwen pulled her bow from her back and sprang into the doorway of the Coffee Dragon. Though she now knew how to make a magical barrier around herself, and the shop itself had some interesting defenses, it was a good idea to take additional cover when facing a drive-by shooting.

Val and Zavryd must not have agreed because Val planted herself on the sidewalk and pulled her pistol from her thigh holster, magical ammunition loaded inside. Zavryd folded his arms over his chest, glowered at the van, and formed a barrier around them.

The goblins who'd driven the delivery truck squeaked and hopped inside, the rear door closing with a clang, seemingly of its own accord. Even though their ogre helper hadn't returned, they drove off.

Instead of whizzing by at top speed with rifle-toting orcs leaning out the door, the van rolled up to the coffee shop. It parked where Father's truck had been.

Though she kept her gun raised, Val arched her eyebrows. "Parking isn't their usual MO."

"Maybe they heard about the arrival of the Donut-O-Matic," Arwen said.

"We *do* have orc customers."

"Those feeble miscreants are doubtless cowed by my presence and aware that they would be foolish to enter into a battle with a dragon," Zavryd said. "If they are wise, they will exit their conveyance, make an offering to me, and leave promptly."

"What kind of offering would you want from mercenaries?" Val asked.

"Meat is always acceptable, though orcs lack the human tendency to spice their haunches, which can make a meal more appealing."

"Spices are civilized."

"I also enjoy the addition of bacon, such as you mix into your meat cubes."

"Meat loaves," Val corrected. "And, yes, bacon makes everything taste better." She glanced over her shoulder at Arwen. "Maybe you could add some to the apple fritters."

"I do have a recipe that includes bacon. Bourbon too."

"Hell, that's going to be a hit." Val's gaze shifted back to the orcs, but she added, "Arwen, you should retire from tracking and farming to come work at the Coffee Dragon full time. Your baked goods could make you rich and famous."

"I don't have a desire to be either of those things, and Colonel Willard hired me for my tracking skills."

"A bacon apple fritter might change her mind about how you should be employed. What are they *doing*?"

Three orcs were packed shoulder-to-shoulder in the front seat —as big as the armored brutes were, they had to be half-sitting in each other's laps. As one, they peered out the window at Zavryd and Val. Their tusked faces scrunched up as they glanced dubiously at each other—until one spotted Arwen in the doorway. They pointed at her and whispered eagerly.

Arwen tensed. Nothing good had ever come from a bunch of people looking at her. Worse, her senses promised there were many more orcs in the back of the van. More than she would have thought could squish into that much space.

One of the front-seat orcs made a fist and thumped on the wall dividing the groups. He shouted something in a pleased voice. Because they'd found the prey they'd been hired to waylay?

"Can you understand them?" Val asked Zavryd.

"No dragon would lower himself to study the language of such an inferior species, but their minds are simple to read."

"Uh-huh, so what are they talking about?"

"Your comrade, Tracker Arwen."

"*I* could tell that much without mind-reading." Val opened her mouth to add something, but the van door on the side slid open, revealing all the orcs that Arwen had sensed.

As the front-seat mercs were doing, they peered out as one. They wore chain mail and bone armor, and many had swords or axes strapped to their waists, but none of them held their weapons. That was probably the only reason Val hadn't yet fired.

The orcs poked each other in the shoulders as they whispered amongst themselves, jerking their chins toward Arwen and also Zavryd. One orc finally hopped out—or was he pushed out by his comrades?—and strode toward the coffee shop. He looked familiar, but that might have been because these orcs had attacked Arwen before.

The chosen representative held his empty arms wide and stopped in front of Zavryd and Val, though he looked at Arwen. If not for Zavryd's barrier, he might have walked straight up to her. Appearing nervous, he touched his bluish tongue to one of his tusks before addressing Arwen.

"I am Brok," he said in heavily accented English, "mercenary warrior and former clan leader. That was before our kind were forced to become refugees on this lowly world. We were driven from our homes by the dragon who made himself ruler of our kingdom. He thrust us out, saying our ways made us criminals."

Those were the most words Arwen had heard an orc string together, at least in English. It was possible they were much chattier with each other in their native tongue.

Even though the orc had been speaking more to Arwen than Zavryd, Zavryd lifted his chin and responded. "Those chosen by the Dragon Council to rule over worlds, always in cooperation with the native rulers, are picked for their fairness and ability to keep order. If they considered you criminals, you *are* criminals."

"We are *not* criminals." Indignation flared in Brok's yellow eyes.

Arwen realized where she'd seen him before. In Pine Ridge Park in Edmonds, lying on his back and bleeding under a bunch of ferns. At the time, he'd only spoken in Orcish as he glowered at her and Azerdash.

"Uh." Val raised a finger. "Your mercenaries have shot up the coffee shop, a tattoo parlor, and you've killed a troll tattoo-artist, among who knows how many others. You've *tried* to kill us." She pointed at herself and Arwen.

Brok tilted his head in puzzlement. "Because we are mercenaries and were hired to do so."

"Oh, sure," Val said. "Riddling people with bullets isn't a crime if you're *hired* to do it."

Missing the sarcasm, the orc nodded in agreement before

pointing at Arwen. "We came to see the mate of the half-dragon, Azerdash Starblade. We wish to swear allegiance."

"Arwen isn't—" Val lowered her gun. "Uhm, what?"

"Allegiance to... me?" Arwen asked.

"To Azerdash Starblade. Already, he made me swear allegiance. And now I know why. He amasses a great army. We wish to help him throw the dragons out of our home world, and then we can return."

When he was in human form, Zavryd's growl wasn't that obvious, but it *was* apparent as his violet eyes narrowed.

The tusked orc didn't acknowledge it. He looked wistfully back at his comrades, and they grunted and nodded.

"We are only twenty," Brok said, "but we are fearless."

"I'm sure Azerdash will be honored to have you join him." Arwen *wasn't* sure of that, but Azerdash had asked the orc for allegiance when he'd healed him. At the time, it hadn't seemed to mean anything, but it was possible Azerdash had been thinking ahead. "He's not here right now, but I can give him a message when he returns."

If he returned. The pessimist in Arwen tried not to imagine Azerdash finding his lost love, reuniting with her, and forgetting all about Arwen. Unfortunately, life had taught her to lean more toward pessimism than optimism.

"You will house us until his return?" Brok asked.

"Ah, house?"

"Yes. In exchange for the right to camp outside your domicile and dine on your food, we will protect you. This is the way of orcs."

"Mooching free room and board is the way of orcs?" Val asked.

"The mate of Starblade will be in danger from those who claim him an enemy. From all dragons. She *needs* protection."

Zavryd raised his chin. "She is not in danger from me."

"Not as long as she makes you rotisserie yeti haunch?" Val asked.

"Not as long as she is your friend, my mate."

"The yeti haunches are just a bonus?"

"A suitable offering for a dragon, yes."

"How about you let me know where you're staying now, and I'll send him your way when he comes back to Earth?" Arwen didn't want orcs camping out in the pumpkin patch.

Brok turned to confer with his comrades.

A familiar red hatchback turned onto the street, and Arwen sensed the quarter-elven aura of Val's daughter, Amber.

"What is she doing? I told her to stay away because we're inundated with orcs." Val touched her temple to indicate telepathy.

"I have observed that your offspring rarely obeys you," Zavryd said.

"Yeah, I've observed that too. She's a teenager and about to be a senior in high school."

Zavryd gazed blankly at her.

"Never mind." Val lifted a hand as Amber got out of the car, wearing a cute knit-trim sweatshirt and denim shorts. Though Val had holstered her pistol when the orcs started speaking of allegiance, her other hand remained on the butt of the weapon, and she kept one eye on the van as her daughter approached.

"Hey, Val," Amber said as she walked up. "I was worried I'd come down here one day and there *wouldn't* be any green, blue, or tusked weirdoes hanging out at your coffee shop."

"You know it's not appropriate to call someone weird because of their skin color or tooth arrangement, right?" Val asked.

The orcs tilted their heads toward the sky. One let out a strange roar-whoop as they all thumped their fists against their chests.

"What about if they do that?" Amber asked. "Did those kooks get overly caffeinated on your goblin-fuel roast?"

"No, they're eager to swear their allegiance to Arwen's boyfriend and enter a war."

"Well, as long as it's something rational."

"A war they will lose." Zavryd sneered at the noisy orcs, sniffed, and walked out into the street to change into his dragon form.

The orcs stopped roaring and chest-thumping to watch him warily. Zavryd ignored them.

I must inform my mother of this new development, he said telepathically. When a car turned down the street, he hopped onto the roof of the coffee shop, his tail dangling over the edge and down to the sidewalk.

"You think she'll be worried about twenty orcs joining Starblade's army?" Val asked.

It is what their willingness to join signifies. They will not be the only ones. Zavryd sprang into the air, formed a portal over Lake Union, and flew through it.

"Maybe the orcs shouldn't have made their intentions known in front of a dragon," Arwen said.

"Maybe *you* should redo the wards around your house," Val said, "so they don't end up camped outside your front door while they wait for their new commander to visit Earth."

"Zavryd is the one who installed the wards. I don't know how to reinforce them."

"You could be out of luck then."

Amber cleared her throat. "I'm going school shopping soon, Val."

"Is that your way of asking for money for clothes?"

"No. Dad forbade me from hitting you up. After he refused to give me any money himself. He thinks that now that I'm a working girl, he doesn't need to give me an allowance. He also said my closet was full of clothes, as if I can wear *last* year's fashions to school. Can you imagine?"

"Nope."

Amber looked at Val's jeans and duster and sniffed derisively, but all she said was, "I came down to let it be known that there's a week and a half before school starts, and I've finished my summer reading list. I'm available for work. *Lots* of work. Providing it's mentally stimulating and doesn't involve breaking nails or getting dirt lodged in crevices that are hard to clean."

"Does that mean you're not letting Matti know you're available?" Val asked.

"Not... *first*." Amber looked hopefully at Arwen.

"The dark elves have disappeared." For good, Arwen hoped. "And nobody's paying me right now to track down bad guys. I'm just baking and helping my father with the harvest. We've got apples ripe already, so we're going to fire up the press to make some early-season cider. We could use help picking and pressing, if you're interested."

"That sounds like it might involve crevices."

"Probably just reaching and lifting. Eventually, the press would need cleaning. *It* has crevices."

Arwen's lip curled. "Are you sure you don't need any *research* done? Or to be driven somewhere? I bet you have a secret desire to get away from this place."

With Zavryd gone, the orcs let out another round of roar-whoops. It was as if they were psyching themselves up for a battle they thought would start at any moment.

"Sorry," Arwen said. "I don't need rides or research right now."

Val's phone rang, Colonel Willard's number popping up.

"Hold that thought," Val told Arwen before answering. "Hey, Willard."

"Do you know where Forester is, Thorvald?" Willard asked.

Val switched her phone to speaker mode. "Standing five feet away from me."

"Ask her why her phone has been off all morning." It was

amazing how well Willard's Southern drawl could come across as scathing.

"On the ride over, it heated up in my pocket," Arwen said. "When I took it out to check on it, the screen flashed three times and hissed at me."

"Her phone still hates her dark-elven blood," Val translated for Willard.

"I thought that might improve now that she got her tattoo removed."

"Apparently not. Maybe you could get a pair of magical communication devices out of your artifact vault and give her one for when you need to contact her."

Willard sighed. "Those are heavy, and the artifacts we find or liberate from criminals aren't technically ours. We keep them to study only until someone who can prove they're the rightful owners of the items come along."

"Your other option is to keep someone on staff who's powerful enough to speak telepathically to Arwen from across town. Zav wouldn't be interested, but there are some orcs here looking for..." While Val groped for the right word, the orcs tilted their heads back and roar-whooped again. "Meaning and purpose in life."

"Just tell her to turn on her phone."

Arwen already had and nodded at Val. For the moment, the phone was behaving, even politely popping up alerts that Willard had called four times that morning.

"I have an assignment for her," Willard added. "Can she hear me?"

"She, Amber, and up to twenty orcs, though they're busy with some kind of ritual."

"Is that what that dying-hippopotamus sound is? I thought a dragon might have dropped off something not-quite-dead for Forester to rotisserie."

Yes, Willard had been at the dinner during which Yendral had

deposited a yeti in the driveway. Dragons *did* tend to bring Arwen
fresh game they wanted prepared.

"The orcs aren't dying," Val said. "They're alive and filled with
vigor."

"Imagine my relief. Okay, here's the deal: numerous young
women have gone missing from the towns of Mountlake Terrace,
Lynnwood, Bothell, and Mill Creek. *So far*, there's no evidence to
tie them in with Forester's relatives, but since you last encountered
dark elves in those tunnels under Mill Creek, I'm highly suspicious that they're behind the kidnappings. They're big fans of
kidnapping."

"And ritual sacrifices," Val said.

Arwen didn't have to see Willard's face to know she winced.
"Let's hope *that's* not what's happening."

Amber was close enough to hear the conversation and
frowned. "Those towns are really close to Edmonds."

"You'd better lock your doors, stay inside at night, and keep
your sword cuddled close in bed," Val told her.

"I'll assume that advice wasn't for me," Willard, who probably
hadn't heard Amber, said dryly.

"No? I think that's good advice for all."

"I don't have a sword."

"You can cuddle with your gun. I'll allow it."

"Magnanimous. Forester, you up for finding these missing
women? And the dark elves who took them? I know the entrances
to their tunnels were magically sealed up, but there ought to be
another way in there."

Arwen took a long, slow breath. The last time she'd been in
those tunnels, she'd had to face her mother, her mother who
wouldn't be pleased that she'd not only removed her tattoo but
had resisted the compulsion to kill Val.

But this was why Willard had hired her, and Arwen knew the
dark elves better than anyone else in the area. Unfortunately.

"I can look into it, ma'am," she made herself say.

"Do you want me to help?" Val asked.

"If Forester figures out they're still down there, I'll send you in," Willard replied, "but, first, I need you to talk your mate into getting you in front of the Dragon Council to deliver a message to the queen."

Val blinked. "From... you?"

"From a number of world leaders, including the president, who are aware of the possibility of a Cosmic Realms dragon war and have concerns that it will spill over onto Earth. We want to open up negotiations and get some assurances that such won't happen."

Val looked in the direction that Zavryd had gone. "I don't think dragons give assurance to lesser species."

"I have orders to get whatever we can, Thorvald, and you're the conduit."

"Lucky me."

When the call ended, Val looked at Arwen. "I'm not sure which one of us got the less appealing assignment."

Maybe it was crazy, but Arwen would rather have dealt with dragons, even if it meant battling them, than her dark-elven kin. "Do you want to trade?"

Val gazed at her, touched her hip—in memory of an injury received during her last confrontation with dark elves?—and said, "No."

"You'll probably need someone to do research on those missing women," Amber told Arwen, her eyes brightening with calculation. "I don't have to remind you of my ability to use the internet like a P.I."

"*You* stay away from this one." Val pointed a finger at her nose. "Your father will kill me if I let you get kidnapped. *Again.*"

"Kill you? Dad doesn't own a weapon. The worst he can do is use his replica cannon to pelt you with dice."

"Dice hurt. I know." Val glanced toward the second story of the Coffee Dragon.

Arwen hadn't heard much from the goblin gamers that always occupied the loft—having roaring orcs out front might have subdued them—but she sensed a couple dozen up there. Every now and then, a cackle of victory floated down the stairs and out the door.

"Dad doesn't even know about the other kidnapping," Amber added.

"Don't remind me that I, in an ongoing effort to win your affection, agreed to withhold that information from him."

"My affection *is* delightful."

"No research. Here." Val pulled out her phone and slid a few twenties out of a pocket in the case. "Go school shopping. Get a cute top on me."

Amber accepted the bills but held them up. "With sixty dollars? I'll be lucky to find a belt for that."

"You could get a number of shirts at Goodwill," Arwen offered. "And jeans and a jacket."

Amber pressed a hand to her chest. "*Goodwill*? That's not last year's fashion; that's last *century's*. And the clothes are *used*." Never had someone holding a fistful of twenties worn such an aghast expression.

"No dangerous research," Val told her again, giving Arwen a warning look too. "The only thing I want you looking up is how to spend less money on clothing."

Amber rolled her eyes.

"I'm sure I can learn about the dark elves on my own," Arwen said.

"When your phone practically blows up in your hand when you touch it?" Amber asked. "Doubtful."

"And," Arwen continued, "I know someone who might be able to help me get into those tunnels under Mill Creek. The dark elves might not be there anymore, but it's a reasonable place to start my search."

"Good." Val opened the door to head inside. "Willard has people who can do research. Leave your phone on, and she'll keep you updated."

"People who are three-and-a-half-feet tall, green, and need to sit on a phone book to drive?" Amber had worked with Gondo before.

"Goblins can be helpful," Val said.

A cackle wafted down from above, and a fist-sized die clattered past Val and onto the sidewalk.

Amber shook her head and met Arwen's gaze, mouthing, "You need me."

Not wanting to go against Val's wishes, Arwen only smiled and shook her head.

But after Val disappeared inside, Amber turned toward her car with that calculating expression in her eyes again.

3

When Arwen arrived at Imoshaun and Gruflen's basement workshop in Bellevue, she sensed numerous gnomes inside and paused before knocking. Was the couple having a party? Or, more likely, a gathering for inventors and scientists?

Arwen bit her lip. Maybe she should have called before coming over.

A muffled beeping came through the door, and she snorted, recognizing the alarm. If the gnomes hadn't sensed her arrival before, they knew she was there now.

The door opened. Imoshaun stood at the top of the steps, wearing denim overalls with the pockets full of tools. She peered at Arwen through her spectacles, the lenses filmed with fine wood dust. "Normally, I wouldn't rush to the door when my dark-elf detector goes off, but I knew it was you."

"I'm relieved that you consider me worth greeting."

"Of course. You're a delightful and wholesome individual who respects gnomes and is a joy to know." Imoshaun peeked around Arwen's shoulder toward her pack. "Did you, by chance, bring any pickled or baked goods?"

Arwen smiled. "Of course."

"Wonderful, wonderful. Come in. Or..." Imoshaun glanced down the stairs to where a few gnomes were visible. Was that Gruflen speaking in their native tongue? "Maybe I'll step outside. So you don't get waylaid."

"Uhm, okay. What's going on?"

"Several gnomes from our home world came to Earth, seeking out the half-dragon, Starblade."

"They don't want to swear their allegiance to him, do they?"

"They wish to build him siege engines."

"Oh. He'd like that. Especially if the schematics were included." Arwen, feeling a twinge of loneliness and longing, looked toward the sky, as if Azerdash might soar over the skyscrapers of Bellevue to join her.

"I am certain of that. Who *wouldn't* enjoy perusing the schematics of a talented gnomish inventor?" Imoshaun touched the front of her overalls. "That is not the problem. That they all wish to use my workshop for their projects is. Even though our people do not take up a lot of space, there is only so much room here."

"They don't have workshops on their home world?"

"Those workshops are currently being monitored by dragons." Imoshaun pressed her lips together in disapproval. "In addition to the Silverclaw dragon currently overseeing our capital, several more of their kind have arrived. They are there to observe the population and ensure that no insurrections arise, as if *gnomes* are warmongers."

Arwen frowned at the revelation that life had grown more oppressive for the citizens of the various worlds in the Cosmic Realms because of what Azerdash had put into motion. Technically, he hadn't wanted to start any of this, but *destiny,* as he'd called it, had convinced him of the need—and that it was his duty to spearhead it. Arwen thought Yendral had influenced him more than destiny but wouldn't try to talk him out of his course of action.

"The dragons are increasing their numbers on all the worlds," Imoshaun said. "They are hunting for Starblade, but they are also making plans to quash his uprising before it begins."

Arwen's heart ached. She couldn't imagine them quashing his uprising without quashing *him*. As she well knew, they had already sent a dragon assassin. Yes, Azerdash and his allies had defeated Saruknorath, but they had also let him live.

If only there was something she could do to help the cause—or help turn it toward a diplomatic end instead of an all-out war. Especially if, as Willard was concerned about, that war might spill over onto Earth. Would Val really be called to help Zavryd fight on the side of the *dragons*?

Imoshaun, perhaps noticing that Arwen was lost in thought, poked her arm. "If you give me the items you brought out here, I won't be pressured to share them."

Arwen smiled and removed her pack. "You think those new-to-Earth gnomes will enjoy pickled watermelon chips?"

That was what she'd brought today, as well as watermelon jam and watermelon honey. Since Azerdash had put in the magical rejuvenation pool, the plants near it had grown even more fruitful than they usually were from Arwen's enhancements. The watermelons and the pumpkins were spreading far beyond their usual patches, and the wasabi, one of the farm's high-value crops, was coming in so vigorously that Father was talking about being able to buy a new tractor. In addition to selling it at the farmers market, he'd made a deal with a couple of restauranteurs who liked to feature fresh, local produce in their dishes.

"I do not know what they will enjoy, but I know what *Gruflen* enjoys." Imoshaun accepted the jars, cradling them close to her chest with a contented smile.

"You're not going to share with your husband?"

"Perhaps a select few samples." Imoshaun considered Arwen over the jar lids. "Other than a desire to ply me with delicious food, there must be a reason you came."

Arwen hesitated, hating to think of her jams and honeys as *bribes*, but she did need a favor. "Do you still have your tunnel-boring machine?"

"Yes. The tunnel attaching this basement to the old dark-elf lair remains, and the borer is parked in an alcove." Imoshaun cocked her head. "Do you need to excavate underground storage for your farm?"

"No, my father put in a root cellar a long time ago. I need to excavate a way into the dark-elven tunnels in Mill Creek."

Imoshaun stepped back, her shoulder blades bumping the door. "That dreadful place? You're not going to challenge dark elves again, are you?"

"I have to, yes. Young human women are going missing, and Colonel Willard thinks my mother's people are responsible. Unfortunately, I agree. I need to find them."

"Being kidnapped by dark elves is most loathsome."

"At least you had a private cell and tools." Arwen almost mentioned that dark elves usually sacrificed those they kidnapped, and Imoshaun had been lucky they needed her skills.

"The *company* made it loathsome."

"I believe you."

"And they forced me to modify—to *corrupt*—my own invention and turn it from a tool to do good into one that can wipe the memories of innocent people." Imoshaun pointed at her, though the gnome hadn't been there when Arwen's mother had threatened to steal Arwen's memory to turn her into a more pliable servant. "Not only that," Imoshaun added, "but they didn't give it back. That was the most heinous part."

Arwen wished she *had* been able to get the device back so the dark elves wouldn't have access to it. Her mother might still plan to use it on her. And what of all those women they were kidnapping? The dark elves might wipe *their* memories to make them more pliable too.

"That's why I need to get into their tunnels," Arwen said.

"To steal back my invention?"

"Among other things."

"Well, you may certainly use my tunnel borer, and I had an inkling that you might be forced to deal with your kin again, so I made you some more arrows with an affinity for dark-elven targets."

"Thank you." Arwen nodded her appreciation, though the thought of aiming at her mother's chest disturbed her on multiple levels.

"I should warn you that the tunnel borer cannot easily be driven from one place to another except through excavation."

"Uh." Arwen imagined a map of the Seattle area in her mind. "Unless I'm wrong, it would take a long time to excavate a tunnel from Bellevue to Mill Creek."

"Yes, that is true. It took a long time to excavate one from my basement to a building a block away. Perhaps if you have a crane? Or even a large conveyance. We could use magic to lift it into the back."

"I... think I know someone who could help."

4

"IMOSHAUN AND I APPRECIATE YOU GIVING US A RIDE," ARWEN TOLD Matti.

They were riding in Matti's truck up I-5 toward Mill Creek, the gnomish tunnel-boring machine strapped down behind them. Arwen had considered calling her father, but Matti's truck was newer with a larger bed. As it was, the boring machine barely fit. Though well secured, its large bit pointed ominously at the vehicles driving behind them, prompting drivers to change lanes frequently and leave a long following distance. At least it wasn't glowing at the moment.

"Her especially, I assume." Matti glanced toward the seat well at Arwen's feet.

Imoshaun sat down there instead of next to them, alternately poking around in the glove compartment and investigating the contents of a large stainless-steel toolbox. Whistling happily as she perused Matti's tool collection, she didn't appear to be listening to their conversation.

Arwen hadn't intended to bring her along, but when Imoshaun had asked if Arwen or Matti knew how to operate a gnomish tunnel borer, the answer had been no. Had Azerdash been there, *he* could have figured it out.

"I think so," Arwen said. "Does Sarrlevi mind watching the twins by himself?"

She would have loved if the former assassin had come too, since, if this worked, Arwen might bore into the top of a tunnel and come face to face with dark elves. But if both new parents had joined her, they would have been toting their kids in slings. A dark-elf lair wasn't an approved field-trip destination for babies.

"Nope. This week, he's creating illusions to instruct Natia and Laki on identifying elven insects and telling them how some Earth species, such as bees, hold similar ecological niches as the bugs he grew up with."

Arwen would have found the topic interesting, but...

"How old are they now? Are they capable of learning yet?" Since Arwen didn't have kids and didn't know that many parents, she wasn't well-versed on how quickly they developed, but she was fairly certain Matti's twins were too young to do much more than eat and poop.

"A couple of months, and they just look at the pictures floating in the air and gurgle. Varlesh, however, is convinced that a proper education starts early. I told him it's unlikely kids of mine will become honors students, but he gave me a blank look and asked if I wanted to include instruction on Dwarven insects, whatever they are. I haven't spent much time on the surface of my mother's world. He's planning to ask her for some books." Matti pursed her lips as she signaled for the exit. "When I was a kid, my grandma plopped me down in front of *Sesame Street* and told me not to lose my temper and break anything. Apparently, I was rough on my toys, snapped my crayons in half, and took out some beloved souvenirs."

"Because of your dwarven blood?"

"Sure, we'll blame that. Elven children, Varlesh assures me, don't swing their Fisher-Price hammers at sentimental and break-able Samoan tchotchkes that were brought to America when their grandparents immigrated." Matti looked at Arwen. For confirmation?

"Dark-elven children are indoctrinated to do worse." Arwen grimaced at memories that flashed through her mind of rituals and sacrifices. "I would have liked toy tools," she added softly.

"Like gardening stuff? I had a plastic rake. I jousted with it while riding a broomstick and assailing my older sister."

"I wonder if Sarrlevi will find raising your children to be chal-lenging."

"I'm positive he will, but he promises he's up for it." Matti swung the truck into the lot for McCollum Park. Since it was a sunny day at the end of summer, it was full of cars, with hordes of kids playing on the sports fields.

"Gnomish children are also difficult to raise." Imoshaun lifted her head and waved a pair of pliers. "Because of their great intel-lect and curiosity. I did not destroy home furnishings with hammers, but I *did* disassemble many appliances to examine how they worked. This was not much different from wanton destruc-tion, as I wasn't skilled at *re*assembling items when I was younger."

"Do you have kids of your own?" As they spoke, Arwen stretched out with her senses, seeking sign of the dark elves or anyone else magical. The last time she'd been here, the assassin dragon had been flying around and pestering her. No, preparing to lure her into a trap so he could use her as bait to lure in Azerdash.

Fortunately, she hadn't sensed any dragons aside from Zavryd for a while. They might all be busy preparing for Azerdash's impending insurrection.

The glum thought that one of them would succeed in killing him and she would never see him again crossed her mind.

"Gruflen and I decided to focus on our work instead of having children." Imoshaun climbed onto the seat to peer out the windows. "Sometimes, I regret that, but I was never very maternal. I do have siblings back home with children, and we visit them and teach them about engineering and science."

"That's good," Arwen said.

"Will *you* have children with the half-dragon?" Imoshaun asked. "Is such a thing possible?"

"I'm not certain." To either question, Arwen thought, but she didn't clarify.

Matti slanted her a knowing look.

Ahead of them, someone pulled out of a spot, and Matti was able to park. "Good thing this tunnel borer fit into the bed so we didn't need a trailer."

"I will levitate it to the ground." Imoshaun climbed over Arwen's lap and let herself out.

After turning off the truck, Matti grabbed her hammer. Arwen took her bow and quiver from the back and slung the weapons over her shoulder, nerves teasing her belly. She'd donned her armored jumpsuit for this foray, but she felt anything but impervious to danger.

Once the borer was on the pavement—only a few people were in the parking lot to gape as it floated out of the truck bed—Arwen pointed toward the trailhead. "I'll lead us through the woods to where the hole was before."

Imoshaun didn't touch anything on the machine, but, at some mental command from her, it rolled faithfully after Arwen. Imoshaun matched its trundling pace.

Matti glanced at Arwen a couple of times as they walked down the wooded trail toward the back of the park, but it was a few minutes before she said what was on her mind. "I met Gemlytha."

"Oh." Arwen kept her tone neutral. She didn't want to talk about the female half-dragon. If Gemlytha hadn't been Azerdash's old flame, Arwen would have been curious to meet another dark-elf mongrel like herself, but his interest in Gemlytha changed that feeling.

"She saved my and Dimitri's lives," Matti said. "Not because she liked us, or even wanted to, but because we managed to win Starblade's respect, I guess, and he asked her to do it. But she died in the process. At least we all *thought* she died. I know Varlesh checked the body. But I hear she might have been revived?"

"The half-dragons heard a rumor about that and are investigating it."

Behind them, Imoshaun cursed in Gnomish. The tunnel borer was wider than the trail, and its treads kept catching on roots. Arwen and Matti slowed their pace.

"I don't know what she's like as a person," Matti said, "since we only met her briefly, but I'll be relieved if she's alive. It bothered me that she died because she came back for us. She might have made it out otherwise."

"Yeah."

"We didn't see Starblade after she died and we escaped, but it probably bothered him too, since he'd requested she help us. Now that I know him a little better, I'm positive that's true."

Arwen nodded. She wasn't going to say anything else, but as the tunnel borer got stuck again, a surge of helpless frustration that had nothing to do with the machine swelled within her. "He loved her," she blurted.

Matti blinked. "Starblade? Loved Gemlytha?"

"Yes. He hasn't said that outright, but he admitted having feelings for her when they served together. He didn't act on them because he was her commander, and it wouldn't have been appropriate, but she loved him. I guess he has all these regrets that he obeyed the rules and didn't let himself have a relationship with her."

Matti gazed at her for a moment before saying, "I did get that she had feelings for him."

"I wouldn't wish anyone to be dead if they could be alive, but..." Arwen spread a helpless hand.

"I can see how this complicates things for you two."

That was an understatement.

The tunnel borer caught up, and Arwen continued down the trail. She didn't know why she'd told Matti about Azerdash's feelings for Gemlytha, other than that it was hard worrying about the future and keeping everything to herself. What if she lost the first man she'd loved and who'd finally admitted he loved *her*?

"You should bake some of his favorite things," Matti suggested. "He likes mushrooms."

"I was thinking cakes and cookies. I doubt mushroom casseroles are a proven way to win a man's heart."

"I doubt it too." Arwen smiled sadly as she headed off the trail toward where the sinkhole had been. This time, the area was devoid of Parks and Rec staff and curious dog walkers. The caution tape and cones had been removed. The earth was churned up, with a barren spot devoid of vegetation, but the hole was gone.

"What if you bake delicious cookies *shaped* like mushrooms?" Matti suggested. "You could frost the tops to make them look like cute little toadstools."

"That's your idea for winning a man's affection?"

"Sure. You need to use your strengths."

"I think mushroom-shaped cookies might end up looking like, ah, something else. Something... anatomical."

"You're talented. You can pull it off."

"I *do* have cookie molds. There are probably mushroom ones available, or I could make something. I suppose it wouldn't be that hard." Arwen envisioned walking up to Azerdash while he and Gemlytha were entwined and trying to lure him away with a tray of fungi-shaped cookies.

"Nope. You can do it. I have confidence that you and your

cookies are *much* more appealing than some overpowered half-dragon chick."

"What about me *without* my cookies?"

"That would lower my confidence level a bit." Matti held up a thumb and forefinger, but then stretched her arms wide.

"Funny." Arwen walked over the churned earth, thumping it with her foot to see if it was solid everywhere. The last time she'd come, she had sensed a hint of dark-elven magic wafting up from below, but she didn't detect anything now. "Have you ever met... I mean, was there anyone Sarrlevi cared for before you? That you were worried would be competition?"

"I've met *way* more of his former lovers than any woman would ever want to encounter. And I've heard about more. He used to be promiscuous. I even got the hint that he'd been with orcs—or at least *some* kind of tusked women."

"Those sound more like flings than romantic relationships."

"You don't think one can fall in love with a tusked lady?"

"I'm sure it happens—especially among orcs—but you probably didn't have much to worry about with such former lovers."

"Maybe not, but that didn't keep me from having all kinds of anxiety. The *elven* lovers were all drop-dead gorgeous, and the Assassins' Guild leader... well, she's part dwarven, like me, but more..." Matti waved vaguely in the air. "*More.*"

"Oh." Maybe Arwen had been too quick to dismiss Matti's experiences. She might understand perfectly well what Arwen was feeling.

The tunnel borer rumbled closer, flattening a few ferns on the way.

"As I recall—" Imoshaun peered around, "—the tunnel ran this way." She gestured with her hands. "I will attempt to angle an excavation downward from over there. The machine is designed to descend and ascend at a gradual slope, not dig straight down."

"Humans—and mongrels—prefer walking slopes to jumping into vertical shafts too," Matti said.

"You don't need to come down," Arwen told her as Imoshaun set up.

"Oh, I wasn't planning on it. But I'm your ride, so I'll wait up here." Matti hefted her hammer. "If any dark elves pop out of the hole we make, I'll crack them on the head. Like a Whac-A-Mole." She pantomimed head-cracking.

Imoshaun let out a startled cry and sprang onto the tunnel borer.

Matti spun with her hammer raised.

"What is it?" Arwen didn't sense anything.

"A huge snake." Imoshaun peered all around the base of the borer.

"The snakes in Western Washington are harmless," Arwen said. "It's probably a garter snake."

"It was *huge*." Imoshaun spread her arms to demonstrate.

"They're usually only a couple of feet long."

"A *gnome* is usually only a couple of feet long. A snake could eat me!"

"Garter snakes eat slugs and earthworms," Arwen said.

"I should have brought the combat armor Gruflen and I made."

"To... defend the slugs and earthworms?" Matti asked.

After giving her a scathing look, Imoshaun, from her safe perch above the ground, set the borer's bit to spinning. It tilted downward, sending clumps of dirt and rock flying as it dug in. The earth vibrated under Arwen's feet.

"That'll have every snake in the park fleeing," Matti said.

"Yes," Arwen agreed.

The dark elves, if they were down there, would hear the borer coming. Not that they wouldn't have sensed it by the magic it emitted anyway.

The machine worked quickly, excavating downward at an angle and rolling into the tunnel as it was made. Aside from the initial dirt that had gone flying, little piled up behind it, and Arwen remembered Azerdash noting that it stored what it bored in an extra-dimensional pocket.

After the machine disappeared, Imoshaun crept into view, holding a hammer and screwdriver aloft as she eyed the brush all around the new tunnel entrance.

"Is she that worried about snakes?" Matti asked. "When dark elves might spew out of the tunnel at any moment?"

"We all have things that bother us more than others." With her fear of crowds—or even small groups of people—Arwen understood phobias well.

Matti must have believed she was still thinking about Azerdash and Gemlytha because she thumped Arwen on the shoulder. "He'll choose you. Don't worry. You're loyal, and guys with troubled pasts like that."

Arwen made herself smile and thank her for the reassurance, but she suspected Gemlytha was loyal too. More, she'd been loyal to Azerdash for decades before they'd been captured and forced into stasis chambers.

"Just in case, I'll make cookies."

Matti nodded. "I would."

5

ONCE THE NEW TUNNEL WAS DUG AND CONNECTED TO THE WIDER tunnel below, Imoshaun extricated her boring machine and bowed out of the adventure. She said she would ensure snakes didn't take over the area while Arwen was gone, but she would rather not encounter dark elves or be thrown into a dungeon again.

"It was more of a tool-filled alcove than a dungeon," Arwen pointed out.

"A cage is a cage, no matter how many tools are in it. Bring my *thyamiliscar* back if you see it."

"Oh, I will." Arwen would prefer the dark elves *not* have access to a device capable of altering—or wiping out—memories.

Despite her promise to stay above ground and play Whac-A-Mole with dark-elf heads, Matti followed Arwen into the tunnel, her war hammer slung over her shoulder. Maybe she worried Arwen would need help.

Though Arwen hated to endanger a mother with babies who needed her, she didn't refuse the company. As a strong warrior and enchanter, Matti was a good ally to have, and they both had camouflaging charms that they activated.

With the smell of freshly churned earth filling their nostrils, and the flashlight on Arwen's multitool turned on, they headed into the main tunnel. Despite the magical sealing of the sinkhole, the passageway remained intact once they got past the rubble that had come down when Arwen and Gruflen had fought the *drykar*.

The withered remains of the giant dead spider dotted the ground. Fortunately, Arwen didn't sense that the barrier blocking the tunnel—the barrier Gruflen had blown away—had been recreated. That was good, though Matti's powerful hammer could likely knock such a thing down as easily as his arm-mounted cannon had.

Surprisingly, they didn't encounter any obstacles as they walked toward the chamber where the kidnap victims had been held. Even before they reached it, Arwen had a feeling the dark elves had abandoned this place. That made sense, but she'd hoped that finding the missing women would be easy.

The tools Imoshaun had used were gone from the alcove. There was no sign of her memory device, nor anything else. Arwen didn't sense magic anywhere.

"Looks like they moved out." Matti eyed the dark corners of the chamber. "I was a little worried we'd run into one of those purple knot-shaped artifacts that curses innocent people." She flexed her hand, and Arwen remembered the glowing mark one such device had left on Matti's palm the year before.

"I've encountered those, and I'm not affected by them." Arwen headed for a tunnel she hadn't been down on her last visit. Her mother had arrived through it.

"*I* am." Matti shuddered. "My eyes would get glazy, and I would run straight for it."

"I would stop you."

Matti didn't say she could kick Arwen's ass, but, with her big war hammer in hand, she *did* raise her eyebrows.

"I'd throw baked goods into your path to divert you." Arwen touched her pack. She'd given most of her goodies to Imoshaun, but she had a tin of Cherries Jubilee cookies left.

Matti snorted. "That might work. Fresh baked goods have *at least* as much magical power as dark-elven artifacts."

They padded through a warren of tunnels and chambers, all with whatever furnishings and magical devices that had been there before removed. Arwen was about to give up and admit this had been a waste of time when she spotted a piece of parchment on the ground in the corner of one chamber. Something that had fallen out when the dark elves had been moving?

"Shopping list?" Matti asked.

"I doubt it." Arwen picked up the parchment.

Of course, the writing was in Dark Elven. Arwen propelled her memory into gear to translate the words, though she had to fill in a few blanks and make some guesses. She hadn't learned every word by age seven and had forgotten many that she *had* learned during the intervening twenty-three years.

"It looks like a report to She Who Leads." Reluctantly, Arwen clarified who that was. "My mother."

"Catchy name."

"It says twenty-seven female humans have been captured and... I think this means they're being prepared to be impregnated with dark-elven embryos."

Matti touched her stomach and shuddered. "Hell."

"I'm not positive on my translation, but it seems to say the embryos were scientifically created, combining ninety percent dark-elven... that probably means genetic material... and the rest from a special mix made from the half-dragon, gnomes, elves, orcs, and others who were captured and had samples of their essences extracted."

"That doesn't make the idea any better." Matti curled her lip. "And where the hell does one go for *essence* extraction?"

"That's what they were doing in the basement of the insurance building in Bellevue."

"An insurance building, sure. That would have been my guess."

"Half-dragon," Arwen murmured. "That would mean the babies would have a bit of Yendral in them."

"So, they'll grow up calling you Chef Arwen?"

"They'll probably grow up programmed to hate all outsiders. They would shoot me."

"Or gore you with their tusks. Did you say *orcs* were in the mix?"

"Yes, probably for their fertility. My mother's goal, I think, was not only to create powerful offspring but more fertile beings since the dark-elves have been struggling with that these past generations. They're slowly going extinct."

Matti grunted. "That's one endangered species that I wouldn't donate to a fund to save."

Arwen rubbed the back of her neck. This was largely information she'd already learned, but she would take the report to Willard. Maybe her translators could pick something else useful out of it. Like where the women were being imprisoned.

She closed her eyes and tried to remember the map of dark-elf hideouts they'd found up in the old mountain lair. There'd been one spot that Arwen hadn't known about, but she suspected Willard had already sent someone to investigate it. Also, the dark elves knew that Arwen had seen that map, so they'd probably gone somewhere new.

"They wanted me to help with this scheme," Arwen admitted.

"Kidnapping women for their wombs?" Matti asked.

"Yes. I guess they're managing fine without me."

"I don't know. They've only got twenty-seven. As horrifying as that is, I think it takes more babies than that to repopulate a species."

"As you well know, one mother can have more than one child at a time, but I was thinking it might be a long-term plan and that they expect to keep the women, to *breed* them, for years. Or decades. It sounded like they're deliberately picking young people."

"Good God, Arwen. That's awful."

"I know." Arwen shivered at the idea of being imprisoned for years in dark tunnels and forced to deliver baby after baby. It had been bad enough spending the first seven years of her life trapped underground with her mother's people.

"Why can't they take fertility tea and deliver their own babies? That's a thing, isn't it?"

"We grow black cohosh on the farm. And chasteberry, which, despite the name, promotes female fertility."

"There you go. You should make them a special tea and trade it for the prisoners."

"I'll be sure to mention that possibility when we run into them." Arwen ran her finger down the parchment. "There's more on the second half. It's in a different ink, so it might have been written on another day. This is about... a possible dragon war. They must have heard about what Azerdash is up to. The writer says a great upheaval and re-ordering may be about to occur. Maybe, in the chaos that comes, the dark elves will be able to take advantage and find a more magic-filled world where they can slip in and make a new home. With the natives of many worlds distracted by war, they may not notice and attempt to drive them out as the surface elves once did."

"I wouldn't mind if they left Earth forever. But we can't let them take kidnapped women with them."

"No. I..." Arwen frowned as, for the first time, she sensed a hint of magic.

Matti must have caught it too. Hammer raised, she turned toward the tunnel.

It didn't feel like a magical being or even an artifact. Just the hint of something.

A faint glowing haze formed in the entryway of their chamber, something similar to an eyeball floating in the middle. Arwen hadn't done anything that should have broken her camouflage, but she rubbed the multitool to activate its magic again. Just in case.

The misty eyeball slowly turned left and right, gazing into the chamber. *Searching* the chamber?

We're still camouflaged, Matti said telepathically, the words reassuring until she added, *Right?*

Yes. Not certain if the eyeball would float inside and get close enough to see through their camouflage, Arwen crouched, ready to flee. *But we may have inadvertently stepped on a magical tripwire the dark elves set to warn them of intruders.*

After a long moment, the eye backed out of the entryway and floated out of view. It headed down the tunnel, the mist trailing it.

Maybe it's searching all the chambers, Matti suggested.

Arwen started to nod, but heat and magic flared in her hands. Startled, she released the parchment and stepped back.

It only fell halfway to the ground before bursting into flame. Arwen gaped as it burned quickly, nothing but ashes remaining.

I guess I won't be able to give that to Willard to check my translation. She rubbed her palms on her jumpsuit, though she'd released the parchment before being burned.

We'd better tell her the dark elves know someone was snooping around in their old base.

Even though they'd been camouflaged, Arwen had a feeling the dark elves knew *she'd* been snooping around.

"What's new?" she muttered.

6

When Arwen and Matti exited the sloping tunnel the borer had made, afternoon sunlight filtered through the branches and dappled the freshly dug earth. They found Imoshaun sitting cross-legged on her machine while munching watermelon chips.

Arwen was about to deactivate her camouflage when she sensed a portal forming.

"Dragon magic," Matti warned.

A silvery disc appeared in the air between two trees. Azerdash flew out, banking hard to avoid another tree in his route. He shifted into his elven form to land in a crouch, a cloak whispering about his ankles and his sword in a scabbard on his back.

Delight filled Arwen—he'd come back to see her!—and she ran toward him, making more noise than she usually would as she crunched through the undergrowth.

"Azerdash," she blurted when he looked around, not seeing her through the camouflage, though he had to *hear* her. "You're here."

He smiled and held his arms wide. "I am here."

"How did you find me in the park?" As Arwen wrapped her

arms fiercely around him, she realized how much anxiety she'd had, how much she'd worried he wouldn't come back, either because he'd been killed or because... he'd found someone else to replace Arwen. Throat tight with emotion, she held him and didn't let go.

Since *he* hadn't worried about whether he would come back or not, his return embrace wasn't quite as hard, but he did hug her fully, still smiling as he rested his cheek against her head.

"I went first to your farm. Your father, after pressing me into magically enhancing his sump pump—I believe that was the term for it—told me you were searching for dark elves, and I recalled these tunnels." Switching to telepathy, he murmured, *I've missed you.*

Azerdash glanced toward Matti and Imoshaun but didn't let their presence deter him from kissing her.

Encouraged by that, Arwen kissed him back with enthusiastic passion, hoping he would enjoy it—enjoy *her*. She wanted him to stay with her, or at least always come back when he left. *I've missed you too.*

He brushed his fingers through her hair, but was his kiss more hesitant than it had been weeks earlier? Before he'd heard Gemlytha might live?

Arwen leaned back and gazed into his eyes, searching for an answer, but she didn't ask the question. Maybe it was her imagination. She didn't want to jump to conclusions or assume anything.

With her dark-elf tattoo no longer guarding her thoughts, Azerdash should have been able to read her mind, but he didn't comment on her concerns.

"I have something for you." Arwen slung off her pack, deciding to be glad he'd come and take a moment to discuss lighter matters. Like freshly baked desserts.

"Oh?"

She dug out the tin and handed it to him. "Cherries Jubilee cookies."

Azerdash accepted the tin but cocked his head. "Jubilee? This word in your tongue means a celebration, does it not? A festive party?"

"The cherries are a party in your mouth."

"Interesting." He opened the tin.

"There's also a definition that means to flambé something with alcohol. Dragons should know all about flambéing."

"Ah, yes. Dragons are experts at applying fire to food. We rarely douse our meals with alcohol first though."

"You'll change your method of flambéing once you've had these. The cherries were soaked in rum."

"I have not consumed any of the alcoholic offerings from this world." Azerdash might have come for a reason, but he plucked a cookie from the tin, momentarily distracted as he examined it. "Is rum potent? Will I experience, as the Study of Manliness called it, a killer hangover?"

"Not from the amount in my cookies, no." Arwen scratched her cheek. "Did that book suggest hangovers were to be embraced or avoided?" Given the other things he'd referenced from that text, she could see it going either way.

"It said alcohol was a suitable way to deal with sorrow and regret and that the killer hangover that followed the next morning might prolong the distraction."

"My cookies are a less painful way to raise one's spirits."

After sniffing the one he'd selected, he took a bite.

Arwen thought about mentioning that she would make a mushroom mold to try on future cookies, but maybe that should be a surprise. Besides, that would work better with a sugar cookie.

Azerdash nodded, finished off the treat, and drew the tin to his chest. "Excellent. As your food always is."

Arwen smiled, always delighted when someone enjoyed what

she made. Matti joined Imoshaun on the top of the tunnel borer, and the gnome pointed to something in the brush. Another heinous snake?

"I will not share these with Yendral and Sleveryn," Azerdash said.

"Good idea. Yendral would eat half of them in one bite."

"Indeed." He smiled back at her.

Was it her imagination, or was it a sad smile?

"Uhm, *are* you feeling sorrow and regret?" Maybe she didn't want to know, but curiosity drove Arwen to add, "Have you learned anything about... Gemlytha?"

"Thus far, we've unearthed only the single rumor that Sleveryn heard, but it is a concerning one. It suggests that Silverclaw dragons at the mountain battle on Veleshna Var were the ones who found Gemlytha and were responsible for reviving her. If they did that instead of killing her, it was certainly not out of kindness. They may have believed they could use her to ensnare the rest of us half-dragons."

"Your enemies are big on baiting traps."

"Yes. Perhaps I should be honored that they believe they must resort to such methodology to defeat me, but... I am not. If they've truly had Gemlytha all this time... I worry about what they've done to her."

"Your battle was almost a year ago, wasn't it?"

"Yes." Azerdash sighed. "We haven't confirmed anything yet, but Yendral and Sleveryn are even now trying to find proof that the Silverclaws have her. My comrades want me to stay away, in case a trap *has* been set. I'm too valuable to the war effort, the Cosmic Realms, right now, they say. My heart doesn't agree, but my rational mind does believe I should remain focused on this greater work. Per their suggestion—their *order*," he amended with a rueful smile, "I am continuing to speak with world leaders and generals of armies."

"The dragons have reputedly heard all about your plans and are taking measures."

"I am aware. That was to be expected. Small sorties into enemy lands might be planned and undertaken in secret, but when one seeks to join together great armies from multiple worlds... That never could have been a surprise effort."

"I suppose not." Arwen pressed the tin in his arms down, lifted the lid, and withdrew another cookie for him. He needed an emotional up-lifting.

"Thank you. The rum-soaked cherries are tart and sumptuous." Azerdash took a bite without hesitation. "I've gained the tentative support of the trolls and ogres, but the elves are refusing to see us, and I haven't yet managed to secure a meeting with the dwarven king." He'd raised his voice for that last sentence and looked toward Matti. "It would be convenient if an acquaintance could arrange an audience with King Ironhelm."

Matti arched her eyebrows. "The dwarves were all perturbed when you escaped from your stasis chamber."

"That was through no fault of mine, though I am pleased to be free. *You* released me."

"Yeah, that's who they were perturbed at. They consider you a criminal."

"Which I am not." Azerdash lifted his chin.

"I never thought so." Matti waved a hand. "I can reach out to my mother, but if you want an audience with the king, you can probably get in by taking him some peanut brittle."

"Peanut brittle," Azerdash mouthed and looked at Arwen.

"I've got a recipe for that," she said. "And I can make other desserts if they'll help. We did talk about wooing world leaders with sweets."

"Yes. You will put rum in the brittle?"

"That... might be possible. I can experiment."

Matti raised a finger. "Just one problem, Arwen."

"What's that?"

"The dwarves like my *grandmother's* peanut brittle. It's dreadful by human standards. You can chip your teeth on it."

"But the dwarves like that?"

"They do. Dwarves are a little weird. They like challenging food." Matti pantomimed taking a bite out of something hard.

"I usually strive to make food that's pleasant to eat, not challenging. Certainly nothing that would break teeth."

Azerdash set down the tin and rested his hands on Arwen's shoulders as he gazed into her eyes. "I have faith that you can make an appropriate dessert to help me win an audience with the dwarven king."

"Challenging, rum-filled peanut brittle."

"Perfect." He kissed her without hesitation, with the same passion she'd kissed him.

A heated tingle ran through her, and Arwen knew she would do her best to fill any order he requested. Somewhere along the way, she'd fallen deeply in love with him. She tried not to think about what would happen if he found Gemlytha alive.

7

As bangs and thumps and an intermittent rumble wafted through an open window from the direction of the barn, Arwen inhaled the smell of sweet peanuts permeating the kitchen. It mingled with the vanilla scent of the buttery shortbread cookies in the oven.

Azerdash had suggested dwarves might enjoy Cherries Jubilee cookies, but Arwen suspected that was more because he had, with her father's help, already polished off the tin she'd given him.

A *kerchunk-thud-bang* from the barn made her wonder what they were working on. Earlier, a truck had delivered a few yards of gravel. Father wanted to get a fresh layer on the driveway before the rainy season came.

Even with all the noise, Arwen smiled, content to be baking while her father and Azerdash tinkered nearby. For the moment, she could pretend they'd solved all their problems and that this was a preview of the peaceful times she and Azerdash might one day have together.

Arwen slid a candy thermometer into the burbling pot of peanut brittle while wondering how Matti's grandmother got her batches so hard that they could chip teeth. At first, she'd thought Matti had been joking, but a text exchange had confirmed that humans found the dessert inedible because it was indeed so hard. Most home cooks Arwen knew erred in the other direction, turning out brittle that was softer and chewier than desired.

"I don't know how to make *inedible* desserts," Arwen grumbled. Nor did she want to learn that skill. "The dwarves will have to enjoy a *non*-challenging dessert."

Maybe if she wrapped the brittle in multiple layers of Saran wrap, they would struggle to open it, and that would satisfy their need for discomfort in life.

Once it was ready, Arwen added the final ingredients and spread the brittle onto warmed baking pans. The oven timer dinged. As she removed the finished sugar cookies, Azerdash walked into the kitchen.

His twitching nostrils suggesting the scents had wafted outside and enticed him to visit. Once the cookies cooled, Arwen would have to take a few to her father. He was working hard at—

Beeping noises joined the rumble she'd been hearing.

"What are you two building?" Arwen thought of Imoshaun's dark-elf detector but doubted her father had felt compelled to install one of those on the tractor.

"Your father informed me that commercial conveyances often beep when backing up, thus to warn pedestrians of the danger of being run over. It was a simple matter to magically add that feature to your tractor." Azerdash stepped close and clasped her hands.

"Yes, but there aren't a lot of pedestrians on the farm, and the bees and chickens are good at getting out of the way." Arwen leaned into him, glad for his touch. What would it be like to be married or, as those from other worlds often said, *mated* to him? To have a lifelong companion and enjoy his company every day?

"The male chicken squawks uproariously at me."

"Horus? He thinks he's in charge. You're not only a dangerous predator who might be a threat to his hens, but he can probably sense your aura and believes you challenge his authority." Arwen had no idea if animals—or birds—could detect magical auras, but they always knew who was a threat and who wasn't. "He would fly away if you backed up toward him beeping."

"Or he would peck my calves."

"Possibly your butt." Wanting to give Azerdash a treat while they waited for the desserts to cool, Arwen removed a jar of pickled watermelon rinds from the pantry, opened it, and offered it to him. "Horus isn't a *good* flyer, but he can reach such a low target."

"I will keep that in mind." Azerdash pulled out a pickled rind and sniffed it. "It would be embarrassing to lead an army from the front when one's butt has been perforated by a chicken beak."

"Yes. I've heard that subordinates don't respect commanders with holey butts." Arwen grinned and leaned the side of her head against Azerdash's shoulder. It felt good to joke about little things. She wished *little things* were all that were on her mind.

"I have missed this," he admitted, perhaps thinking something similar.

"My arms around you or the smell of my desserts cooling?"

"Both." Azerdash squeezed her and popped the watermelon into his mouth. "This is excellent. Crisp and refreshing. Is it a fruit? Or a vegetable?"

"Watermelons are fruit—my bees pollinate the flowers early in the season—but some gardeners think of them as vegetables since they're in the same botanical family as squash, cucumber, and pumpkins. They're the state vegetable in Oklahoma. They can grow quite large in the long warm summers of the South. The last I checked, the world record for heaviest watermelon was logged in Tennessee at three-hundred-and-fifty pounds." Realizing she'd given him far more information than he'd asked for, she leaned back to check his expression.

He was smiling. He even seemed appreciative of the data. Maybe the pickled rinds were giving him an interest in the fruit.

"My interest is in you," he murmured and nibbled on another rind. "I enjoy when you burble about your passions."

Arwen decided not to be embarrassed about her burbling. Not if he liked it.

She leaned against him again and strove to relax and not think about Gemlytha or the dark elves, to enjoy the moment— enjoy him. For an entire minute, she succeeded. Then her phone rang.

If she hadn't been on a mission for Willard, she would have ignored it, but she made herself slip from Azerdash's embrace and grab the phone from the other room. Amber's name appeared on the display, and she answered before the call dropped to voicemail.

"Hi, Amber."

"About time. I have information for you about the kidnapped women."

"I... don't believe I hired you to work on this assignment." Arwen remembered the calculating look that had been in Amber's eyes when they'd parted ways at the coffee shop. "That reminds me," she murmured, lowering the phone and looking toward Azerdash, who was waiting in the doorway. "The orc mercenaries who've killed innocent people on Earth and shot up a tattoo parlor and the Coffee Dragon want to join your army."

Azerdash blinked a few times as Amber answered.

"You didn't say you wanted to hire me, but I could see the angst and overwhelm in your eyes and knew you needed me."

"Your mother specifically told me not to get you involved with this assignment."

"Looking stuff up on the internet isn't *getting involved*. I'm in the safety of my room." Amber sounded like she was smiling when she added, "I *do* have an idea if you want to hear it."

"I do not. I can't go against your mother's wishes. She's a friend. Also, she could kick my ass." Arwen had little doubt she could best Val in an archery contest, but in hand-to-hand or sword-to-multitool combat? She wouldn't want to get in that fight.

"She can kick everybody's ass. It's what she does."

"Yes."

"Fine, I won't tell you my idea. I'm still refining it anyway."

A vroom sounded as Father drove past the window on Frodo. The tractor was no longer beeping, but a plow attachment glowed blue.

"You *do* want the information I gathered, right?" Amber asked.

Arwen hesitated. As much as she didn't want to get Amber involved, it would be unwise not to accept information that could help her rescue the kidnapped women.

"I'll only charge *five* percent this time," Amber added. "A back-to-school special."

"You must really need money for clothing."

"Nah, I've got money from my other work this summer. I just..." Uncharacteristically, Amber hesitated. She was always so blunt and direct that the pause surprised Arwen. "Look, I'm a little embarrassed and chagrined that Gondo and I—especially *I*—got kidnapped last month. And then that artifact took over my brain and almost made me a liability to you. I'm smart and capable and *not* a liability, Arwen."

"I believe that to be true."

"But I let myself be *kidnapped*, like some knuckle-dragging, mouth-breathing *sidekick*." Amber sounded genuinely distressed, like she'd been thinking about it ever since it had happened.

The rare display of self-doubt and uncertainty made Arwen realized that, deep down, Amber probably had the same insecurities as she did. That made her want to help Amber.

"Let me give you what I'm able to find with research," Amber said. "You *need* my help. And I won't get kidnapped again. I'm sleeping with my camo charm now. Even though Val originally gave it to me with *bloodstains,* and having it touch my skin seems so gross. I sanitize it daily."

"It's difficult being a teenager, isn't it?"

"*Obviously.*"

"I'll take your information, but I can only offer three percent."

"*Three?*"

"Plus four jars of pickled cherries and two batches of your choice of cookies."

Amber hesitated. Azerdash raised his eyebrows again.

"Make it *four* batches of cookies, and you have a deal. I have moochy family members."

"Deal." Arwen telepathically told Azerdash, who was watching the call, *I'm working on my negotiating skills and developing confidence in my worth.*

Excellent. Such abilities will come in handy when we see the dwarven king.

You're taking me to see him? I thought only my peanut brittle was going.

If you complete your quest and are available, I am certain you would be an asset.

Arwen resisted asking him if she would be as much of an asset as Gemlytha and hated that the thought had popped into her mind. She had a long way to go in the self-confidence department.

His smile turned a touch sad, and she worried he'd gotten the gist of her thoughts.

"I'm going to send the information over to your email address. *Don't* forget to check it. I know how seldom you fire up that computer. Why you people added a satellite dish to your corn crib, I don't know." Amber's vulnerability and self-doubt had disappeared. "It's the names and ages of the people who have been kidnapped, and I've mapped out where they all went missing and triangulated a few square miles in the center. Maybe you could fly over the area with a dragon and see if you sense any magic? The dark elves don't *need* to be hunkering down in the center, but it's possible they're grabbing people from all around their lair."

"It does make sense to check that area." Arwen wondered if Azerdash would stick around long enough to fly her about. Covering a few square miles on dragon back wouldn't take that long. Of course, if this lair was similar to the others, the tunnels would be camouflaged and difficult to sense until one was inside them.

"The oldest of the captured women is nineteen," Amber said. "It's creepy that they're swiping teenagers."

"I think they want people with a lot of childbearing years ahead of them. They're planning to use them as surrogates."

"That's even creepier. To be kidnapped for your *womb*? To *breed*? Completely primitive."

Arwen didn't disagree. Even if she understood that the dark elves were desperate, this was far from an acceptable way to go about increasing their population levels.

"I'll see what else I can find and send it over. I intend to *earn* my cut and do well enough that you won't try to negotiate my pay downward next time." Amber sounded affronted, enough so that Arwen felt guilty and almost blurted that she would part with five percent. But with Azerdash watching, she held firm. Amber was a bit of a price gouger. She *deserved* to be negotiated with.

"Thank you," Arwen said and ended the call.

She slipped past Azerdash to return to the kitchen, needing to get another batch of cookies started. As he trailed her in, Azerdash's nostrils twitched again, but he didn't poke his finger into anything hot. *Yendral* might have.

"Yes," Azerdash said, reminding her that he could read her thoughts. He'd offered to teach her how to erect mental defenses to keep people from doing that, but they hadn't had a lot of time for magic lessons since then. "Do you have a moment to talk?" He waved toward the living room.

Arwen set down the stick of butter she'd grabbed and nodded, following him to the couch. The next batch could wait.

"About more than butt perforations?" she asked.

"I believe we covered that sufficiently."

They sat shoulder to shoulder, and he took a deep breath. Arwen kept from grimacing, but she was afraid all her thoughts about Gemlytha made him feel compelled to bring her up.

She rubbed her face, wishing she'd been able to keep her insecurities out of her mind. Of course, if he hadn't been rudely snooping in her thoughts, he wouldn't be aware of them.

She squinted at him, said nothing, and waited to see what he would say.

"It *is* rude of me to read your mind without permission." Azerdash took her hand. "But, as I've admitted before, it's hard not to catch your thoughts when we're close. Also, you project them somewhat."

"So it's my fault you're a snoop."

He smiled. "Undoubtedly." His expression grew more sober. "I understand that you're concerned that, if Gemlytha does end up being alive and we can rescue her, it'll change something between us. About how I feel about you."

"You did care for her long before you met me."

"That is true."

He paused. Considering how to put his words delicately?

"Do you think you'll still care for me?" Love me, Arwen thought, but didn't say. He'd used the word right before he'd heard the rumor of Gemlytha's revival.

"Yes." His lack of hesitation might have cheered her, but he added, "And that's the problem. Even though she and I never..."

Well, I told you that we never consummated a physical relationship."

Not because they hadn't wanted to.

"But she was a comrade for a long time, and I knew she loved me. If I found her, and then immediately flew off with you, it would feel like a betrayal. It would hurt her."

"I can see that." Arwen waited for him to say the same thing about her, that if he flew off with Gemlytha, it would hurt *her* and feel like a betrayal.

He didn't. Instead, what he whispered was, "I haven't been able to stop thinking about you." He clasped her other hand and shifted to gaze into her eyes. "During the day, while working at other tasks... while in the middle of negotiations... and even while fleeing from dragons who wish me dead, I think about you. And at night, I dream about..." Was that a hint of pink flushing his cheeks? "I dream about being with you."

Arwen swallowed, touched and a little aroused by the heat in his eyes, the warmth of his hands wrapped around hers.

"I've had dreams about you too," she whispered, lifting her palm to rest it on his chest.

The memory of him standing naked in the rejuvenation pool flashed into her mind, of him levitating her into his arms, of her wrapping her legs around him as they'd shared a kiss like no other she'd experienced. She'd dreamed often of that night, of things that might have happened if the dragons hadn't interrupted them.

"That is also in *my* dreams," he said, his voice husky.

He lifted a hand to her face. They moved as one, coming together for a kiss.

He still wanted her. Maybe the reappearance of his old comrade would complicate things, and Arwen understood that, but he was here with her. He had to want...

I do, he whispered into her mind as his warm lips caressed hers, and his hand slid around her waist, pulling her closer.

Outside, the tractor rumbled past a window, a reminder that they were on her father's couch, but Arwen didn't care. As Azerdash's hands roamed, tendrils of titillating magic accompanying his touch, zipping along her nerves and lighting up her senses, all she could think was that she wanted him to stay, at least long enough that they could spend a night together. After all, he couldn't leave until the peanut brittle hardened, right?

Azerdash must have caught that thought. He chuckled into her mind and spoke telepathically: *Certainly, I could not gain access to the dwarven royal halls with a soft dessert. Would you like to go to your abode?*

Do you need something from there? Not certain what she might have in her home that he would want, Arwen pulled back enough to look in his eyes.

They crinkled at the corners. *I need* someone *in there.*

It took her a moment to realize...

"Oh, you want to come too? With me. To, uhm..." Even though they'd been kissing and speaking of erotic dreams to each other, her cheeks flushed madly with embarrassment. Or uncertainty. She didn't know, but anxiety and anticipation and emotions she couldn't name jumbled together to make her feel self-conscious about her inexperience.

"We do not have to," Azerdash said gently, watching her. "But from your thoughts and actions, I believed you wish to be with me."

"Oh, yes," she blurted. *That much* she wasn't confused about.

Looking a little smug, he let his gaze drift to her chest as he massaged her hip with his hand, his thumb slipping under her shirt to brush bare skin. A hot tingle zipped to her core, and she caught herself shifting toward him, wanting his touch elsewhere. Wanting him.

Another rumble wafted through the open window, and gravel crunched.

"I thought you might desire more privacy and also to be in your own abode," Azerdash murmured, bending to nuzzle her neck.

With the most delicious sensations coursing through her body, Arwen let her head fall back as she pushed her fingers up his head to rub his scalp, his soft hair brushing her skin.

"It is true that... I would feel weird... having sex... on the couch where my father watches *Jeopardy*." Her eyes rolled back in her head as his nuzzling turned into light teasing nips. The sensations ignited every nerve in her body. "But are you sure that you won't regret... I mean, you were talking about feelings of betrayal."

Arwen shouldn't have brought that up. She didn't want to remind him. She *definitely* didn't want him to stop.

Azerdash hesitated, lips pausing on her neck, and she gripped the back of his head, wishing she could retract the words, that she hadn't even had the thought. She returned to kneading his scalp, hoping deep down that he would find her too enticing to leave even if he *was* conflicted. She didn't want him to feel he was betraying someone he cared about, but *she* wanted to be the one he loved, the one he wanted more than any other.

Fingers curling into his hair, she turned her lips toward his ear, kissing the lobe, then drawing it into her mouth to promise... she didn't know what, but she'd heard elven ears were sensitive. And she wanted to please him so badly, to make it so he would stay. Always.

Azerdash growled as he tasted her skin and inhaled her scent. She didn't know if the growl indicated indecision and frustration over his conundrum or pleasure from her ministrations.

I came back for you. I will have you. His hand shifted, and he pulled her into his lap.

Arwen could feel the hard heat of his body through their clothing and promptly wished there *were* no clothing. She didn't care where they were. She wanted him.

I'm ready. She nibbled on his ear, then traced the pointed tip with her tongue.

This time, when he growled, she had no doubt what it meant. He liked that. And he wanted her.

That has been true since you first stepped naked into my rejuvenation pool. He returned his lips to hers, this time kissing her hard, his need plain in his hungry mouth and his taut muscles. *And more every time you fought at my side.*

His admissions made her want him even more.

Still kissing her, he leaned her onto the couch, bringing his body down with hers, leaning atop her. A whisper of magic came from him, and the locks on the doors clicked. A promise that they wouldn't be interrupted. And that she wouldn't escape?

She smiled. As if she ever wanted to escape from him.

Using his hands, or maybe his power, he unbuttoned her blouse and cupped her breast. He brushed his thumb over her nipple, sending a tingle of magic straight to her core. Such pleasure rocketed through her that she gasped and arched into him. Her bra loosened, slipping off her shoulders, and baring her breasts to his touch, his pleased perusal.

Excitement and anticipation coursed through her, ruling over other emotions, and she pushed her hands under his shirt, eager to feel him, to be with him. She felt daring, running her fingers boldly over a man's bare chest, and he seemed to enjoy it as much as she. Their kisses grew hungrier, breathless with need. Her body throbbed with desire, and she pressed herself up into him, wanting him inside of her.

Her waistband loosened, and she trembled, willing his touch lower, willing him to fill her. His hand slid tantalizingly from her breast and down her abdomen to slide her jeans and panties off her hips. He brushed her sensitive core with his thumb, and she bucked up into him, gasping at the surge of pleasure his touch brought.

Instead of moving atop her so that they could join, as she'd expected, he drew his lips from her mouth to trail down her body. Her belly quivered at his light teasing touches, and she shifted her legs apart, wanting whatever he would give.

Hands to either side of her on the couch, he nuzzled her exposed flesh. She squirmed as desire built, making her arch into him again, needing so badly for him to satisfy her as only he could.

Smiling against her, he stroked her with his tongue. He observed her as he licked and nuzzled—pleased by the way she responded to his touch? Yes, his eyes were intense with arousal, and was he breathing quickly too?

She was surprised he didn't yank down his trousers and take her fully, but this was so amazing that she didn't want it to stop. Soon, she was panting as she writhed and thrust, needing—

His strokes shifted to an exquisite sucking that took her from building desire to an explosion of pleasure such as she'd never felt before. She cried out his name, holding onto his powerful shoulders as waves of ecstasy swept through her.

He watched her with hunger in his eyes and shifted a hand toward his own waistband and the hard bulge restrained by his trousers. Realizing he still needed to sate his desire, Arwen shifted up, finding her grip on his shoulders again and kissing him, wanting him to know she was ready for more. She would *always* be ready for him.

With that growl rumbling through him again, he pushed her back on the couch, bringing his body atop hers. *I've longed for you and will have you,* he whispered, his kisses and touches growing frantic with need.

She returned them eagerly, hoping she could make him enjoy this more than he'd ever enjoyed being with—

Ah, Azerdash? came Yendral's voice from startlingly nearby.

Arwen froze, feeling like they'd been caught doing something illicit.

Azerdash also tensed in surprise. Yendral must have been camouflaged as he approached. Hell, how long had he been on the property?

Go away, Azerdash told him. *I need—*

He didn't articulate to his comrade, but his hard kisses told Arwen exactly what he needed. And she wanted him to have it— to have her.

Could they ignore Yendral? Ignore the whole world and finish what they'd started?

Before you, ah— I thought you'd want to know... Yendral spoke more circumspectly than Arwen had ever heard him. *We've confirmed that Gemlytha is alive. The Silverclaws have her.*

8

Arwen let Azerdash go outside first, in part because she dreaded hearing news about Gemlytha and in part because she needed a moment to fix her clothing and find her equanimity. His step had a hitch to it, his body tight with the tension he hadn't been able to release, and she knew he hadn't wanted to stop. He'd brought such pleasure to her, and she regretted that he hadn't gotten to satisfy his own needs.

When she eventually stepped onto the porch, Azerdash and Yendral were talking in the driveway. They paused to look at her. Did they want their conversation to be private?

Yendral's face was grave, but he managed a smile. "I was hoping you'd bring some cookies out. The ones with the blue fruits inside."

"If you'd come an hour later, I might have been in a better state to consider the cookie desires of those around me."

"*Three* hours later." Azerdash smiled, though he appeared more aggrieved than amused.

When their gazes met, he looked away. Was that a hint of doubt or even anguish in his eyes? Was he imagining explaining to

Gemlytha that he hadn't been faithful? Surely, one wasn't expected to be faithful to someone everyone had believed to be dead.

Azerdash was, however, a staunch devotee of loyalty. Maybe he did believe one should be faithful, at least for a time, to the deceased.

"Only three?" Yendral smirked at him. "I'd hoped you would have the stamina to reward Chef Arwen for her loyalty and delicious sharing of food for a far greater amount of time than that."

Azerdash squinted at him. "You said you have news."

"Yes." Yendral dropped the smirk and extended a hand toward Arwen. "Do you want to include…"

Azerdash hesitated, again looking at Arwen but not holding her gaze. Finally, he nodded. "She is making desserts to assist us in wooing the dwarven king."

Yendral opened his mouth and closed it, not seeming to know if that answered his question. Arwen didn't know either.

"I can start another batch of cookies." She pointed back into the house.

Yendral nodded.

But Azerdash lifted a hand. "She has a right to know if… *why* there might be a delay."

"In your three hours?" Yendral asked.

Azerdash glared at him.

"I'll go inside." Arwen waved and hurried in, closing the door behind her.

If he wanted to explain *delays* to her later, he could. But, as she pulled the ingredients out of the fridge to start another batch of cookies, their voices drifted through the open window to her. Surprisingly, they hadn't switched to speaking in Elven.

"You're sure the Silverclaws have her?" Azerdash asked.

"Yes. The rumor was apparently true. Eager for revenge, they searched the rubble of the fiery collapsed mountain more assiduously than the other dragons or the elves. It makes sense that they would have found her body and immediately started plotting. By then, they probably knew you had escaped."

"*We* escaped."

"Yes, but you were in charge of us and therefore the most loathsome. They would have found your escape most detestable."

"This sounds like speculation," Azerdash said. "Are you *sure* Gemlytha lives and is their prisoner?"

Arwen cracked eggs softly, not wanting them to hear her in the kitchen and realize she could hear *them*. She hadn't intended to spy, but now her curiosity made her want to hear the whole story.

"Yes. As you ordered, Sleveryn and I continued negotiations with the gnome rulers and head engineers to acquire magical machinery that could aid us against the dragons. While we were on their world, an escaped gnome arrived. Since he was a cousin of the gnomish ruler, he was taken to the royal hall, where we heard his story. He'd been a prisoner of the Silverclaws, forced to work for them and maintain a gnomish stasis chamber with a special prisoner in it."

"Gemlytha."

"He did not know her name, but he described her. She is the only half-dark-elven half-dragon in the Cosmic Realms, so there is no chance he was mistaken. He said she's alive inside the chamber. The Silverclaws plan to use her against you to force you to call off the war. Apparently, some dragons, though they'll never admit it to outsiders, believe we may have a chance of winning."

"They will threaten to kill her if we don't comply with their demands?" Azerdash guessed.

"I believe so. The gnome wasn't privy to all their conversations, but he got the gist."

"And then happened to escape and show up in the place where you and Sleveryn happened to be this week? Is it possible this is all the setup for a trap?"

"It is certainly the setup for a trap, but... we have to save her, Azerdash."

"I know, I know, but I do not wish to do something foolish, such as leading us all to our demise."

"It would be a tragedy for the only remaining half-dragons to all perish. Perhaps I should stay here and sample Chef Arwen's baked goods while you retrieve Gemlytha."

Arwen couldn't see them through the window, but the way they paused made her guess they were looking toward it, perhaps noticing it was open...

They switched to Elven and walked away from the house.

Heat warmed Arwen's cheeks. They must have realized she could hear them and *was* listening.

It wasn't her fault. They were the ones who'd stood close and spoken in English... Even so, she felt as if she'd been in the wrong. She *could* have moved to another part of the house while they had their conversation.

Arwen worked for a few minutes and was about to place a couple of pans of cookies in the oven when Azerdash spoke into her mind.

Arwen?

Yes? she replied warily, though she doubted he would chastise her for listening—or being understandably curious about Gemlytha.

You may wish to come outside. There is something concerning out here.

More than my father oiling the apple press and requesting you give it a sentience?

That would not be concerning but natural. He shared an image of the road in front of the farm and something floating and glowing near the driveway. *You will wish to see this.*

Arwen wiped her hands and jogged outside, joining Azerdash and Yendral in the driveway.

"I can destroy it," Azerdash said, "but presumed you would want to know of its existence."

A glowing haze floated near the mailbox, something similar to an eye in the center, an eye turned toward the farm —toward her.

Arwen swallowed, recognizing it. It was the same eye that had searched for her in the tunnels under Mill Creek.

"It's dark elven," she said.

"Yes." Of course, Azerdash had already been able to tell that. "I believe it is here to spy on you."

"You don't think it's here to spy on *us*?" Yendral touched his chest.

"I doubt the dark elves care about our plans," Azerdash said.

"I wouldn't assume that." Arwen remembered the parchment she'd found and wished it hadn't been destroyed. "They at least want to take advantage of the chaos in the Realms that your insurrection will cause—is *already* causing."

Power surged around Azerdash, and, with a flick of his fingers, his magic obliterated the hazy eye.

"I guess they don't have another special telescope to use to spy on me from a distance," Arwen said, "and don't care about being subtle anymore."

Either that, or the eye had followed her from the tunnels.

Azerdash frowned at her with concern. "Have your people spoken to you since the half-troll removed your tattoo?"

"No, but I'll bet they know about it." Arwen sighed. "And I doubt they've given up on using me."

"Perhaps you should kidnap her and bring her with us," Yendral said. "We could keep her safe from the dark elves."

"As we infiltrate a Silverclaw stronghold and possibly battle a whole clan of dragons to reach Gemlytha?" Azerdash asked. "That would be an even greater danger."

As Arwen had thought before, she would rather battle dragons than her mother and the dark elves. Not a rational thought but a true one.

"Perhaps she could be of assistance," Yendral said. "She has proven resourceful, and her arrows enjoy pronging dragons between the scales." His eyes glinted as he looked at her with appreciation. "And in the ass."

"We must consider her safety. You only wish her along so she would feed you desserts."

"That is not *all* she could do." Yendral stepped closer to Arwen and rested a hand on her shoulder. "Perhaps, should you return to Gemlytha and leave Chef Arwen, she will be bereft without the companionship of a half-dragon and will be driven to turn to another to sate her needs."

Arwen froze, not able to tell if he was joking or not.

Azerdash's eyes flared with violet light, and he growled, clearly not taking it as a joke. "You will *not* start harassing her again. Release her."

"No female has ever considered my touch *harassment*. Goodness, Azerdash, you are so sanctimonious. I only wish to ensure Arwen is not emotionally distraught over all this. The stars know, you haven't been the clearest with her when it comes to your feelings." Yendral turned a surprisingly gentle and sympathetic expression toward Arwen.

Unexpected emotion welled in her throat. She didn't want to be weak or distract Azerdash from his quest—*quests*—but this *was* distressing her.

Azerdash stepped toward them, using not a physical touch but his magic to shove Yendral back. The great power whispered past Arwen without disturbing her. It sent Yendral stumbling back and made him raise a defensive barrier.

"I have *not* been perfect in expressing my feelings for Arwen," Azerdash told him without apology, "but she will *not* be distraught over this. I am not leaving her."

He spun toward Arwen so abruptly that she jumped. Tension bunched his shoulders, his aura crackled with intense power that buzzed at her skin, and his eyes still glowed.

Arwen almost took a step back, but she didn't fear Azerdash. She knew he wouldn't hurt her.

And he seemed to realize he'd been abrupt. He paused and softened his features before gently taking her arm and pulling her toward him. She went willingly, especially when his aura grew more tantalizing than alarming, caressing her skin and reminding her of their all-too-short moments on the couch.

Her arms wrapped around his shoulders as he lowered his mouth to kiss her. It might have been to show Yendral as much as Arwen, and maybe she should have objected, but she couldn't. She kissed him back hard, willing her magic and her body and her desire into her touch so that he would leave knowing she wanted to be with him. And that she was worth coming back to, proclaiming his love to. The passionate way he kissed her made her believe he still wanted her, that he *would* come back to her.

Maybe Azerdash had started out trying to show Yendral something, but as his arms wrapped around her, his body pressed against hers, she believed he forgot Yendral, that she filled his thoughts.

"Neither woman will allow you to claim them both." Yendral didn't sound impressed or moved by the display.

The words sprouted a new concern in Arwen. Would Azerdash think to try that? Had he mentioned the idea to Yendral?

It wasn't as if men throughout history hadn't kept multiple women as lovers. But Azerdash wouldn't think Arwen would be okay with that, would he?

Azerdash sighed and broke the kiss, though he cupped the back of Arwen's head and kept her close as he looked at his comrade. "I have no intention of claiming them both."

"Then you have made your feelings clear to Chef Arwen?" Yendral squinted at her, as if trying to determine that.

Did he truly care? Or was he setting himself up as a possible backup if Azerdash walked away from her? She couldn't tell, but she didn't want that. She wanted Azerdash.

"My feelings are clear." Azerdash looked at Arwen again, but he didn't state that he loved her or make a promise that he would be with no other. Oh, how she longed for him to do so. His dedication to loyalty would make her believe and trust him fully if he did. Instead, he looked toward the road, though the dark-elven eye hadn't reappeared. "We will not take you into a Silverclaw lair with us, Arwen, but I urge you to take precautions here to be safe and avoid your mother's people. I would not forgive myself if you were hurt while we were away on another mission."

"I... will take precautions." Arwen made herself smile, but she felt more conflicted than before he'd come. Further, the fact that Willard had hired her to find the missing women would make it hard to take as many precautions as he would wish. But she had to continue with her life. She *would* be careful.

Azerdash hesitated, perhaps catching some of her thoughts, but then nodded. Maybe he had to go, no matter what she said. If his comrade was in Silverclaw clutches, she understood perfectly well.

"Go rescue her." Arwen patted his chest, then made herself step out of his arms.

"I will. And I will not forget that you were the one to make it easier for us to sneak in and do so." Azerdash touched his pectoral where his tattoo had once been.

"Good."

Yendral formed a portal.

"Wait." Arwen ran inside, grabbed some fresh cookies, and put them in a bag and handed them to Yendral and Azerdash. "For the road."

"The road?" Yendral looked toward it.

Azerdash tilted his head. "You wish us to leave an offering on the pathway in the hope that the dark elves will not again conjure spy magic upon it?"

"That *would* be nice. I meant that they're for you on your journey." Arwen waved them toward the portal.

"Ah. Of course. Thank you." Azerdash touched her cheek before leaping through the portal.

Yendral clutched the cookies to his chest and bowed to her. His expression wasn't flirtatious, nor did he promise to be there if Azerdash abandoned her for another. Instead, as he turned to follow his commander through the portal, his eyes were grave and concerned for her.

9

Before dawn, Arwen woke from a troubling dream with her blankets tangled around her body and sweat making her pajamas stick to her skin. It had started out erotic, a demonstration of where her unconscious mind imagined her couch interlude with Azerdash could have gone if they'd been permitted to finish. Then a hooded woman had arrived, her face hidden, and pulled Azerdash away. Arwen had leaped to her feet, demanding to fight for him, but the woman had been too powerful and had knocked her flying before leading Azerdash through a portal.

Arwen rubbed her face, wondering why she couldn't have normal dreams, ones where things worked out for her. But it wasn't like that for anybody, was it? Weren't dreams a reflection of one's anxieties?

She swung her legs off the bed, intending to dress and harvest vegetables for her father to take to the market, but her phone rang from the bedside table. Given the early hour, she grabbed it, expecting Willard. Surprisingly, it was Amber.

"Hello?" Arwen answered warily, knowing Amber was never

up this early. What if she hadn't come home the night before, and this was her father, calling everyone while looking for her?

"Hey, Arwen." Amber yawned. "I was up all night, but I've dug up some more information for you."

"Oh, thank you." A rush of guilt swept through Arwen. She'd forgotten to check her email the day before. Everything with Azerdash had distracted her. "What is it?"

"You probably know that hiring out your womb and having some rich people's babies is a thing, right? Like on Earth with humans, not in weird dark-elf experiments."

"Surrogacy, yes." Arwen hadn't heard it described as *hiring out your womb* before. It wasn't as if the womb could leave its body and do its own thing. "I don't know any of the details about the process, but I've heard of it."

"Right. Apparently, it costs like fifty thousand dollars. I'm not sure how much the baby mom gets, but some decent compensation, I guess. I can't imagine wanting to do that myself."

"It's more of a commitment than giving someone a ride but possibly less dangerous."

Amber snorted. "Less dangerous than giving *you* a ride, for sure."

Arwen wished she could deny that, but...

"Anyway," Amber continued, "I found some online groups where people thinking of doing it or who've done it share information. There are some right here in the Seattle area. All the companies that I saw listed looked legit, like they've been at it for years and have real addresses and stuff. Addresses that aren't former insurance buildings turned into dark-elf lairs. I decided to look up some of the women who'd been active in the groups but then stopped posting abruptly. I found a few like that. I dug around on their profiles and Googled them for news. There are a number who were recently reported as missing."

"I think Willard already has a list of the missing women."

"Yeah, yeah, and I've got that, and there are some matches." Amber didn't say *how* she'd gotten the colonel's list, but maybe it was in the email. "But does Willard know what those girls were posting about right before they went missing? There's one that was asking about doing it outside of the system and linking up directly with a rich couple to make more money. She asked if anyone had heard of the people and thought it was weird that they wanted to meet on their yacht down by Olympia. In another group, one of the *other* now-missing women mentioned a meet-up at sea. That's not normal, Arwen. Not unless you're going to sail out of US territory to do something that would be *illegal* here."

Arwen combed her fingers through her hair, debating how the dark elves might be tied in with that. "My mother's people wouldn't be on yachts or any other ships. Their eyes are too sensitive for them to be out in daylight." But why was Olympia familiar? The city had come up recently, hadn't it? "I suppose they could have orcs doing their dirty daylight work again."

Except those orcs now wanted to work for Azerdash. Maybe the dark elves had found another group to hire down by Olympia.

"If I showed up to hire out my womb, and the doctors had tusks, I can't tell you how fast I'd run the other way."

"Me too. I—" Arwen lurched to her feet as she remembered why Olympia was ringing a bell. The map. "Was the location by a peninsula *near* Olympia rather than right in the city itself? Or its waterfront?"

"The woman's post wasn't that specific, and Olympia only came up once. The other people who mentioned yachts didn't say whether they were supposed to meet up at a marina or out at sea or what."

"Remember that map in the underground chamber you took me to?" Arwen asked. "One of the circles that showed dark-elf lairs was down in that area."

"You think they would use a place they know you saw on their map?"

Arwen sat back down. "Maybe not. I'll have to ask Willard if she checked on that area. I bet she did, and I would have heard about it if they'd found a lair."

"Well, look, I have an idea about how to find out where all these women are being taken. I made accounts in some of these groups and started posting for information. I made sure to include my age. You know, how *young* my womb is."

Arwen stared at her phone in horror, an inkling of what Amber might be thinking coming to her.

"A couple of people already replied that you have to be eighteen, but that's not who I'm hoping will reach out to me."

"Please don't do anything to put yourself in danger."

"I'm not. I just thought whoever is shopping for women might see my post and message me. I didn't use my real name or anything. It's a burner email address. If they give me a place to meet them, I'll send you and Val instead. That ought to surprise the heck out of those orcs."

Arwen shook her head, not wanting there to be any chance that Amber would be wrapped up in this. "Maybe *I* should be the one signing up for these groups and making posts."

"Your womb is too wrinkled and old."

"I'm only *thirty*." Not to mention that her elven blood ought to convey longer than usual life, if she didn't get herself killed along the way. "Dark elves don't even consider you an adult until you're thirty."

"Yeah, yeah, I'm joking, but they want human teenagers, right? I'm the perfect demographic."

"Amber..."

"It'll be fine. I'm not dumb. My real name, address, and phone number aren't tied to the accounts. I'm going to bed, but I'll let you know if I hear anything or learn anything else."

Though reluctant to have her involved, Arwen said, "Okay."

This could be the lead she needed.

"Hopefully, they'll reach out right away," Amber said. "We need to get this wrapped up soon."

"Because those women are in danger, I know."

"And because school starts soon. I can't be on my phone, making posts about my womb, during Physics class."

"Yes, I hear teachers frown upon that."

"They frown upon *everything*. Bye."

After Amber hung up, Arwen stared at the phone, debating on calling Val to let her know what her daughter was doing. As much as Arwen appreciated the help, she didn't want to risk Amber being hurt.

Since it was still early, she texted instead of calling. She also texted Willard, not about Amber's plan but about what she'd shared. She also wanted to know if Willard's agents had found anything in Olympia.

Three seconds after the message sent, the phone rang. Willard.

"You can call anytime in the morning if you have dark-elf news," she said without a greeting.

"I wasn't sure if you'd be awake, ma'am."

"I'm always awake early. Now, if you call me after nine p.m., something better be on fire."

"Understood." Arwen relayed the information in more detail. She was tempted to withhold where she'd gotten it, since it felt like a betrayal to Amber, but it would be best if Val and Willard knew. They would be better at talking Amber out of taking risks than Arwen.

"Why is that girl always getting herself involved?" Willard asked with a sigh.

"She likes giving me rides and doing research more than she likes carrying heavy things around and getting her nails dirty for Matti."

"Well, that's expected, but did you *hire* her for this?"

"I'm... not entirely sure. She kind of hired herself."

Willard sighed again. "I'll talk to Val later. As for Olympia, I did send agents to the marked spot to look for sign of tunnels, but they didn't find anything. There weren't any recent sinkholes to conveniently mark the spot."

"Wasn't Val responsible for the sinkhole in Mill Creek?"

"Yes. I suppose I could send *her* to that peninsula. It's not actually in Olympia. It's a semi-rural area between there and Shelton."

Arwen tried to remember the map in her mind. "The circle was by the water, wasn't it?"

"It *is* near the coastline, yes. There wasn't a road directly to the spot, and my agent had to tramp across someone's private forested property to do his search. I didn't authorize that, mind you. We don't tell people to trespass. But he took initiative."

"Would someone see more by *yacht* than by land?"

"I don't know. Do you have a yacht you'd like to volunteer to take down, Forester?"

"No, ma'am, but I assume you have more resources than I do. Don't you have access to a submarine?"

"Yes, yes. Let me make some calls. It might be worth poking around further."

A knock at the door startled Arwen. She opened it to find her father frowning darkly.

"Are you upset that Azerdash left before magicking up the apple press?" she asked before noticing he gripped his rifle.

Uh-oh. What now?

"No. Did you invite company to stay on the farm without asking me?" He squinted. "*Tusked* company?"

She'd been about to say *no* but paused at the addition. "Orcs?"

"Yes, orcs. They *say* you're the mate of Azerdash Starblade—" Father's eyebrows twitched upward, "—and that they're joining his army and you promised them they could stay here."

"All I told them was that I'd tell Azerdash that some orcs are looking for him."

"They think Starblade's *mate* is obligated to give them a place to stay." His eyebrows were doing all *kinds* of twitching during this conversation.

"Don't they *have* a place to stay? At the least, they have a van."

"There are a lot of them for one van. They also said you're supposed to feed them. It's part of their culture that the female of the chief feeds the warriors. It seems they know all about the excellent food you make and want to enjoy some."

When had those orcs had her food? Their kind occasionally visited the Coffee Dragon, along with trolls and ogres, but she hadn't ever seen the mercenaries inside. Given how many drive-by shootings they'd done of the coffee shop, she couldn't imagine Nin allowing them to amble up for a cappuccino.

"You'd better talk to them. With your bow in hand." Father pointed his rifle toward the front of the property. "I think the only reason we haven't already been invaded is the magic your dragon ally put around the place."

"Okay." Arwen hurried to dress and grab her weapons. She paused at her kitchen counter, where a few raspberry-almond kisses from a recent batch of cookies rested. After all, one had to sample one's goods before sharing them with a dwarven king, right? "Do you think I should give the orcs some sweets since I'm going to refuse their request to stay here? A consolation prize?"

"*No.* You making good food for people is what's got us in this mess." Father whirled to stalk to the front of the property but paused, squinted at her and into her kitchen, then strode in to grab a couple of the cookies for himself. Head high, he *then* stalked away.

Arwen hardly thought her baking was the reason the orcs had come—or any other trouble had found her lately—but she didn't take any cookies to share. It might be harder to get rid of the orcs if they thought she would feed them regularly. Images of squirrels and crows that she'd unwisely shared nuts with in the past came to mind. They'd turned into her wildlife stalkers.

Before she rounded her father's house and walked up the driveway, she sensed the orcs. There were more now than there had been at the coffee shop, but she recognized the leader among them. Brok. Arwen recalled that she'd *requested* Azerdash heal him since she'd wanted to question him. Maybe that had been a mistake.

"Claimed mate of the half-dragon leader, Starblade." Brok grunted and bowed to her. The rest of the orcs did the same.

Their politeness didn't keep her from noticing their armor and weapons—and did that one have blood on his tusk?—not to mention how *many* of them there were. Thirty? Forty?

Lately, she'd gotten a little better at dealing with crowds, but that familiar feeling of panic crept into her as she considered them lined up in the road and facing her. Every set of orc eyes focused on her. Her father stuck to her side, not leaving her to face them alone, but they had no interest in him. All those eyes were unsettling.

"Uhm, hi." Arwen tried to smile as she stopped at the end of the driveway, but it might have come out as a grimace. "Did I... tell you where I live? I'm rather positive that I did not."

"The farm of Starblade's mate is known to many," Brok said.

"Wonderful," Father said.

"You will allow us to build our portable huts here and stay until Commander Starblade returns and we can join him?"

"He's busy right now, and I'm not sure when he'll be back. He's on a special mission."

Brok frowned. "On such a mission, he could have used our help."

Arwen imagined the orcs attempting to storm a dragon lair. "Possibly so, but you just missed him."

"You will allow us to stay here until he returns for us." Brok pointed at the front of the property, the field to the left of the driveway, beehives poking above the edible ground cover.

"Uh, you can stay out *here*." Arwen pointed at the road. Out of the corner of her eye, she saw her father's eyebrows fly up. Maybe she should have directed the orcs to a campground. "There are wards on the property that don't allow strangers in, and I don't know how to adjust them."

Technically, true, though Zavryd had told her she could grip someone's arm and say a word in the dragon tongue to bring a guest in.

"Yes, we sense the wards. It is important that the mate of Starblade be protected."

"Yes, it is," Father said.

"But not from us."

"I'm afraid there's nothing I can do about the wards." Arwen attempted to look sad.

The orcs rumbled and conferred among each other in their language. Finally, Brok pointed at the road and gave a few orders. The orcs removed packs and dug out the equivalent of pop tents.

Hand on Arwen's arm, her father drew her up the driveway for privacy. "How are we going to explain a legion of orcs camped in the street to our neighbors?"

"The same way we've explained all the dragons flying over our farm?"

Admittedly, only one of their neighbors had a smidgen of magical blood and had noticed the dragons, but from what Arwen had heard, he'd been gossiping to everyone around.

"By avoiding eye contact when we see them?" Father asked. "And pretending we don't see them waving?"

"Exactly. It'll be fine. When Azerdash comes back, he can take these guys with him."

Father grunted dubiously and walked away. As Arwen watched

the orcs set up, she wondered if her life would ever return to normal.

10

THE NEXT MORNING, A REQUEST FROM VAL TO MEET AT THE COFFEE Dragon prompted Arwen to get a ride into town with her father. He grumbled about traffic, bad drivers, and—*especially*—the rows of hide huts in the road that made getting out of the driveway an obstacle course.

"Maybe we *should* have let them camp on the property," he'd said. "It would have been less obnoxious."

"Not to the bees," Arwen said. "I didn't like the way they were looking at the hives."

"You thought they'd raid the honey? They look like meat eaters to me." He used a finger to pantomime a tusk growing from his jaw.

"Bears eat meat, and they're the biggest raiders of beehives in the forest."

"True."

Arwen had been more worried that the orcs would prove they were still enemies if they were let loose on the property. Given her history with the mercenaries, she didn't trust that they'd reformed themselves and were eager to join Azerdash's army. It was as likely that they were spies for the dark elves.

Her father stopped the truck in front of the busy Coffee Dragon as two goblins with multiple ice-cream cones from the shop next door met two goblins with to-go cups stacked precariously in their grips. They did some licking and sipping to consider each other's offerings, then juggled their goods around. One would think it would have been so that each goblin had one coffee drink and one ice-cream cone, but it turned out that some preferred two coffees and no ice cream and vice versa. They were still sticking their tongues in each other's cones when they ambled around the corner and out of view.

"You have no idea how weird that looks to someone who can't see this magical coffee shop," Father said.

"It looks weird even if you *can* see it." Arwen wondered if the green-skinned patrons had appeared to step out of thin air to him. "Goblins are unique souls."

"Uh-huh."

"Thank you for the ride. If I get done early, I'll swing by the market to help out." Arwen gestured toward the coolers of produce in the truck bed.

Father grunted and waved in what might have been dismissal. Again, she felt guilty that she'd been too busy lately to provide as much help as he needed.

Inside, Arwen found Val waiting at a table for her, a can of sparkling water her only beverage. Surprisingly, a young woman with raven hair and the aura of a shifter sat across from her. A werewolf? Their kind occasionally visited the coffee shop, but Arwen hadn't seen Val socializing with them.

Arwen waited for them to finish their conversation, but Val spotted her and waved her over.

"Willard is arranging our boat ride, and I'm expecting her to message us soon with the details." Val raised her phone. "I don't know if it'll be the sub or a motorboat or a two-person kayak. In the meantime, Winter here could use any information you have on dark elves."

Arwen blinked at the human name attached to someone with the aura of a werewolf, a powerful one, her senses promised. Though Winter appeared young—early twenties?—and fit anyone's definition of beautiful, she had the dangerous vibe of a predator, something typical for their kind. And when she smiled, her canine teeth were longer and sharper than those of a mundane human.

"Especially information related to being kidnapped by dark elves," Val added.

"Is that an aspiration of yours?" Arwen asked Winter.

"Apparently, it is." She smiled. "I'm trying to get out of the family business, but my mom, grandma, and sisters, who *all* think they have a say in my life, won't let me leave unless I'm bringing in money from another source. A reliable and reputable source. Mom particularly forbade me from hooking up with whores and gigolos, even though *I'm* not the sex-crazed one in the family. Summer is the one who boinks that half-dragon when he comes by, pretending he cares about our wine. I think even Autumn slept with him."

"Half-dragon?" Right away, Arwen assumed Yendral, as she couldn't imagine Azerdash cozying up to werewolves, though if the sisters were as pretty as Winter, any heterosexual male might be tempted.

"It sounds like Yendral is a frequent visitor to Wolf Winery in Woodinville," Val said.

Winter nodded. "*Frequent.*"

"From what I've seen, he's on the libidinous side," Arwen said.

"Yup," Winter said. "He's not the only horny male who shows up at the winery for more than our award-winning Pinot Noir."

"What do you want to know about dark elves?" Arwen asked.

"I haven't personally been kidnapped by them, but they've lured me into traps and harassed those around me."

"Zoltan feels so harassed that he's packed up most of his laboratory and is searching for alternative lodgings. Oddly, most landlords want him to pay rent, so he hasn't found anything yet." Val extended her hand toward the werewolf. "Winter is trying to get a job working for Willard as an operative. Willard says she doesn't *need* anyone else on the payroll, and complained vociferously about the amount of money her office is already spending on contractors and informants—she has to justify her expenses to her higher-ups, after all. She *did,* however, admit she doesn't have any shifters and that someone with ties to their community might be valuable."

"I'm here to prove myself," Winter said. "Even though I'm just out of college and have mostly worked at the winery, pushing brooms and explaining tasting notes to visitors, I know how to fight. I also know every shifter within a fifty-mile radius, including who's a decent person and who's a jackass."

"What's your degree in?" Val asked.

Winter's lips flattened. "Viticulture and Enology."

"Oh." Arwen brightened. "We could talk all about growing grapes and wine making. Technically, I'm more versed in making *jam* than wine, but my father and I have experimented on the farm. Our Catawba, Jupiter, and Concord grapes do well in this climate, and we made a chardonnay last year."

"I'm more interested in talking about *dark elves.*" Winter leaned forward. "And kicking their asses after they kidnap me."

"Worthy topics of conversation," Val said.

Winter nodded firmly.

A half-troll whistled as he walked past their table, giving Winter *and* Val thumbs-ups. Val ignored him, and Winter bared her canines at him. He scurried past.

"When Willard and I discussed Amber's crazy plan," Val said, "which I expressly forbade her from undertaking, Willard admitted that having someone young enough to entice the dark-elf scientists and get kidnapped so she could find out where the lair is could be useful. At the same time, Winter was in the office, looking for a new career..."

Arwen scratched her jaw. If she were given the choice, she would choose a career involving winemaking over being kidnapped. But when Winter looked intently at her, blue eyes eager with the desire to *prove herself*, Arwen started explaining dark elves, the type of magic they used, the demons they worshipped, and everything else about them that might be useful.

About ten minutes into the spiel, Arwen sensed Amber arriving. She strode directly to their table, folded her arms over her chest, and jutted one hip forward as she glared at Val.

"*This* is who Willard wants to replace me with?" Amber jerked her chin toward Winter. "She's barely older than I am."

"She's graduated college," Val said.

"*So*? Like that's hard? I took Running Start classes all last year. They were easier than my AP stuff."

"You're seventeen, and you're not being replaced, because you were never hired to start with."

Amber looked at Arwen.

"By *Willard*," Val clarified. "And Arwen doesn't want you getting yourself kidnapped by dark elves either. Or being impregnated by them." An aghast expression twisted Val's face.

"But she wants *her* being kidnapped?" Amber pointed at Winter, who leaned back in her chair with her chin raised and also folded her arms over her chest. "And—" Amber's lip curled with deep distaste, "—*impregnated*?"

"If any guy tries to impregnate me, I'll get furry and rip his balls off." Winter snapped at the air.

"Usually, the higher-ranking dark-elven scientists who would do such work are female," Arwen pointed out.

"Females have parts that can be ripped off too," Winter said.

"Your werewolf side is showing," Val told her.

"I assume that's the side your colonel is thinking of hiring."

"True." Val looked at Amber. "If you want to be helpful, you can tell Winter anything else you've learned that you didn't report to Willard or Arwen. Such as specifics on how to get in touch with the dark elves—or whoever is working as their intermediary to find appropriate women for their needs."

"I didn't tell you what I found so Willard could give my job away," Amber told Arwen, accusation in her eyes.

"It's not your job," Val said as Arwen winced, feeling she had betrayed Amber. "Even if you were older, it wouldn't be," Val added.

"It's messed up AF that you want to pump me for information and then won't let me do this. That doesn't hit right, Val."

"Sorry, but you're my kid, and it's my job to protect you."

"I want to earn my three percent. And, and..." Amber threw an exasperated look at Arwen.

Arwen remembered her saying she wanted to show that she was capable, to redeem herself after her *last* time being kidnapped. Winter wasn't the only one who wanted prove herself.

"Look," Val said. "It's not that I don't think you could do this. It's that Thad and I want you to see your eighteenth birthday. Not only that, but you're my daughter, and the dark elves might be able to figure that out."

"I'm not using my own name."

"That doesn't matter. You can't hide your aura. They may be able to tell by looking at you that you're my daughter."

"I can tell from your scent," Winter offered.

That prompted another lip curl from Amber. "Gross."

Winter smirked. "I've smelled worse."

"If they *do* figure out that you're my daughter, and they've got you in their clutches, not only would the ruse be up, but they might torture and kill you solely to hurt me. Or they might use you as bait in a trap to lure me in."

Amber issued a disgusted noise and stalked to the coffee counter.

"I'm not sure you'll be able to get any more information out of her," Val told Winter.

"That's okay. Willard sent a lot." Winter pulled out her phone and showed them a text that took up the entire display. No... She scrolled to show that it filled much *more* than one page of the display. "And I have an idea about how to attract fertility scientists. All I have to do is put it out there that I'm interested in being a surrogate and that my family is huge. Do you know how many sisters and brothers and cousins I have? We're a fertile people."

"Aren't werewolves a somewhat promiscuous people?" Val asked.

Winter flashed her canines. "That does help with fertility."

"That's not *all* you'll have to do," Amber said, walking back past the table with a to-go cup in hand. "You'll have to know who to contact and where to post. If you need that information, it'll be two hundred dollars. Val and Arwen know how to reach me." She sniffed and walked out of the shop.

"Sorry about that," Val told Winter. "If you get stuck, let me know, and I'll figure out how to wheedle the information out of her."

"It's not a problem. My aunt would like her. She approves of anyone with a capitalist streak."

"Except whores and gigolos?"

"*Grandma* is the one who objects to them. She's very proud and doesn't believe in selling your body for sex. I think it's just because she's gotten old and isn't as interested in sex anymore. *She* didn't find the half-dragon's allure appealing. She smacked him on the wrist when he tried to take too many cheese samples."

"Did that stop him?" Maybe Arwen should have whacked Yendral's wrist when he'd been vacuuming up her cookies.

"She smacked him on the wrist with a serrated knife," Winter clarified.

"Your family sounds interesting," Val said.

"Yes."

Arwen's and Val's phones buzzed at the same time with incoming texts.

Arwen's hissed at her and flashed several times before turning off.

Fortunately, Val, whose blood was not loathed by technology, was able to read hers. "Our yacht is ready."

11

THE "YACHT" TURNED OUT TO BE A TWO-PERSON SUBMARINE WAITING for them at Shilshole Bay marina. As Arwen and Val drove up in her Jeep, a steam-powered wagon that might have been state of the art at the turn of the *last* century was leaving, a hoist dangling a hook from the back. The green-skinned goblin driver saw them—he had to be sitting on a box or phone books to see over the wheel—and blew Val a kiss before waving and pulling out of the drop-off area.

"Was that goblin flirting with you?" Arwen asked.

"That kiss might have been for you."

"I don't get a lot of men blowing me kisses."

"That's one of the gamers from the coffee shop. He's probably had your strawberry shortcake."

Arwen was fairly certain he'd been gazing with the romantic longing of poets and painters at *Val*, but she didn't argue further, instead eyeing the submarine curiously. "Is that what we almost rode in the night of the big dragon fight in Edmonds? When we found Azerdash's sword?"

"It's the submarine I arranged transportation for and drove

across the city to Edmonds only to find out you'd already gone free diving and *found* the sword, yes."

"Sorry about that." Arwen had already apologized, but she always felt guilty about inconveniencing people. "The dragon battle pushed things along and made me feel short on time."

"After what happened to the kayak you borrowed, Willard is *glad* you didn't go out there in her submarine." Val parked and got out.

Arwen followed her along one of the docks framing the boat launch, the water placid thanks to the breakwater farther out. The submarine floated next to the dock, the hatch open and waiting for them.

"It looks less flammable than the kayak," Arwen offered, considering the metal and glass frame.

"Dragon fire burns at a temperature that makes *anything* flammable."

"True." Arwen thought of the various things, including a brick wall, that she'd seen Azerdash incinerate.

Val climbed in, stashed her sword scabbard behind the seat, and took the controls.

Trusting she had experience navigating the craft, Arwen did the same with her bow and quiver and slid into the other seat. A hint of bleach and other chemicals promised it had been cleaned recently. Arwen suspected the goblins were only the drivers and didn't care for the submarine, since their idea of cleaning usually involved grease to put a nice sheen on metal.

At a touch from Val, the hatch came down, and the scent of bleach intensified. She wrinkled her nose as she navigated them out of the marina. "It may *look* like a civilian submarine, but you can tell the Army owns it—and that Willard demands it be kept in an impeccable state of cleanliness."

"I've ridden in her SUV." Arwen remembered how tidy it had been.

"Yup. She's made comments when she's ridden in mine. About the dog hair and tiger fur."

"How does she feel about the piña colada air freshener?"

"She hates it almost as much as Sindari does." Val touched a button, and they descended below the surface. That was surprising, since it was quite a ways to Olympia from there, but the submarine picked up speed as soon as it submerged, so maybe it could travel faster underwater. "I changed the piña colada to something else, by the way. I'm not convinced that assassin dragon wasn't tracking us by the scent."

"That does seem possible. Those air fresheners have a strong odor. What is it now?"

"True North."

"What does *that* smell like?"

"According to the package, the scent was inspired by Canada's snow-capped mountains, and it brings to mind crisp, arctic air and frosted pine needles."

Arwen was skeptical an air freshener could capture that but offered, "That could be nice."

"Sindari says it smells like a sasquatch fell in a campfire." Val grinned wickedly at her. She'd probably delighted in sharing the scent with her tiger companion.

"Have you noticed that you have an antagonistic relationship with a lot of your allies?"

"Yeah, but I'm sure it's them, not me. I'm a delight."

Deciding it would be impolite to refute Val's statements, Arwen gazed through the glass hatch. They weren't far below the surface, so enough daylight trickled down to highlight schools of fish and kelp forests. Once, an orca whale swam by, indifferent to their passing. The sea life in Puget Sound had to be used to a lot of marine traffic.

When Val brought them to the surface again, they weren't far from land, the tree-filled shoreline far less filled with houses and buildings than in the area they'd left. Ahead, islands—or maybe peninsulas?—rose up from the water.

"We're going into Totten Inlet. The circle on the map is near the shoreline somewhere up there." Val pointed toward a heavily forested area with more cliffs than beaches. "The dark-elven map wasn't even vaguely accurate, so it's hard for me to guess exactly where, but I'm planning on cruising close to the shoreline and hoping to sense magic or spot something out of the ordinary."

Arwen nodded. "I'll keep an eye out."

"It's mostly private land all along here, and roads don't go down to the water in many places, so Willard's operative didn't get a thorough search in."

Arwen spotted a few houses perched atop cliffs with views of the water. "Will the landowners object to us floating by and peering into their trees?"

"I think landowners only object if you peer into their bathrooms."

"I doubt the dark elves would be in there."

"Let's hope not. Lots of people kayak out here, so homeowners have to be used to having their lands admired by floating visitors." Val guided them along the shoreline, the instruments warning them if the water grew shallow.

Arwen reached out with her senses as she peered toward the cliffs, searching for caves, natural or recently added. Most likely, the dark elves would have camouflaged any entrances with magic, so she didn't expect to spot anything. So far, she hadn't detected anyone in the area with a smidgen of magical blood.

"This may turn out to be a waste of time," Val admitted after they'd gone as far into the inlet as they could. Even though the map had marked the peninsula they'd examined, she navigated them up the opposite shoreline to check there as well. "That lair was probably abandoned decades ago."

"Could be, but it's the only one that was right by the water. I told you what Amber dug up about the yacht meeting point for potential surrogates, right?"

"Yes, and she gave me some tidbits herself before she decided to start charging for information." Val frowned. "I don't usually mind my daughter's efforts to make money, but it would have been nice if she'd been less of a dick to Winter."

"I think she's upset to have what she was thinking of as *her* job given to someone else."

"It was never going to be her job. She's just a kid. I don't know why she has this sudden interest in getting involved in the magical community, anyway. You can't be *that* fun to drive around. No offense, Arwen, but I've ridden with you."

"Are you sure your *allies* are the reason you have antagonistic relationships with people?"

"Hm, maybe not."

"Amber seems to be enjoying the research," Arwen offered. "She's figured out she's good at it. She was saying that, in addition to having a career in the fashion industry, she might want to be a private investigator on the side."

"I can just imagine her opening up that business with Gondo."

"He might not be her first choice in partners."

"Poor Gondo. He gets that from all the ladies." Val squinted at a damp cliff, roots dangling down from above, but must have decided it didn't hold anything of interest. She navigated them into a cove to eye a couple more rock faces. "It's a little depressing when your kid opens up to other people more than you. I wasn't a part of her life for a long time, so I get why I'm not her favorite blood relation, but... we've been doing better lately. I thought."

"She'll open up to you and appreciate you more when she's older."

"You think so? How *much* older?"

"Probably after your death."

"Oh, great. Maybe she'll come to the cemetery and keep my

tombstone company." As they exited the cove, Val waved at open water ahead. "That's the end of the inlet."

"Should we submerge and check near the circled area again?"

"I guess that makes sense. We *do* have a submarine, after all."

"I was surprised you didn't go down already."

"In most spots, it was too shallow. You saw all the mudflats to the south, right? People farm oysters down there." Val took them back across the inlet toward a cliff, the closest rock face near the marked spot on the dark-elf map, and descended.

The silty water kept them from seeing far. If there were caves anywhere, they never would have known. The submarine had headlights, but they did little to pierce the hazy water. Val poked around for a bit, ascended, then stopped the submarine. Water lapped at the glass.

"It'll be sunset soon," Val said. "I'm tempted to wait, since night would be the time for dark-elf activity."

"You think we'll see a yacht dropping off unsuspecting women then?"

"Maybe. We could attempt to camouflage ourselves and hang out." Val rubbed her charm. "Zav's still back home, doing who knows what for his mom, so I don't have evening plans."

"Do you two go out on date nights?" Arwen had a hard time imagining Val getting dressed up. Further, Zavryd's black elven robe and fluorescent-yellow Crocs might not meet the standards of fancier restaurants. Val seemed more like a fish sticks from Ivar's Seafood Bar kind of gal, anyway.

"Now and then. We even double-date with Matti and Sarrlevi."

"Is that hard with them being mortal enemies and starting duels on a regular basis?"

"*Very* hard. We've found that they enjoy hockey games though. We also went ice skating once, though Zav got huffy and said such an un-engaging sport was beneath dragons. He only called it that after Sarrlevi picked it up instantly and danced across the rink like an Olympic figure skater. Zav fell on his ass. The *ice* is what was beneath a dragon."

"I can't imagine a dragon doing something as ungraceful as falling. They're so majestic and beautiful when they're flying."

"It's a different story when they're shape-shifted. And on ice." Val thumped her on the shoulder. "After all this is over, we can go on a date with you and Starblade, and you can see."

Arwen smiled wistfully.

Val lowered her hand and glanced up as a heron landed on the hatch. "I don't think our camouflage is extending to the submarine."

Arwen activated hers and rested a hand on the frame, willing her power to flow into the craft and hide it. Since nobody had taught her how to do that, and her tattoo was no longer around to help her, she didn't know if the effort was effective. Regardless, she didn't lament the loss of the spider mark.

As the sun sank below the Olympics, the heron folded one leg up, lowered its neck, and went to sleep. Val slumped back in her seat with a sigh and glanced at the clock on her phone several times as darkness descended over the water.

For the first time, something magical plucked at Arwen's senses. It came from the cliff.

Val sat up.

"Did you feel that?" Arwen asked.

"Yeah, a hint of something. Like a portal forming, maybe."

"Someone arriving for the evening's events?" Arwen peered around the inlet but didn't spot any yachts heading in their direction. A couple of kayakers remained out, but most had headed for shore to call it a night.

Val and Arwen said little more, only straining their senses to try to detect something else as night deepened.

"The tide is going out," Arwen observed, wondering if that might reveal anything along the cliff.

"Does that look like a crevice?" Val pointed toward the vertical rock. "Or just a shadow?"

It had gotten too dark to tell.

"I'll get us a little closer." Val reached for the controls, but something wavered on the cliff a few dozen yards to the side of the crevice she'd noticed. It was like a mirage in a desert, rippling over the rock. "Illusion magic."

"Something's coming out." Arwen almost reached for her bow before catching herself. It wasn't as if she could fire through the glass. Though if they popped the hatch, she could stand up and fire at— "Is that a boat?"

"It looks like a *yacht*." Excitement infused Val's voice for the first time. "Can you tell if we're legit camouflaged? I felt you do something, but I'm not sure we've got more than the sleeping heron to make us blend in."

"I'm not sure either."

The yacht appeared to emerge straight from the cliff. With an all-black hull, it blended in with the deepening night. No lights brightened the craft, but Arwen could make out crates loaded along the deck. They stood out since it wasn't a cargo ship.

"I sense a couple of orcs onboard." Val nudged the submarine slowly forward.

"So do I." Arwen thought of the orcs camped out in front of her farm. Were these from the same mercenary group? And still working for the dark elves? "Maybe we should question them."

"Exactly what I was thinking." Val put them on a course to intercept the yacht. It was already swinging out into the inlet, its helm pointing to the north and Puget Sound.

A whisper of magic—no, that was another magical being— back at the cliff made Arwen lean forward in her seat. "That's a dark elf." A *familiar* dark elf. "Harlik-van."

"Your asshole brother who attempted to kill me while his demon-octopus was trying to devour my flesh?"

"It wanted your soul, not your flesh."

"I wasn't eager to part with that either."

Arwen bit her lip. Should they go after the orcs and the yacht, a yacht that might be on its way to kidnap more unsuspecting women? Or—

The submarine lurched as Val accelerated, not after the yacht but toward Harlik-van. The heron, who hadn't minded that its perch was moving when it had done so slowly, left amid a great flapping of wings.

"Uhm." Val lifted her hands from the controls. Magic rippled over them—*dark-elven* magic.

"Can you turn us?" Arwen didn't know if it would be better to go after the yacht or her brother, but she didn't like that they weren't getting a choice.

Val tapped at the controls. "No." She leaned back and grabbed her sword scabbard. "That's okay. This'll give us a chance to finish off that bastard this time."

Nerves fluttered in Arwen's belly. Harlik-van would be a more dangerous opponent than the orcs, and if he was manipulating the submarine, he was prepared for them.

Still, it would be all right if they could get the best of him. The kidnapped women might be inside that cliff somewhere.

Arwen's mother and all those serving her could be in there too, a thought that intensified the rattling of nerves battering Arwen's insides.

They couldn't see Harlik-van—couldn't see anything but the cliff—but he had to be in whatever cave was hiding under the illusion. He might be looking right at them.

Abruptly, her brother's aura vanished. Had he camouflaged himself?

If you seek to lend your womb to our repopulation efforts, Harlik-van spoke into her mind in Dark Elven, *I am certain our mother would allow that.*

Arwen groaned.

"What?" Val asked as the cliff loomed closer, the submarine carried inexorably toward it.

It appeared very solid, and Arwen shifted in her seat. Even though they'd seen the yacht emerge from the cliff, she wasn't certain they were heading for that exact spot.

"He knows we're coming," she said.

"I figured."

The submarine accelerated toward the cliff.

12

THE CLIFF FILLED THEIR VISION AS THE SUBMARINE CONTINUED toward it.

The grim set of Val's face as she gripped her sword said she didn't mind. She wanted to take out Harlik-van bad.

Arwen, who'd shot her brother between the shoulder blades the last time they'd met, worried he wanted to take *them* out just as bad. Worse, he had the advantage. This was his lair.

Though the illusion of rock never wavered, the submarine glided into the cliff without slowing. Magic rippled over Arwen's skin as they passed through. It wasn't unpleasant, but an angry buzz that followed was.

Like an intense static shock, it knocked her back in her seat. Lights flashed on the control panel before everything went dark. The engine cut off, but their momentum took them into an underground pool.

"Do you sense your brother?" Val asked. "Did he say anything to you?"

Arwen licked her lips, peering around, but it was pitch black inside the cavern. Behind them lay the cave opening, not hidden from within. In the distance, the dark shore on the opposite side of the inlet was visible, but since night had fallen outside, no light filtered in.

"He said our mother would let me donate my womb to their project."

"Gee, what an offer. No interest in mine? Am I too old?"

"Probably."

"My elven blood is supposed to keep me spry and fecund for longer than the typical human."

"Do you want me to tell him that?"

"Nah. It's better to keep one's enemies in the dark in regard to one's fertility."

"I've heard that."

The submarine, which had continued to glide forward with the engine off, scraped twice on a shallow bottom, then hit something with a jolt. Metal wrenched, and Arwen pitched out of her seat as the craft bounced back, rocking violently.

Arwen grabbed her bow and quiver, glad for the four new dark-elven arrows Imoshaun had given her. She couldn't sense Harlik-van or anyone else but had no doubt enemies were about.

Val tapped the controls of the submarine, but they remained dark. "Guess if we have to leave in a hurry, it'll be a swim."

A rumble followed by a thump came from behind them. They peered backward, but the view of the inlet had disappeared. The *exit* had disappeared.

"I don't think swimming is an option either," Arwen murmured.

"Not until we deal with him."

Them, Arwen's mind wanted to correct. She anticipated multiple enemies. Maybe *many* enemies.

Val pulled on an emergency lever, one that didn't require power, and popped the hatch.

She switched to telepathy to say, *Camo yourself. We'll hop out so they don't know where we are.*

Okay. In the dark, Arwen had no idea if there was a ledge or protruding rock on which to hop, but Val was already springing out of the sub.

She landed with a soft thud instead of a splash, so that was promising.

"*Eravekt,*" Val whispered as Arwen slid down the nose of the sub, landing one foot in the water and one on a rocky protrusion about twenty paces long and ten wide.

Val's sword glowed blue, illuminating an underground chamber filled with water, save for a few other large rocks poking above the surface and a ledge with a dock at the far end. Was that a tunnel at the back of the ledge leading off into darkness?

Will the light break your camouflage? Arwen asked, worried Val was a beacon.

No. And you'll have to stick close if you don't have a light of your own. Once I'm out of range, it will disappear to you.

Got it.

I'm surprised that yacht was able to tie up in here, Val said telepathically as she looked around. *It's shallow if we scraped the bottom in that little sub.*

Maybe there's a deeper channel for those who know where.

I suppose. Even if power returns to the sub, we might not be able to escape if the tide goes out farther. Val looked toward the other end of the pool, but whatever door had closed blended in with the natural rock. *We might not be able to get out, period,* she amended. *Not until we find the dark elf and make him open the door. If my hand is around his throat, maybe he'll be amenable to doing that.*

If we see Harlik-van, I'll deal with him. Could she? Arwen didn't know if he would avoid attacking her this time. Before, she had been able to take advantage because he'd considered Val far more of an enemy than she, but that might have changed since she'd shot him. *He's my brother,* she added to explain why she felt responsible for him.

Oh, I know, but he has a powerful aura. Assuming he shows up again, we might need to work together against him.

One of us needs to find the kidnapped women.

We'll kill him and find them. Willard likes operatives who can multitask.

Val nodded toward the dock. A hint of magic came from the tunnel in that direction. From devices, Arwen decided, not people. Her brother had either left or remained camouflaged.

Val slid off their rock island and into the water. It lapped at her hips, and she strode gamely toward the dock.

Arwen crouched, intending to follow her, but paused, something plucking at her instincts. A warning. She still couldn't sense anyone, but she had the feeling of being watched. Harlik-van.

I'd put a barrier up if I were you, Arwen warned Val, imagining her brother poised in the shadows with some of his throwing stars.

Yeah. You'd better do the same. Maybe Val also felt they were being watched.

Arwen summoned a magical barrier around herself. Between one blink and the next, darkness smothered the cave again.

She twitched in surprise before remembering Val's warning. Right. She'd moved out of range and was now as camouflaged to Arwen as anyone else.

Arwen almost waded after Val, but her instincts made her believe Harlik-van was in the other direction, over by the entrance. Maybe that door hadn't closed automatically over the cave entrance. Maybe he'd been the one to trap them inside.

Though she'd activated her camouflage earlier, Arwen did so again. Just in case. She also readied one of her new dark-elf arrows.

You've removed your tattoo, Harlik-van spoke coolly into her mind.

Arwen's sleeve wasn't up, and he shouldn't have been able to see it—or sense it—through her camouflage. That made her wonder if he'd noticed them cruising around in the inlet earlier. They hadn't been magically hidden then. He might also have gotten the information from the eyeballs spying on her.

Her first thought was to remain quiet, but if she kept him busy, Val could hunt for the prisoners.

It didn't go with my look.

She Who Leads wishes me to capture you.

Arwen licked her lips. *I'm right here.*

She could tell from his telepathic voice that he was close.

I see, he said. *Well, I don't see at the moment, but I* know.

Are you okay, Arwen? Val asked. *Are you behind me?*

I'm still by the sub. Harlik-van is talking to me. He's in this cave.

That sounds like a good reason to leave.

I'll keep him distracted. You find the prisoners.

Harlik-van spoke again. *When she has you again, She Who Leads will use the memory-wiping device on you. She regrets that she did not do so last time. She believed the compulsion she placed on you would be sufficient, that you would eagerly obey her wishes. I did not believe so and said as much. But she thought you would be more useful with your memories intact and that your human half would make you have feelings for her, that you would wish to obey your mother.*

She doesn't know me very well.

Clearly. Harlik-van chuckled aloud, and she heard it. It sounded like he was floating above the water between her island and the hidden entrance.

Arwen pointed her bow in that direction, but it was so dark that he could have been levitating ten feet away without camouflage and she would have struggled to see him.

Arwen risked lowering her bow so she could activate the light on her multitool. Unfortunately, it operated like a flashlight instead of glowing like Val's sword. Arwen would have to hold it to direct the beam. Since she needed both hands to shoot, she set it down, pointing the light in Harlik-van's direction.

It revealed a black haze floating over the water and nothing more. But she trusted her instincts and what she'd heard. He was there, watching her. She lifted her bow again.

We have found enough useful magical beings who can go out in the light and are willing to work for us that I don't believe our mother needs you, Harlik-van said. *It may be stubbornness that makes her desire to have you with us, walking at her side. She has forbidden me from killing you.*

Because she cares for me? Arwen highly doubted that and wasn't surprised when he snorted.

That sound was slightly closer than the laugh had been.

Arwen swallowed, nerves making her palms damp. Since she had extra arrows, she could risk guessing with a shot. But she hated to lose even one of the valuable gifts. It would only be worth it if she could succeed in taking her brother out of the equation.

Because she set her plan in motion more than thirty years ago. She wishes it to be fruitful. Even though our people are long-lived, nobody wishes to believe they've wasted three decades on a project.

I feel for her.

I believe you are trouble, far more trouble than you and your womb are worth. She Who Leads would be better off focusing on our mission and forgetting about you. He was even closer. *Of course she does not listen to me. She has bartered for a dragonish way to earn your willing cooperation. You hardly seem worth the effort though. Or cost.*

Dragonish way? What did *that* mean? Something to do with Azerdash?

Thanks so much. Arwen's arm quivered from holding the bow taut for so long, and she had to fight the urge to fire. If she did and missed, he might be close enough to prevent her from nocking another arrow in time. Hell, with his power, he might be able to do that from anywhere in the cave.

I believe, Harlik-van whispered into her mind, *that I would be doing her a favor by killing you, by removing the distraction.*

How about I kill you *instead?*

You have tried and failed. Even with the assistance of a supposedly great warrior and her pet cat.

Sindari was hardly that. Arwen wished she had the great magical tiger at her side now.

Harlik-van fell silent. She still couldn't see or sense him—sense *anything*—but her instincts warned her that he was creeping closer. That he meant to attack.

Something plunked into the water behind her. A distraction.

She jumped to the side and risked firing at the spot she thought Harlik-van was. Her arrow sailed into darkness, then clattered into a stone wall.

Something struck her multitool, knocking it spinning, the flashlight fluctuating wildly. A rubbery tentacle. Or was that a long fin?

Terrified the treasured gift would fall into the water, Arwen almost sprang for it. But she could now sense a magical creature in the water behind her. A lesser water demon. Harlik-van had summoned it. And he—where was *he*?

She nocked another arrow. Power surged, and a shadow moved not five feet in front of her. Arwen sprang to the side an instant before something whizzed past her ear—a throwing star.

She fired at the shadow—at *him*—as splashes came from the water behind her. Her arrow deflected slightly, and a faint grunt sounded. Harlik-van. She'd struck him, but that could only have been a glancing blow.

A tremendous wave of power slammed into her. *Angry* power. Even with her barrier up, it knocked her back.

She stumbled several steps, her heel coming down in the water at the edge of the island. The creature's rubbery appendage brushed her calf. She leaped and dove, rolling across the hard rock, and heard another throwing star whisper past above her.

Arwen spotted the multitool tilted into a divot and snatched it, relieved it hadn't been knocked into the water.

"You want to talk about relying on a *pet* for help," she barked as she sprang to her feet.

Finally, the cloaked and hooded Harlik-van came fully in view, crouching on the island with her. If she'd injured him, he didn't show it. He carried a sword, but he blasted her with magic instead of attacking with the blade. It knocked her back before she could turn her bow toward him. This time, the power not only sent her stumbling, but it ripped her barrier to tatters, leaving her vulnerable to him—and the demon in the water. Two glowing yellow eyes were now visible in a dome-shaped head, and thick fins stretched toward her.

Arwen scurried away from her enemies, juggling bow and multitool. She managed to re-form her barrier before another blast of power struck her.

Harlik-van hadn't taken a step, hadn't even lifted a finger. He merely stood there, his intent crimson eyes upon her, as he called upon his magic.

She gripped the multitool tighter, thinking to draw upon its magic to reinforce her barrier. She'd lost her tattoo, but Azerdash had made the gift, imbuing it with some of his power.

A great splash came from her right, and the demon propelled itself out of the water. A blobby body, four prehensile fins, and a maw filled with fangs flew toward her.

Arwen dropped to her belly and rolled away.

Her concentration lapsed—and so did her barrier. The demon sailed over her head, but one of the fins struck her, knocking her flying as surely as her brother's power had. She landed half in the water as Harlik-van chuckled.

The urge to flee, to try to reach Val for help came over Arwen, but she made herself get to her feet and face him.

The demon landed on the other side of the island with a great splash. Remembering the way her supernatural arrow, Ghoster, had once destroyed a tiny creature summoned from another dimension, Arwen fished in her quiver for it. With water dripping from her hands, she nocked it.

Harlik-van stepped toward her. *I should make your death look like an accident, I suppose, or at least have it appear that I was forced to defend myself. She Who Leads will enjoy it when I bring her the Ruin Bringer's head, but she mustn't believe I killed you when I knew her wishes were otherwise.*

"Yeah, don't piss off Mommy."

As I said, she has a new plan to bring you to her side—and deal with that half-dragon you've befriended as well.

Frowning, Arwen was about to ask what he meant—as long as he was volunteering information, she would be a fool not to listen. But the demon flew out of the water toward her again.

This time, Arwen was ready. She fired Ghoster into its maw.

It wouldn't do anything to stop the huge creature's momentum, so she also dodged out of the way. Instead of obeying her instincts and rushing backward, she made herself leap toward her brother.

His eyes widened slightly under his hood, but he glanced at her bow, saw she didn't have an arrow nocked, and simply reinforced his barrier. She swung the multitool toward him as the demon sailed over the island behind her. It landed with a great splash that sent droplets of water flying at her and her brother.

The flashlight beam hit his eyes.

Harlik-van winced but only briefly before laughing and pulling his hood lower to block it. *You think I don't have ways of protecting my eyes from light when I know I'll encounter you?*

Arwen hadn't expected the flashlight to do much to him, but she activated the powerful beam she'd used before to tunnel her way out of rockfalls. When it hit his barrier, Harlik-van stopped laughing.

At first, the beam was deflected, burrowing into the roof of the cave and bringing rocks down. Some landed on the demon, and it swam away. Ghoster was lodged in its throat, but she hadn't killed it. It flapped at its head with a fin, trying to remove the arrow.

Val, Arwen called telepathically as she willed all of her power into the multitool and for the beam to break through Harlik-van's defenses. *I could use some help out here.*

Maybe she should have started with that.

Her brother lifted a hand, as if to send another attack at her, but she channeled her power into the multitool, and the beam intensified. He grunted and stepped back, forced to put all his energy into maintaining his barrier.

Scowling, he yanked out another throwing star and hurled it at her face. Its glow made it possible to track, but it was more luck than skill when she jerked her bow across and deflected it.

"More power," she whispered to the multitool, managing to keep the beam focused on Harlik-van. Was it her imagination or was it eating into his barrier? "Please."

A roar came from the tunnel. Sindari?

Harlik-van glanced at his demon, but it had sunk below the surface, nursing its wound.

I'll deal with you later, Harlik-van told Arwen.

He sent a final blast of power at her, knocking her barrier and multitool aside, then dropped his own to form a portal. Though pushed off-balance, Arwen swung her bow back in line and nocked an arrow. For an instant, she had a fatal blow lined up, a shot that could have pierced his neck, but she hesitated. Despite her earlier brave words, the thought of killing her own kin repulsed her.

She shifted her aim toward a less vital target, but the delay cost her. Harlik-van sprang through as she fired, and her arrow whizzed through his cloak, leaving a hole in the fabric but doing nothing to hurt him.

He disappeared, the portal disappeared, and the demon also faded from Arwen's awareness as it returned to its own dimension.

"Arwen?" came Val's call from the tunnel.

Sighing, Arwen lowered her bow. "I'm okay."

The blue light returned to the cave as Val dropped her camouflage and appeared at the dock, her sword in hand. Sindari was crouching at the end, as if he'd been about to spring, but he looked around, straightened, and sniffed disdainfully at the cave.

"He's gone," Arwen added in case Val hadn't seen Harlik-van leap through the portal.

"Too bad we couldn't catch him to question."

Arwen had been too busy trying to stay alive to consider how she might have done that.

Val shook her head, pointing over her shoulder. "There's nothing back there."

Arwen pushed damp hair away from her face. "*Nothing?* I sense magical artifacts."

"You sense what I think is magical science equipment." Val grimaced. "There are some doodads and what were living and sleeping areas, but almost everything has been cleared out. There weren't any dark elves or human women. There wasn't *anybody*."

Arwen slumped. She'd challenged her brother and bought time for nothing?

"Remember the crates?" Val pointed toward the inlet. "The dark elves must have guessed we would check this place. They probably decided to clear out a while ago, and that was the last or maybe second-to-last load." She looked around. "Did you learn anything from Harlik-van?"

"Just that my mom wants me alive, plans to wipe my memory, and is open to adding my womb to the pile."

"It's nice to be loved."

"Hardly that. Harlik-van was contemplating killing me. *He* doesn't have any use for me in his plans—and thinks my mother would be better off giving up on me since I'm trouble."

"Yeah, *we're* the ones causing trouble."

After sweeping the cave with her senses to make sure the demon was gone, Arwen lowered herself into the water so she could retrieve her arrows. To her surprise, she found Ghoster floating near one of the others. The demon had either succeeded in tearing it out, or magical arrows couldn't travel to other dimensions. Not caring which it was, Arwen kissed it before returning it to her quiver.

"An interesting battle tactic," Val said. "Does lip residue improve the accuracy of your weapons?"

"Yes. Don't you kiss your sword?" Arwen waded wearily through the hip-deep water toward the submarine. She almost plunged in up to her shoulders as she encountered a deeper pocket where the demon had originally appeared.

"I've hugged it and snuggled with it a few times, but it's sharp. Lip contact isn't recommended." Val waded out, joining her at the submarine. "I can wait if you want to take a look at the laboratory area back there, but I've got a bunch of photos. I took pictures of everything in case there's a clue about where they went. Unfortunately, I think we're out of marked spots to check from that map you and your dad found."

"We are."

Arwen trusted Val had gotten as much information as she would from the laboratory and instead swam for the cave exit, which Harlik-van had rudely not unblocked before leaving. She still couldn't see a door or any cracks or signs that would have indicated one.

"Any ideas about how to get us out of here?" she asked.

The aura of a dragon reached her senses. Zavryd.

"Yup." Val pointed upward with a smile. "My mate has come looking for me."

Arwen wished *her mate* would come for her. Granted, she and Azerdash hadn't called each other mates yet, and he was off searching for another woman, but she would love to see him again.

"Stand back," Val said. "He's going to blast us out of here."

Arwen alternated swimming and wading back to the submarine. Before she reached it, tremendous power struck their hidden cave from outside. Rocks flew inward, and boulders and dirt tumbled down from above.

The disturbed water surged about, sloshing against Arwen and knocking her into the submarine. Val, who'd already climbed inside, leaned down and grabbed her.

In the aftermath, Arwen could again see the inlet and the opposite shoreline. The entrance was much larger now.

You are welcome, my mate. Zavryd's black-scaled head appeared in the opening, violet eyes turned toward Val.

"Always good to have you back on Earth," she told him.

Yes. I came from the canyon of the Dragon Council. The Silverclaws were called away because there is some trouble on one of the worlds they claim as their own. His gaze shifted toward Arwen.

"Azerdash is trying to find someone they kidnapped," Arwen said. "Uhm, how *many* Silverclaws left?"

Six.

Arwen looked bleakly at the slowly calming water. That was far, far too many dragons for Azerdash and Yendral to handle, even if their other half-dragon comrade was with them. Far too many. She remembered Azerdash's musing that the Silverclaws had set a trap for him, and feared he'd been right.

13

Days passed without word from Azerdash, and if Zavryd delivered any more updates, Val didn't share them. The only person who contacted Arwen was Willard, letting her know that more teenage women had gone missing and were believed to have been captured by dark elves. Willard didn't mention if her new werewolf operative had managed to get herself kidnapped yet.

Arwen made more peanut brittle and baked every dessert she could think of that might help Azerdash win over world leaders, but she worried that he'd been captured—or killed—by the Silverclaws. It was possible she was baking for nobody. That thought filled her with bleakness.

"I can always have Nin sell my desserts at the coffee shop if he doesn't come soon," Arwen told herself. "They're best fresh, after all. Though maybe the dwarves would prefer their baked goods to be a few days old. So they're *challenging*."

She tried to smile but instead found her hand straying to the multitool. Azerdash's gift. No matter what happened, she would have that. And the rejuvenation pool on the back of the property too.

"Did you say challenging?" Her father walked into the kitchen and washed his hands, not bothering to dig out the dirt under his nails. That usually took more than a little soap, as Arwen well knew.

"Yes. Dwarves have strong jaws. I'm told they like their desserts —or at least their peanut brittle—hard."

"Huh. How do orcs feel about challenging desserts?" Father waved toward a window facing the road, one of the huts visible beyond the beehives.

Since Zavryd had flown Arwen home after the submarine adventure the other night, she had been able to bypass the orcs, though she'd noticed a couple leaning out of their hide-and-bone dwellings to look up at her passing. She didn't have any updates on Azerdash, so she didn't know what she would tell them if they insisted on speaking. Immersed in her baking, she hadn't left the property and had to deal with them.

"I haven't discussed sweets with the orcs," she said.

"You think they can use those tusks to open cans?"

"I believe they use them to open suits of armor. While their enemies are wearing them."

"I brought the orcs up because..." Father glanced toward the window, as if spies might lurk outside the house, and lowered his voice. "You're in the back of the property, so you wouldn't have noticed, but the last couple of nights, I went out and caught a couple of them poking at the magic that's protecting our borders. Like they were testing the whatchamacallits."

"Wards."

"Yeah. The orcs got buzzed, and a few sparks lit up, so they backed off, but it made me suspicious."

"Just two were doing it? Was Brok one?"

"I don't know their names, but it wasn't the leader who spoke to you. A couple of the subordinates."

"Did their eyes seem glazed?"

"I didn't get close enough to peer into their eyes."

"I ask," Arwen said, "because some of those very orcs were working for the dark elves and attacked us a while back."

Father stared at her, and she realized she hadn't shared that information before.

"Maybe not those *very* orcs," she amended, waving toward the road, "but some from that mercenary outfit."

"So, their buddies."

"Yeah."

"And you invited them to camp here."

"To camp in the road." Had Arwen even invited them to do that? She wasn't quite sure how this had happened.

Father scowled out the window. "The next time one pokes at the wards, I'll lob a grenade into their camp."

"That's one method of dealing with itinerants."

"You should take more grenades with you on *your* missions." Grumbling, he grabbed a cookie and stalked out of the kitchen.

Since grenades might have helped against her brother, Arwen didn't deny the assertion. Magical grenades, anyway. She doubted mundane explosives would have done anything to lower Harlik-van's barrier or distract him.

Arwen stepped closer to the window and caught one of the orcs standing at the front of the driveway, scant inches from the wards, and staring at the house. From this distance, she couldn't tell if his eyes were glazed.

What if the orcs had lied, fully knowing Azerdash wasn't on the planet, and they were biding their time until they could find a way onto the farm to attack?

Magic flared at the back of the property, and Arwen ran toward a window that looked in that direction. Was that a portal?

She glimpsed a silver disc floating in the air above the trees and sighed in relief when Azerdash flew out of it. *He* could deal with the orcs.

He headed toward her house, but did his flight seem lopsided? Had he been injured?

Yendral soared out of the portal behind him, and that gave her more relief. If Azerdash and his staunch ally were both alive, things couldn't have gone too badly.

She grabbed a paper towel, tucked raspberry thumbprints and blackberry white-chocolate-chip cookies into it, and hurried out to meet them.

Azerdash alighted on the roof of her small home. Yendral, however, flew around the property, lingering over the road and the orcs.

Arwen. Azerdash's violet eyes met hers as she hurried down the path toward him. A deep gouge on his snout wept blood, his scales were charred, and one of his eyes was half shut. *Swollen* shut?

Azerdash, what happened to you? Do you need my first-aid kit? The rejuvenation pool? Arwen lifted the bundle she'd made. *Cookies?*

All of that. Even through telepathy, his tone came across as weary and pained.

He shifted into his elven form. Usually, he would have leaped down from the house and landed easily, but he gripped the gutter and lowered himself gingerly to the ground.

His clothing was torn, and numerous wounds leaked blood. It soaked the side of his shirt. He retained his sword, the big magical weapon in its scabbard on his back, but his shoulders bowed, as if the weight of it were greater than usual.

Arwen hurried forward and wrapped an arm around him, careful not to touch his wounds. "Come inside. Let me tend you."

"Gladly." He slumped against her, limping as he let her guide him into the house.

"Did you run into the Silverclaws? Zavryd said six left the council to deal with you."

"It could have been six. It could have been sixty. We were outnumbered, regardless. Our attempts at stealth were limited in effectiveness. They knew the gnome had escaped—I think they *let* the gnome escape so he could leak the news that Gemlytha was alive."

Arwen directed him to a chair and started for her first-aid kit, but Azerdash waved a hand and pulled his travel tin of elven regeneration bandages out of thin air. Not certain if that cleaned wounds as well as healing them, she grabbed her first-aid kit anyway.

"Is Yendral okay?" Arwen sensed him swooping about, like a guard on patrol. Maybe that was exactly what he was.

"He informed me, as we were fleeing from four bitter and angry dragons who obliterated our camouflaging magic, that he was feeling weak and not flying as effectively due to a lack of cookies and other delicious foods from Chef Arwen."

"So, he's fine?"

"Just a couple of scratches, I believe. The Silverclaws all targeted *me*. They know I'm the leader of the movement and believe that if they can get rid of me, all their problems will be solved."

They were probably right. Arwen didn't know his comrade Sleveryn that well, but she couldn't imagine Yendral taking over an army and wooing world leaders.

"I'm glad you escaped." Arwen held up her clean, damp towel and a tube of antibiotic ointment. "Take your shirt off, please."

Azerdash smiled slightly, as if he might make a comment about her wanting him out of his clothes, but he complied without remarking on it. Too exhausted for jokes, perhaps.

"Thank you for tending my wounds and..." His gaze shifted to the paper towel. She'd wrapped it so that it hid the contents, but his nostrils twitched. "Are those for me?" he asked.

"For you and Yendral. I thought you could both use some cookies."

"Doubtless so."

While she washed his wounds—damn, he was bleeding a lot, especially given his magical power and ability to regenerate quickly—he opened the bundle. He was more interested in the contents than what she was doing.

She'd inadvertently grabbed an odd number for her impromptu gift. He selected two thumbprints and two blackberry cookies, placed them in front of himself, then put two of each aside for Yendral. One raspberry thumbprint remained on the paper towel.

"A conundrum." A muscle ticked in his jaw as Arwen dabbed a deep wound, but that was the only indication he gave of his pain. "As the commander, it could be argued that it's my right to take the extra. But Yendral was pivotal in helping me escape and is now guarding the premises and mind-scouring the legion of orcs camped in front of your property." He frowned at her. "Perhaps you will tell me *why* orcs are camped in front of your property."

"They're the ones I told you about. They say they want to join your army and drive the dragons from the orc home world. Maybe Yendral's mind scouring can determine if they're telling the truth."

"Likely." Azerdash's gaze drifted back to the problematic single cookie on the paper towel.

"Will I fix your conundrum if I eat that?" She supposed she could also fetch a knife to cut it in half.

"Yes. Though I was going to suggest that I might levitate another out here to make an even number." He looked thoughtfully toward Father's house—specifically toward the kitchen.

"You can levitate a whole pan of them back if you want." Arwen paused cleaning his wounds to rest her forehead on his shoulder. As relieved as she was that he'd survived and come here, she hated seeing him in pain.

"That would not be presumptuous?" Azerdash rested his hand on the back of her head and leaned his cheek against hers. "I assume you baked them for a purpose, not so that wandering half-dragons would show up and slurp them down."

"I baked them for *your* purpose. For the dwarf king and whoever else you need to woo. Per your request."

For a moment, he didn't reply, though he tenderly rubbed the back of her head. "You are... perfect," he whispered.

"Hardly that," Arwen murmured, but his words filled her with such warmth that her chest ached. She wanted to be perfect in his eyes, for him to appreciate her over all others.

But the reason he was injured came to mind, reminding her there *was* another.

She leaned back to finish cleaning his wounds but caught herself looking around with her eyes and senses. She didn't *think* anyone else had flown through the portal behind them, but she'd been distracted when she'd noticed Azerdash's lopsided flight.

"We weren't successful in finding Gemlytha," Azerdash said, watching her face—and probably her mind.

"I'm sorry." Arwen strove to mean it. She had nothing against the woman she'd never met, and would be happy if more of the half-dragons had survived than they'd thought, but she couldn't help but acknowledge that things would be easier for her and Azerdash if Gemlytha weren't ever found.

If he caught that thought, he didn't comment on it. "We *did* find evidence that she'd been there, a prisoner on their home world. We located a number of stasis chambers, as the gnome described, but one was missing from the middle of the grouping, the dust still on the ground where it had rested. In that empty space, we sensed the remnants of her aura. We think she left—or was moved—only a couple of days earlier."

"Do you think they moved her after the gnome escaped?"

"After the gnome was permitted to escape as part of a trap for me, yes." His mouth twisted, probably in disgust because he'd flown into that trap.

She had little doubt that he'd made some plans and been clever, else he wouldn't have reached the stasis chambers and escaped with his life, but the incursion clearly hadn't gone as well as he'd hoped. If they'd found Gemlytha and made it out with her, he would be far more pleased.

"Is there another Silverclaw stronghold?" Arwen asked. "Somewhere else they might have taken her?"

"Sleveryn is asking around, but we—"

Have you patched your wounds yet, Azerdash? came Yendral's telepathic voice from the front of the property. *Our meeting with the dwarven king that you worked so hard to arrange is soon.*

I am aware, Azerdash replied, including Arwen in the response.

Are you also aware that a number of orcs have invaded Chef Arwen's land, claiming they wish to join your army?

Have you ascertained whether that desire is in earnest?

The one in charge—Brok—is in earnest. You used elven regeneration bandages on him at one point, so he has fond feelings for you.

Interesting.

I thought so, Yendral said. *Who heals orcs?*

Are the rest of his people as dedicated?

They are not. Some are. Some he wheedled into joining. One has lustful thoughts about our chef and has considered trying to thwart the wards to intrude upon her home when she sleeps and have his way with her.

What? Azerdash sat rigid, and his eyes glowed.

I have considered smiting him myself. Had he so much as touched her...

Arwen scratched her jaw. Was *that* what had been on the minds of the orcs her father had seen?

A tusked marauder springing into her home in the middle of the night would have been alarming, but she found it less disturbing than the thought of her brother controlling them all.

There is another who had thoughts of a male dark elf in his mind, but he's a little hard to read. It seemed like a memory from the past. He was thinking about how he'd lost a friend when they worked for the dark elves.

Thank you for checking on them. None of the tension had gone out of Azerdash's body, but his eyes did return to normal as he turned his gaze on Arwen.

If you wish, Yendral said, *I can go ahead to the meeting. It's important not to be late or miss it. If we can get Ironhelm, King Eireth may be more tempted to give troops to our cause. As strange as it seems, elves and dwarves are allies in this time.*

I know.

And if we get Eireth, we might be able to get more assistance from the gnome ruler too. Yes, they've agreed to give you siege equipment, but they have that fascinating armor as well.

Arwen lifted her eyebrows, thinking of the suit of combat armor that Gruflen had invented. Maybe he'd built something that was already known and popular back on his world.

We can't do this with just trolls and orcs, Yendral added.

Don't forget the ogres.

Yes, dragons quake when ogres wave their clubs at them.

We won't be late, Yendral. I'm gathering a few sweets to soften the moods of the dour dwarves, and we shall go. Azerdash met Arwen's eyes. "We do have to leave to meet with King Ironhelm shortly, but, afterward, I'll return for the orcs and take them to another world where they can join my army if they wish. At the least, they will be away from Earth where they can't pester you or your father."

"I would appreciate that, but you're leaving already?" Arwen had barely gotten a chance to see him, to talk to him. "I thought you needed to use my pool. And we haven't put the pads on you yet."

"I have a few minutes before we need to leave." He smiled at her, took one of the pads from the tin, and waved for her to apply it. "Also, I'm hoping that you will, as we discussed, come *with* me to see the dwarven king. After all, it was only after I mentioned that you were a friend of his granddaughter that we were able to finagle a meeting."

"Oh. I can come." Arwen gently laid the pad on one of his wounds, and it adhered to his side. "Though you might get more mileage out of taking Matti. If you stood next to her in the king's court—" Arwen had no idea if dwarves *had* courts in the human sense, "—and praised her and her children, the king might look fondly upon you. She might even be able to take them some of her grandmother's peanut brittle."

Azerdash sniffed. "I am certain *your* desserts are superior." He bit into one of the thumbprints and chewed contently. "*Most* superior."

Arwen almost said she was less certain of that, especially since she'd been unwilling to ruin the brittle to get it hard, but a pan of cookies floated through the open door, distracting her.

"Those are... for the dwarven king?" She raised her eyebrows.

"They are not." Azerdash floated the pan to the table, selected a cookie, and rested it next to the odd one he'd identified earlier. Thus assured that he and Yendral would receive equal amounts, he set the rest of the pan aside, though he did cast a few contemplative looks at it. "You are an excellent ally. The dwarven king will be pleased to meet you, and you will assist us with negotiations."

Arwen tried to smile, but the thought of entering a castle and being surrounded by a bunch of strange dwarves and expected to *negotiate* filled her with angst. Or maybe that was panic burbling up. She wanted to help Azerdash, but a part of her would rather stay home, even if she had to deal with lusty orcs.

14

ARWEN STEPPED OUT OF A PORTAL TO THE DWARVEN HOME WORLD with so many cookie tins and boxes of sweets in her arms and pack that she felt like a FedEx driver during the holiday season. Yendral had headed off to another world, or she might have pressed him into carrying some of her treats. Since Azerdash was here as an important war leader with an appointment to see the king, she decided that turning him into a delivery boy wouldn't be appropriate.

She found herself by his side in a huge cavern, the air a mix of earthy fungi scents and machine oil. Behind them, the ground was level with rails and a road running off into what looked like an underground wilderness. Ahead, a great wall stretched from side to side of the cavern, and armored dwarves gazed down from towers perched atop it. The flat roofs of buildings were visible beyond the wall.

Wide, shallow stone stairs led up to a gate framed by two more armored dwarves bearing axes, the blades larger than Arwen's head. Their beards and red hair flowed down to their belts.

The dwarves frowned at Arwen. Though the cavern was

spacious and open, anxiety crept into her. Between the gate guards and the tower guards, there were too many sets of eyes upon her. She'd thought Azerdash would command the dwarves' attention, but maybe they'd never seen a human with dark-elven blood. Would they allow her to enter their city with him?

Her bow and quiver were slung across her back, but she hadn't brought any of the grenades that her father had suggested. As she'd assured him, she was going to meet friendly people, not enemies. At least she hoped that would be the case. She was glad she'd insisted on stopping in Green Lake to convince an ally to join them. Just in case the cookies and brittle weren't enough.

Matti came out of the portal beside Arwen, clanking like a gnome in battle armor. She not only carried her war hammer but had a backpack full of who knew what. Secret weapons, she'd told Arwen with a wink. Whatever she had, Arwen believed her presence would help.

Azerdash stood straight with his chin up as the gate guards descended the stairs. They nodded solemnly at Matti, glared suspiciously at Arwen, and frowned at Azerdash.

We have an appointment to see King Ironhelm, he told them telepathically. *I am Azerdash Starblade.*

A war criminal from another era who escaped from our stasis-chamber prison.

Predictably, Azerdash's chin roes even higher. He always hated being called a criminal. *I was a general fighting in a war against your people. I was* never *a criminal. And now I seek to unite many against our dragon overlords.*

We have heard what you wish to do. It is foolish.

Nonetheless, I have an appointment to see your king. Azerdash's eyes flared violet with irritation. *You will take me to see him, or I will go on my own.*

Arwen, who didn't think *threats* should be a part of negotiations, stepped forward and rested a hand on Azerdash's forearm.

"Hey, guys." Matti, who probably thought the same, stepped up to the dwarves, rested her hammer on the ground, lifted a hand to them, and pulled off her pack. She rummaged inside, withdrew a tin not dissimilar to the ones Arwen stored cookies in, and opened it for them. A rather dry-looking peanut brittle lay inside, the edges crystalized.

Arwen curled a lip, but the dwarven guards leaned forward with interest, each taking a piece. They chomped down, broad jaws working hard to break the stuff, and loud cracks and snaps sounded as they chewed. Contented smiles grew visible through their beards.

Matti winked at Arwen and Azerdash, giving them a thumbs-up.

"Maybe I'll only share my cookies with them," Arwen said, feeling her own peanut brittle might not appeal to them as much. "I also made biscotti."

"What is that?" Azerdash watched the chewing dwarves.

"A sweet, crunchy almond biscuit. Because they're hard, you're supposed to dip them in your coffee, but these guys may prefer them as they are."

"A challenging dessert." Azerdash nodded as the dwarves took more pieces of brittle.

One leaned forward, kissed Matti on the cheek, winked, and said something in Dwarven to her.

Wearing a bemused expression, she closed the tin and joined Arwen. "This is the only place where I get hit on regularly. It's a lot more infrequent on Earth. Dwarves appreciate a stout woman with curves, and they don't mind a little hair on her upper lip. And elsewhere."

Arwen eyed Matti's upper lip, but it was devoid of hair.

Perhaps guessing her thoughts, Matti said, "My electrologist is in my will."

I will accompany you to the royal quarters. One of the dwarves started up the stairs, tiny amber shards of brittle in his beard, and the gates opened.

Azerdash looked at Matti, perhaps rethinking his objection to stopping to pick her up.

"You can put me in *your* will." Matti winked at him before following the dwarf.

"I own few belongings." Azerdash let her follow their guide before falling in behind her. "Arwen will be the recipient of my manly project."

"Your what?" Matti asked over her shoulder, glancing at Arwen.

"It's an airplane," she explained. "He's reconstructing the engine."

"Well, I guess you have the room on your farm for such a thing."

"Yendral will deliver it upon my death," Azerdash said.

"Glad you two have it all worked out."

"Yes." Azerdash, chin up again, looked pleased with himself.

Arwen smiled, though she hoped Azerdash lived a long life and she would never have to make room for that airplane. She had, however, considered that she could use it like a trellis and grow grape and kiwi vines over it.

"Really," Azerdash murmured, apparently catching the stray thought.

"*You* have stuff growing on it now."

"To camouflage it from enemies, so they believe it a hulking wreck and don't realize I've ensorcelled it with numerous magical defenses."

"Grape leaves are also good camouflage."

"Hm."

The dwarf led them toward a raised trolley stop. Magic-powered cars zipped along tracks that ran all over the city, which was far more modern than Arwen had expected. Some of the stone, brick, and cement buildings rose up to ten stories, and electricity, rather than magic, powered the lamps that brightened the streets.

Citizens on foot or levitating motorcycles looked curiously at Azerdash and suspiciously at Arwen. As if *she* were the criminal who'd escaped from their prison.

She sighed, thinking Azerdash had been silly to believe she could help with negotiations. When they filed onto a trolley car already occupied by three dwarves, it felt crowded, and Arwen's shoulders bunched. She looked back with longing toward the gate, wishing she could run off and wait in the empty wilds beyond the city.

Azerdash rested a hand on her shoulder. Maybe a touch should have made her even more tense, but his aura wrapped around her, warm and appealing, and she leaned into him. His aura also kept the dwarves, who didn't think anything about crowding each other and Matti, from getting too close. A couple eyed him warily and got off at the next stop.

The trolley swept them through the city, past industrial areas full of clangs from smiths and machinery, and to a lake outside of a sprawling building at the back of the cavern. It was made from white stone different from the building materials used in the city. Or was that crystal? Here and there, it glittered as it reflected light.

"It's salt," Matti told her. "And you're not allowed to lick the walls."

"Did you ask about that?"

"Of course I did. I was curious."

"Did you lick them anyway when nobody was looking?"

"You know me kind of well considering how little time we've spent together."

"It was a hunch. You seem rebellious."

"That's about right." The trolley stopped in front of a path leading to another set of wide, shallow stairs that rose to what was presumably the royal quarters, and Matti hopped off. "I hope this doesn't take long. I've got to get back to Natia and Laki soon."

"To feed them." Arwen nodded and also jumped off, not wanting to keep Matti.

"That and to rescue them from reading time. Sarrlevi got some books from his mom. They're meant to teach young elves about botany, geology, and the versatility of vines—one entire book is seriously just about vines."

"You don't approve?"

"Oh, it's fine, but even his mom said they're books for school-age children, not babies. There are hardly any pictures at all—a cross-section of a vine does *not* count. The twins are way too young to find those books anything but gobbledygook." Matti whispered, "They're gobbledygook to me too, even when he translates them into English. I got some books from my sister, Penina, that she read to her kids when they were little. Things like *Moo, Baa, La La La!* and *Knuffle Bunny.* Varlesh thinks those are far too basic for children spawned from his loins."

"He has a high opinion of himself, doesn't he?"

"He's an elf. It's required."

Azerdash considered them as they conversed but didn't comment, though his eyebrow twitched at the line about elves. Arwen wondered what kind of father he would be. Two dwarves from the royal quarters came down before she could ask his opinion on reading to babies, but he'd already mentioned a fondness for military history. He would doubtless quote ancient commanders to his children.

The dwarves led their trio inside. After traveling down a wide hall, and passing what might have been staff or residents—one female made what was probably the local equivalent of a hex sign at Arwen—they entered a cavernous audience chamber. The stone throne at the end was empty, but to the right of the doorway stood a dwarven woman Arwen recognized as Matti's mother. She pounced on Matti with a hug.

"You didn't bring the babies with you, Nika?" She gripped Matti's shoulders and looked her up and down. "You know I'd like to see them again."

"They're at home anytime you'd like to visit, Mom. I didn't think squalling babies would be welcome at a formal negotiation."

"They are squalling? Is something wrong?"

"Well, Varlesh is reading to them."

Matti's mom—Princess Rodarska, Arwen recalled—pursed her lips. "Not from that thick science book about vines, I hope."

"He *was* fondling that one when I left."

"They are far too young for such tomes. I will send a translation of *Boom, Boom, Bang, Bang Go the Rocks* with you."

"That does sound like something they'd appreciate it."

"*You* did." Rodarska grinned. "And thumped on the walls with your toy hammer while I read to you."

"I'm sure," Matti said.

Rodarska stepped back from her daughter and looked Azerdash over, then pointed toward an alcove to one side of the chamber. A waiting area? It had furniture made from stone and covered with pads one might optimistically call cushions. A stout red-headed dwarf with gray in his frizzy beard lifted a hand toward Matti from the alcove. Was that the king?

It was hard to see Matti in either her mother or her grandfather, but *they* appeared related. Matti had to take after her father. From what Arwen had heard, human genes were dominant, at least when it came to physical traits, in mixed-blood offspring. Arwen had always been thankful for that. Interactions with mundane humans were already difficult enough without having albino skin and red eyes.

Before Azerdash took more than a step toward the king, Matti said, "Hang on," and lifted the peanut-brittle tin.

Arwen withdrew one of her own tins, the one with biscotti, and also gave it to her. She thought about piling more into her arms but, perhaps for the first time since she'd been a little girl, she had doubts that the baked goods she'd made would be well received.

"I've got this too." Matti pulled a thermos from her pack. "Some of the goblin-fuel blend from the Coffee Dragon."

Rodarska pointed to it. "My father is getting old. You do not think that will be too much for his heart, do you?"

Ironhelm's eyebrows flew up at the word *old*. Did he understand English? He said something tart to his daughter in Dwarven.

Unfazed, Rodarska held up thumb and forefinger. To suggest he only drink a little? He flipped his beard in what might have been the dwarven equivalent of sticking one's tongue out. Maybe not, but it didn't look like the most mature of gestures. Arwen hoped it meant the king had a sense of humor.

Matti piled the tins and thermos on a table in the seating area. Several guards stood against the wall in the alcove, but they didn't bat their eyes at the food delivery. Maybe they were only there to protect their monarch from weapons, not taste his food to ensure it wasn't poisoned. Not that the king's granddaughter would be deemed a likely person to poison him.

Ironhelm nodded contentedly at the food, but when Azerdash stepped forward, standing with his hands clasped behind his back instead of presuming to sit with the king, his expression grew cooler, the earlier humor evaporating. Though Ironhelm occupied something that looked like a Flintstones sofa, he didn't invite his visitor to sit.

Matti drew her mother aside and murmured, "The negotiations might be less tense if your father showed Starblade some of his hobby projects."

Rodarska cocked her head. "The half-dragon has an interest in... engineering?"

"That's my understanding." Matti looked to Arwen, who nodded.

"Especially gnomish engineering. Hopefully, he won't say anything snooty or haughty about dwarven engineering." Arwen bit her lip, not certain Matti's idea would work.

Given how stiff Azerdash and Ironhelm were as they discussed whatever they were discussing, it might cause the situation to deteriorate. Interestingly, Ironhelm was speaking in Dwarven, and Azerdash was responding in kind, though with short answers and hesitations that suggested he wasn't as fluent in the language.

A few tense minutes later—why didn't Ironhelm try the desserts?—the chamber doors opened. A number of dwarves pushed in a wheeled wagon with a mechanical contraption on it. Arwen had no idea what it was, but it had two shovels, a giant screw, and a flywheel, so she assumed it dug... something. A couple of small embedded components emanated magic.

Ironhelm asked his daughter a question. Rodarska smiled and shrugged, as if the staff had randomly decided to bring in the digging machine on their own. He squinted suspiciously at her, but she only smiled wider.

"It was built long ago, in the days before portal magic was invented and dwarves battled only other dwarves," Rodarska told Arwen and Matti. "It's for sapping under city walls. My father has been rebuilding it as a hobby."

Azerdash asked a question, pointed, and looked at the king. Ironhelm glanced at him in surprise and asked a question of his own. Azerdash nodded, held up a finger, then opened his cloak. A couple of the guards stepped forward, half-drawing their weapons. Azerdash withdrew...

Arwen groaned. Was he *still* carrying around that note-filled roll of toilet paper? The magic the gnomes had imbued it with had to add substantial durability for it not to have fallen apart over the weeks that Azerdash had been toting it everywhere and consulting it.

Arwen watched warily as he unrolled it partway to show the king a diagram-filled square with a shovel on it. Would Ironhelm be offended that Azerdash was comparing a dwarven machine to gnomish schematics? Hopefully, Azerdash wasn't saying how much better the whatsit would have been if gnomes had built it.

Rodarska gripped her chin as she watched them talk, both gesticulating now. Their postures were less stiff. Maybe this *had* been a good idea.

Matti watched smugly, as if she'd known all along that a mechanical construct would be an icebreaker. "My grandfather should be ready to grant Starblade a few legions of troops by nightfall."

Still gesticulating, Ironhelm paused to open the dessert tins. He smiled when he spotted Matti's peanut brittle and took a piece, then waved for Azerdash to do the same. Azerdash eyed the extra crunchy shards and selected one of Arwen's cookies instead.

"Maybe by lunchtime," Matti said.

Rodarska nodded.

"And here Azerdash thought *I'd* be the one to help with his negotiations," Arwen said. "Thank you, Matti."

"You're welcome. I owe you."

"I don't think that's true. You made us a key to get into the chest that held Azerdash's sword, even though you'd just delivered your babies. *We* owe *you*."

Matti shook her head. "You've given me more gourmet food than I could ever afford on what my business makes. Have you seen how much pickled vegetables cost at the co-op by Green Lake? You can't get all the exotic stuff that you make either. And what they do have isn't nearly as good."

Arwen almost scoffed at the idea of her food being considered gourmet, but if Matti wanted to feel grateful for the munchies and help her out, Arwen wouldn't object.

"That is not a very dragonish half-dragon," Rodarska observed, watching Azerdash unroll more toilet paper and point to another schematic. He gestured expansively, as if to include the entire chamber—or maybe the entire dwarven city—while Ironhelm combed his fingers thoughtfully through his beard.

Dragonish. Someone else had used that made-up word not long ago. Who?

Oh, right. Harlik-van.

"The other half-dragon was odd too," Rodarska said. "Overly sexed. He flirted with me, I thought in an attempt to flatter me such that I might be willing to help him get an audience with my father, but then he flirted with my maid too. From what I heard of the battle on Veleshna Var last year, the female half-dragon was the fiercest of the bunch. I'd heard she died, but now there's a rumor that she lives." Rodarska looked to Arwen. "Maybe *she* should have been leading their army."

As she spoke, Harlik-van's words replayed in Arwen's mind. *She has bartered for a dragonish way to earn your willing cooperation.*

Did that mean they'd acquired a dragon-made artifact? Or... the assistance of a dragon?

"Oh, I don't know," Matti responded after watching the two hobby engineers discussing matters. "Starblade seems to be getting along well with my grandfather. Would the dark-elven half-dragon have shared opinions on ancient dwarven siege engines?"

Arwen, replaying Harlik-van's words in her mind again, didn't chime in. The urge to go home and check in with Val and Willard distracted her. They might have some thoughts on what *dragonish* assistance the dark elves could have acquired.

15

When Arwen returned to Earth with Matti—Princess Rodarska formed a portal to send them home—Azerdash remained on Dun Kroth, finalizing the commitment of troops and resources from King Ironhelm. The last Arwen had seen, they'd been noshing on cookies and peanut brittle, and drinking coffee while chatting amiably. She was glad it had gone well but couldn't help but dwell on the dark-elf situation here.

Her phone popped up messages as soon as she landed on the pavement between Matti's and Val's houses. Willard wanted to see Arwen and Val at the coffee shop. Val wasn't home, so she was probably already there.

"I'm going to see if Varlesh finds this reading material acceptable." Matti lifted the picture-filled book her mother had given her, complete with a translation into English. "There are only rocks on the front, no trees or plants."

"Or vines."

"He'll probably think it's primitive."

"No doubt." Arwen started to head off but paused as a thought came to her. "Matti?"

"Yeah?"

"I know Sarrlevi is retired, but... does he ever accept gigs? For his, uhm, old line of work?"

"He uses his skills for Willard, but that's not quite the same. Why?" Matti raised her eyebrows. "Do you need to hire an assassin?"

"Does it... cost a lot?" Arwen didn't know even a ballpark of how much to offer, but she remembered her hesitation when fighting Harlik-van. If she hadn't shifted her aim at the last second, he might not have escaped. He might not have *lived*. But it had been harder than she'd expected to aim at a vital target.

"I think so, especially if you go through that Assassins' Guild, but he's not a member there anymore. Maybe there's a friends-and-family rate." Matti smiled, but, when Arwen didn't, her expression sobered. "Is this about the dark elves?"

"I know he's capable of handling them. And I... I'm not sure I am. Two specifically."

"Your mother and brother?"

"Yeah. I don't care for them—they're loathsome, and I hate them—but I feel..." Arwen groped in the air. "Conflicted."

"I get that. I had an evil aunt. Sarrlevi was kind enough to behead her for me so I didn't have to do it myself."

If Arwen hadn't heard that story before, she might have been horrified. But in this context, it was encouraging.

"Did he give you a friends-and-family rate?"

"I paid him later with sex."

"I... was thinking more like cookies and goat cheese."

"Yeah, I think he'd accept that." Matti touched her arm. "I'll talk to him. Right now, you don't know where they are though, right?"

"That's right, but I'm working on it. Thanks."

Matti gave her a thumbs-up before heading inside.

Arwen took a determined deep breath, then jogged off, glad the Coffee Dragon wasn't far.

When she reached the shop and stepped inside, she found Val and Willard at a table in the corner. Surprisingly, Amber sat with them, as if she was part of what looked like an official work conversation since Willard wore her Army fatigues.

"You should have let *me* go in," Amber was saying when Arwen reached the table. "I've had *years* of sword-fighting lessons. I would have been way more capable an operative than some pretty-girl werewolf who studied *grapes* in college. Like that's a major that's going to get you anywhere."

"Her family owns a winery," Val pointed out.

Amber sniffed.

Willard frowned at her. "Have you unearthed any more information about where the women are meeting the dark elves' handmaidens before they're swooped off to the new laboratory-lair?"

"Just what I told Winter. She called me, you know. She intuitively knew that I was a good resource."

"Your daughter is lippy, Thorvald," Willard said.

"I hadn't noticed." Val looked up at Arwen. "Winter is missing. She's not answering her phone, and her family hasn't seen her in two days. We think she believed Amber's plan was a good idea and decided to try it herself."

"It *is* a good idea," Amber said.

"Not if you end up imprisoned and unable to escape yourself."

"What exactly did you tell her?" Willard sounded like she was struggling for patience as she addressed Amber.

"I shared everything I dug up in the forums and online groups. Nobody's messaged me yet about volunteering, but I know Winter set up a profile on one of the sites. Maybe they messaged *her*. I saw her post. It mentioned her werewolfness. The other would-be mothers scoffed and gave her thumbs-downs, but that's because they're mundanes and are oblivious to the existence of shifters. Whoever is looking on behalf of the dark elves would know werewolves exist. It might have been a selling point. You said they're fertile, right?"

"They tend to have multiple babies at once," Willard said. "Like actual wolves. I suppose that could be seen as a bonus for dark elves looking to repopulate their species."

"It sounds like a lot of work to me," Val said. "Ask Matti how she likes being the mother of twins."

"I think Sarrlevi is exasperating her more than the babies," Arwen said.

"That might be true."

"Send me all the information you've gathered." Willard waved toward Amber's phone. "I'll have my people comb through it for clues."

Amber replied, but Arwen missed it, because a weird chill went down her spine.

The front door opened. She didn't sense anyone coming in, but a hint of black mist flowed into the coffee shop.

"Uh." Arwen recognized it, something that often accompanied the use of dark-elven magic. But it was the middle of the afternoon. There couldn't be a dark elf standing on the sidewalk, casting spells.

"That is not normal." Amber had spotted it too.

"I'll have to ask Nin," Val said, "but I don't think we serve mist."

The hairs on the back of Arwen's neck rose as the magic outside intensified. Something floating beyond the door? She dropped her hand to her multitool. If one of those eyeballs formed, she would zap it with a beam this time instead of letting it stare at her.

Not an eyeball but a golden orb floated inside, wisps of black mist flowing from it to join what gathered on the threshold. Patrons seated at tables near the door scooted their chairs back or got up fully and moved to the back of the room. Nobody had missed this strange entrance.

Ignoring them, the orb floated toward Arwen's table. Of course. Who else was targeted by dark-elven magic?

Multitool in hand, Arwen stood.

"I think that's a communications device," Val said. "I've seen something similar before, though it was on a desk, not floating creepily in misty air."

"My mother's people like to add flair," Arwen murmured.

"I guess if regular technology heats up and explodes in your grip, you have to make your own phones with magic," Willard said as the orb came to a stop directly over the table.

When Arwen took a step back, it moved the same distance with her. A step to the side prompted it to shift in that direction.

"Looks like it's for you," Val said dryly.

Arwen bared her teeth at it. More black mist flowed out of the orb, wreathing the table.

Willard curled her lip and moved her coffee mug, putting a protective hand over it.

"Hopefully, that's a low-calorie additive." Val smirked at her.

Arwen, thinking it was more likely to be a *toxic* additive, hoped Willard dumped the coffee out.

"Maybe you should take your call in the back room," Val suggested, glancing at the patrons in the shop. Every eye was turned toward their table.

Arwen didn't yet know if it was indeed a communication device, but she did head for the hall. If it was a magical bomb or something else inimical, she didn't want it going off where it could hurt innocent people.

Like a faithful hound, the orb followed her into the back room, the mist trailing it. She stood so that it would float over the table and considered how to activate it. It merely hovered in the air and oozed mist.

"What do you want?" When nothing happened, Arwen reluctantly repeated the question in Dark Elven.

Some of the mist wafted upward, forming a black background above the orb. Two hooded heads formed. She could make out just enough of their faces in the shadows to identify her mother and her brother. Great.

"It is good to know you remember your native tongue," her mother said.

"I remember a lot." Arwen answered in English. "Aren't you glad you didn't wipe my memories when you had me?"

"That may have been a mistake." Her mother continued in Dark Elven without commenting on Arwen's language choice. "We shall see. It has occurred to me that I have not been properly motivating you to wish to return to the fold."

"Honey does work better than vinegar," Arwen murmured.

"We have neither. What we *do* have is a newly acquired prisoner."

"A *dragonish* prisoner." Her brother smirked.

Arwen's concerns about that word flooded back to her. They had kidnapped a *person*? Could they be referring to the werewolf girl? Winter? No, she wouldn't be considered dragonish.

"Oh?" Arwen prompted, careful not to show much interest.

"Yes, *oh*." Her mother shifted, extending an arm, and the viewpoint drew back to show more of the underground chamber around them. A tall cylindrical device against a stone wall glowed, illuminating a woman inside. A woman with albino skin and a more muscular build than typical for those with elven blood.

"Gemlytha?" Arwen whispered.

"The half-dragon half-dark elf," her mother agreed.

"But how—" Arwen cut herself off, not wanting them to realize how bewildered she was. How could they have gotten the Silverclaw clan's prisoner?

Maybe they were showing her an illusion. Maybe they'd heard

about the Silverclaws' prisoner and thought they could trick Arwen.

"Why are you telling me about her?" Arwen did her best to feign indifference. "I've never met her."

"And yet, she is important in your life." Her mother looked at Harlik-van, who nodded in confirmation.

How could her brother have figured out who Gemlytha was and that there was any link between her and Arwen? He had, she'd assumed, only spied upon her from afar. Was there some conversation he'd overheard between her and Azerdash? The idea that he might have been camouflaged nearby and spying on them during a private moment made Arwen grimace deeply.

"She is your competition, is she not?" her mother asked. "The one who held the affection of the male half-dragon before he grew interested in you? Perhaps it was because he believed her dead that he turned his eyes upon you. Another with dark-elven blood who might sate his needs."

Damn, she knew way too much. Arwen didn't think *that* was what had drawn Azerdash to her—he hadn't wanted anything to do with her at first *because* of her dark-elven blood. Still, she couldn't be certain it hadn't played into his eventual attraction.

And, whether Arwen wanted to believe it or not, Gemlytha *was* competition. Though Azerdash had thus far hinted that he wanted to remain with Arwen and only worried about betraying Gemlytha, he also hadn't seen the woman face to face yet. He hadn't seen even a glimpse of her. It was possible that once they were reunited, he would realize he still cared for her. He'd admitted he regretted that they'd never been together physically. What if he wanted to be with Gemlytha to see if there was magic between them before he committed to Arwen?

She tried to keep her thoughts off her face but feared her mother caught some of them. Her expression was smug, like someone who'd played a trump card.

"As you can see," her mother said, "we acquired her unconscious inside her stasis chamber."

Arwen barely kept from swearing as the realization that this was the truth thundered into her. It wasn't an illusion. If they hadn't been involved, they wouldn't have known that Gemlytha's stasis chamber had been missing when Azerdash and his allies found where she'd been held. Even if Harlik-van had been spying on Arwen, it seemed a lot to believe he would have caught that quietly uttered tidbit.

"Why did the dragons give her to you?" she asked.

"They wished to hide her where Starblade wouldn't find her, *and* we paid handsomely for her. We are not without means."

"Why would you spend your means on their prisoner?" Arwen asked, though she'd already gotten the gist that her mother thought she could use Gemlytha against her.

"Because it was a way to get you," her mother said.

Her brother didn't quite roll his eyes, but he did lift them upward and sigh slightly. He'd been clear that he didn't think Arwen was worth the effort, and she had little doubt that he would again attempt to end her life.

"Should you *voluntarily* return to your people, to *me*—" her mother rested her hand on her chest, "—I will ensure Gemlytha's life is ended. While she is unconscious, it would be a simple matter to slide a dagger into her heart and sacrifice her soul to the demons."

Arwen gaped. "You think I want her *murdered*?"

"Sacrificed."

"There's not a difference."

"Oh, but there is. When you return to me, I'll continue your education on such matters."

"I don't want her killed," Arwen said.

"So you say, but you acknowledged, with your eyes if not your words, that she is competition for the male half-dragon's affections. If he finds her alive again, he may forget about you and claim her for his mate."

Arwen swallowed, hating that her mother, her mother who was a stranger to her, had read her so easily.

"I don't want her killed," she whispered.

"Are you sure?"

"Yes."

And she was. She just wanted Azerdash to... make the right choice. Her.

But what if he didn't?

"Why are you doing this?" Arwen asked. "You've clearly got someone handling your kidnapping already. Where are you taking all those women anyway?" She doubted her mother would cough up that information, but it would be nice if Arwen could get some intelligence out of this conversation, something that would help with recovering the young women.

"A half-dragon loyal to the child I birthed could be a boon to our people," her mother said without acknowledging the second question. "I have been close enough to him to sense his power— and that of the sword you helped him recover."

The hood shadowed her forehead, so it might have been Arwen's imagination that her mother's eyebrows rose. But maybe she wondered why Arwen hadn't kept the galaxy blade for herself. As if Arwen would know what to do with a sword or had the power to keep the half-dragons—or anyone more powerful than she—from taking it from her.

"Should he succeed in uniting the lesser species against the dragons, perhaps there would be more room in the Cosmic Realms for dark elves. We must think ahead. Once we've regained our numbers, we will need more than these savage wild-world tunnels in which to make our home."

"Azerdash isn't going to be your real estate agent."

"He could be yours," her mother said without missing a beat, though Arwen doubted she knew what a real estate agent was. "And you will be ours. In exchange for getting rid of the competition." She gestured toward Gemlytha again.

"No," Arwen snapped.

"It is your wish."

"It's not."

Her mother gazed at her for a long moment. Trying to determine if she was lying? "Do you fear that he'll read your thoughts and see the betrayal in them?"

Arwen hesitated. Since she wasn't planning to betray Azerdash, she hadn't considered that, but she shuddered at the idea that he would see into her mind and believe she had, for even a second, contemplated what her mother was suggesting. Simply being a part of this conversation could be deemed a betrayal. And Azerdash valued loyalty above everything else.

"No." Arwen worried the word wasn't convincing.

Harlik-van looked at Gemlytha, her eyes closed in the stasis chamber, and then thoughtfully at Arwen before finally whispering to their mother.

Despite her keen ears, Arwen didn't pick up the words. They might as well have spoken telepathically.

"Interesting," her mother murmured. "But would that bind the half-dragon to our people in the same way?"

Harlik-van shrugged. "Perhaps. Perhaps not. But it would bind *her*, and he might feel indebted to her."

Arwen didn't want to show her curiosity and refused to ask what he'd said, but she caught herself holding her breath and leaning forward.

"Will you return and serve us loyally for the rest of your days," her mother said, "if we *don't* kill her?"

The "What?" that Arwen had intended to keep to herself came out.

"Your brother believes you might selflessly step aside and

make way for the two half-dragons to be together. Perhaps you wish us to let Gemlytha live? Even to let her go so that she might return to him. Then he could be happy, and you... you would step out of his life and come to us." Her eyes narrowed as she watched Arwen.

Arwen fought the urge to slump over and grip her knees for support. She understood now. The new twist on her mother's threat. And her brother was right that this was more... Maybe tempting wasn't the right word, but it wouldn't be a betrayal to Azerdash. Only to herself.

She shook her head bleakly. "You started this call saying you'd kill her and get her out of the picture if I agreed to work for you. Now, you're going to kill her if I *don't* come to work for you?"

"We are an adaptable people, Vleesha."

Arwen, not wanting to cave in to either of the *deals* they were offering, tried to pierce the shadows behind Harlik-van and her mother, to figure out where they were. Another maze of tunnels, of course, but near which city?

Unfortunately, the dark rock walls behind them gave away nothing. Powered by magic rather than electricity, that stasis chamber could have been set up anywhere.

"I will give you two days to decide," her mother said.

"Decide what?"

"Do not be obtuse. If you wish her to live, you'll come to us and swear your allegiance to me. If you do not, I will drive a dagger into her heart and sacrifice her."

Panic clutched Arwen's chest. "Come where? You didn't tell me how to find you."

"The werewolf girl found us." Her mother's eyebrows rose in a challenge. "She was your ally, was she not?"

Was? They'd killed her?

"I barely knew her. She was working for— someone else."

"The human military leader and the Ruin Bringer. Yes, we

learned that when we questioned her. She found us. I'm certain you can. If you cannot..." Her mother looked at the stasis chamber. "I'm afraid the male half-dragon will be terribly bereft. And, when he sees into your thoughts, thoughts your tattoo would have kept hidden, he will realize his loss is your fault. Unless you give yourself to us to save her."

Arwen reached out, as if she could grab her mother through the device and stop her, but their images disappeared. The golden orb stopped glowing, thunked down on the table, wobbled off and onto the floor, then rolled to a stop at the wall.

An unsettling vision of her mother beheading Gemlytha came to Arwen.

"Damn it." She dropped into a crouch and grabbed the back of her head with both hands.

What was she supposed to do?

16

Birds chattered and warm afternoon sun beat down on Arwen's back while she knelt in the tomato beds, pulling weeds with such frustration that her tosses sent them far past the wheelbarrow to litter the pathway. The chickens were out, pecking for bugs, and investigated the discarded clumps.

Now and then, one of the orcs camped in the road watched Arwen. She didn't care. With her mother's deadline looming, Arwen alternated between wanting to call Amber to see if she knew how to get kidnapped and respecting Val's wishes to not get her daughter involved. Three times, she'd jerked out her phone and started to make the call—a woman's life was at stake—and three times, she'd shoved it back into her pocket.

She had two days. Maybe she could find out where the dark elves were without Amber's help. But she didn't know where else to look. She was out of maps and out of clues.

It occurred to her that Amber might be able to set things up, and then *Arwen* could show up at the meeting point to get herself kidnapped. Then there would be no need to endanger a teenager. But the switch would only work if the kidnappers were drugged or too obtuse to realize Arwen had the aura of a half dark-elf. Maybe if they were mundane humans...

"Unlikely. I would need a disguise."

Did such a thing exist? She had the camouflaging charm. She could be invisible when her would-be kidnappers showed up, then follow them back to the dark-elf lair.

The encamped orcs stirred, several stepping out of their huts to peer down the road. Arwen sensed Val's aura before she heard the Jeep.

As she stood, dusting off her trousers, Arwen considered that the orcs might be the spies she'd been thinking about. As she'd considered before, one or more of them could still be working for the dark elves. But Yendral had read their minds and hadn't mentioned picking up on that. Only that a couple were lusting for her. But had he checked every orc?

They ambled slowly out of the way as the Jeep approached, but they watched Val coolly, their hands on their weapons and their eyes narrowed. She deliberately drove through a puddle and sprayed a couple of them as she turned into the driveway. One snarled and strode after her but halted abruptly when the wards buzzed. Forced to stay where he was, he glowered after the Jeep while caressing the haft of his axe.

Horus crowed and shooed his hens out of the driveway.

Arwen made herself smile and wave when the Jeep parked, but she worried that Val somehow knew Arwen had been contemplating calling Amber. Maybe she'd come in person to reinforce the notion that she didn't want her daughter involved with dark elves.

That was okay. Arwen's latest iteration of the plan wouldn't involve endangering anyone else.

"If you've decided to start a campground here, those aren't the most amenable guests you could have invited." Val waved toward the orcs. "I hope you're charging them a lot."

"They're Azerdash's volunteer army, but he keeps forgetting to take them with him when he goes."

"Maybe he doesn't want them. *I* wouldn't." Val bared her teeth at the one fondling his axe.

The orc flicked his tusk in what was probably the equivalent of giving the middle finger.

"Next time he comes, I'll tell him to take them whether he wants them or not. I was just worrying one or more might be spying for the dark elves."

"We're out of earshot, and they don't have a view of much from there." Val gestured to indicate the length of the driveway before pointing at the trees to one side and field of edible ground cover and bee forage to the other. "Just those boxes."

"Those are my beehives."

"Are you worried they'll be able to tell how much honey you're getting this year?"

"Funny."

"Yup. My wit is what keeps me in business. Employers love it." Val stepped closer and frowned at Arwen. "Are you okay? You rushed out the back door of the coffee shop so quickly that I worried. How'd you get home so fast, anyway?"

Val looked around, probably noting the lack of a vehicle in the driveway. As far as Arwen knew, her father was at the farmers market.

"I took an Uber. Amber showed me how a while back. She said I would hate it because the driver wouldn't have as quality—or straight fire—a vehicle as she, but I might need it once she started school and couldn't drop everything to come take me places."

Arwen rubbed the back of her neck, feeling guilty that she'd made Val worry. After the ultimatum from her mother, Arwen had been so distressed that she hadn't wanted to talk to anyone or do anything but escape to think.

"*Did* you hate it?"

"The vehicle was fine—it even had butt coolers and warmers —but it was weird riding with a stranger. He asked me what I do for a living, and I almost had a panic attack."

"That's a pretty common ice breaker."

"Strangers prying into my life make me uncomfortable."

"So, you don't want your ice broken."

"I just want it left alone." Realizing she might be making Val feel unwelcome, Arwen hurried to clarify. "By strangers, I mean. I appreciate you coming out to check on me. I'm fine, but..." Her miasma of emotions threatened to bubble up and over again, and she bent forward and grabbed her knees.

"What did the dark elves—that was your mother and brother, right?—say?" Val gripped Arwen's shoulder and guided her to the picnic table.

"It was. Did you hear any of it?" Arwen had been too focused on her kin to pay attention to auras of people who might have been in the hallway, listening in, but she knew Val had a translation charm.

"I tried to hear *all* of it, but they rudely weren't speaking loudly enough, so the conversation wasn't enlightening." Val sat with her on one of the benches, their backs to the table. "I only caught your half, though you got quiet at the end when you switched to answering in their language."

"Did I?" Arwen didn't even remember deciding to do that.

Val looked at her, hopefully not in judgment.

"There's a lot from my youth that I wish I could forget but can't." Arwen wistfully imagined using the memory device to erase those first seven years from her brain. What would it be like to remember nothing from one's youth? Would it change who she was today? Would she forget basic skills like language?

"Yeah. What did they want from you? Willard wants to know if anything would be useful, if the dark elves shared any information about where they are. Where their *prisoners* are."

"I wish. I did ask, but all they wanted..." Arwen blew out a slow breath. "Somehow, assuming it wasn't an illusion, they traded for or *purchased* Gemlytha."

Val blinked. "The dark-elven half-dragon?"

"Yes."

"Are they... going to impregnate her? She's pretty powerful for their plots, I assume. I didn't meet her, but I know Matti did. And I've met Starblade and his oversexed buddy, of course."

"Funny how many people describe Yendral that way."

Arwen wondered if he'd hit on Val. A lot of guys did, so it wouldn't be surprising. Arwen decided Yendral's attention hadn't been all that flattering. Azerdash, on the other hand... who'd never hit on anyone in her presence...

She stared at the gravel driveway and shook her head. She didn't want to see him hurt, to let the dark elves kill Gemlytha. For the universe to have given her back only for him to lose her before he got to see her again? That would be dreadful.

"She's in a stasis chamber," Arwen said, aware of Val waiting for details. "And unconscious. I assume she has been the whole time, at least since the Silverclaws gave her up."

"I'm not a science—or magic—expert, but I wouldn't think you could be frozen in hibernation while gestating a baby."

"No, that's not why they want her. They're using her as bait in a trap. Or, well, to manipulate me, I guess."

"They still want you back and working for them? Badly enough to buy a *half-dragon*? I can't imagine they come cheap."

"My mother has developed a new... hypothesis. She thinks if they can coerce me into promising my loyalty to them, they might get Azerdash's loyalty too. Because he cares about me."

"Like... you two would get married, and he'd be in-laws with them, so he'd be forced to help them out?" Val's expression grew skeptical. "Their plots aren't exactly the equivalent of moving into a mother-in-law cottage in one's backyard."

"I know." Arwen summed up the rest of the conversation, including the twist where, thanks to her brother, her mother had decided to dangle Gemlytha's life in front of Arwen. "If I... go to them, promise to work for them, they'll let her go," she finished, "so she can live and be with Azerdash, and they can be happy." Her voice lowered to a whisper. "And forget about me."

"Nobody's going to forget about you, Arwen." Val slapped her on the arm. "They're *definitely* not going to forget about your food."

Arwen couldn't manage a smile, though she knew Val was trying to be a friend and lighten her mood.

"And Azerdash is falling for *you*, right? I've seen the way he looks at you. Not to mention you two lip wrangling on the steps to my basement."

"He knew her first."

"Knew or *knew*?" Val made a vague gesture that Arwen had no trouble interpreting.

"From what he said, they were never romantically involved, but Gemlytha always wanted them to be. Azerdash held back, since he was her commander and their rules said fraternization wasn't allowed, but he was aware of her feelings and cared for her too. When he thought she was dead, he admitted to me that he'd regretted being a rule-follower and not acting on their feelings. He'd always wondered..." Arwen turned her palm toward the sky.

"Ah."

"I want to be with him, but I also want him to be happy. He's had a hard life."

"*You've* had a hard life. You deserve to be happy too."

Arwen twitched a shoulder. "Maybe that's not meant to be."

Val blew out an exasperated breath. "You're *not* thinking of giving in to them, right?"

"I'm contemplating ways to find them, free Gemlytha, and hopefully get them out of my life forever."

"Well, good."

Val might not think it good if she knew Arwen was thinking of calling Amber.

"They said they have the werewolf— Winter."

"Shit. I'll tell Willard. She was hesitant to bring in someone so young and inexperienced, but since those are the kinds of women the dark elves are seeking out..." Val shook her head. "I kind of talked Willard into it. Winter came to me at the shop and asked about working for her. She brought me four bottles of wine. I don't even drink wine, but she was very earnest and complimented my tiger, so I put in a word for her."

"Who knew the way to your heart was through tiger compliments?"

"Sindari likes it when people call him a badass, and I like to keep his morale up. It makes him more willing to go into insane battles where we're outmatched."

"The car air fresheners don't harm his morale?"

"Nah. Those just keep him snarky. I like that in a service animal. Don't tell him I called him that. It makes him batshit."

"You two have an interesting relationship."

"Yup." Val gripped her shoulder. "Listen, don't do anything silly like contemplating selfless sacrifice, okay? Let me talk to Amber and Gondo to see if either of them has dug up more information on the location of the dark elves. All we need to do is figure out where they are, and we can go get Gemlytha and everyone else they've kidnapped out. Then we can collapse their tunnels on their heads and bury them once and for all."

They both knew it wouldn't be that easy—Val had been wounded and almost lost her Jeep the last time she'd confronted a handful of dark elves. And Arwen had been knocked unconscious and had her mind tinkered with. Her mother could have as easily killed her that night.

"All right. I had been thinking about calling Amber." Arwen looked sidelong at Val. "I wasn't sure if you'd approve."

"I don't want her volunteering herself to be kidnapped, but if she's dug up information that we can use, that's fine. I'll even pay her. We need help, especially since Zav isn't around. His mom has him back home, preparing for war. I'm having to walk a fine line, pretending not to have anything to do with Starblade—or the people he cares about." Val gave her a pointed look. "Zav was trying to forbid me from speaking to you, but I told him we're on a mission together to find the dark elves."

"And that worked?" Arwen imagined a dragon would prioritize *his* people's problems.

"Yeah, but I'm forbidden from speaking to you once our mission is over."

"Sad. Can I still have food delivered to your home?"

"Absolutely. Especially meat. I—"

The ground trembled, making Arwen feel off-balance, even though she was sitting. The windows in her father's home rattled, and the birds chattering in the trees fell silent. Only Horus had something to say. The rooster crowed his disapproval loudly.

"What now?" After glancing at the camp in the road, Val ran to her Jeep to grab her sword.

The orcs stood with their arms spread, looking around in bewilderment.

Intending to snatch up her bow, Arwen also stood, but the trembles subsided, the ground stilling.

"Earthquake?" She looked around uncertainly, half-expecting a giant demon worm to burst out of the ground and eat them.

"I think so." Sword in hand, Val returned. Judging by the way she peered around, she expected enemies too. "But was it natural? Or are your people up to something?"

"I don't know."

Earthquakes did occasionally happen in the Seattle-area, but they weren't as common as in California.

"I'm going to head back and check on the Coffee Dragon." Val considered Arwen, like she might be contemplating a kidnapping of her own.

"I'll stay here." Arwen didn't want to return with her, especially if it was because Val thought she needed a babysitter to keep her from doing something unwise. "I don't want to see that communication device again."

"I doubt it'll automatically flare to life with nagging messages from your kin just because you're near."

"You never know."

"It might have fallen and broken in the earthquake."

Arwen snorted. "I'm sure that wouldn't destroy it."

It had fallen on the floor earlier, and that hadn't left a dent.

"When I left, the goblins were contemplating adding it to one of their games and chucking it across the room in a dice-launching catapult."

"That might do it."

Val continued to hesitate but finally said, "I'll let you know what I learn from Amber and Gondo. Don't do anything rash, okay? We've got two days to figure this out."

If the dark elves had been telling the truth. Arwen couldn't assume that about anything they said. She couldn't even know for certain that they had Gemlytha. Harlik-van had used illusions to manipulate her before.

Arwen needed to find their new lair and see for herself if Gemlytha was there. And if she was... Arwen couldn't let them kill her. She couldn't let that happen to Azerdash.

"Nothing rash." Arwen made herself nod.

Val squinted at her and sighed before driving off.

Arwen waited until the Jeep was out of view before pulling out her phone. One of the orcs looked in her direction. Even though he was, as Val had noted, out of earshot, Arwen walked around the house to the back of the property to make her call.

"Hi, Imoshaun," she said when the gnome answered. "I could

use some more dark-elven arrows if you can make them quickly. I'm planning an incursion into one of their compounds." As soon as she could find it.

"*Another* compound? This is a most unsettling hobby you've picked up."

"Tell me about it."

"Some humans and mongrels enjoy word puzzles or painting and knitting."

It took Arwen a moment to realize Imoshaun was suggesting such activities as an alternative to dark-elf-lair infiltration. "Mrs. Zuber showed me how to knit when I was a girl. I made a cover for my quiver."

"You are drawn to violence, even in peaceful pursuits."

"It may be my dark-elven blood."

"It sounds inconvenient." Imoshaun sighed—with pity? "Do you still have the arrows I made for you? How many more do you need?"

"I do, but I'll take as many as you can make. And if you have any secret weapons lying around that could give me an advantage, I would accept those too." Arwen hadn't bested her brother with the arrows before, and chances were that she'd have to face him *and* her mother if she found her way to Gemlytha and the kidnapped women.

"Let me contemplate what we could make. Weapons are not a gnomish specialty, other than the occasional siege engine. I suppose you do not wish one of those."

"Something I could fit in my pocket would be ideal. Or at least my backpack."

"How soon do you need the items?"

Arwen looked at the sky. Her mother had said two days, but something told Arwen she didn't have that long.

"By tonight."

"*Tonight?*" Imoshuan asked. "Gnomish brilliance takes more time than that to manifest into useful tools."

"I'll bring you munchies."

"You will bring the contents of your entire pantry!"

"Whatever it takes." Arwen thanked her and hung up. As she lowered the phone, she repeated, "Whatever it takes."

17

Too agitated to relax, Arwen had weeded almost every garden bed when she sensed Azerdash and Yendral approaching. The sun was sinking low toward the Olympic Mountains, and she'd intended to talk her father into giving her a ride to Imoshaun's workshop when he got home, but maybe one of the half-dragons would take her. And maybe they would stay and help her find and infiltrate the dark-elf lair. Azerdash, when he learned that Gemlytha might be on Earth, would surely want to stick around to search for her.

Arwen's nerves tangled at the thought of explaining everything to him. Even though she'd done nothing wrong, and she didn't think even her thoughts had been that treacherous, she couldn't help but think that it was her fault that Gemlytha was in the dark elves' clutches. If not for Arwen, they wouldn't have cared one whit about purchasing a stasis-frozen half-dragon.

Arwen didn't believe Azerdash would blame her, but she couldn't kick aside the fear that he would. Maybe because she was having a hard time not blaming herself for the situation.

The half-dragons glided into view, and Azerdash landed in the driveway while Yendral dropped down among the orcs. At first, they scattered, ducking behind the trees across the street, but a few stepped out and faced him. He flicked his silver tail and formed a portal to the side of their encampment.

Azerdash shifted into his elven form. His shoulder-length black hair was mussed, and was that a fresh cut on his collarbone?

"What happened?" Arwen touched his arm. "When you sent me home, you and the dwarven king were getting along well. His digging machine didn't attack you, did it?"

"It did not. Ironhelm and I *did* get along, and we reached an agreement that he would commit troops, though he assured me he would deny having ever met me if the dragons showed up to question him. Understandable, and I did not object to that." Azerdash touched his collarbone. "As to this, Ironhelm suggested I try again to get King Eireth of the elves to commit troops, as spies had reported that the dragons were sending several of their kind to Veleshna Var as well as Dun Kroth. They believe that by making their presence more known and more ominous, those who promised allegiance to us will change their minds and realize it's not worth the risk. When I took a portal to Veleshna Var, I was wise enough not to come out near the capital but instead by geysers and burbling pools that are rarely visited by more than scientists. It is within a short flight of the capital so it seemed a possible staging ground, but a dragon must have thought the same. I had the misfortune of flying out of our portal and almost into his maw."

We *had that misfortune,* Yendral stated telepathically from the road.

"Yes," Azerdash murmured. "We escaped but not without fighting. Further, there were four other dragons already perched in the trees around the capital. They started flying over as soon as we arrived. They might have been placed there to keep me from attempting to recruit the elves. We had no chance to speak to the king. We formed portals back-to-back to three different worlds so that they couldn't track us here, but it's inevitable that they'll think to check Earth eventually, so I won't be able to stay long." He sighed. "It would have been convenient if Eireth had joined my cause the first time I went to see him."

In the road, Yendral lifted a wingtip and pointed toward the portal. Was he going to take the orcs to add to their army?

"Can you win a war without the elves?" Arwen didn't know if Azerdash and his army could win a war *with* the elves, but she would be optimistic for him. Besides, he had to believe there was some chance of success, or he wouldn't be leading so many into a battle.

"If we must, we will try, but it would be easier with elven mages and warriors riding their *evinya* with us. Among the lesser species, elves are the most powerful, and there are enough of them to give the dragons pause. I'm certain."

Yendral, Arwen said telepathically to him, noticing him ushering the first orc toward the portal. *Would you search the minds of the orcs again?* Maybe it didn't matter, now that they were leaving, but it would be good to know if they *had* passed along everything they'd seen in the days they'd been near the farm. *I have reason to believe at least one of them has been spying on me and sending information to the dark elves.*

Hm, there was one before that I recall being unable to read. He had some trinket that protected his thoughts. Such items are not uncommon, so I did not think much of it, but let me see if I can find him...

"Do you want to use the rejuvenation pool?" Arwen asked Azerdash, wondering if he had other wounds under his clothing— or if the ones they hadn't had time to fully treat earlier were still bothering him.

"Yes. With you." Azerdash smiled sadly at her. Or maybe that was a tired smile. He probably hadn't slept much for a long time. "But there is unfortunately not time. I came because... Well, I hate to attempt to use you for your connections, but you are friends with the half-elven daughter of the king."

"Val, yes. And you can use me in any way that I might be helpful." After all, she'd used *him* for his ability to fly and create portals. More than once, she'd felt guilty giving him gifts of her food and asking for favors, afraid he would see them as bribes.

"Do you think she could get a message to the king? That I request Eireth or one of his representatives slip off to another world so I might make a proposal? Even if she would only deliver a handwritten message to the king for me, that might work. The dragons should not think anything of Eireth's daughter visiting, should they?"

"I'm not sure, but I don't think Val can guard her thoughts from mind reading."

"Few but powerful mages can. If she would risk it..." Azerdash spread his palm. "I know she has no allegiance to me. *None* of the elves in this era have shown allegiance to us, even though our kind once battled and died for them."

"I can ask, but I can't promise anything. Since she's mated to Zavryd, the dragons are counting her as being on *their* side. I don't know how she feels about that, but..."

"Asking is all that I request." Azerdash took her hands and nodded to her. "I believe we have little time before the dragons engage my forces."

His warm gaze and touch sent a tingle of pleasure through her. But she couldn't enjoy it, remembering what she needed to share with him.

"We have a time crunch here too," she whispered. "It's about Gemlytha."

"Go ahead."

"You can read my mind if you need to, but know that I don't trust everything they showed me or told me." With that said, Arwen shared the call from her mother and brother, how they'd sought to manipulate her through Gemlytha. She did her best to remember and relay everything, and she tried to open her mind so he could see her every thought, hoping he would appreciate her honesty and wouldn't think that anything she'd considered was a betrayal.

Azerdash exhaled slowly, released her hands, and took a few steps away, eyes unfocused as he stared at the driveway. "Never would I have guessed she would be on Earth."

"It's become a popular spot for magical beings."

Something Willard wasn't happy about.

When Azerdash didn't answer, merely staring, lost in thought, Arwen asked, "Do you want to stay and help me find her?"

"Yes." He managed a slight smile as he turned back toward her. "But you don't know where the dark elves are yet, right?"

"I'm working on it."

"I don't know how much time we have out there." He waved toward the sky—the galaxy. "If we can't talk the elves into helping before the dragons attack, we may lose before the war has started. They've sent their kind to the capital cities on numerous worlds, and, at a word from the queen, they could attack at once, devastating those cities with their power. We have to be ready. I..." He trailed off as he touched his chest, but there was only determination in his eyes. "I have to gather every ally I can to strike before they do, and I still need to come up with a plan, some way to gain an advantage." He lowered his arm and paced. "This is difficult for me. I *do* long to find Gemlytha with every ounce of my being."

Because he loved her, Arwen thought but did not say.

"But she would be the first to call me foolish if I risked the greater mission—the greater good of the entire Cosmic Realms—for one person." His voice lowered to a whisper as he added, "Even one I've known for a long time and care deeply about." He looked sadly at Arwen.

Her fear that she would lose him to Gemlytha reared up, but

his forlorn expression tugged at her soul. Longing to fix things for him—or at least this *one* thing—she said, "Do what you need to do to help the Realms. I'll find Gemlytha before the dark elves can make their threat a reality. It's my fault that they have her."

"It is not."

"If I did not exist and I had not... defied my mother..." Arwen glanced at her forearm, her skin bare to the evening sun. "They never would have thought to bargain for Gemlytha. She might still have been in the Silverclaws' talons when you reached the depths of their lair."

"That is perhaps true, but it is not the same as this being your fault." Azerdash stepped close to her and took her hands again. "Your support means a great deal to me. More than I know how to say." He bent and touched his forehead to hers, closing his eyes as he rubbed his thumbs over the backs of her hands.

"I'll get her for you," she whispered.

Even if she worried Azerdash would be more conflicted about how he felt once he came face to face with Gemlytha, Arwen couldn't do anything less. She would fight her for him if she had to, but she couldn't sabotage Gemlytha's opportunity to do the same. Arwen hated her mother for putting her in a situation where that might be a temptation.

"You will not have to fight her," Azerdash said softly, lifting a hand to her cheek as he gazed into her eyes. "You are—"

A screech of pain in the road made them jump back, hands reaching for their weapons.

Yendral, still in dragon form, stood atop an orc, pinning the big male with his talons. Several of their kind had disappeared through the portal he'd made, but others remained, and they raised their weapons uncertainly. One of the orcs—that was Brok —demanded something in his tongue. Probably wanting to know what Yendral was doing to one of his troops.

Yendral looked coolly at him and then toward Azerdash. *There is a spy among them.*

Without releasing the orc, Yendral lifted one foot. A magical amulet dangled from his talon. Was that the device he'd mentioned that had kept him from reading the orc's thoughts before?

That one is reporting to the dark elves? Azerdash glanced at Arwen.

There wasn't any judgment in his eyes, but shame washed over her. What an idiot she'd been to allow the orcs to camp at her doorstep. It was true she hadn't given her permission, but she could have told them to get out of there. And perforated any who didn't obey with a round of arrows.

Not to the dark elves, Yendral said. *To the dragons. To the Storm-forge queen specifically.*

Zavryd's mother.

Arwen stared at the orc. It wasn't that she was shocked, but she wouldn't have guessed the dragons would make use of orcs to do their spy work. Maybe they had believed that mercenaries from the area would fit in. Might Zavryd have suggested it?

He was instructed to report to a dragon who would visit this world now and then for updates. They want to know when Azerdash is here.

To trap me? Azerdash asked.

The orc doesn't know if that's the reason, just that he has to learn what he can about your movements and those of your female, and report that information to the dragon who comes. He's saying he had no choice, that the dragon used compulsion magic to insist.

What dragon is he reporting to? Zavryd? Arwen told herself it wouldn't be a betrayal if Zavryd was working against them—as his mother's son, he had little choice but to do what she wished, and he would naturally want to protect his kind. Even if his kind were big bullies that enforced their rule on worlds that didn't want it.

No, Arwen couldn't blame Zavryd, but, going forward, she would have to be careful about what she said to Val when he was around. Hell, she might have to be careful about what she said to Val at any time.

She shook her head bleakly, hating the idea of being on the opposite side of a friend. But she knew Val also didn't like the situation.

Yendral must have questioned the orc further, because another minute passed before he answered her.

It is not Zavryd. The orc was specifically instructed not to report to him.

Uh-oh. Did that mean the queen had reason to doubt her son's loyalties? Arwen told herself it wasn't any of her business if she did.

He does not know the dragon's name, only that she is a member of the Stormforge clan.

She? Arwen had no doubt there were many female dragons from that clan, but she had to ask... *Does she have lilac-colored scales?*

After a pause to question the orc, Yendral said, *She does.*

It's Zavryd's sister then.

You can let him go, Yendral. Azerdash waved for him to release the orc. *We had better not linger on this world.*

I came only for cookies from Chef Arwen. Yendral turned his eyes upon them as he lifted his foot, letting the orc roll away. *Cookies and meat.*

She forced a smile, though a dozen worries waltzed about in her mind. *I can get you some of both.*

"I'd better not risk going with you to hunt for Gemlytha." Azerdash had already said as much, that he had to sway the elves to his side while there was still time, but maybe he'd been going back and forth with himself while Yendral questioned the orc. His heart and mind might be arguing. "I will accept your offer to find her. I *need* you to find her. If she is killed, I... will have failed her twice." He closed his eyes to hide the anguish in them.

Arwen clasped his hands. "I'll find her. I promise." She would. One way or another. "And hold on." She lifted one finger and dug for her phone to dial Val. "I'll see if we can get your message to the elven king."

Fortunately, Val answered right away.

"Any chance you'd like to visit your father this evening?" Arwen asked.

Val hesitated. "That is not what I expected you to ask."

"I have someone here who needs a note delivered to him."

"And *someone* can't fly it there himself?" Val clearly knew exactly who Arwen meant.

"There are dragons guarding the capital on Veleshna Var. He was attacked when he showed up earlier and barely escaped with his life."

We *were attacked,* Yendral interjected from the road. He'd formed a new portal and was ushering the rest of the orcs through while he kept tabs on their conversation.

"Yendral was also attacked," Arwen said. "An outrageous affront. I'm going to give him extra meat and cookies."

Azerdash, you don't know what an excellent female you have found, Yendral said.

I do know. Eyes still closed, Azerdash brought Arwen's free hand to his mouth and kissed her knuckles.

"When you say the dragons are *guarding* the capital," Val said, "does that mean they're not letting anyone in or out? Or are they sunbathing themselves in the trees and attacking select irritating half-dragons that show up?"

"I don't know."

"I do not know either," Azerdash said. "They didn't take the time to clarify their position before attacking us."

"I don't visit that often, and the queen doesn't like me," Val said. "They might send me away. Also, the dragons might find it suspicious that I want to visit at this particular time."

"Even though you're Zavryd's mate and should clearly be an ally to the dragons?"

Val snorted. "I've gotten the gist from what Zav has said that the queen questions where my loyalties are. She's deliberately leaving me out of the loop. Even Zav isn't as much in the loop as he would be if he hadn't married me."

"Hm."

That, unfortunately, lined up with the orc reporting to Zondia instead of Zavryd.

"I should point out that Zav isn't here right now either, so I don't have any easy way to get to Veleshna Var, unless you guys can wait until he comes home."

"Time is of the essence," Azerdash whispered.

"Waiting isn't ideal," Arwen said. "There's no chance Matti could open a portal? She has that artifact her mom made, right? Does it go to Veleshna Var?"

"I think so. You know... It may go to the goblin home world too."

Arwen frowned at her phone, puzzled. "I don't think Azerdash's victory depends on goblins joining his army."

"Oh, I'm sure it doesn't. His army will probably be more effective *without* goblins mucking things up, but my half-sister Freysha is there, working on a joint goblin-elf engineering project."

Arwen would have found the notion bewildering, but she remembered Val once saying that her half-sister had a passion not only for plants and gardening—as many elves did—but for engineering—something fewer elves were into. Freysha had learned the goblin language so she could study goblin engineering. Though they'd only crossed paths a couple of times when Arwen had been at Val's house while her sister had been visiting, she did remember Freysha tended to wear clothes as full of tools as Imoshaun's overalls.

"Neither the dragons nor the queen would question Freysha if she went home for a visit," Val added. "Maybe Starblade could find her on the goblin world and give *her* the message."

"Ah? Would that work?" Arwen was asking Azerdash more than Val.

He remained close, her hand in his, and his eyes closed as he listened to both sides of the conversation.

"I can't make any promises," Val said, "but Freysha knows you, so if you go along, she'll probably listen to Azerdash. And I doubt the dragons are worried about a huge goblin insurrection. I wouldn't be surprised if they don't have any of their kind placed there at all. I seem to remember that one of the dragons only visits their world infrequently to receive offerings and make sure their rule is properly imposed."

"Thanks, Val," Arwen said. "We'll find out."

She hadn't planned to go with Azerdash tonight, but maybe this wouldn't take that long. After hanging up, she offered, "I'll bake some cookies that I know goblins like."

Arwen didn't have any roadkill that she could decorate them with—and had no plans to acquire any—but, according to Nin, the goblin gamers at the Coffee Dragon were particularly fond of her lavender shortbread cookies. Apparently, they adored eating desserts with flowers embedded in them. Or maybe it had been the purple sugar crystals she'd sprinkled on top that had won their delight. Either way, she could make a batch the cookies. The season for flowers in the garden was over, but she had some frozen lavender buds she saved for such purposes.

"You are magnificent." Azerdash opened his eyes, such appreciation in them that her throat thickened with a tangle of emotions she couldn't name. All she knew was that she loved him and had to do everything she could to help him. In all aspects of his life.

18

When Azerdash flew out of his portal on the goblin world, Arwen riding on his back with her weapons and fresh cookies, heavy clouds filled a gray sky visible between the branches of trees similar to great redwoods. With trunks wider than cars—some wider than houses—they were spaced far apart in the forest, and Azerdash flew between them without trouble. The air smelled of campfires, and hundreds of torches burned in the distance, noticeable in the shadows of the forest.

Orange and yellow mosses draped the branches of the trees, adding unfamiliar scents to the air, but it all smelled comforting to Arwen. As a forest should.

The birdsong that wafted from the treetops was more screechy than musical, at least to Arwen's earth-based ears. She wasn't positive the creatures making the noises *were* birds. Maybe some other type of creature filled that ecological niche on this world.

As they flew over mossy roots and needle-dusted earth, they glimpsed statues on the forest floor, some carved from stone but most assembled from what one might call recycled junk. Arwen had a feeling that not all of the building materials had come from this world. In particular, she spotted a dwarven shield with a hammer and mug on it, some magic protecting it from rust. The skull of a massive dinosaur-like creature perched atop another statue.

Have you been here before? Arwen asked as they flew closer to the encampment—or was that a city?

A few times. Mostly to hunt the zlegarus. Azerdash's head tilted briefly toward the skull on the statue. *They are spirited prey and bite hard if the kill is not swift. Even dragons are wary of them.*

Can goblins kill them? Even though she'd heard that goblins hunted as well as scavenged, and could wield spear throwers and other projectile launchers, Arwen had a hard time imagining even a clan of them taking down prey that a dragon would deem *spirited.*

They tell stories that promise they have, usually by luring them into traps in canyons, but I've not seen it done and am skeptical.

Arwen sensed magic as they drew closer to the campfires and torches, numerous artifacts as well as the auras of hundreds of goblins living in the area. Someone blew a horn—an alarm? Azerdash wasn't camouflaging himself, so the inhabitants would have sensed his approach.

Arwen almost suggested that he *should* camouflage himself but doubted he wanted to skulk around like a criminal. They might have to speak with the inhabitants to find out where Freysha was. Val probably hadn't had a recent update on her sister's adventures. It was possible she wouldn't even be here. What if Freysha had been called home when all the dragons arrived on the elven home world?

I do not sense the aura of an elf yet, Azerdash said, monitoring her thoughts, *but there are many,* many *goblins in the area. Not only those that live in the stone huts on the surface but hundreds, maybe thousands, more in caves below. There are many layers of subterranean chambers and tunnels, connected by boxes similar to your elevators.*

Yes, now that he pointed it out, Arwen could sense that too. *They're packed in down there like sardines.*

Goblins are not creatures who desire to spread out and have privacy. They think little of sleeping in piles for warmth and camaraderie.

Must be why there are so many goblins in that sanctuary on Matti and Val's street. The last Arwen had heard, there were at least twenty living in that house.

Azerdash tucked his wings in, angling downward over the largest statue they had yet seen. Carved from striated stone, it represented a dragon perched on two legs with its wings stretched wide, its maw open as it towered over the nearest of the goblin huts. Yellow glowing eyes surveyed the city, as if it were alive. A stone slab rested horizontally like a table between its feet, the surface piled with roasted and dehydrated meat, some looking like it had been there for a while.

Azerdash landed in a square in front of numerous bald and wispy-haired goblins that looked to be elders. The surrounding huts were larger than many of the others, and the elders wore clothing adorned with metal gears, screws, and other gizmos Arwen couldn't name. A sign of wealth and status?

Welcome, half-dragon Azerdash Starblade. One of the elders stepped forward, a female with bracelets made from chains that clattered when she lifted a staff with a glowing wrench attached to the top. *We have given the day's offerings to the Watcher—* She pointed her staff toward the towering statue— *and we dare not assume the dragon who rules here won't visit to consume them, but we can make more meat for you. Fresh meat.* She looked hesitantly toward Arwen.

Arwen braced herself for a comment about her dark-elven heritage.

Your mate would be welcome to consume our offerings as well.

You are gracious, Grand Work Leader Griga, Azerdash said, more polite and less haughty than Arwen had witnessed him being with strangers—strangers who weren't dragons. Maybe he was learning diplomacy as he sought to get people to pledge troops to him. *We do not come for offerings, however. We have, in fact, brought gifts for you and your people.*

Taking that as her cue, Arwen slid off his back. A few goblins fingered weapons—and more reached for tools—as they watched her warily.

Having them touch their weapons didn't bother her, but all those gazes upon her made her skin scrawl. Half the goblins in the city were drifting in this direction. They kept a distance from Azerdash, but their respect—and maybe fear—of him didn't keep them from looking at him. And at Arwen.

She slowly removed her pack to draw out tins of cookies. *These are desserts that are popular with the goblins who visit an establishment known as the Coffee Dragon on Earth.*

The goblins murmured to each other in their own tongue. Arwen had no trouble understanding the telepathic words, but she didn't grasp any of their spoken language.

The elders accepted the tins and allowed her to remove the lids. A couple bent their heads to sniff the contents with interest, but nobody reached for a cookie.

They are mistrustful because of your heritage, Azerdash, who could read their minds, said. *They are concerned that the gifts may be poisoned.*

Maybe you *should have given them the tins.*

It is unlikely they would have believed that one with dragon blood had baked sweets.

Because baking is beneath dragons?

Because dragons do not have ovens. There is no need. His eyes glinted with humor, and a trickle of smoke wafted from his nostrils, a reminder that he could incinerate things.

A few startled exclamations came from the goblins at the wafting smoke, and they skittered backward. One fumbled a cookie tin but didn't drop it, instead clutching it to her chest. Maybe they'd liked what they'd smelled and *wanted* to enjoy the treats.

Azerdash, perhaps realizing he'd alarmed them, shifted into his elven form.

In addition to bringing these gifts, which you'll find are delicious— he stepped forward and took a cookie from a tin, lifted it in a salute, and bit into it, *—I am seeking the elven princess Freysha. Is she in the area? I was told she was learning engineering from your people.*

Princess Freysha is working with my sons on an underground aqueduct using goblin engineering and elven magic.

Will there be vines? Arwen wondered.

The goblins looked curiously at her.

Never mind.

A couple of the elders had been watching closely as Azerdash ate the cookie. They pointed at him, the tin, and whispered to each other. One selected a cookie, sniffed again, and nibbled on the edge. His buddy took the cookie from his hand, stuck the whole thing in his mouth, and smirked a goofy smirk that made him look like a six-year-old instead of the sixty or more he had to be.

Arwen smiled, though Azerdash was looking toward one of several cave entrances around the area. Recessed in it were metal doors that *did* remind her of an elevator. When they slid open, she almost expected a ping announcing the arrival of a car. But a *cart* was what hung inside with rotating gears set against the wall behind it. A blonde-haired elf and a goblin sat in the cart.

"Tracker Arwen?" Freysha asked curiously before looking toward Azerdash. Dirt or maybe grease smudged some of her locks, and she also wore clothes decorated with gears and screws. Her crudely-spun oversized tunic might have been a gift from the goblins. "Do you... need something translated?"

"Not at this time. Azerdash is hoping you can deliver a message to your father."

Freysha climbed out of the cart with her goblin comrade, who tapped her arm and pointed at Arwen.

"That is the friend of Plumber Puletasi," he announced in English, then repeated it in goblin. A number of oohs, ahhs, and clanking of tools came from the surrounding goblins, along with approving murmurs of, "Plumber Puletasi." Those who'd been wary about sampling Arwen's cookies came forward and dug into the tins, eating without hesitation.

"I had no idea Matti's name would win us favor on the goblin home world as well as Dun Kroth," Arwen said.

"Matti is known to be a friend to Earth goblins," Freysha said as she approached. "And word has gotten back to this world. Goblins are chatty."

Gossipy bigmouths was the term Arwen had heard Willard use. Somewhat fondly since she'd gained a lot of useful intelligence through Gondo and his goblin connections.

The work leader holding one of the few tins with cookies remaining held it out toward the elven princess. Freysha lifted a hand, as if to pass, but her nostrils twitched. And here Arwen had thought the sniffing and nose waving came from Azerdash's *dragon* half.

"Are there flowers in that biscuit?" Freysha asked.

"Yes," Arwen said. "Lavender."

Arwen fished in her pack and found a bag with a few extras to give to Freysha.

"Elves often cook with flowers." Smiling, she nibbled on a cookie before turning a more solemn expression toward Azerdash.

I am not certain if she will be willing to help, Azerdash told Arwen telepathically as he waited for Freysha to speak. *The elves have not assisted us yet, and she may not wish for her people to get involved in a war that could be devastating for them.*

Are you reading her mind? Arwen replied.

No. She is capable of protecting her thoughts. Also, it would be improper to attempt to fish in the thoughts of a princess.

But it's okay for random dark-elf mongrels in the wilderness. Arwen thought of their first encounter.

Certainly. Especially mongrels who are suspiciously denuding the forest of mushrooms.

Denuding, really, Azerdash. I inoculated those trees with truffle spores. We had every right to harvest them.

"Val said you two are mated?" Freysha asked curiously.

"She used that word?" Arwen asked.

"I believe her term was... shacking up. I interpreted it as mated. Or even *Vyseria hyleeth s'ah.*"

"That's Sarrlevi's term for his relationship with Matti, isn't it?" Arwen remembered Sarrlevi explaining the tree fusing to Amber, who'd rolled her eyes. Arwen thought it was romantic, and the idea of being figuratively fused to Azerdash appealed to her. Unfortunately, they weren't even *shacked up* yet.

"It is an elven term, so it does not surprise me that he would use it." Freysha nibbled on the cookie, appearing very young when she stuck her tongue out to lick the sugar crystals. "I had planned to return home shortly, due to the uncertainty in the Cosmic Realms at this time." Freysha turned toward Azerdash. "Also because my father recently sent a messenger and *ordered* me to return home." She smiled wryly. "I can deliver your words for you, Commander Starblade."

Azerdash blinked. He'd already opened his mouth, maybe planning a rebuttal or the start of some bargaining, but he closed it and looked at the cookie and then Arwen, as if the treats were responsible for Freysha's willingness to help.

"That is good," he said when he recovered from his surprise. "There are many dragons poised around your city, so it is not safe for me to visit there to speak with the king and queen in person."

"Should you get a chance to talk to my parents, I would suggest trying to get my father alone. He is more understanding and sympathetic to the plight of your people."

"Is he? When I visited before, he did not suggest that to be so. He would give us neither sanctuary nor information."

Freysha hesitated. "Was my mother at his side when you spoke?"

"Yes."

"She is... I would not say she is the one in charge, but she has always believed it wise to serve and be loyal to the dragons. One of the reasons my father was chosen as the elven king, after the last monarch was involved in a rebellion and ousted by the dragons, was their certainty that Mother would never betray them. My father has said in private to me that he wishes he could help you, but as long as the dragons rule and consider you an enemy, he dares not. Not when she..." Freysha lifted a hand and waved away whatever she'd thought to say. Out of loyalty to her mother?

"I see," was all Azerdash said. "Will you relay a verbal message then? Perhaps it would be safer for you if you did not carry anything."

Freysha grimaced. "I would hope the dragons wouldn't search me, but I believe you are right that it is safer if you speak your message. I will hope the dragons guarding the city will consider it impolite to mind scour a princess." She bit her lip, not appearing confident in that belief.

Arwen hoped the dragons wouldn't somehow find out Azerdash had met with her.

Nodding, Azerdash extended his hand toward a somewhat secluded nook. The goblins didn't seem to have a concept of giving people privacy and continued to watch the exchange as they noshed the last of the cookies. Azerdash and Freysha switched to telepathy as they moved away.

Left alone in the middle of the square, Arwen shifted her

weight and tried not to be uneasy. Now, most of the goblins were watching Azerdash and Freysha instead of her, but it was hard not to feel hemmed in and self-conscious. At least her dark-elven tattoo was gone, so she didn't have to worry about it glowing purple and alarming anyone.

To distract herself from the goblin gazes, Arwen looked around the city. Now and then, clanks came from the caves—the elevators—and something rumbled and hissed below the ground, causing it to vibrate. She would be curious to see what inventions and mechanical things existed below the surface.

One of the glowing yellow eyes in the dragon statue seemed to wink, and that startled her until she realized something had flown across it. A bat? This world's equivalent? Whatever it was, the black-winged creature continued through the village.

As Arwen regarded the statue, a weird little premonition came over her. She couldn't sense any change in its magic or anything around it, but her instincts said there was something off.

She looked toward Azerdash and Freysha, but their heads were bent toward each other as they engaged in their telepathic conversation. They didn't appear to have noticed anything amiss. None of the goblins were looking at the statue either. A few insects buzzed around the meat on the slab, but nothing else moved in the area.

Arwen was about to dismiss her premonition, deciding she was on edge because having so many people around always gave her anxiety, but magic swelled in the air between the elders and the statue.

Azerdash spun toward it, drawing his galaxy blade.

A portal formed in the air, a portal emanating dragon magic.

The goblins scattered, running into the forest or diving into their huts. Arwen nocked an arrow and aimed it at the portal, though she wondered if she and Azerdash should run, escape through their own portal before anyone arrived.

A roar came from behind the statue, and the aura of a dragon immediately registered. It hadn't come through the portal. No, it was behind the huge statue.

With another roar, a blue-scaled dragon sprang into view. He leaped onto the head of the statue, pinned Azerdash with an icy silver gaze, and flew through the portal.

He was gone so quickly that Arwen didn't think to loose her arrow. She hadn't even recognized the dragon, but...

"A spy," Azerdash stated grimly. "He was camouflaged so I didn't sense him."

Squinting, he gazed around at the goblins who remained in view. Most of the elders were peering out from the doorways of their huts. Freysha, a hand to her chest, appeared to be as startled as Arwen.

We didn't know he was here, the goblin work leader who'd spoken before said. *That is the dragon who oversees our world and comes for the offerings.*

Does he report to the Dragon Council? Azerdash asked.

"All of the dragon rulers do," Freysha said. "Will you create a portal to send me home, Lord Starblade? The dragons will soon know I've met with you. I'd best get back as soon as I can and explain... as much as I can to my father."

"Will the dragons also demand an explanation from you?" Azerdash frowned but did as she asked and formed a portal to the elven home world.

"Unfortunately, they may, but I'll pass along your message first." Freysha waved a goodbye to her goblin friends and ran for the portal, springing through as if an army was on her tail.

Arwen worried that one soon would be.

19

"I HAD BETTER GET YOU BACK TO EARTH." A TROUBLED FURROW creased Azerdash's brow. "I need to check in with Yendral and Sleveryn and get an update on what other worlds have been invaded by dragons."

He didn't mention Gemlytha, but she had to be on his mind too.

"I'm ready," Arwen said.

"Thank you for assisting me with this." Azerdash nodded toward the goblin city, most of the inhabitants still in hiding as they eyed their statue warily. Maybe dragons didn't typically camouflage themselves, then spring out from behind it. Azerdash shifted forms, switching to telepathy to add, *When the dragon issue has been resolved, I intend to free you of dark-elf interference in your life.*

"That would be nice." Arwen smiled but wouldn't hold her breath for the *dragon issue* to be resolved anytime soon.

Azerdash levitated her onto his back, and magic trickled from him to form a portal.

"Will you take me to the farm?" she asked.

His magic faltered. Had he planned on another destination? They still didn't know where the dark elves' latest lair was.

"I asked Imoshaun to make me secret weapons," Arwen said. "I don't know if she's had time to do so, but I promised to bring her some goodies."

"Of course."

His magic swirled as he created the portal, and they flew through. The disorientation and sensation of floating outside of her body was familiar to Arwen, but the ride ended unexpectedly as something arrowed into them when they arrived. A dragon.

Acting on instinct, Azerdash raised a barrier while barrel-rolling to evade talons slashing toward them. Arwen started to fall, but he used his magic to keep her in place.

As they rolled, the cloudy night sky and a few lights spinning, Arwen clutched her weapons to make sure she didn't lose any arrows. She would *need* her arrows. Her senses told her this wasn't the only dragon. There were three present, banking and swooping about over the farm.

Shit. This was her fault. She'd forgotten about the orc spy when she'd asked Azerdash to bring them here.

Magical attacks lit up the night sky, fireballs and silvery bolts streaking toward them from multiple sources.

"I'm sorry, Azerdash," Arwen blurted, reaching for an arrow.

There are too many. He came out of the barrel roll and flew behind a copse of trees, but dragons surrounded the property, and he couldn't escape. More attacks chased after him, pummeling his barrier. Already, it wavered, not a match for such great power. *We need to make a portal and flee.*

Wait. Leave me here. I'll get Gemlytha, just like I said I would.

It's too dangerous. They'll attack you.

I'll camo myself as soon as I land. Half-tempted to jump, Arwen eyed the ground, but it was forty or fifty feet below. Could she even leap off while his barrier was up? Or would it catch her and keep her with him?

No. They could raze your whole farm.

Azerdash flew around more trees, skimmed over the corn crib, and formed a silvery portal over the road. He flew toward it, tilting and diving in an attempt to evade more attacks.

I'll run away from the farm so they won't have a reason to, Arwen said, the wind whipping at her hair, knocking her bun loose. *You need to stay away from Earth. They're expecting you here now.*

They're expecting me everywhere, he replied grimly.

Two of the dragons dove, on courses to intercept Azerdash and block his route to the portal. He flapped his wings, flying harder in an attempt to reach it first.

A fireball blasted into his side. His barrier dropped.

Almost there. He arrowed for the portal.

One of the dragons was almost upon him. Would he make it through?

Afraid that Azerdash wouldn't be able to return, and afraid the dark elves would kill Gemlytha, Arwen leaped from his back.

In the air, she twisted to loose an arrow at a dragon blocking the portal. A lilac dragon. Hell, was that Zavryd's sister?

Her arrow glanced off the dragon's barrier without doing damage, but it did distract. Icy eyes shifted toward Arwen as she landed on the driveway, rolling to soften the impact.

Azerdash blasted Zondia with fire, with everything he had, then curved around her and made it to the portal. She whipped her head toward him, jaws snapping, but he escaped before she could make contact.

Zondia landed in the road, spinning toward Arwen as another dragon flew through the portal after Azerdash. Arwen snatched the multitool from its belt sheath and rubbed the oval that activated the camouflage.

A second dragon flapped his wings to follow Azerdash, but the portal disappeared first.

Heart pounding, Arwen resisted the urge to sprint, knowing it would break her camouflage. Instead, she crept toward the trees to the side of the driveway.

The dragon who'd missed going through the portal screeched in frustration.

Eyes glowing, Zondia sprang into the air, flapping her wings to hover over the spot where Arwen had landed. The dragons must have destroyed the wards around the property, because nothing opposed them. Zondia blasted the gravel driveway with brilliant flames.

Arwen had moved far enough that the fire didn't strike her, but that intense heat almost scorched her back, even from a distance. These dragons would kill her if they could.

With two remaining, Arwen didn't dare attack again. Maybe it had been foolish to shoot Zondia even once, but Azerdash had gotten away. It had been worth it. Now, Arwen had to figure out how to stay alive long enough to get Gemlytha for him.

Roaring, Zondia blasted the driveway again. Plants and trees along the sides charred, instantly blackened, or they outright burst into flame.

Zondia'qareshi, called a telepathic voice in the distance. A familiar one. Zavryd flew into view beyond the property line. *You will not destroy the human farm. Or the mongrel dark elf.*

Arwen glanced back but she kept going, slipping through the trees toward the neighboring property. The more distance she could put between herself and the dragons, the better. She wished she had a way to drive them away. Damn it, those flames were encroaching on the beehives. And where were Horus and the chickens? Had they been smart enough to flee or hide in their coop?

Zondia stopped spewing flames but only so she could glare

defiantly at her brother. *She flies with that traitor, Starblade. She aids him at every turn. She has declared herself an enemy to dragons.*

Zavryd flew down to land on the main house. Through the trees, Arwen could see her father's truck in the driveway, and she winced, hoping he hadn't been hurt. She doubted he'd been foolish enough to fire at the dragons, but had he found a safe enough hiding place?

Starblade is not a dragon, nor was he raised by our kind. He owes no allegiance to our people and is thus not a traitor. Once he perched on the roof, Zavryd sent cool magic toward the flaming trees, putting out the fires.

He carries the blood of a dragon, of our very own uncle, Zondia replied with indignation. *How can you defend him?*

I do not defend him. I merely note that the word traitor is not applicable. After all, he also carries the blood of an elf.

The elves have not spoken of raising arms against our kind nor done anything to declare themselves enemies.

Not yet. Zavryd sounded grim. Just because he didn't want to see Arwen and her farm destroyed didn't mean he was on Azerdash's side. *Our spies say that he visited King Ironhelm. The dwarves may be ready to join his side, and, if so, it is possible the elves will follow. Our mother needs us back at home in case... Well, I believe she has made a decision. The coming days will be challenging.*

For our enemies, perhaps, Zondia said.

If we must make war on a dozen worlds to retain our control, it will be a challenging matter for all. We are not nearly as many as the lesser species, and we would have to deliver great destruction to their lands and cities, doing damage and killing many. When we have taken similar actions in the past, it has created resentment. We would place dragons in their minds as enemies, perhaps forever more, and have to deal often with insurrections.

The words you speak, brother. Do not tell me you are afraid to defend our rule.

I am not afraid, and if the queen and the council decree it, I will fly into battle. Zavryd gazed around the farm. *But we will not attack those who have not attacked us.*

Even allies—lovers—of that one? Zondia spat like a llama.

Arwen almost sighed. It should have been the last thing on her mind then, but she wished she and Azerdash actually *were* lovers. Especially if she was to be condemned for it.

Yes, Zavryd said.

If she rides on his back into battle and fires upon our kind, she will declare herself an enemy. Then we may rightfully attack her.

She has *shot her damnable arrows into dragons,* the other male said as he circled slowly around the back of the property.

Silverclaw dragons, Zavryd pointed out. *In self-defense.*

She just fired at me. Zondia roared in disgruntlement.

In defense of Starblade, Zavryd said. *My mate has attacked Silverclaws to defend me. I do not believe we should consider self-defense or the defense of one's mate to be an act of war.*

Zondia didn't spit again, but she issued a disgusted noise and sprang into the air. Another portal formed, this one over the beehives.

We will return to Mother and see what her wishes are. With luck, Yedronarik will have caught and killed Starblade. She flicked a wingtip toward the road where the other dragon had disappeared through Azerdash's portal after him.

Arwen prayed Azerdash had expected pursuit and made another portal in time to escape again. Though he might be crafty enough to survive a battle with one dragon, she couldn't be certain of that. He'd taken a lot of magical blows in a short time and might have been injured again.

Not waiting for Zavryd's response, Zondia flew through her portal. The other dragon circled the farm again, nostrils flaring.

Arwen tensed. Was he trying to catch her scent? Hoping they might yet capture her?

If they did, she knew well that she would be effective bait if they wanted to lure Azerdash into a trap.

She drew an arrow and nocked it.

Let us go, Zavryd said, though he didn't yet leave his perch on the house. Was he making sure the other dragon departed first?

Arwen didn't know why Zavryd would care about her and the farm, other than that he considered her "the friend of his mate," but she appreciated his intervention.

The remaining dragon finally left, flying through the portal after Zondia.

Zavryd gazed into the woods in Arwen's direction. She held her breath. Did he know where she was? Even though he'd helped, she worried he would forbid her from continuing to assist Azerdash. Or might he even cart her off somewhere for her own good? She couldn't let that happen. She had to find Gemlytha tonight.

The mate of Starblade, Zavryd said, his eyes not focused exactly on her spot but in her direction, *would be wise to avoid him and have nothing to do with him until this matter is resolved. I am respected among my clan, but I may not be able to deter my kin if they again have Starblade in their view.*

Arwen didn't know if she should reply. It seemed safer to stay quiet.

Perhaps the mate of Starblade could remain in her domicile and bake something.

Oh, sure. She would stay home and make cookies while her mother murdered Gemlytha and every dragon in the Realms went after Azerdash.

With his message delivered, Zavryd flew through the portal before it disappeared.

Arwen slumped against a tree and wiped cold sweat from her forehead. She reached into her pocket for her phone, intending to check in with Imoshaun about secret weapons, but a message that Amber had called popped up.

A sense of foreboding filled Arwen. The message had come in an hour earlier.

"Hey, Arwen. I emailed you some more deets, but I wanted to let you know they contacted me with a meetup location. I'm going to check it out. You guys lost the werewolf. You need me to do this, and I *can* do it. I'll help you get those girls back. Nobody should have to endure that, and I'm... Like I said. I'm your best bet."

Arwen groaned. By now, Amber might already have been kidnapped.

20

On the way into her father's house, Arwen dialed Val's number, but the call dropped immediately to voice mail. She tried Willard.

"What is it, Forester?" Willard answered, sounding cranky.

Feeling cranky, or at least frustrated, herself, Arwen summed up Amber's message. When she opened the front door, she almost dropped her phone. Her father stood inside, his rifle in hand. He glanced past her shoulder toward the sky.

"Are you okay, Arwen?" he asked.

"Shit," was Willard's reply to the summation. "I sent Val off to look for the werewolf girl—Winter Moonclaw. If she's not answering, she might be in the middle of a fight. Or at least in a tunnel without reception."

"I'm okay." Arwen patted her father's arm, knowing he was worried about the dragons and wondering if some were still lurking. If he'd seen them try to fry Azerdash—with her on his back—he would be doubly worried. "I'll explain more later."

Arwen jogged to his office and turned on the computer. The power button sparked at her touch, and she jerked her hand back.

It had better not complain about her blood now. She needed to see whatever *deets* Amber had emailed.

"I'll keep trying Thorvald," Willard said. "You see if you can find her daughter. You can track, right?"

Arwen hesitated. "Probably not all the way from Edmonds to... wherever she went, not if Amber took her car. But I'll do my best."

"Don't let that kid get killed. Please."

Arwen had never heard Willard say *please* before and felt compelled to reassure her. "I won't."

She hoped that would prove true.

Finally, the computer came on. Arwen hung up and delved into her email, ignoring messages with updates to farmers market hours in favor of—

"There."

Amber's message was on top, a forward from Interactive Health and Pregnancy Solutions.

"Yeah, right."

Arwen skimmed through the brief email. It was typed in perfectly normal English, not Dark Elven with pictures of flames and demons mixed in. Not that Arwen had expected that, even if it would have been appropriate.

Thank you for reaching out, it read. Had Amber found an address to reach out to, or had they contacted her based on her posts in those groups? *We are indeed paying fifty thousand dollars for appropriate surrogates. If you are under twenty-one years in age and in good health, please visit us tonight at the Gasworks Marina. We have invited our clients who may be interested in employing you for surrogacy for drinks and information on our company's yacht. We're also inviting you to come and meet them and learn more about the process.*

"The process in which you'll be kidnapped and locked up for years—if not decades—while you birth dark-elven babies," Arwen muttered.

Arrive by nine p.m., the message finished. *The name of the yacht is the* Teakstar *and will be waiting in dock for you.*

Arwen glanced at the time and swore. It was already eight-thirty.

With a dragon's help, she could have flown there in minutes. Why did Azerdash's war have to interfere with her attempts to keep her mother's people from being loathsome villains who were a plague on Earth?

"Father?" Arwen called before realizing he stood in the door-way, watching her with concern. "Will you give me a ride to Gasworks Park at Lake Union? Amber's either been kidnapped or is *about* to be kidnapped."

She braced herself, expecting him to ask for an explanation, one there wasn't time to give, and was about to promise to tell him more on the drive over.

All he asked was, "Sigrid's granddaughter?" and nodded.

Weapons in hand, they ran outside and leaped into his truck.

Arwen glanced at his rifle—his mundane rifle with bullets that wouldn't pierce a magical barrier—and hoped she could convince him to stay in the vehicle when they got there. He knew how to fight and had grabbed grenades too, but if the yacht was still there, Arwen planned to camouflage herself to get aboard, not lob explosives at it. Who knew how many innocent women might be there? That message hadn't said Amber's name specifically. An identical email might have gone out to a dozen potential surrogates.

Arwen texted Val that Amber might be at Gasworks Park while she shared what she knew with her father.

"It's time to put an end to them once and for all," he said with resolution. "I wish the Seattle area weren't infested with dragons at the moment." More than once, he glanced upward through the windshield as he drove.

"They took off after Azerdash."

Unfortunately, that didn't mean they wouldn't be back.

Her father slanted a flat expression toward her. She worried it meant he thought she should put an end to things with Azerdash.

It was late enough that there wasn't much traffic, but it was still forty-five minutes into the city. Arwen was tempted to have her father stop at Imoshaun's workshop in Bellevue in case she'd managed to put together some useful weapons, but she couldn't take the time. It was possible it was already too late to catch Amber, but Arwen didn't want to risk a situation where they drove up five minutes too late and watched the yacht pass into the ship canal and out of reach.

Arwen's phone rang. Val.

"I *told* her not to get herself kidnapped," Val stated without preamble.

"I know." Arwen, worried Val would blame her, added, "I just got back from talking to Freysha or I would have messaged earlier. She's supposed to be meeting a yacht at Gasworks Park at nine."

"The same yacht we watched take off with crates and probably a bunch of kidnapped women?" Frustration made Val's words come out harshly and quickly.

"I think so." Arwen wished they'd been able to go after the yacht that night instead of getting in a fight with her brother in an abandoned cave.

"I was following a dubious lead up in Everett, but it sent me on a wild goose chase. I'll head to Gasworks now. That marina isn't very big. I wonder where the hell they're going from there. If it's out to Puget Sound, then why would they have chosen a pickup location that requires them to go through the locks? I wonder if we could catch them there. Yeah, I'll drive there just in case, all right? You go to the marina."

"Okay." Arwen would have liked to charge onto that yacht with Val at her side, but she understood the logic in trying to guess their enemies' route and cut them off, especially since they were going to be late to the party. "You don't think they're going into Lake Washington?"

"Hell if I know where they're going. I'll see if Willard can drive to Portage Canal and look for yachts passing that way. I hope they can't camouflage their ship. And that we're not too late. Damn it, Amber. And damn it, Zav, I need your help. Why can't you stay on Earth for more than two minutes when I need you?" Clearly not expecting an answer from Arwen, Val hung up.

Arwen rubbed her neck. She'd never heard Val so frustrated but understood perfectly. Even though she didn't have children, she could imagine what it would feel like for one of them to be in grave danger.

Her father remained calm, driving over the speed limit when it was possible but not going so fast that they were likely to get pulled over. "Do you want me to drop you off right at the marina? Or close?"

Arwen activated her camouflage charm but was never sure how well it worked, if at all, when she was in a vehicle and moving fast. She called up a map of the marina on her phone, not being that familiar with the area. It was next to Gasworks Park and, as Val had pointed out, not large.

"Better make it over at the park. If the yacht *is* still there, we don't want them sensing me or being suspicious of a vehicle roaring up this late."

"I don't think it's that late by city standards but will do. I'll park and *we'll* get out together and check on the marina." Maybe Father thought she meant to ditch him once she was camouflaged, because he gave her a stern look. "Let me help. I've known Sigrid as long as you have and don't want anything to happen to her granddaughter."

"I want to sneak aboard, if possible. Can you stay at the truck and make a distraction if I give you a signal? If they have ways of detecting camo magic, it could really help out."

His stern look didn't fade. "Stay in the truck? I can handle myself, girl. And you don't have backup this time, right? Your allies are going to different places."

"I know, but they won't be far. And I don't want anything to happen to you. Besides, I don't have another camouflaging charm that you can use." Arwen didn't even know if mundane humans could use such magic.

"You don't think something might happen to me if I start lobbing grenades from the parking lot?"

"I said make a distraction, not lob grenades."

"I have limited tools at my disposal. I doubt standing on the truck and playing armpit music is going to deter dark elves."

Arwen's jaw dropped at the image.

She must have given him a bewildered look because he added, "You learn a lot of less useful skills in the military when you're on long deployments."

"I... guess so. Maybe you could flash your headlights and honk a few times."

His grunt didn't convey acceptance of the idea, and he glanced at the gear he'd thrown into the back, including ammo and grenades.

They were almost to Gasworks, so Arwen didn't have time to argue further. As soon as he slowed down in the parking area, she activated her camouflage again and grabbed her bow and quiver. She opened the door before the truck came to a complete stop, an act that earned her another dark look.

Forcing herself to walk instead of sprinting down the street to the harbor, Arwen stretched out with her senses, hoping to catch... She didn't even know what. Orcs? The dark elves had made use of them often, but that mercenary company was off somewhere with Yendral now. Further, Arwen couldn't imagine women being lured onto an orc-filled yacht, even for the promise of fifty thousand dollars.

Arwen hoped she wouldn't sense Amber since that would mean she wasn't camouflaged. Arwen assumed Amber's plan hadn't been to amble openly up to the yacht and let herself be kidnapped. She'd mentioned wanting to get an invitation but only to learn their location.

As Arwen rounded a large building, and the pier and a couple of houseboat-lined docks came into view, she sensed numerous beings with magical auras. Not orcs. They were half-bloods, like Arwen. A half-dwarf, a half-troll, and was that a half-elf?

Arwen couldn't imagine such people voluntarily working for dark elves, but if they were like the orcs, they might be under a magical compulsion. Overall, half-bloods made sense for this since they would look like normal humans and not alarm the young women who showed up.

She walked toward the longest dock but also considered the others. The blocky houseboats had no resemblance to yachts, and she assumed the black one she'd seen was the only vessel the dark elves had, but she didn't see it anywhere. A hulking freighter was tied up parallel to the pier, and a couple of small white yachts were moored at a shorter dock near it. Was one of them the *Teakstar*? Maybe the dark elves did have two.

It was only once she started up the longest dock that she realized the auras she sensed were out in the water off the end. Though she had reasonably good vision, even at night, it took her a moment to pick out the all-black vessel. As when she'd seen it before, it lacked running lights. Or lights of any kind.

Had the crew grabbed Amber, left the dock, and turned off the lights so nobody would see it?

But it wasn't moving away. It was anchored about twenty yards out. Close enough that Arwen could swim to it.

A car drove up behind her, making her pause. The windows were down, and a black-haired young woman in the passenger seat peered out. Another woman drove, gesturing and speaking to her, then stopping the car without parking.

Were these also potential surrogates who had been invited?

As if in answer to her question, the lights came on in the black yacht. Magic flared to Arwen's senses, as if artifacts had gone from dormant to active.

No hint of engine noise reached Arwen's ears, but the yacht glided toward the end of the dock. Propelled by magic, it navigated deftly into a spot that didn't look like an official slip. There wouldn't have been room for the black craft, but it slid in at an angle, positioning itself so that it could extend a gangplank.

"How much do you want to bet they didn't pay for a slip?" Arwen muttered.

"Arwen?" came a whisper from farther up the dock.

"Amber?" Arwen whispered back.

"Yeah. I can't see you."

"I can't see you either."

"Good," Amber said. "That means you can't stop me from doing this."

Arwen eased closer, certain she *could* find and stop Amber based on the location of her voice. The dock wasn't that wide. Even if Amber saw Arwen when she closed to within five or six feet, Amber would have a hard time getting by.

"I've got my sword," Amber added, as if she knew what Arwen was thinking.

"Is that a threat?"

"To them, yeah. I can handle this." She'd moved farther down the dock.

Two couples strolled onto the deck of the yacht, men in suits linking arms with women in cocktail dresses. With phony smiles plastered on their faces, they gazed toward the car.

Since Arwen was in that same direction from them, she froze. Amber had affirmed that her camouflage charm was working, but

Arwen's instincts warned her to be careful when magical beings were looking at her.

Her senses told her the couples were half-bloods, but, as she had assumed, they looked like normal humans. The women in the car wouldn't know they had otherworldly power. The women's conversation had ended, and both were looking toward the yacht.

"Don't do this," the driver whispered loudly enough for Arwen to hear. "It's not worth it."

"If it's legit, it is," the passenger said.

"That doesn't *look* legit."

"It's fine." The passenger got out, a long dress swishing around her ankles, and closed the door.

Her driver scowled after her but didn't stop her. As the woman approached the dock, Arwen realized she would pass close enough to see through camouflage. Arwen climbed onto one of the small white yachts moored next to her.

An older woman in jeans and a white lab coat joined the couples on deck. A half-dwarf with the build of a bodybuilder and a scar on one cheek, she seemed an unlikely candidate for a nurse or doctor or whatever she was supposed to be portraying, but the approaching woman nodded, as if comforted by her appearance.

"Good evening." The half-dwarf lifted a clipboard, like she was a bouncer with a list of names. There was probably nothing more than a hangman game drawn on the paper. "Are you Camille or Leah?"

"Camille."

Was Leah the name Amber had given?

When the woman—Camille—didn't pause anywhere along the way to the end of the dock, Arwen assumed Amber had also gotten out of the way.

"Welcome," the half-dwarf said. "Come aboard, and I'll introduce you to everyone. And you may wish to enjoy a drink. If you agree to carry one of the babies to term, we'll insist that you follow a healthy diet and consume no alcohol, but there's nothing wrong with a few libations tonight."

Was Camille *old* enough to legally drink? She was Amber's age, maybe sixteen or seventeen.

"You may be nervous," the half-dwarf added with a smile.

"A little." At the base of the gangplank, Camille paused and glanced around.

Don't go in, Arwen urged silently, then hopped off the yacht she'd climbed on. She was tempted to rush forward, pull Camille out of the way, and leap into a fray with anyone aboard the yacht who challenged her. But her senses detected at least a dozen magical beings in addition to those visible, and the half-orcs might be the trained muscle. It would be a lot for Arwen to take on by herself, and the best she could achieve was to save Camille. She needed to find Gemlytha and everyone else the dark elves had kidnapped.

"Come aboard," the half-dwarf repeated.

"Okay." Smiling nervously, Camille walked up the gangplank.

A waiter in a white tux came out with a tray, offering a drink in a martini glass or a bottle of water with an ice-filled tumbler. After hesitating, Camille chose the water. Arwen wagered both drinks were drugged.

She padded down the dock, intending to find Amber and keep her from boarding. Hopefully, she could do that without making noise or breaking either of their camouflage spells. How much would Amber fight her? She wouldn't draw her sword on an ally, would she?

The waiter led Camille inside while the half-dwarf remained near the top of the gangplank. Arwen stopped a few feet from the end of the dock, not wanting to risk those on the deck seeing through her camouflage.

Amber? Arwen asked silently, imagining her face to make the telepathic communication pinpoint. Though the half-bloods didn't have auras any more powerful than hers, and *shouldn't* have been able to pick up a telepathic comment not directed at them, Arwen was wary. If she didn't make any mistakes, she might be able to sneak aboard the yacht and ride along with Camille to the new dark-elf lair, but she had to be careful.

One of the men stepped away from his partner to stand at the top of the gangplank with the half-dwarf.

Arwen wished they would move away. She couldn't sneak aboard until she found Amber and ensured *she* didn't get on the yacht.

"Do you have a phone number for the other one?" The man was a tall half-troll with a beard that would have impressed a dwarf. "She sounded like exactly what they want, and we won't get paid if we don't bring her."

A chill went through Arwen. They meant Amber. *Leah.*

"I'm aware of that, and you know we don't get phone numbers. This is far from a legitimate business." The half-dwarf shrugged. "If the girls don't show, they don't show."

"She was pretty hot in her picture."

Arwen grimaced, hoping Amber hadn't sent her *own* photo. If she'd thought she would need to be identified to get on board, she might have.

"*You're* not going to be the one impregnating her," the half-dwarf said.

"Nah, I just like to flirt with them."

"Is *flirting* what you were doing to the blonde girl before she went in the pod?" The half-dwarf scowled her disapproval at him. "The dark elves don't want these women hurt. You'd better watch out if you value your life—and your penis."

Arwen's fingers curled into a fist. The thought of a bunch of young women with these loathsome people—who'd been hired by her loathsome kin—made her want to leap into a battle with them even more.

"She liked it," he promised.

The half-dwarf shook her head and looked toward the parked car. Camille's friend hadn't driven off.

"We could get that one and say she's Leah," the half-troll said. "The dark elves wouldn't know."

"They *would* know. They're very specific about what they want. That's why this is taking so long." The half-dwarf looked at the time on the phone. "It's past the meeting time. Just the one will have to do for tonight."

"The pay for one doesn't go a long way when it's split between all of us."

"You'll survive."

"Good thing this job has other perks." He adjusted himself and strolled toward the door the waiter had led Camille through.

Arwen's fist tightened again, her mind conjuring fantasies of springing on him and making sure he didn't *flirt* with anyone else.

The half-dwarf moved away from the gangplank. She didn't leave the deck completely, and the other couple and woman remained, but they were far enough back that Arwen could risk finishing searching for Amber. Amber, who hadn't responded when Arwen had reached out to her. That worried her.

The driver of the car took off, maybe concerned about the people who kept looking in her direction.

Arwen made it to the end of the dock without spotting Amber and backtracked, hopping onto the handful of moored vessels to search their decks.

Amber? Arwen whispered telepathically again.

The people on deck ambled toward the door. The vessel was getting ready to depart.

You're not stopping me. Amber's voice came from the yacht.

Damn it.

I'm going to find out where these creeps are taking everyone. Then I'll text you and Val.

The half-dwarf went inside, and the gangplank withdrew.

Arwen swore to herself. Going as fast as she dared without breaking her cover, she hurried toward the yacht.

Before the gangplank finished retracting, the black vessel started gliding away from the dock.

With little choice, Arwen ran the last ten feet and sprang across the water. She reached the railing, grabbed it, and vaulted over, landing in a crouch. She hadn't made a sound, but—

"I saw something," a half-orc said from just inside the doorway.

Arwen hurried to reactivate her camouflage but worried it was too late.

21

I SAW YOU, AMBER TOLD ARWEN, HER TELEPATHIC VOICE COMING from a lifeboat mounted toward the bow of the yacht. *I think they did too.*

Thanks for the tip.

Camouflage activated again, Arwen moved away from her landing spot as quickly as she dared.

The half-orc who strode out, followed by another, had the height and bulk of a yeti. They carried axes in their hands and automatic rifles slung across their backs.

Don't come toward me and mess up my hiding spot, Amber said.

Arwen *had* been heading that way because she wanted to protect Amber if necessary, not to lead anyone to her, but she paused. Instead, she climbed onto the roof of the cabin. She almost tripped over a paint bucket and brush someone had left up there. Or was that a waterproofing varnish? In the dim lighting, she couldn't tell. She skirted it and crouched in the middle of the roof.

The half-orcs reached the spot where she'd been and peered around. Arwen froze, glad they weren't full-blooded orcs. She doubted half-bloods would have noses or other senses much keener than humans.

They split up and strode in opposite directions, following the railing. Arwen hoped Amber was able to stay far enough from them that they wouldn't glimpse her.

Arwen thought about trying to signal to her father to provide a distraction, but the yacht was gliding farther into Lake Union while the half-orcs searched. Since he didn't carry a phone, she didn't know how she *could* signal him from there.

She eased her own phone out of her pocket. Once she knew which way the vessel was heading, she would text the information to Val and Willard. With luck, they were both in position with spots overlooking the canals.

Music started up inside the cabin, and someone shut the door. Arwen was surprised the half-bloods were keeping up their cock-tail-party charade to fool Camille and hadn't grabbed her, gagged her, and tied her up. Maybe the dark elves didn't want the future surrogate mothers of their children to be manhandled.

"Someone camouflaged?" one of the half-orcs asked when they came back together on the far side of the yacht.

"I don't know," the other said. "Are you *sure* you saw something?"

"Yeah, it was a redhead."

Arwen winced.

"That other one we were waiting for?"

"I don't know. She disappeared."

The half-orcs split again and did another pass, this time zigzagging across the deck and peering into every nook and cranny. One headed toward the lifeboat, crouching to peer under it.

Afraid they would spot Amber, Arwen grabbed the varnish bucket. When their backs were to her, she heaved it into the water off the back of the yacht. It was a long shot, but maybe the half-orcs would believe someone had jumped overboard and was swimming away.

When it splashed into the lake, they spun, raising their weapons, and ran toward the stern railing. Even in the dim lighting, Arwen could make out the bucket floating and almost groaned. That wouldn't fool anyone. Worse, they would realize a stowaway *was* onboard.

Arwen willed an illusion to cloak the bucket, to keep them from seeing it, but she had little experience with such magic, and she no longer had her tattoo to help her in a pinch. The half-orcs met at the railing, gripping it and peering over.

"That's not—"

A shadow stirred behind him, emitting a soft, "Hy-yah!"

Amber. Her movement broke her camouflage as she kicked the speaker in the lower back. Hard.

The half-orc lurched forward. If he'd been a normal height, the railing might have saved him, but he struck it mid-thigh and pitched into the water with another splash.

The second half-orc had time to react and whirled toward Amber with his axe raised. She ducked, lifting her sword to parry, and Arwen winced at the clang that rang out.

Traffic rumbled nearby—the yacht was heading under a bridge—but that might not be enough to cover the noise. Too late to be useful, a horn honked.

Pulling her bow off her back, Arwen leaped down to the deck to help. Amber deflected the axe but staggered back, probably not used to blows that heavy when she sparred with her mother.

Snarling, the half-orc swung again. This time, Amber dodged and evaded the axe completely.

Before he spotted her, Arwen leaped in from the half-orc's side and swung her bow like a staff. It cracked him in the forehead. The bow lacked the heft of a real blunt weapon, and he didn't stagger back. Arwen whipped it down, smacking his knuckles. He dropped the axe.

Amber leaped in and kicked him in the gut. As one, she and Arwen surged into the half-orc, shoving him over the railing.

Again, the splash was loud, and the first guy shouted from the water.

Afraid the music and closed door wouldn't be enough to drown that out, Arwen whispered, "Watch the cabin," to Amber and nocked an arrow. She pointed it between the noisy half-orc's eyes, hoping he could see her in the dim illumination provided by the running lights.

Shout again, and I'll end your life. Arwen did her best to include both half-orcs in the telepathic threat without projecting toward the cabin. The shouts stopped, both thugs glowering at her.

"Who the hell are you?" one asked aloud, the words barely reaching Arwen over the roar of traffic. Maybe he didn't know how to project his words telepathically. She hoped that was the case. Then he wouldn't be able to warn those inside.

Someone who doesn't want to see the dark elves succeed. Arwen didn't want to speak to them or answer their questions, but if they were talking, they weren't shouting. And the yacht was drawing farther away. Soon, it would be too late for them to get the attention of the captain or anyone inside.

"You're part dark elf!"

Which is why I don't want them to succeed. Arwen wouldn't have cared if her mother's people figured out a way to make themselves more fertile so they could have more babies, but she *would* stop this plan.

The half-orc might have been puzzled by the answer, but all he did was slap the water and start swimming toward shore. The other one did too.

"They might warn the ones inside telepathically," Amber whispered, rubbing her camouflaging charm.

"Yeah." Arwen frowned, not sharing her hope that the half-orcs couldn't use telepathy. That might be wishful thinking.

They might already have warned those inside. Short of shooting them in the backs of the heads, Arwen couldn't stop them. And she couldn't murder people for hiring on as security guards.

"Val and Willard are in the area. I'll let them know we're going..." After reactivating her own charm, Arwen paused to look around and get her bearings.

Where *were* they going? They had sailed west, under the Fremont and Aurora bridges, the traffic noise wafting down from above. Arwen started to text Val that they were heading into the ship canal, but the yacht was gliding toward shore, toward warehouses that loomed adjacent to it.

The vessel slowed, again guided by magic, and stopped. A gangplank extended toward a patch of trees. Was that the Burke Gilman Trail running in front of that warehouse?

Arwen's phone buzzed in her hand, a text from Val popping up. *Do you have an update? Did you find Amber?*

The gangplank extended, and the music inside the yacht stopped as the door opened. The half-dwarf strode out, her clipboard abandoned. The half-troll followed her, Camille unconscious and slung over his shoulder, his hand on her ass.

"I want to *kill* that guy," Amber whispered, waving her sword.

I know. Me too. But we need to follow them first.

Yes. One sec. Arwen wanted to text a more thorough answer to Val, but that would have to wait. If the gangplank retracted, she doubted she and Amber could make the leap to shore without breaking their camouflage.

Two more half-orcs walked out after the pair. They looked around, foreheads furrowed. They had to be looking for their buddies.

Arwen grimaced, but the half-dwarf called back to them, and they strode after her.

Arwen and Amber waited only long enough to make sure nobody else came out, then crept onto the gangplank after them. Before they'd reached shore, it started to retract. Arwen grabbed Amber by the wrist and jumped. She made it, but Amber only got one foot on land, the other slipping off toward the water. Arwen pulled her to safety.

The rearmost half-orc looked back, raising an axe. Arwen froze, again worried about being seen. Or maybe he'd heard them?

Arwen and Amber—who had proven herself a decent fighter —might be able to take the group, but they were so close to finding out where the kidnap victims were being taken that Arwen didn't want to risk missing that opportunity.

The half-orc grunted but must not have seen through their magic. He lowered his axe and continued after the others.

Behind Arwen and Amber, the yacht glided away, the lights once again extinguishing.

The group reached the paved bike trail. Arwen expected them to follow it toward a door in the closest warehouse, but they went straight toward a wall.

The half-dwarf rested a hand on it. A soft glow formed around her fingers, and a hidden door swung inward. The group headed through it into a pitch-dark interior.

As badly as Arwen wanted to charge in so the door wouldn't close and lock them out, she couldn't draw too near. Keeping a ten-foot distance, she waited until the last half-orc disappeared inside to advance. The door started to close.

Arwen reached for it, trying to catch it first. Amber was the one to lunge forward and thrust her sword tip in.

The door clinked softly when it hit the metal. Arwen winced. They'd moved far enough from the bridge that the traffic noise wasn't that loud now.

Pulling out her multitool, Arwen hurried to push open the door and step in ahead of Amber. Expecting to find a half-orc waiting, Arwen braced herself for a fight. But the security guys must not have heard the noise. Nobody was waiting to spring at her.

Nobody, Arwen realized with a sinking stomach, was inside at all. A moment ago, she'd sensed everyone in the group. Now, she didn't sense anyone.

"Crap," she breathed as Amber slipped inside, the door shutting behind her and leaving them in complete darkness.

22

AMBER TURNED ON THE FLASHLIGHT ON HER PHONE, SHINING IT around the windowless room in the warehouse. The walls, ceiling, and even the floor were painted black. Arwen didn't see the outline of any doors or access panels.

"There has to be a door." Arwen walked along the walls, sliding her fingers over them. "They disappeared so quickly."

"Even if they disappeared *slowly*, there would be a door," Amber pointed out.

"They could have made a portal. But I would have sensed that. And I haven't heard of any half-bloods with the power to do so. Even Matti can't make them on her own, and she's talented with her magic." Arwen touched the floor, confused about the abrupt disappearance of the party's auras. If they'd gone through a door, she should still have sensed them. Maybe the walls were insulated with something that blocked senses?

Amber tried the door they had come through. "This is locked now. I should have kept my sword in it." She rolled her eyes at herself. "I'm about to get concerned."

"More concerned than when the half-orc security guys were peering under the lifeboat where you were hidden?"

"I'd already scooted away when they were doing that. You didn't need to throw a *bucket* in the water." Amber gave her an exasperated look. "That guy I kicked was about to yell, I'm pretty sure."

"Sorry. I was worried about you."

"Adults worry *way* too much."

"About people they care about, yes."

"About *everything*. My dad has been wandering the house, lamenting the execrable state of global relations and our country's politics."

"Those are some good vocabulary words."

"I aced the SAT."

"You did well with the half-orcs too." Arwen did a slower search of the walls, patting along them while Amber shined the flashlight for her.

"I did okay. I think I would have been in trouble if you hadn't helped." She sounded so grudging. "Thanks," she muttered, even *more* grudging.

"You're welcome."

"I wasn't planning on taking on two guys. I just had to react before they yelled. And they were right at the railing, already leaning over, so..."

"It was the right decision." Arwen smiled at her, trying to be encouraging, though she was worried. Not about global relations and politics—at least not at that moment—but that the half-bloods were pulling farther and farther away with their captive. If magic was involved, or transportation in a vehicle, Arwen might not be able to track them when they found a way out of the room.

"It was okay." Amber pulled out her phone. "You said Val is nearby?"

"She was going to wait somewhere along the ship canal with a view. We thought the yacht would head into Puget Sound or maybe Lake Washington, not to a warehouse a few hundred yards away."

"She hasn't texted for a while. Not since she forbade me to go on a yacht or anywhere else with a stranger." The flashlight beam whipped about as Amber held up the display to show Arwen. "That was two hours ago."

"You were expecting more texts of forbidding?"

"Of *course*. That's how parents work. At least she hasn't told Dad, and *he* isn't calling and forbidding." Amber frowned at the display. "I don't have any bars."

"Maybe these walls insulate against cell signals as well as magic." Arwen crouched to peer along the floor again. There *had* to be a secret door. "Were you thinking of calling her to help?"

"If we exhaust every possibility and are still stuck in here, yeah. Her sword is bigger and more magical than mine. I'm sure it can hack down a door." Amber stuck her tongue out at the one locking them in. "I'll try my sword first though. Just in case it can break the lock."

Arwen didn't want to get out of the room, not through the door that led out to the trail. And she hated the thought of having to tell Val and Willard she'd been right behind the kidnappers and had lost them. If she'd thought that would happen, Arwen would have attacked outside to free at least one victim. And maybe she could have questioned one of the half-orcs.

"I want to find those kidnapped girls though." Amber pointed her flashlight toward where Arwen was searching again.

"So do I. My mother and brother are responsible for that. And for taking Gemlytha too."

"Who's that?"

"A half-dragon... friend of Azerdash's."

"A friend or a *girl*friend?"

"She was his subordinate." That was the exact word Azerdash

had used when he'd first explained Gemlytha to Arwen. Of course, his eyes had promised she'd been much more to him.

"That does less to answer my question than you'd think."

"Sorry."

It occurred to Arwen that she could use her soul-tracking magic in the room and might be able to see where the prints had disappeared. The group had been inside so briefly that she probably wouldn't get much, but she would try.

"Aren't you and him hooked up now?" Amber asked. "Mated or claimed or whatever dumb term dragons use?"

"We've been trying to *hook up*, but we keep getting interrupted."

Still kneeling on the smooth black floor, Arwen rested a hand on it and called upon her ability to see the essences of souls that people left behind when they passed. Her vision shifted, growing darker.

In the already dim room, it was alarming, as if she was going blind. Amber disappeared, but a few very faint photoluminescent partial prints came into view. At first, she saw only Amber's and her own, which made sense since they'd been in the room tramping around longer, covering up other sign, but a couple of fainter prints led from the door to the center of the room.

"You're probably going to get interrupted a lot more," Amber said, "if he gets his old girlfriend back. Are you *sure* you want to find her?"

The words refreshed Arwen's anxiety about that—about her mother's flexible plans to let Gemlytha live or to kill her, depending on what would force Arwen to do her bidding.

"I think he loves me," she said. "The challenge is that Azerdash doesn't want her to feel that he's betraying her. He's a staunch believer in loyalty. When he thought she was dead, he wouldn't have felt that moving on was a betrayal. But if she's alive, and she sees that he's gone on to someone else, he'll feel... I don't know.

Bad, I guess." That wasn't the most accurate term to describe feelings, but it was what came to mind.

Arwen looked up, realizing she hadn't considered the ceiling. There weren't any prints up there, not that she would have expected them, but might someone have dropped a ladder down through a trap door?

It was hard to imagine four people climbing up in the short time that Arwen and Amber had lost sight of them, but maybe they'd *levitated* up.

"His feelings might switch once he sees her," Amber pointed out. "Is she hot?"

"Probably." Arwen hadn't gotten a good look at Gemlytha in the stasis chamber.

"Well, I guess it would be wrong to suggest you *don't* rescue her and let some dark elf with a vendetta take her out, but it sounds like things would be easier if this Gemlytha didn't reappear."

"Will you shine your light up there, please?" Arwen willed her vision back to normal, hoping to pick out the outline of a trapdoor.

"Is that your way of saying you won't do the easy thing?" Amber pointed the light at the ceiling. "The *smart* thing?"

"It's my way of saying... I have to do the *right* thing. Anything else would be a betrayal to Azerdash and to myself."

"Betrayal comes up a lot for you."

"My life has gotten complicated of late." Arwen didn't see any lines to indicate a door and debated if she could climb up to check. The walls were smooth and without any handholds.

Amber walked toward her so she could more directly shine the light overhead. When her foot passed over a spot in the center of the room, a glowing purple spider appeared on the floor.

"Shit!" Amber leaped back.

After a couple of seconds, the spider disappeared.

"That's weird," Arwen said.

"You think?"

"I've walked across that spot a dozen times in my search." Arwen hesitated, then stepped into the center of where the spider had appeared. Nothing happened. She looked at Amber.

"I'm not walking there again. Nothing good comes from spiders."

"In nature, spiders are very helpful. They feed on a lot of the pest insects that can plague your garden."

"That wasn't a *natural* spider, and you know it. It's one of those nasty dark-elf demon things."

Arwen smiled sadly. "Yes, but it may be marking a doorway. Will you stand on it again? I wonder if it's triggered because..." She waved vaguely at Amber's midsection.

"I have a *womb*? You may have noticed you have one too."

"They've been looking for people of a specific age though."

Amber made a disgusted noise. "You'd better protect me if a spider comes to life and tries to eat me."

"I'll throw a bucket at it."

"Oh, great." Sword in hand, Amber stepped forward.

The glowing spider appeared again, about four feet by four feet, almost exactly in the center of the room. Magic swelled, and black mist appeared from nowhere, curling across the floor in the room.

On impulse, Arwen stepped forward and gripped Amber's wrist. None too soon. A purple flash filled the room, the solidness of the floor disappeared from under their feet, and queasiness assaulted Arwen's stomach as the world warped around them.

23

DISORIENTED, SIMILAR TO THE WAY SHE WAS DURING PORTAL TRAVEL, Arwen flailed for balance, but she didn't let go of Amber's arm. She tightened her grip, afraid they would be parted or that she would be left behind.

Abruptly, there was a hard floor underneath them again. No, that was the *ground*. The packed dirt of an underground chamber with two dark tunnels on opposite ends leading out of it.

Light and magic emanated from pods lining a wall carved from the earth. The pods, similar to stasis chambers, held unconscious young women. Two dozen? Three? All except one were mundane humans, but Arwen sensed a familiar aura at the end. Winter, the werewolf, was also unconscious.

Unconscious but not frozen the way they would be in stasis chambers. These pods were different, with magical IV tubes delivering fluids to their veins. Water and nutrients to keep them alive? Or drugs to keep the occupants knocked out? Maybe both.

Arwen tried to tell if the dark elves had already impregnated the girls, but she didn't think so. Not yet. Since the intended babies would be magical beings, she would have been able to sense them.

She grew aware of other magical beings behind her and halted her inspection. The two half-orcs. And they weren't unconscious.

They stood ten feet apart, aiming rifles at Arwen and Amber. No, just at Arwen. Maybe they thought Amber was their missing *Leah*, or at least someone the dark elves would want for their experiment.

"I knew we were being followed," one snarled, his finger tightening on the trigger.

Arwen raised a magical barrier that included Amber, glad she still had a grip on her wrist so she couldn't pull away.

"Uh." Sword in one hand and phone in the other, Amber crouched and glanced around, as if to dive for cover.

"You're protected," Arwen promised her.

The half-orc's rifles were mundane, and she didn't sense anything special about the bullets.

Her words didn't keep them from firing. Amber lifted her sword, as if it might deflect bullets, and squinted her eyes shut.

Somewhere along the way, Arwen had grown confident in her abilities—at least her ability to deflect mundane attacks with her barrier—and she stared defiantly at the orcs.

Their bullets pinged off and ricocheted around the laboratory. Several hit the walls, and one lodged in the earthen floor. Another struck a pod and was deflected, but not without a flash of light and an angry buzz. One bullet slammed into a beaker on a counter, shattering the glass. A yellow liquid spilled, dribbling onto the floor. Smoke wafted up from the mess.

"Stop, you idiot," one half-orc said, lowering his rifle, as if he hadn't also been firing. He grabbed his buddy's arm. "She's powerful."

If only that were true. Arwen might have stronger magic than they, but when she came face to face with a dark elf, she would be outmatched. Fortunately, she didn't sense anyone other than the half-orcs stirring in the chamber. Of course, Harlik-van could be in the area and camouflaged.

"She's one of *them*." The half-orc squinted at her. "At least partially."

"Do you think we can take these guys?" Amber whispered, her eyes open again as she eyed the half-orcs, maybe thinking of the others they'd kicked overboard.

Arwen released Amber to draw an arrow, knowing she could fire through her barrier. Before she drew it, a new voice came from the tunnel, someone approaching.

"What the hell is going on in here?" It wasn't a dark elf but the half-dwarf in the white lab coat.

Arwen licked her lips, growing less certain of her barrier and her ability to keep it up as more enemies presented themselves. She was also nervous at the idea of shooting these people since she didn't want to kill anyone. But if she didn't, they would raise an alarm. They might already have done that.

"And how did they get through the transporter?" The half-dwarf frowned at Arwen, but her eyes brightened when she noticed Amber. "Oh, she's another one who fits the dark elves' desires, isn't she?" She waved toward a counter opposite the pods, a shadowy area that Arwen hadn't noticed right away.

The other girl—Camille—lay on her back upon it, still unconscious. The half-dwarf must have been about to prepare her for... for what? Why were they putting the girls to sleep and pumping concoctions into them?

Arwen scanned the long row of prisoners again, and her breath caught. One pod was different from the others. That one *was* a stasis chamber, and its green light shone onto a white-skinned woman with elegant features and pointed ears. Unlike the others, she was frozen, her aura diminished to a speck, making it seem she was barely alive. That was why Arwen hadn't noticed her at first. But this had to be Gemlytha.

Would the dark elves attempt to impregnate her too?

Fury built within Arwen as she imagined all these poor women forced to carry and deliver babies they hadn't bargained for. Babies that might even be dangerous to them. Arwen's mother had admitted the dark elves had used the essences of many types of beings in an attempt to make superior children. These women were being turned into science experiments.

Jaw clenched, Arwen raised her bow and pointed it at the half-dwarf.

Maybe she should have targeted the half-orcs with the rifles, one of whom was poking into drawers and probably looking for something that could cut through Arwen's barrier. But *they* weren't the scientists. They were only the brute force.

"Release those women from those chambers, or I will end your life." As Arwen aimed between the half-dwarf's eyes, she wasn't sure it was a bluff.

The half-dwarf snorted and created a barrier of her own.

Arwen hesitated. Would her magical arrow pierce it? She didn't know.

"You'll have to talk to the dark elves about that. I don't know how to work their machinery. I only know how to put new girls in it and start preparing them for the seed." The half-dwarf glanced toward what looked like a mini fridge under the counter, but, like so many things in the laboratory, it was magical. Maybe it held the embryos that would be used? "And I know how to monitor them and let the dark-elven scientists know if anything is amiss."

"If you can put them in, you can take them out." Arwen squinted at the half-dwarf, willing herself the power to rake through her mind and read her thoughts. She'd done it before but not since her tattoo had been removed. She tried anyway, needing to know if the half-dwarf could help.

"No, I really can't."

Arwen couldn't read every thought, but she got a hint, enough to know that the words were a lie.

"Like I said, you'll have to talk to the dark elves." The half-dwarf headed for a section of the counter with shelves on the wall above it. She rose on tiptoes, reaching for a golden orb identical to the one that had floated into the Coffee Dragon to enable communication between Arwen and her mother. "But I warn you they won't want to be bothered. They've got another project going on tonight."

One of the half-orcs pulled a box out of a drawer, one that held... Was that magical ammunition?

"We'll deal with this ourselves," he said.

Arwen was on the verge of shooting the orb, but a rumble sounded, and the ground shook. Glass containers clinked on the shelves.

Another earthquake?

The half-orc chuckled as he loaded bullets into his rifle. "Yup, another project."

The words made Arwen wish she had checked the news after the first earthquake to see if anything odd had been reported about it.

"Shoot them, Arwen," Amber whispered. "Shoot them before they shoot us."

Arwen nodded, whispering, "If my barrier fails, duck behind one of the empty pods for cover."

Amber glanced toward Gemlytha's stasis chamber and a dark and empty one beside it. "I can't help you if I'm hiding."

"Being out of the way where you can't be hurt is helpful. Trust me."

The half-dwarf had set the communication orb on the counter and rested a hand on it. Her barrier protected it. It started to glow, and Arwen loosed her arrow, willing her own power into it and aiming for the scientist's wrist.

The half-dwarf saw the release and jerked her hand back but not quickly enough. The arrow pierced her barrier and drove through her palm.

Screaming, she reeled back and clutched her hand to her chest.

The half-orc had finished loading his rifle with the magical ammunition, and he aimed at Arwen. She whirled and loosed another arrow before he could fire. He lifted his rifle like a shield and got lucky, deflecting the arrow toward a wall. Thanks to its magic, it gouged deep into the earth, only an inch of the fletching visible.

Instead of shooting again, his buddy ran toward the tunnel. To flee? Or get help?

Arwen swung her bow and shot him in the calf, sending him sprawling. Bullets hammered into her barrier. Again, they were deflected, but their magic gave them more power. Her barrier sparked and wavered.

Feeling it giving away, Arwen lowered her bow to focus on her magic. She tried to feed more power into her barrier, but the half-orc kept firing, the magical bullets depleting it.

"Shit." Amber darted away from Arwen's defenses.

Fear leaped into Arwen's throat. Fortunately, Amber ran toward the pods, squeezing between the empty one and the one holding Gemlytha.

The half-orc remained focused on Arwen. Willing her barrier to stay around her, Arwen aimed for his chest. She still didn't want to kill anyone, but they were trying to kill her and might hurt Amber. What choice did Arwen have?

Before she fired, the half-dwarf used her good hand to grab and throw a beaker full of a magical liquid. Most of it flew out before reaching Arwen, but some splattered on her barrier.

Not worrying about it, Arwen loosed her arrow, but the half-orc was on the run now. He dove behind one of the pods, one with a woman in it, and the arrow only clipped his shoulder. It must have hurt, because he cried out, but he still had his rifle and wasn't out of commission.

An image formed in the air over the communication orb. Was that Harlik-van's hooded face? Damn it.

Arwen pulled out another arrow, willing her power to infuse it and make it stronger, and fired at the orb.

The crystal, or whatever it was made from, didn't shatter, but the projectile struck hard enough to crack it. The image disappeared, the orb stopped glowing, and it clunked to the floor.

The half-dwarf shot Arwen a scathing look, but Arwen didn't know if she'd succeeded in cutting off the communication in time. Even if the scientist hadn't spoken to Harlik-van, he might have guessed something was up.

Footsteps sounding in the tunnel made Arwen whirl, afraid an army was already rushing in. It was the half-orc she'd shot in the calf. He'd pulled the arrow out and clenched it, his face contorted with rage.

The other half-orc was behind the pods, trying to use them for cover as he maneuvered toward Amber. Her back was toward him. She was squatting and fiddling with something inside an open panel.

"Amber, that looks like a bad idea." Arwen aimed at the half-orc angling for her, but she couldn't get a clear shot.

His buddy in the tunnel threw her arrow, distracting her.

"It's a *fabulous* idea." Amber glanced toward the approaching half-orc. "Especially if you can keep that guy off me for a minute."

Arwen wanted to, but he was crouching behind a pod with an occupant. She didn't dare shoot.

The half-orc leaned out with his rifle and fired at Arwen. Expecting her barrier to protect her, she didn't duck and almost fell over when a bullet skimmed past her head close enough to stir her hair. Only then did she notice smoke wafting from the place in her barrier where that liquid had struck—struck and made a *hole*.

The half-orc fired again, but his rifle clicked. He was out of ammo.

Before Arwen could feel any relief, he roared, pulled out a knife, and charged out from behind the pods toward her.

As Arwen drew another arrow, she struggled to re-form her barrier, to fill in the holes. He reached her first, leaping through the gap to tackle her.

Her arrow flew from her grip. Desperately wielding her bow like a staff, she blocked a slash to her head. Though she deflected the blade, the half-orc bore her to the ground.

She pulled her multitool out before he crushed her with his greater size and weight but didn't have time to open one of the blades. All she could do was jab the blunt end into his gut.

The blow didn't faze him. He snarled, knocked her bow away, and pinned her before bringing his knife toward her throat.

"Arwen!" Amber cried. "I need your help with this guy."

The other half-orc was running toward her. Forced to move away from the open panel, Amber ducked a grab for her hair—or maybe her throat.

"I can't right now," Arwen answered, the guy's knee on her gut. Her words came out as a wheeze. "Use your sword. Remember, the pointy end goes in the bad guy!"

"That's shitty advice."

Forced to focus on her own battle, Arwen silently ordered the multitool to send a beam lancing into the half-orc's ribs. But would that work when it wasn't open? She'd fired from the bottle opener once, but that wasn't the same as having all the tools tucked away.

The half-orc's knife came to rest on her throat, the blade icy against her flushed skin.

"Do I kill you or hand-deliver you to their leader to kill?" he whispered, glancing at his buddy. The other half-orc was in a dance around the pods with Amber, trying to catch her as she ducked behind them.

The beam didn't shoot out. Again, Arwen could tell she didn't have as much power to call upon without the help of the tattoo. Gritting her teeth, she attempted to dredge up everything she could to pour into the multitool, to mingle her power with that which Azerdash had infused his gift.

"Better kill you to be safe." The half-orc looked back to Arwen.

Behind him, the half-dwarf had set the communication orb on the counter again and was rummaging in a drawer. What if she was able to fix the device?

The knife blade bit deeper into Arwen's throat, but her power —or her fear and desperation—must have fueled the multitool sufficiently. Magic surged from it and into the half-orc. She wasn't sure if it was a beam or raw energy. Either way, her opponent screamed, dropped his knife, and rolled away.

A clang and Amber's cry of, "Hy-yah!" came from the pods.

The half-orc fighting her yelled in pain. "Bitch!"

Before Arwen could check on Amber, the half-dwarf threw something at her. The orb? No, another beaker filled with that magical liquid. That magical *acid*.

Arwen rolled away as the beaker struck the ground. It shattered, and shards of glass flew along with droplets of liquid.

She'd put enough distance between herself and the beaker that most of them missed her, but a few struck her exposed skin, immediately searing her to the core. She cried out and almost dropped the multitool. But she'd already lost her bow. She couldn't lose that too. Tightening her grip, she pushed herself to her knees and looked for her bow.

A tremendous explosion came from where Amber was battling the half-orc.

Had he thrown a grenade? In the middle of a laboratory full of women the dark elves had carefully selected and prepared for their plot?

The shockwave caught Arwen, knocking her across the chamber. She tried to twist to come down on her feet, but she slammed into a cabinet first. The side of her head struck the hard counter, and blackness sprang into her vision. As gravity took her to the floor, she blinked, trying not to lose consciousness.

A roar of fire filled the chamber, and she groaned. What now?

Arwen expected the flaming attack to strike her, but, as her vision cleared, she could see the gout of fire crossing the chamber toward another target. Fear slammed into her chest like a wrecking ball. Amber?

"No," Arwen rasped, trying to push her battered body to her feet.

But great magical power wrapped around her and pinned her to the ground. Confused and helpless, she peered into smoke and flames.

That was far more power than a half-orc or half-dwarf should have been able to summon. She was right. They weren't the ones striding toward her.

Gemlytha was awake, out of her stasis chamber, and furious.

24

GEMLYTHA'S AURA MIGHT HAVE BEEN DIMINISHED WHEN SHE WAS frozen in the stasis chamber, but it flared around her now, crackling with barely restrained fury. Her power had to be as great as Azerdash's. And she was using that power to keep Arwen pinned.

Gemlytha spoke, that same fury in her words, but Arwen couldn't understand. Was that Elven?

"I'm not with them," Arwen croaked, afraid Gemlytha saw only her dark-elven blood and believed her an ally of the clan. After all, all the other half-bloods down here *were* working for the dark elves. As power tightened around her, Arwen hurried to repeat her words telepathically and added, *We came to rescue you.*

Arwen couldn't see Amber from her position on the ground and hoped they still *were* a we. There. Arwen sensed her crouching by one of the counters. She'd left the pods because— Damn, they'd exploded.

Rescue me? Gemlytha spat. *Your kind have tormented me as much as the dragons did.*

I'm not one of their kind. I'm like you, your *kind.* Arwen didn't know if she could get through to Gemlytha, or if it was possible to rationalize with someone consumed by such anger. She lifted the multitool, the only weapon she had left to defend herself, and groped for the power to summon a protective barrier again.

Gemlytha's furious eyes—as red as those of a full-blooded dark elf—locked on the tool. Arwen thought she might melt it with her gaze. Or incinerate it. Arwen hoped Azerdash's gift could withstand that.

Long seconds passed, the crackle of flames dying down in the laboratory. Arwen realized she still sensed Amber but not anyone else with magical blood. The half-orcs and half-dwarf had either fled or... Gemlytha had killed them.

The fiery gaze shifted from the multitool to Arwen.

Azerdash made that, Gemlytha stated telepathically, a question in her eyes.

Unexpected emotions stole Arwen's tongue—even her telepathic tongue—at the reminder that this powerful being cared for Azerdash. *Loved* Azerdash. She'd used his first name, not Commander Starblade, as one might expect from a subordinate.

When Arwen didn't respond, Gemlytha scowled and shifted her focus from Arwen's face to the top of her head.

Magical power scraped through Arwen's mind, and she gasped. A mind-reading. Or a mind-*scouring*? Gemlytha had the rough touch of a full-blooded dragon.

"He's a friend," Arwen blurted, then repeated the words telepathically.

Her first instinct was to try to wall off her mind, but she realized the truth might convince Gemlytha that Arwen was an ally, a friend of Azerdash's who'd come to find her.

Only after she'd slumped back, intending to let Gemlytha see whatever she wished without fighting, did Arwen realize that might be a mistake. If Gemlytha saw how close she was with Azerdash, how much they'd come to care about each other that summer, she might make the choice that Arwen hadn't.

The *smart* one, as Amber had said, to get rid of the competition.

Right now, it wouldn't be hard. Weary and wounded from the battle, Arwen couldn't raise her barrier, much less defeat someone so powerful.

Gemlytha's eyes narrowed. If she decided to kill Arwen...

"Is everything okay?" Amber called uncertainly across the chamber.

The raking faded, and Arwen sensed Gemlytha's presence withdraw from her mind.

Arwen licked her lips. "I'm not sure."

"If it was a mistake to turn off the stasis chamber, I'm sorry," Amber said, "but I heard more guys coming, and I figured she could help."

More guys coming? Arwen risked glancing toward the tunnel. There were charred bodies on the ground in it. In the chaos, Arwen hadn't sensed their arrival and didn't know if they had been more mixed-bloods or dark elves.

Gemlytha raised a hand.

Arwen jerked her gaze back to her and lifted the multitool to defend herself. Gemlytha merely arched her white eyebrows. It took Arwen a moment to realize she was offering a hand up.

Arwen tucked the multitool into her belt and accepted it. Gemlytha's time in the stasis chamber hadn't diminished her strength, and she easily pulled Arwen to her feet.

Thanks.

Gemlytha's expression wasn't warm—how much had she seen in Arwen's mind about her relationship with Azerdash?—but it wasn't furious anymore. That was something.

Amber walked warily over, eyeing Gemlytha and keeping her distance. Even though Amber, with her six feet in height, was taller, she had to sense the great power that the dark-elven half-dragon commanded.

When Arwen stood straight, she realized that she and Gemlytha were the same height. Something about all that power and her fiery intensity made her seem much taller.

Do you know how to release these women? Arwen asked her. Or... "Do *you*?" She looked at Amber, remembering that she'd had the panel open. "Did you or the half-orc accidentally free her during your skirmish?"

"*Accidentally?*" Amber propped a fist on her hip. "Do you know how much poking around I had to do in there? It's a good thing I thought to take a photo of this." Amber held up her phone to a close-up of schematics. "Willard got these from your gnome friend."

"Imoshaun?"

"Yes. She gave them to *Winter*." Amber rolled her eyes, but then turned smug. "Who I convinced to share them with me."

"Ah."

It made sense that Willard would have wanted Winter to be able to free the women if she found them.

"The schematics are for stasis chambers." Amber lowered her phone. "The pods are a little different, but we need to figure out how to get the girls out. Are they already impregnated, do you think? If so, that's so totally illegal. I really doubt they were actually paid. Even if they were, they wouldn't have signed up for *that*." Amber flung her arm toward the pods.

"I agree, and I don't think they have been yet." Arwen looked to Gemlytha, groping for a way to sum up their problem and ask for her help in a few sentences.

Arwen worried more reinforcements would be sent soon. She was surprised the dark elves hadn't been here, guarding the women personally, since this represented the culmination of their work for years, if not decades. But she remembered the half-orc saying something about another project occupying them tonight and grimaced, hoping they weren't after Val again. They had it out for her.

I understand, Gemlytha said before Arwen managed to articulate anything.

Even though the mental claws had stopped raking through Arwen's mind, Gemlytha might be able to read her surface thoughts.

I am not an engineer, she added, *but I will see if these devices can be destroyed in such a way that the occupants aren't harmed.* Gemlytha started toward the pods but paused and looked back at them. *What world am I on?*

Earth.

That prompted a puzzled crease to Gemlytha's brow.

"The elves call it *Yee Slysora,*" Amber said.

"How do you know that?" Arwen hadn't heard the term before.

"My grandfather is the elven king, remember."

"I didn't know that meant you'd studied their language." Remembering poor Camille abandoned on the counter, Arwen grabbed her bow and went to check on her.

"I haven't, but when he came to Green Lake, we bonded. We inline skated, and he learned that you can't pay for ice cream with gold coins here." Amber looked at her phone and curled her lip. "I still don't have any reception. Where do you think we are? Did we really get teleported? I thought that only happened on *Star Trek.*"

"I believe they're transported on *Star Trek,*" Arwen said, though she wasn't an expert.

"Like it matters." Amber walked over to the pods and examined them. Searching for access panels to see if she could turn them off or short-circuit them or whatever she'd done to the stasis chamber?

Arwen brushed dark hair back from Camille's face, but the young woman didn't stir. Whatever they'd drugged her with had been potent. Arwen eyed the IVs delivering who knew what to the women in the pods. Maybe it was the same drug.

"At least when you wake up, you won't be with a child you probably don't want," Arwen whispered.

None of them are with child, Gemlytha said.

Arwen exhaled slowly, relieved to have that verified. "I'm glad, but that's a little surprising. They've had some of these girls for a while. Did they want to start the pregnancies all at once?"

"That would be weird," Amber said. "I don't think the term *economies of scale* applies to babies. The more babies you have, the more of a huge chaotic mess it has to be."

"Matti seems to be doing okay with two."

Since there wasn't anything she could do for Camille, Arwen walked around and retrieved her arrows, grimacing since the bodies of those she'd shot were so charred as to be unrecognizable. The scent of burned meat wafted up from them, turning her stomach. Azerdash wasn't the only half-dragon prone to incineration when his temper was roused.

"How would she do with *thirty-two*?" Amber might have counted the captives, because that seemed about right. "Sarrlevi's homemade vine baby carrier is maxed out at twins. I'm positive."

"Sarrlevi? Matti?" Gemlytha spoke aloud for the first time, her voice not as stern and forbidding as her visage. *I have met them. I...* Gemlytha rested a hand on her abdomen, frowning down at herself. *I died for them. At least, I thought I did.*

Her troubled frown suggested she hadn't spent a lot of time conscious since her revival. Had the Silverclaws stuffed her immediately into that stasis chamber without explaining anything? Probably.

As Arwen retrieved her last arrow, Gemlytha scraped through her mind again. It wasn't pleasant, but Arwen tried to keep her hackles from rising. As she knew from her first meeting with Azerdash, half-dragons could be as presumptuous as full-bloods and didn't think much of the privacy of lesser species. Given that they might not have much time before the dark elves came to check on the laboratory, mind-reading was faster and more efficient than speaking anyway.

The Silverclaw dragons revived me? To use against Azerdash? Because he's... started a war with every dragon in the Cosmic Realms? Gemlytha's mouth drooped open.

I tried to tell him it was a bad idea, Arwen said. *One that might get him killed, but once he found his galaxy blade, he figured it was his destiny.*

Gemlytha considered that before laughing shortly. *It likely will get him killed, but he's right. It is what he was made for. I'm glad he's doing it.*

Arwen didn't know how to respond to Gemlytha's approval, but worry wormed into her stomach. Even though Arwen had always been supportive of Azerdash—she'd helped him find that sword, after all—she'd also made it clear she thought taking on the dragons was a bad idea. Would he be moved by another woman—the first woman he'd cared for—approving of his choice? A woman who was, despite her earlier fury and sternness, as beautiful as Arwen had feared.

Yes, Azerdash might value loyalty over looks, but Arwen had a feeling Gemlytha, as his faithful officer, had supported him throughout his whole career. Loyally.

What if Arwen's mother was right that it would be a greater gift to Azerdash to step aside for him to be with Gemlytha? The thought pained her like a dagger to the heart.

If Gemlytha was still monitoring Arwen's thoughts, she didn't respond other than to narrow her eyes slightly. Thoughtfully?

An ominous *click-thunk* echoed in the chamber.

"Uhm." Amber knelt in front of one of the pods with a panel open. "I thought I was turning this off, nothing else."

The noise hadn't come from the pod but the walls or maybe

the ground. A buzz of magical energy rippled through the chamber.

Gemlytha turned away from Arwen and dropped into a crouch, her fists raised. Two more *click-thunks* sounded, and the energy sizzling in the air went from low to so high that the hair on Arwen's arms rose.

Thick metal doors she hadn't noticed before dropped from the ceilings of the two tunnels and clanged down so hard the ground shook. They were magical, far more magical than they had been a moment before. It was as if the whole chamber had been in hibernation and had come awake.

We should get out of here. Gemlytha strode toward one of the doors.

"That was more of an option ten seconds ago," Amber said.

Gemlytha lifted a hand, power radiating from her core. A wave of energy roared toward one of the doors, flames dancing at the periphery. When it struck, the flames turned into an inferno that battered at the obstacle.

From across the chamber, Arwen felt the heat and raised a hand to protect her eyes. Orange brightness drove back the shadows, highlighting the faces of the women still suspended in their pods. The flames crackled as if they were burning through a forest, not beating against a metal object.

"We have to free the girls before we leave," Amber called.

The fire died down, the heat and brilliance fading. The door remained, not so much as charred. Arwen slumped. They weren't going anywhere. With as much power as Gemlytha had, Arwen wouldn't have guessed much could stand up to her, not anything made by dark elves.

I do not know if either will be an option, Gemlytha said telepathically, understanding Amber even though she spoke aloud in English. *If this project is as important to the dark elves as you believe—*

she looked at Arwen, —*it is surprising that it is not protected by more than a handful of weak mongrels.*

Arwen couldn't keep from glancing at the charred remains of one of those *weak mongrels.* She didn't point out that, if Gemlytha hadn't killed them all, they might have questioned one. After all, Gemlytha had helped her out.

"So, what?" Amber asked. "They're going to keep us trapped in here until they have time to come deal with us?"

The light emitted from the pods and various artifacts around the chamber dimmed, and the air grew foggy. A purple glow came from the floor, outlining a vaguely triangular shape. It brought to mind the dark-elven rituals Arwen had witnessed in her youth.

The shape didn't form in the spot where they'd arrived, so she didn't believe it had anything to do with the spider that had transported them here. It was something else. It was—

The greater demon, Yeshelee vun, Gemlytha said grimly. *Very powerful. It would have taken numerous dark elves working together to summon it—or build a summoning shape through which it could be brought into this world.* She pointed at the floor.

"A demon?" Amber asked. "Coming to the room we're trapped in? That can't be good."

No. It is not.

25

"I AM UNABLE TO MAKE A PORTAL TO ESCAPE FROM THIS PLACE," Gemlytha said, eyeing the walls and ceiling.

Arwen grimaced, not surprised. The dark elves wouldn't have wanted it to be easy for magical beings to come and go.

Her throat felt raw as she watched the purple glowing shape on the floor, but a demon hadn't yet coalesced above it. A faint pulsing came from the spot, like a bell being rung. Was it a call to the demon?

In her seven years with the dark elves, she'd never seen an automated summoning like this. Usually, demons were only called for rituals, to receive offerings—or sacrifices—and dark-elven priests formed a ring to invite them into the world.

Yeshelee vun will be too powerful for me to fight. Gemlytha glanced at Amber's sword and Arwen's bow but didn't amend her words to say *us.* Her lip didn't curl in dismissal, but it *did* twitch.

Arwen doubted Gemlytha believed they could be any help. Maybe she was right. Arwen didn't have an arrow crafted to have greater power against demons.

"I'm all for leaving." Amber pointed at the other door. "Any chance that one can be incinerated?"

Doubtful. Gemlytha headed toward it anyway, giving the triangular shape on the ground a wide berth. She paused before reaching the door and considered the wispy fog flowing around her legs. *My senses tell me this fog is dangerous to breathe.*

Gemlytha rubbed her thumb and fingers together as if she might determine more from feeling the air between them. She formed a magical barrier around herself.

Arwen didn't think her barrier kept out air molecules—and the fog was already wrapped about her, regardless—but she stepped close to Amber and also raised one. She glanced toward the unconscious Camille, then gripped Amber's arm so she could walk close enough to the girl to include her. Hopefully, the pods protected their occupants. Since this project was so important to the dark elves, they shouldn't have booby traps that would hurt their subjects.

"My throat itches." Amber wiped her watering eyes. "Is your barrier doing anything?"

"Probably not." The rawness in Arwen's throat grew more pronounced, and her lungs ached. Was that fog more than just dangerous to breathe? Maybe it was *deadly.*

"Maybe we should put her in one of the pods." Amber pointed at Camille. "You know *they* have air filters."

Arwen drew back, repulsed by the idea of helping the dark elves ensnare women, but Amber was right. The air inside the pods appeared clear, bright under the glow of magic.

"Maybe *we* should get in them too," Amber rasped.

"Then we'd be trapped." Arwen set her bow aside and gripped Camille under the armpits, shifting her off the counter.

"I've got a newsflash for you, Arwen." Amber took the girl's ankles.

"We're not defeated yet." A round of coughs attacked Arwen,

and she tried to believe her own words. As long as they were standing, they could fight.

"I'd pay all my driving money for a HEPA purifier right now," Amber said.

I am uncertain how to use my magic to filter the air. Gemlytha also coughed.

With tears running down her cheeks, she watched them carry Camille toward a pod, then faced the door she hadn't yet tested. Once more, she sent a tremendous blast of fiery power at it, the brilliance lighting the chamber.

All that light did was make the fog more apparent. It didn't wither or wane at the flames.

Once again, the inferno was ineffective at destroying the door blocking the tunnel. Grunting in irritation, Gemlytha tried blasting into an empty section of the wall. Magic swelled under her assault, providing protection from damage.

The pod accepted Camille, almost sucking her in, like a starving animal, then activated on its own. Amber jerked her hand back. Given the chance, it might have sucked *her* in too.

Gemlytha roared in frustration as she continued to hurl her flaming power at the wall.

On the chance it might work, Arwen fired an arrow at the door. It pinged off, as if she'd hit it with a stick instead of a magical projectile, and clattered across a counter.

She drew her multitool and activated the beam, trying it on the door. It also deflected off, hitting a beaker. The glass exploded, and liquid spattered.

"Oh, sure," Amber said. "Add *more* noxious gunk to the air."

"Sorry." That didn't keep Arwen from trying again, this time channeling some of her own power into the multitool to enhance its strength. It had worked before when she'd needed to tunnel through rockfalls, but *magical* boulders hadn't been piled in her way.

Again, the beam only glanced off the door. This time, it deflected across the chamber, skipping off Gemlytha's barrier before hitting the ceiling, which it also didn't damage.

"Sorry," Arwen blurted again, jerking her hand down as she deactivated the tool.

I do not blame you for trying. Gemlytha lowered her arms, stepping away from the undamaged wall.

"That's one way to get rid of the competition," Amber muttered.

Arwen blanched, having no such thoughts.

Gemlytha only snorted.

The outline on the floor brightened. What did *that* mean? That the demon was closer to arrival? Maybe it was finishing dinner and letting out the dogs before ambling over to Earth to utterly destroy dark-elf enemies.

"Can one of you magical types blow this fog into a corner or something?" Amber coughed and wiped her eyes again.

Arwen wiped her own. Her barrier was doing nothing to protect them from the bad air.

Gemlytha considered that, then used her power to conjure a wind. It swirled through the chamber, stirring up the fog and making Arwen's throat hurt worse, but it eventually blew the thicker air toward one corner. The mist around them lessened. The rawness in Arwen's throat didn't subside, but the air around her *did* seem less tainted.

A decent idea. Gemlytha nodded to Amber. *But I must continue to concentrate to keep my wind pushing in that direction.*

Meaning that if something distracted her, it would inundate them again.

"You'd think a good laboratory would have ventilation of its own. If they're working with hazardous materials down here, there could be a spill that would threaten their own people." Amber eyed the broken beaker.

Dark elves do not care about the safety of the minions who work for them. Gemlytha eyed the outline on the floor, then stalked around the chamber, considering everything while avoiding the fog her wind continued to push to one corner.

Arwen also looked around, groping for inspiration. She beckoned Amber to step in the spot where they'd first arrived, vainly hoping that the spider outline would pop up, offering to whisk them back where they'd come from. But it looked to be a one-way transporter. The dark elves wouldn't have wanted their surrogates to escape, not for a decade or two, not until they'd made all the babies they could. Maybe not even then.

I wish I could telepathically contact Azerdash. He likes puzzles and building little contraptions. I always thought it a silly use of his time, but perhaps he would make a gnomish fan or filtration device. Gemlytha waved toward the fog, then looked toward Arwen. *Is he on this world?*

I don't think so. Arwen shifted uneasily at the reminder that Gemlytha knew Azerdash as well as she did. Probably much *better* than she did. They'd served together for decades, hadn't they? *I'm not even positive* we're *on Earth,* Arwen added, the thought occurring to her for the first time.

What if the spider had transported them to an entirely different world?

Amber looked at her phone, as if that would give them the answer, but they'd lost reception before they'd left the warehouse.

I believe we are on your lowly wild world, Gemlytha said. *The amount of natural magic in the ground—the amount I can draw upon to enhance my power—is poor. I've heard your world is like that. There is a reason neither dragons nor dwarves nor elves desired to colonize it. I am surprised the dark elves came here.* Gemlytha glanced at the glowing outline. *Perhaps that is why the summoning of their demon is taking so long. Dark elves originated on Veleshna Var.*

"We're real choked up about the delay." Amber eyed the outline, then left the protection of Arwen's barrier.

Arwen almost grabbed her wrist again to keep her close, but maybe she could figure something out. Besides, Arwen didn't know how their situation could get much worse, not until that demon showed up.

The dark elves, from what I've been told, Arwen said, *were driven off Veleshna Var and other worlds where they had outposts.*

Yes, even in my time, that was happening. They have never been loved by the other intelligent species. Gemlytha prowled from door to door, testing them with other types of magic as she kept the wind blowing the fog into the corner. *Were you born among them?* She looked at Arwen. *How did you come to be?*

Memories of Arwen's childhood came to mind, of the tattoo she'd been given, the rituals she'd been forced to participate in, the education she'd had to endure. Finally, she remembered the day her father had helped her escape, the great fire he'd set to distract the dark elves as he ran down the mountainside with Arwen in his arms. The years after that were filled with more pleasant memories of her father educating her and teaching her to track and hunt in between their farm work. Fondly, she recalled teaching herself how to bake from cookbooks a neighbor had brought over after learning that Arwen had never had a cookie or a cake.

She didn't know if the thoughts had come unbidden, or if Gemlytha had stirred them up to read her mind.

I see, Gemlytha said. *Are you certain Azerdash has feelings for you? I do not mean to be insulting, but you are... a simple creature. And a weak mongrel since your human blood conveys no power.*

What kinds of things did she say when she *wanted* to be insulting?

Someone once suggested my human blood gifted me the ability to bake. Arwen remembered Azerdash standing in the kitchen next to her, trying her strawberry shortcake and saying nothing about it but resting his hand on hers and gazing into her eyes with appreciation.

Gemlytha's lip twitched again in a not-quite-disdainful curl but close. *If that is the kind of female he wishes, he could have had his pick from many who offered such services over the years.*

Arwen didn't know how to respond to that.

"I'm sure their food wasn't as *amazing* as Arwen's." Amber had found a screwdriver and was poking gingerly into an open panel. It wasn't in one of the pods—maybe she'd decided not to try to free the girls while the air was tainted—but in a wall.

"Thank you," Arwen murmured, surprised by her support, since Amber usually called her a weirdo, but glad for it.

"*And* he made her a fancy elven hot springs," Amber added. "Zavryd says that means he cares."

Elven... hot springs? A yavasheva? Gemlytha asked.

"On the back of my property, yes," Arwen said. "I helped him in a battle, and he made it for me."

"They're definitely hooked up." Amber poked something, and the pods dimmed and brightened a couple of times.

Hooked up? Gemlytha raised her eyebrows. Because she didn't know what the term meant? Or because she didn't believe it? *Your memories suggest the* hooking *has always been interrupted.*

Arwen grimaced. Gemlytha had grasped exactly what the term meant. And far more about it than Arwen would have wished.

There are some races who believe that if you have not consummated a physical relationship, Gemlytha added, *then your claim on each other is incomplete.*

Arwen hesitated. She and Azerdash *hadn't* promised to be together forever—or even long-term—yet. He'd only just said he loved her and that had been before he'd heard Gemlytha might be —*was*—alive.

Sex isn't required for people to be devoted to each other, Arwen said. *Dragons claim each other before having physical relationships.*

She wasn't a hundred percent positive on that. Val had told her the story of how Zavryd had claimed her to protect her from other dragons—much as Azerdash had offered to pretend to claim Arwen to keep Yendral from making advances.

Dragons don't care a whit about physical relationships. They engage in coitus only to fertilize eggs. Unless you count the mild craving for physical touch that they feel during molting season, it's only if they shape-shift into other forms that they take on the characteristics—and often the desire to rut—of that species. Abandoning the door, Gemlytha strode toward Arwen with her eyes hard, some of that fierceness back on her face.

Grip tightening on her bow, Arwen stood her ground and trickled more magic into her barrier, though the more powerful woman could rip it to shreds if she wanted. If Gemlytha started something, Arwen would point out that she and Amber had *freed* her. But would that sway her? Or had she now decided to get rid of the competition?

Gemlytha stopped at the edge of Arwen's barrier, her red eyes intent. *Since I've been given a second chance at life, I intend to take a second chance with Azerdash. I will fight for him. Especially now, he needs a warrior to stand at his side. Not a baker.*

Arwen's heart pounded more than when she'd been in battle. Did *fight for him* mean Gemlytha wanted to fight *Arwen* for him?

Arwen made herself gaze steadily back into Gemlytha's eyes. *I am both.*

You are—

"What's happening?" Amber blurted.

At first, Arwen thought she was asking about her and Gemlytha, but Amber pointed at the ground with wide eyes. What had been a purple outline had filled in, and black mist flowed out of it, denser than the fog still being blown to the far side of the chamber.

An intensely powerful aura formed above the mark on the ground, growing stronger with each passing second. Already, it felt the equal of a dragon.

Gemlytha turned to face it while increasing her wind. Trying to push away this fog as she was doing the other?

It didn't work. The fog thickened, coalescing into a dark shape that towered over them, like a mountain with a head and arms. Growing to the ceiling, it reached out with those arms, claws forming. There was nothing like legs, but it floated above the ground and was doubtless capable of moving. Black eyes outlined in red burned from its head.

The demon has arrived, Gemlytha said.

26

Though she had no weapon, Gemlytha strode forward to face the demon.

Arwen readied her bow, intending to prove that she was indeed a warrior, though she feared her arrows wouldn't harm the demon. She hadn't even harmed the *door.*

"Stay back, Amber," Arwen whispered as the demon solidified and came fully into their world.

"You think?" Amber asked in a squeaky voice.

All black except for an outline of glowing red—almost like flames—the demon had to be fifteen feet tall and wide. A total of six thick arms ended in amorphous paws with clearly delineated claws longer than scissor blades. Its aura—its raw *power*—felt even greater than that of a dragon. It inspired such fear in Arwen that she had to will strength into her legs to keep her knees from buckling under the urge to fall to the ground and beg for her life. Or to promise to serve it. That was what demons wanted, wasn't it?

Fearless, and certainly not falling to the ground, Gemlytha spread her arms and spoke in the Dark Elven tongue. "Great Yeshelee vun, I have foolishly presumed to call you forth to this lowly world. I did not expect you to come, but I am greatly honored by your willingness to appear. I seek your assistance with a task. Is there a reward you would accept in exchange for helping me?"

Her words sounded so sincere that Arwen almost believed Gemlytha had indeed been the one to summon the demon—maybe to crush the life out of Arwen so she would never bake for Azerdash again. But that was a silly thought. Gemlytha could kill Arwen on her own if she wanted. Summoning demons was far too dangerous to risk unless one truly required their great power.

No, Gemlytha was lying. Hoping to trick the demon.

Certain something that powerful could read minds, Arwen attempted to keep hers blank so it wouldn't see her thoughts. She lowered her bow though she kept her arrow nocked. Chances were this wouldn't work, but she didn't want to be the one to ruin the ploy.

Sacrifices, the demon whispered without lips, without a mouth. The word managed to sound raspy and ominous even though it sounded only in their minds. *Many sacrifices for this inconvenience, my servant.*

The red-lined eyes looked toward the pods. Amber crouched behind one, the side of her blonde head barely visible.

These are for the spawn of my followers. The demon's eyes swung toward Arwen. *A mongrel enemy may be sacrificed. She has some power and the blood of a dark elf, but she is not one of them.*

Finally, someone realized that.

Gemlytha looked over at Arwen. Hopefully, not in agreement that she was a worthy sacrifice.

You will open these doors, Gemlytha told the demon, *and I will arrange numerous sacrifices.*

The doors close when threats arrive to the future mothers of the spawn. The demon shifted back toward Gemlytha, its body growing even larger and its power swelling as it considered her.

You are also not one of my followers. You seek to fool one of my power and wisdom? I will slay you for your impudence.

Gemlytha reinforced her barrier an instant before the demon lashed out, magic pummeling her like a hurricane gale while all six of its clawed limbs raked toward her. She raised her arms, as if they might protect her.

Doubting even a half-dragon was strong enough to defend against the demon's might, Arwen fired an arrow toward its amorphous head. The eyes weren't looking toward her, but maybe it had a brain in there, something vulnerable.

Surprisingly, the arrow sank in, but it didn't appear to affect the demon in any way. Claws raked and magic hammered Gemlytha's barrier, making it waver under the assault. Gemlytha stepped back but only to brace herself, clenching her jaw and thrusting more power into her defenses.

Black mist formed, not around the demon but around Gemlytha, as she called upon her magic, that which was inside of her and what she could siphon from the ground below. It was pure dark-elven magic, Arwen noted as she nocked another arrow. Gemlytha didn't try to alter it into dragon magic or anything else.

Did the insidious voices of demons not call to her when she used that power? Did they not try to tempt her to serve them? Every time Arwen used her magic without altering it, they were there, whispering to her, imploring her to embrace her heritage. To gain more power by swearing allegiance to them.

Hoping to find a more vulnerable target, Arwen fired again. Blue light streaked through the misty chamber as her arrow sped through the haze and sank into the broad black torso. Again, it did nothing to affect the otherworldly being. How could Arwen hurt a demon?

While maintaining her barrier, Gemlytha launched a fireball at their towering foe. Flames engulfed it, swallowing the demon from view.

A round of coughs assaulted Arwen's raw throat, making it hard for her to determine if the fire magic was any more effective than her arrows. With Gemlytha's focus on the demon, the wind had abated, and the noxious fog had returned to the chamber.

The demon emitted an indignant keen that chilled Arwen to her core. Did that mean it was hurt? That Gemlytha's magic *was* affecting it?

Its powerful aura didn't change to indicate it had grown weaker, and its claws swept out from behind the fire engulfing it. One hit with enough strength to shred Gemlytha's barrier. Arwen fired at the stout arm, hoping to distract the demon from its attack if nothing else. Again, her arrow landed but did no good. The claws slashed at Gemlytha.

She tried to spring back, but her legs might have been weakened from calling upon so much power. Instead of leaping away, she stumbled, and those claws sliced into her, drawing blood as they knocked her into a counter.

"No!" Arwen lowered her bow and yanked out the multitool, opening one of the blades.

She raced toward the demon, ordering the tool to launch its beam. Amber ran from hiding and toward their enemy from behind. She swung her sword at its backside.

Afraid the demon would slay Amber with a thought, Arwen pointed the beam at its face to keep its attention in her direction, even if that meant it would continue after Gemlytha. And it did. The beam did no more than the arrows. Arwen snarled in frustration. What could she do to hurt the thing?

Gemlytha pushed away from the counter, managing to get a barrier back up. The demon lifted its arms to strike again. She lifted her own arms, fingers pointing at it, and fire streaked from them.

The gouts of flames flared when they hit the demon, again engulfing it. It paused in its attack.

Sweat dripped down the sides of Gemlytha's face. The keen came from the demon again, but it was far from defeated. It levitated itself upward, head half-disappearing into the ceiling, then pitched down, slamming its body into the ground as it unleashed magic that made the chamber quake.

Gemlytha and Arwen wobbled but kept their footing. Amber, who'd hacked at the demon with her sword but been unable to hurt it, lost her balance and rolled away.

Arwen lowered the multitool. Gemlytha was the only one who'd harmed the demon, but her power was waning, exhaustion setting in. If she was lost, they would all be lost.

Arwen willed some of her own power into her new ally, hoping it would help.

Ignoring Arwen, the demon swept toward Gemlytha with its claws again, raking into her barrier. But Gemlytha immediately put Arwen's extra energy to work. She reinforced her barrier and also cast more flames at their assailant. Again, the demon disappeared behind the curtain of fire surrounding it.

It keened and then spoke. *My followers call upon me.*

The chamber quaked again, and stone snapped above their heads.

Reflexively, Arwen, who'd been in far too many rockfalls of late, lifted her arms and reinforced her own barrier.

The demon backed away from them. *Enemies of the dark elves seek to end them, but I will not fail my followers. I will lend them my power, and they will prevail.*

Abruptly, the demon dissolved into inky blackness and flowed upward. A crack had opened in the ceiling, and its ethereal form wafted into it. The demon disappeared but not from Arwen's senses. It wasn't leaving to go back to its own dimension but wafting off to help with whatever the dark elves were doing.

"Nothing good, I'm sure." Arwen wiped her brow.

Gemlytha dropped to one knee, pressing her knuckles into the ground for support. Arwen coughed again, wishing the *fog* would float upward as well.

With a flick of her fingers, Gemlytha created wind again. It rounded up the fog and sent it whispering into the crack in the ceiling.

A honk came from somewhere above, startling in its mundanity. After the terrifying encounter, traffic noise was the last thing Arwen had expected.

Amber, sword in hand, walked to stand under the crack. "Yup, we're still on Earth."

"Can you see anything?" Arwen rasped.

The air was clearing, fortunately, but her throat and lungs felt like they'd been scored. Hopefully not permanently damaged.

"No. It's jagged, so I can only see some dirt and darkness." Amber waved at the crack. "But it sounds like we're under the city. Somewhere."

"Yeah." Arwen wished they *weren't* on Earth, because that demon hadn't left. Though she didn't know what else the dark elves were up to tonight, something told her that her friends were in danger.

"Uhm, half-dragon lady, can you widen that?" Amber pointed upward. "Maybe we can get out that way."

Still on the ground recovering, Gemlytha glared at her, as if Amber had asked her to move the world. As exhausted as she was, it might feel like it. More than that, she dripped blood onto the floor, the gouges from the demon doubtless painful.

Though Gemlytha might reject the offer, Arwen stepped toward her and lowered her hand. Gemlytha had let her barrier drop when the demon left, so Arwen was able to get close.

Gemlytha stared at the hand before looking up at her, meeting her eyes. After a long moment, during which who knew what thoughts went through her mind, Gemlytha accepted the offer, her hand damp with sweat and blood.

Arwen pulled her to her feet.

Thanks for lending me some of your power, Gemlytha said. *It wasn't as insignificant as I expected.*

"I'll take that as a compliment," Arwen said dryly.

Gemlytha nodded. *Yes. Do.*

Arwen snorted and released her hand, reminded of Azerdash. None of the half-dragons had a lot of experience with Earth phrases or Earth humor.

Ignoring her wounds, Gemlytha pushed her hands through her sweaty white locks. She either didn't know that blood smeared them—and now her hair—or didn't care. After taking a deep breath, she joined Amber under the crack.

A faint rumble made its way down. A truck passing?

I can sense... Gemlytha closed her eyes. *The demon went north. It remains in this world.*

North? If the transportation magic hadn't taken them far, and they were still near the ship canal, that could mean Val's and Matti's houses.

"Is it wide enough for us to escape that way?" Arwen asked, assuming Gemlytha could levitate them.

As Amber had pointed out, the crack twisted, and it was dark up there. They couldn't see how far down they were or how wide the gap was. Unlike the demon, *they* couldn't turn into mist to get out.

It will be. Gemlytha lifted her hands, using her power to widen the gap.

"Don't make it too much bigger," Arwen said. "We could be right under a street."

When Gemlytha looked blankly at her, Arwen imagined cars falling into a hole and landing on their heads.

Gemlytha grunted in what might have been acknowledgment and took care with her magical excavation.

"Should we let the girls go before we leave?" Amber looked toward Camille.

Arwen still felt bad that they'd put her in that pod but reminded herself it had been to protect her from the fog.

The poisonous air continues to flow into the chamber, Gemlytha said. *Once we leave, my magic will not be able to continue to whisk it out.*

"We'll come back once we make sure our friends are okay and that the demon isn't wreaking havoc on the city," Arwen said.

Once we deal with your kin, Gemlytha added, giving her a pointed look.

From her mind reading, she'd figured out how Arwen was linked in with the chaos.

"Yeah," was all Arwen said aloud. Silently, with the words only for Gemlytha, she added, *Do you have any challenges with using your power? Your dark-elven power?*

Arwen sensed that Gemlytha was using dragon magic now and had when she'd been attempting to incinerate the doors, but she'd called upon dark-elven magic to battle the demon. Since she had two magical heritages to draw upon, maybe it didn't matter that much.

Challenges? Gemlytha, focused on widening the gap, only glanced at her. She was using far more care than when she'd thrown her power against the doors. Maybe she sensed that there *was* a street up there and, after Amber's warning, worried about cars falling onto their heads.

Like... when I don't try to twist my power to use it as a surface elf would—to make things grow or do things in nature—I get a voice speaking from the back of my mind. It seems like the voice of a demon, trying to lure me to embrace my heritage and use my magic to serve its wishes. It's... seductive sometimes. I don't know if the voice is something my subconscious conjures based on the memories of my childhood, or if a demon actually wants me. I guess that's silly, huh?

Gemlytha glanced at her again, her face hard to read.

Arwen felt foolish for asking the question. Of course, demons weren't watching her every move and speaking to her every time she conjured a wisp of power. How self-centered of her to believe that. Why she had brought it up to Gemlytha, a woman who'd admitted she would fight her for Azerdash, she didn't know. Fate had set them up to be rivals, not sisters who shared their secrets.

That thought made Arwen feel wistful. Having a sister, someone who had blood like hers and understood her challenges, would have been nice. It was something she'd wished for more than once as a child.

It's not silly. They also talk to me.

Arwen blinked. *They do?*

The dragon-half has opinions too. Gemlytha smirked.

Arwen couldn't tell if she was joking or not. Azerdash had mentioned that his dragon blood gave him urges—tendencies toward wanting to solve problems through incineration—but he'd never spoken of voices.

It could come from my subconscious. Gemlytha shrugged. *I think it's from the blood though. Being magical means putting up with quirks that mundanes don't have to endure. I ignore the voices and tell them to shut up. You should do the same.*

A honk came from above, and she turned her attention back to the hole.

Amber pulled her phone out and waved it toward the gap. Hoping to catch some reception?

Nothing bad has come from you using your dark-elven power? Arwen asked, struggling to let things go. She finally had a resource to draw upon, someone who was also half-dark elven. While she had the opportunity, didn't it make sense to ask Gemlytha questions?

No. I understand what you mean about the seduction, but we have to be stronger than it. Willpower. It doesn't make sense to not use one's power just because it comes with some temptations. Trust me. Gemlytha wiggled two fingers.

Arwen thought it might be the equivalent of a thumbs-up gesture until a whisper of power swept around her and lifted her from her feet. A surprised squawk came from Amber as she also rose into the air.

Up we go. Gemlytha levitated herself as well, leading the way into the hole. *After dealing with the dark elves, we can return for the women.*

Arwen nodded and tried not to feel she was abandoning the captives, but once her mother and brother had been stopped, it would be easier to figure out how to avoid the chamber's booby traps—or whisk the women out before the poisonous air could bother them.

The rumble of traffic grew audible as they floated up farther than Arwen expected. The crack was as crooked as a mountain stream, and Gemlytha had to shift their bodies around boulders jutting out.

When they neared the surface, stars in the sky promised it was still nighttime. Arwen glimpsed Amber's phone and was surprised to find it wasn't yet 11 p.m. They rose through a fissure in an alley, not a main street, but traffic did rumble past nearby.

Exclamations, and whispers of, "Look!" came from a corner roped off with chairs and tables for outdoor dining. Despite the late hour, it was a weekend, and people were still out, sipping wine and cocktails while they gaped at the appearance of three people in the shadows.

The earthquake and opening of a fissure in the alley appeared to have *drawn* spectators rather than sending them scurrying for home. A number of the observers stood without drinks in their hands.

Having no idea what the proper social protocol was, Arwen waved at them before peering at the street signs on the corner.

"I think we're in Fremont," she mused, surprised.

Maybe it made sense that the transportation magic wouldn't have taken them far—not to an entirely different world, as she'd wondered earlier. But what had prompted the dark elves to create their laboratory under a busy part of town? Had something already been hollowed out down there? Given how close they were to sea level, Arwen was surprised that area hadn't filled with water, but magic could fix problems like that more easily than a sump pump.

"Look at that woman," one of the drinkers said. "She's completely white. Like albino."

"Maybe she's a Goth," another said.

"Nobody is into Goth anymore. I don't think that's makeup either."

I sense Azerdash. Ignoring the murmurs and points from the onlookers, Gemlytha gazed toward the dark sky. For the first time, a smile stretched across her face. *He's sensed us too, and he's flying this way. Everything down there must have been insulated, because I couldn't detect anything outside until the crack opened up.*

At first, Arwen shared Gemlytha's smile, delighted that Azerdash was on Earth and on his way to them. Hopefully, no enemies were on his tail so he could help with the dark elves.

But Arwen's smile faltered when she noticed Gemlytha's eyes gleaming with emotion as she kept looking to the sky, waiting for him to appear. She was about to come face to face with the man she'd loved for years—or maybe decades—the man who'd admitted to having feelings for Gemlytha and who regretted that he'd never acted on those feelings.

With Arwen and Gemlytha standing side by side, would Azerdash choose Arwen? Or Gemlytha?

27

AMBER PACED IN THE ALLEY WITH HER PHONE TO HER EAR. ARWEN wiped her moist palms, her nerves making her bounce up and down as she waited for Azerdash to appear. The spectators in the corner dining area sipped their drinks, most going back to their conversations, though some kept eyeing Arwen's little group. A hint of music wafted out from the restaurant, increasing in volume anytime someone opened the door.

"Why isn't she answering?" Amber muttered.

Val?

Arwen checked her own phone. She had to tap it several times before it sluggishly came on, and a message Val had sent earlier came up.

I need to go. Emergency at the Coffee Dragon. Find Amber. Please!

Arwen started to tap a reply, but a black winged form glided into view, coming over the surrounding buildings. Azerdash.

He looked down at them, his eyes glowing briefly violet, before tucking his wings and descending toward their alley.

Arwen's phone warmed, then flashed twice and turned off. She would have to trust Amber was trying to reach her mom and would find out if Val needed help.

Azerdash shifted into his elven form and landed in a crouch in front of Arwen and Gemlytha.

He nodded at Arwen, looking her up and down—to check for injuries?—and touching her arm, but then he turned to Gemlytha and whispered something in Elven. Still smiling—damn, she was beautiful when she smiled, white skin and all—she wrapped her arms around him for a fierce hug.

It's wonderful to see you, Azerdash said telepathically, leaning back and clasping her hands. Was he using telepathy to include Arwen?

At the moment, he wasn't facing her, and Arwen's gut twisted as she watched them together. Gemlytha didn't look like she wanted to break the hug. She looked like she wanted to do a lot more than *hug* him.

Arwen had the urge to spring between them and push her away. She stomped that down, telling herself not to be juvenile. Azerdash was understandably delighted to see his old comrade again, his comrade he'd believed dead. And Gemlytha was... Well, she'd leaned back to gaze at him with such love and adoration that Arwen didn't know how Azerdash could have ever been oblivious to her feelings about him. Maybe she'd hidden them better earlier on.

If I'd known there was a chance you could be revived, Azerdash continued, *we never would have left you. I saw in the half-dwarf's memories that you'd fallen, that the elf Sarrlevi had seen you die, and I thought that was the end of it. That we'd lost you.*

I thought I was dead too. Gemlytha twitched her shoulder. *Only powerful dragon-resuscitation magic brought me back, but as soon as they healed me, they forced me into a stasis chamber. Those loathsome things.*

Yes. Agreed.

I knew nothing except for unpleasant nightmares, as we've discussed before happens in them...

Azerdash nodded. Arwen tried not to think anything of their shared experience—of all their shared experiences over the decades they'd served together. She also tried not to feel threatened, but it was so hard. She'd promised Gemlytha that she would also fight for Azerdash, but this wasn't the time. She couldn't be jealous and interfere with their reunion.

But when *would* the appropriate time be? How would she know when to act?

...and eventually I woke here. Gemlytha pointed around at the buildings and then toward the crevice. *Actually, in a cave down there. Some of the Earth females are prisoners to be used in a dark-elven plot, I gather.*

They also planned to use you *in a dark-elven plot,* Arwen added, though she felt she was interfering with a private conversation. Still, Azerdash had made a point to speak in a way that Arwen could understand, so she didn't think he would mind.

So I gathered, Gemlytha said.

We will free them. Azerdash nodded to her and also to Arwen, though he didn't take his gaze from Gemlytha. *And then I hope to have your assistance on Veleshna Var. I've been uniting the lesser species, and things are coming to a head there. We spoke to Princess Freysha, King Eireth's daughter, on the goblin home world, and when she returned, the dragons guarding the city there captured her and mind-scoured her before she could reach her family.*

Arwen raised her eyebrows. That must have happened while they'd been trapped below.

The elves were livid, Azerdash continued. *I believe that act, more than the message I sent through Freysha, has convinced them to join our side. The dragons may realize that, because they've been bringing more of their kind to Veleshna Var. Yendral is assembling our troops near the elven capital, and I've sent Sleveryn on a special mission, but it may not work, or it may be too late. The battle is going to erupt soon.*

I'm ready to fight at your side, Gemlytha said.

Thank you. We will need every advantage we can get. I only broke away because I needed to check on you and Arwen. Azerdash stepped back and turned toward Arwen.

She met his gaze with a smile, hoping he was done holding hands with Gemlytha and planned to make it clear that he loved Arwen. Her mind knew this wasn't the time to hope for or worry about that, but her heart... her heart ached so much a piano might have lain on her chest.

Gemlytha stepped forward, tightening her grasp on Azerdash and keeping him from moving away. She lifted a hand to his chest and curled her fingers into his tunic. *Arwen is a baker, Azerdash. You need a warrior.*

He tilted his head in puzzlement.

Arwen wasn't puzzled. She realized with dread, before Gemlytha made another move, that she'd already started her fight for him.

Gemlytha took another step and kissed Azerdash square on the mouth, her hand shifting from his chest to wrap around his shoulders. She seemed to have surprised him, because he stood there with his eyes open for a moment, not reacting at all.

Arwen wanted to blurt for him to push her away—*Arwen* wanted to push her away—but his shoulders slumped. In relaxation? Defeat? Arwen didn't know, but he didn't break the kiss.

Swallowing, she looked away, hurt, confused, and not sure what to do. Amber was still trying to call her mother and wasn't paying attention. A few of the onlookers murmured, one asking where *the dude* had come from. None of them had magical blood, so they hadn't seen Azerdash arrive in his dragon form.

Azerdash finally leaned back, breaking the kiss. Maybe Arwen should have stepped farther away and given them privacy, but she couldn't help but watch out of the corner of her eye.

Azerdash rested a hand on Gemlytha's shoulder and gazed at her as he started to say something in Elven.

But Amber rushed over, waving her phone, and interrupting him. "Val's in trouble. They *all* are. At the coffee shop. There's—"

The ground shook, and Arwen spread her arms for balance. These *couldn't* be natural earthquakes.

The diners scattered, some running for cars and others diving under tables or into doorways. Tires screeched in the street.

Unlike during the other quakes, the ground continued to shake, with long seconds passing. Glass shattered. Something large fell in the nearby street, crunching onto the frame of a car. A lamppost? A traffic light?

"It's the Big One!" someone cried as Arwen peered around the ally for something sturdy to take cover behind.

Azerdash raised a barrier, and she remembered that she could too. Arwen gripped Amber, intending to protect her, but Azerdash stepped close to her and extended his barrier around them. He included Gemlytha, though she arched an eyebrow at him, her expression suggesting she didn't *need* his protection.

Though Arwen could make her own barrier, she wouldn't object to his assistance.

"This isn't the first earthquake tonight." She didn't know how long Azerdash had been on Earth. Probably not long considering dragons hadn't hunted him down yet. "And there was one the other day too. Could magic be causing these?"

"I cannot determine the source to check," Azerdash said. "It is possible the dark elves or another party discovered an existing fault line and found a way to activate it."

"Oh, it's absolutely the dark elves," Amber said. "They're the ones attacking the coffee shop. And it sounds like that *demon* might be there now too. Val hung up before she explained it all. Or something *caused* her to hang up." Though Amber usually only had snarky comments when she spoke about her mother, genuine anguish and concern came through in her voice.

"Will you take us there?" Arwen asked Azerdash.

She believed she could find the way and run from their current location, but flying by dragon back would be faster—and less dangerous when the ground was shaking. How long would this quake last?

The lights went out in the surrounding buildings and on the street. The music stopped playing.

"Yes." Azerdash levitated to a flat rooftop and shifted into his dragon form.

I do not know this area, Gemlytha spoke telepathically, *but if you lead, I will follow.* So softly that Arwen almost questioned hearing it, Gemlytha added, *Always.*

Thank you, Azerdash said. *We do not need to fly far.*

Gemlytha also levitated to a rooftop to shift forms. She became a beautiful white-scaled dragon, her eyes the same crimson as when she was in her dark-elven form.

"You're welcome," Amber whispered to Arwen as the ground finally stopped quaking. Even spoken softly, her words sounded loud in the abrupt silence.

"What?" Arwen whispered back.

"It wasn't intentional, since Val really is in trouble, but you're welcome for breaking *them* up. Didn't you say you were going to fight for him?"

Levitation magic wrapped around them, lifting them into the air.

"Yes," Arwen said, "but that didn't seem like the time. They just met after— He thought she was dead."

"Well, you'd better figure out *the time* before they get married and have kids."

Arwen grimaced but didn't say anything else. Azerdash angled her and Amber onto his back, then sprang into the air, with Gemlytha following behind.

"Shit," Amber said, "the power is out in the whole city."

As they rose above the buildings, they could see nothing but darkness, not a single traffic light on or a single lamp glowing in a window. It was eerie, but worse was when Azerdash headed north. Ahead of them, a bright spot stood out in the darkness, flames leaping high above a building. *Red* flames. It looked like a chasm to Hell had opened, and a block in Fremont was in the middle of it.

Arwen's heart sank. With certainty, she knew that was the Coffee Dragon.

28

Bow in hand, Arwen waited for an enemy to shoot. As the half-dragons flew closer to the coffee shop, she sensed magical beings ahead, full-blooded dark elves and...

"You were right," Arwen told Amber. "That's where the demon went."

"No kidding. The coffee shop didn't spontaneously light *itself* on fire," Amber said.

"We'll have more help battling it this time." Arwen rested a hand on Azerdash's scaled back, bolstered by his presence, though she couldn't help but wonder if it would be enough. Gemlytha hadn't been strong enough to defeat the demon, and there would be dark elves, as well, this time.

"Can you sense Val?" Amber peered past her shoulder toward the flames. "Or are we too late?"

I sense her. Azerdash was the one to answer. *Also the elf assassin, Sarrlevi, and many goblins and half-bloods, though they seem to be scattering.*

"You'd think they would fight for their favorite hangout," Amber said.

As they sailed closer to the flames burning all around the building like a giant bonfire, Arwen worried it was too late to save the coffee shop. She picked out Val's aura, not as powerful as that of the full-blooded dark elves, and Sindari was with her. Though flames blocked the view, Arwen sensed them on the rooftop.

The demon, back in its corporeal form, filled the alley between the coffee shop and the ice-cream parlor. It faced Val and Sindari. Had the dark elves called it specifically to kill her?

"Val needs help," Arwen said, though it was a statement of the obvious.

She picked out Sarrlevi's aura, but he was inside on the bottom floor, hopefully not with burning beams falling on him. Some of the dark elves were inside too. Battling him? Trying to reach the stairs to climb up to attack Val? She was the only reason Arwen could think of that the dark elves would have targeted the coffee shop. Her mother had wanted revenge on Val for a long time.

Have you fought demons before? Arwen asked Azerdash as he flew toward the rooftop.

I have not. Have you?

Other than this one twenty minutes ago, just lesser demons. Arwen remembered battling the tentacled beast that Harlik-van had summoned in the waterfall cave. But she'd mostly been sneaking up on her brother while Val handled that one.

I believe this is not a lesser *demon,* Azerdash said.

It's not. Gemlytha had difficulty with it.

She is admitting that to me.

Arwen tried not to bristle at the knowledge that they were having a private conversation of their own. Azerdash could speak to whomever he wished, and, of course, he was trying to figure out what had happened to Gemlytha and what she knew about the dark elves' plot here.

I apologize, Azerdash said quietly into her mind, almost a whisper.

For talking to her? Assuming he'd read her thought—her childish thought—Arwen winced.

For the kiss. It was not my intention... I do not wish to hurt you in any way.

If they hadn't been soaring into battle, Arwen might have come up with a more thoughtful response, but all that came to mind was, *We can figure it all out later.*

Yes.

She wished he would have said that there was nothing to figure out, that he loved *her*. But as he banked to carry them around the flaming block and determine how best to help with the battle, she pushed all such thoughts from her mind. Right now, her friends were in danger and were her priority. And her kin...

She winced, noticing her brother's aura on the first floor of the Coffee Dragon. And her mother... Yes, she was there too. Not in the shop but in a long gap—no, a *chasm*—that had opened in the street out front. The red flames were leaping out of it, though they had spread to wrap around the shop itself.

Surprisingly, the building didn't appear to be burning yet. Arwen remembered that it had defenses of its own, but they had to be struggling to keep the otherworldly power from getting through.

Azerdash tucked his wings and dove toward the demon, its towering body allowing it to attack Val from the alley. It was even bigger than when Arwen and Gemlytha had faced it in the underground chamber.

One of its clawed arms swept toward Val, far too powerful to block. She raised her sword as she dodged and tried to slice a chunk out of it. Her blade glowed blue and flared even brighter when it made contact, but the demon only swiped at her again, not feeling any pain.

Arwen aimed an arrow but hesitated since her weapons hadn't done anything against the demon before. Instead of firing, she rested her hand on Azerdash's back and funneled her power into him, hoping to give him more that he could use to harm their enemy.

Wind whipped at her face and hair as they plummeted toward the demon. It might have been her imagination, since it was hard to see anything through the flames, but Arwen thought two crimson eyes looked at her from the chasm. Her mother's eyes.

You thought to thwart our plot, and you roused a demon, she spoke calmly into Arwen's mind.

What, was she trying to blame Arwen for this carnage? Doubtful. She probably reveled in this.

You're the one who arranged for the demon to pop up if someone walked into that lab.

Someone attempting to steal our wombs, her mother corrected.

Azerdash struck at the demon with magical energy while he also breathed fire. Gemlytha landed on a building across the street —and the chasm—from them, talons curling over the edge as she raised a barrier. Dark elves in the street, able to show their faces since the power outage had made the night so dark, hurled magic at Gemlytha while firing magical crossbow quarrels.

They're not your wombs, Arwen told her mother. *You kidnapped those women.*

They will be treated well as they birth offspring to ensure the continuation of our species.

In pods? And unconscious for the rest of their lives?

Your sanctimonious and disrespectful tone is not proper for addressing a superior being and certainly not your mother.

I'm so terribly sorry. Arwen felt Azerdash draw on some of her power as he swept around, barely avoiding swipes from three demon limbs. One set of claws grazed his barrier.

"What are you doing here, Amber?" Val yelled, the crackling red flames almost drowning her out. "I told you to stay away!"

"I came to help you!" Amber yelled back.

When Azerdash banked to come around again, Amber surprised Arwen by sliding off his back to land on the rooftop next to her mother. Horror, not gratitude, twisted Val's face.

The demon hurled power, not at Val and Amber but at Azerdash. His barrier remained up, but the blast rocked his flight, and Arwen almost lost her bow as she grabbed onto him with both hands.

You will be sorry, her mother spoke into her mind. *I have the* thyamiliscar *with me, and I will use it on you. Tonight. Once your recalcitrant human memories have been taken, I will teach you to be respectful, as a daughter should be.*

With anger, frustration, and the terror of the demon's attacks fueling her, Arwen drew an arrow, one of her *dark-elven* arrows. Letting her senses guide her, she fired it through the flames and into the chasm at her mother's position.

She doubted anything would come of the attack, especially when her mother had to be looking right at her and prepared, but it felt good to try to stop her. And to be blatantly disrespectful. Arwen curled her lip.

The arrow disappeared into the flames. Her mother laughed shortly into her mind, and Arwen didn't need to see her to know the projectile hadn't landed. She would have to go down there herself to have a shot at stopping her mother.

But what if she failed? Her mother would wave that device at her and erase her memories, all that made her who she was.

Arwen shook her head. She couldn't let the chance of that deter her.

Azerdash flew in low, diving closer to the demon this time. Instead of using magic and fire, he snapped at its hulking, red-lined black form with his jaws.

When he made contact, a jolt went through his body as if he'd bitten into a flow of electricity. The shock coursed through to Arwen and knocked her off his back.

Startled, all she could do was flail and try not to lose her bow as she tumbled away. She glimpsed Azerdash ripping a chunk out of the demon—*good*—but he tossed it aside and twisted in the air, his eyes tracking her.

Arwen! Azerdash cried.

Before she would have hit the ground, his power wrapped around her and levitated her carefully to the sidewalk. She appreciated that, but the distraction cost him. While he was focused on her, the demon smacked him with its clawed limbs and its dark, malevolent energy. He went flying, tumbling over Val and Amber on the rooftop of the shop and smashing into the building on the other side.

Azerdash! Arwen called telepathically. *Are you okay?*

Yes, he replied as the demon shifted its attention to Val and Amber, launching a swirling blast of energy at them. *That thing hits hard for a blob.*

A blob with six arms full of claws! Arwen couldn't see Val and Amber, but she sensed them being knocked back.

Sindari roared and ran across the rooftop to spring at the demon. A window shattered on the ground floor of the shop, and Sarrlevi somersaulted out, hurled by a magical attack. Despite the glass flying all around him, he managed to twist in the air and land on his feet with his twin longswords in his hands. He ran back inside through the front entrance—someone had ripped the door off its hinges.

I did notice those, yes. Azerdash recovered and leaped onto the rooftop to help Val and Amber.

Arwen thought about climbing the side of the building to join them, but she sensed movement behind her—movement and *power*. It was her mother's aura as well as those of several other dark elves.

They floated out of the chasm, passing through the red flames without flinching, and landed on the sidewalk not ten feet from Arwen. Shit.

Azerdash was battling the demon while dark elves threw attacks at Gemlytha. Arwen was on her own.

Grimly, she faced the dark elves. Her mother carried Imoshaun's invention—the memory-stealing device—and was ready to wipe away Arwen's entire past. Worse, four powerful dark elves strode beside her, bodyguards carrying magical swords.

"Look out!" Val cried to someone on the rooftop.

Arwen sensed their battle, the demon lunging toward her friends, but she dared not look away from her mother. Instead, she wrapped the most powerful barrier she could summon around herself and raised the multitool. Her arrows hadn't worked. Maybe this would.

She started by summoning light with a terse command of, "*Eravekt*," and shone it into her mother's face. The demonic red glow from the flames wasn't bothering her, but maybe this would hurt her sensitive dark-elven eyes.

Her mother snarled and jerked a hand up to block the light. *All* the dark elves did, and Arwen felt a second of triumph. Then her mother lashed out with a mental attack.

It went through the protective barrier to strike Arwen's brain and nervous system, and her entire body spasmed with the pain. Her fingers loosened before she could stop them, and the multitool clanked to the ground, the light shining off behind Arwen.

The dark elves lowered their arms and advanced.

Gritting her teeth against the agony coursing through her body, Arwen backed up and tried to grab the multitool without taking her eyes from them. Unfortunately, her mother and bodyguards stood right outside her barrier now. Even as she snatched up the tool, they used their power to tear at her defenses. With her mother's attack distracting her, Arwen couldn't remake the barrier.

A flick of power snaked through her waning defenses and

struck the tool, almost knocking it from her hand again. It *did* knock out the light.

Afraid it wasn't enough of a weapon anyway, Arwen switched to the beam.

A keen of pain came from the demon—the first she'd heard here. Azerdash was in the alley, grappling with it, but a powerful blast knocked him back again.

As he tumbled away, the demon levitated up to the rooftop. Gunfire sounded—Val shooting it. Arwen didn't have to see to know that her magical bullets wouldn't be enough.

Longing to survive and help them, Arwen managed to rekindle her barrier, to halt the advance of the dark elves.

We will prevail, her mother said, smiling tightly. *You will be ours, and the Ruin Bringer will be dead.*

She lifted a hand, the gnomish device cradled under her other arm, and tore the remade barrier asunder. Arwen aimed the multitool's beam at her, but it struck her chest and deflected into the building next door, blowing a hole in the brick wall.

An orange glow on the side of the device pulsed. A wide white beam shot out, hitting *Arwen* in the chest. It didn't hurt, but somehow it was more terrifying than if it had. It shifted to crawl up her chest to her face and her forehead. The beam stopped there, ominous warmth coming from its magical touch.

Arwen ducked away from it, but her mother's power swept in. The bodyguards took advantage of her downed barrier and also rushed in, physically grabbing her.

Speaking in Dark Elven, her mother ordered them to hold her still.

A roar came from the building above—Azerdash looking down at them with fury in his glowing violet eyes. He crouched to spring down to help, to abandon the demon battle, but a portal formed over the chasm and made him pause. It floated in the air thirty feet up. Only a flying being would form one at that elevation. Had the dragons figured out that Azerdash was here and decided to come for him again?

Arwen's mother stepped closer, lifting the device and pressing it to her forehead. The gnomish magic humming against Arwen's skin.

Terrified to lose her memories—to lose *everything*—she bucked. She still had the multitool and tried to turn it on her mother, but one of the bodyguards ripped it from her grip. They pinned Arwen so that she couldn't move, couldn't escape.

29

Azerdash! Arwen cried, unable to pull free from the dark elves—or the cursed device her mother held to her forehead.

Before he could answer, a dragon flew out of the portal hovering over the chasm. Zavryd.

Had he come to help? Or to arrest—or kill—Azerdash? Arwen worried it was the latter, that he was here to serve his queen.

Eyes flaring with violet light, Zavryd arrowed toward the rooftop, toward Azerdash's battle.

One moment, Azerdash replied to Arwen, but a whirlwind of power flowed from the demon, and she knew he wouldn't be able to help.

Gemlytha? Arwen tried.

Never would she have believed she would ask her rival for help, but the magic humming against Arwen's skin grew stronger, and her brain grew foggy, thoughts—*memories*—threatening to scatter. She didn't have much time.

Yes? A screech came from the rooftop across the street, promising Gemlytha was under attack too.

Can you use your magic to make a blinding light? Something that will hurt dark-elven eyes more than ours?

After a pause, Gemlytha said, *Yes. I should have thought of that.*

White light burst from Gemlytha's rooftop. The brilliance made Arwen squint her eyes shut, and it was harsh even through her lids. It affected the dark elves even more. They released her and reeled back, trying to protect their sensitive eyes. A clatter sounded—the memory device hitting the sidewalk.

Arwen stumbled back, wanting to put space between her and her mother—and that device. Her heel bumped something. Her bow. She didn't remember dropping it, but she whirled, snatching it up.

Dots floated through her vision as Gemlytha's light continued, brighter and more blinding than the sun. Arwen couldn't see her mother—couldn't see *anything*—but sensed her.

Arwen rushed forward, swinging her bow like a club. It connected with her mother's chest. She staggered back. Arwen swung again, hoping to knock her mother into the chasm. She had to be fast, though, before the dark elves recovered.

But it was too late. Magic swelled in front of her. Despite her curses at the light, her mother managed to get a barrier up. The bow bounced off.

Arwen groped in her quiver for one of the dark-elf arrows, hoping it could slice through. But the bodyguards were recovering, conjuring magic. Gemlytha's light disappeared, the street plunging into darkness again, save for the red flames that continued to leap from the chasm.

"Look out!" someone cried in Dark Elven.

Gemlytha was taking advantage of the reprieve she'd gotten from her own attackers. Still in her dragon form, she dropped down from the rooftop. Arwen thought she would dive into the chasm, but she spread her wings to halt above it—right behind Arwen's mother. Gemlytha's neck snapped forward, and, with a surge of power, her great fangs sliced through Arwen's mother's defenses.

The dark-elven bodyguards whirled toward the white dragon, casting magical attacks. That didn't keep Gemlytha from wrapping her jaws around Arwen's mother's waist and crushing down. Gemlytha lifted her head—and her captured prey.

Arwen's mother had to be in too much pain to concentrate on her magic, but her bodyguards unleashed everything they had at Gemlytha. She snarled as their combined power tore down her defenses, but she didn't let go. Gemlytha descended, dragging Arwen's mother into the chasm with her. More fire flared, not red but yellow-orange. Dragon fire.

Arwen fired at one of the bodyguards attacking Gemlytha. Focused on attacking, he wasn't funneling much power into his barrier, and her magical arrow pierced it, thudding between his shoulder blades. He pitched forward into the chasm.

Despite the threat Arwen represented, the others didn't turn toward her. They continued to throw attacks at Gemlytha, trying to free their leader.

Arwen reached for her quiver, but her fingers grasped at empty air. She'd run out of arrows.

Her multitool lay on the charred sidewalk. She snatched it up and called upon her innate power as she targeted her enemies with it.

Remembering Gemlytha's words about ignoring the demonic voices in her mind, Arwen didn't try to alter her magic from dark-elven to anything else. She simply gathered it at her core, poured it into the multitool, and unleashed it.

A beam shot out, thicker and brighter than she'd ever seen, with her power infusing it. Surprisingly, no voices spoke in the back of her mind, trying to persuade her to devote herself to the demons, to fully embrace her heritage.

She turned the beam on any dark elf who rose up to attack her or Gemlytha. It was powerful enough to slice through some of their barriers and strike vital targets. More than one enemy tumbled into the chasm.

As one female dark elf fell, she cried out to the demon on the rooftop for help.

It left its battle with Val, Zavryd, and Azerdash, smaller than it had been before, as if they'd torn away pieces of it, but it still radiated power as it floated down toward its caller.

Arwen took aim at another dark elf, but an explosion came from the chasm. Had that originated with her mother? The demon? Or Gemlytha?

She couldn't tell but a huge gout of fire roared upward as the earth shook again, the quaking so hard that it knocked Arwen to the sidewalk. Rock snapped, and cement crumbled. She tried to roll closer to the building, to what she hoped was safety, but the ground fell away under her, the chasm widening.

She flailed as she fell and managed to catch a ledge. Not willing to drop her weapons, to risk losing them, she dangled from one hand. With the flames leaping, she had no idea how deep the chasm was, but, for all she knew, it could be bottomless or drop away to another dimension.

Below her, Arwen sensed Gemlytha's aura diminishing. She peered down, afraid the dark elves or the demons had landed a fatal blow.

Gemlytha had shifted into her dark-elven form—or been knocked out of her dragon form?—and lay on a narrow ledge ten or fifteen feet beneath Arwen.

With flames still leaping, Arwen couldn't see the demon. She didn't sense her mother either. Had she been killed?

The piece of sidewalk she gripped cracked, threatening to give way.

Azerdash leaped off the building to fly above the chasm. He looked down and saw Arwen and Gemlytha.

Without hesitation, he wrapped his levitation power around Arwen, pulling her from the precipice and sweeping her onto his back.

"Thanks," she rasped, plastering her body to his scales. She added, "Gemlytha needs help too," though she knew Azerdash had seen that.

Yes. Azerdash dodged a gout of flame that belched up from the chasm, then banked to fly back over it and wrap his levitation magic around Gemlytha. *She was not close enough to you that I could pluck you both up at the same time.*

Gemlytha floated up to settle on his back behind Arwen. Her eyes were glazed, and blood smeared the side of her sweaty face, but she managed a nod to Arwen.

A roar came from the rooftop of the Coffee Dragon. Two dark-elven bodies flew into the chasm.

A second later, Zavryd sprang after them, descending into the flames. He landed on the demon, and great power flared. The red flames waned, and the demon's aura grew less significant.

Let him finish that thing, Azerdash said wearily.

He flapped his wings slowly and flew around the battle scene before angling toward the Coffee Dragon.

"I thought Zavryd came to kill you," Arwen admitted.

I think he was sent to get me, but when he saw his mate in danger, he forgot about me and let the battle lust take him.

"Good. Maybe you should leave before the battle is over." Arwen rested a hand on his scales. She didn't *want* him to go. She wanted him to change back into an elf so that she could hug him and kiss him—whether Gemlytha was standing there watching or not.

Yes, Azerdash agreed.

Instead, he landed on the roof. The street was ravaged, the chasm stretching two blocks in either direction from the Coffee Dragon. The fiery opening had swallowed not only the pavement and sidewalk but all the cars parked there. Farther down the street, a building tottered, on the verge of collapsing into the chasm.

Val and Sindari, both bloody and soot-covered, limped to the edge of the roof to join them. A crossbow quarrel stuck out of Val's shoulder. That had to hurt like hell.

All she did was gaze down at the carnage and say, "That's obnoxious."

"The dark elves or the demon?" Arwen asked.

"The chasm. It was already a pain in the ass to find parking in this neighborhood."

The flames burned lower, some going out, and the demon disappeared, save for black mist that wafted up. With the fire dying down, Arwen could see to the bottom of the chasm. It wasn't as bottomless as she'd feared when she'd been about to fall, but it *did* drop forty or fifty feet into the earth. Charred bodies were visible at the bottom. Arwen was fairly certain one belonged to her mother.

She is dead, Gemlytha told her. Reading her thoughts?

Gemlytha swung her leg over Azerdash's back and slid to the rooftop, though her legs almost gave out, and she had to use him for support. Arwen understood the feeling perfectly.

I made sure to take care of her, Gemlytha added, meeting her gaze.

Arwen didn't know how to respond. *Thank you for killing my mother* was a weird thing to say, even if Arwen doubted she could have done it herself. Gemlytha had done her a favor. Yet it was distressing that it had been the only option. Why couldn't her mother have left Arwen and her friends alone?

Her feelings a tangle, all Arwen managed was a nod for Gemlytha. It seemed to be enough. Gemlytha nodded back, then watched warily as Zavryd flew out of the chasm.

Arwen eased off Azerdash's back in case he needed to take off in a hurry. As she landed, she glimpsed movement in the doorway of the Coffee Dragon. Only then did she remember that her brother and other dark elves had been inside.

She tensed, half-expecting Harlik-van to spring out and attack her, furious about their mother's death. But she didn't sense him, neither walking out nor inside the building. The person who did step out was Sarrlevi, his swords in their scabbards on his back and something dangling in his grip.

Arwen stepped back, pressing a hand to her chest. It was her brother's head.

Sarrlevi looked up at her and nodded gravely, much as Gemlytha had done. Telepathically, he added, *Per your request.*

It took a stunned moment for Arwen to remember her conversation with Matti about hiring Sarrlevi.

Val grinned, as if all these bodies—and a decapitated head—were all a part of a day's work. She thumped Arwen on the shoulder. "Isn't it great having powerful friends?"

"I..." Arwen rubbed her face. "Yes."

"Just FYI," Val said, "we *are* going to expect cookies after all this."

"*And* caramel apples." Amber joined them, a cut on the back of her hand the only sign that she'd participated in the battle. Her mother had likely done everything in her power to protect her. "And didn't you mention apple cake before? And apple betty? I *love* streusel toppings."

"Don't we all," Arwen murmured.

Zavryd circled the area—looking for more dark elves that might be a threat? Maybe he'd communicated with Azerdash and they'd declared a momentary truce, because Azerdash risked shifting into his elven form.

Arwen couldn't resist the urge to step forward and hug him.

"Thank you for helping," she whispered.

He returned the hug *and* kissed her. Almost fiercely. *I thought you would fall in before I could reach you. I thought...*

Me too, she whispered in response, returning the kiss.

I love you, he added. *I could not lose you.*

I love you too. Arwen was so happy to have him holding her that she forgot about everything else that had happened. As she gripped his shoulders, basking in the warmth of his aura and his body, she forgot about Gemlytha too. At least for a moment.

Maybe he had too, but a hint of hesitation came to the kiss, and Azerdash drew back. He clasped her hands, however, like he didn't mean to let her go. Arwen *hoped* he wouldn't let her go.

He looked over at Gemlytha and nodded toward her, not as if he'd remembered he also loved her but more in apology. At least that was how Amber interpreted his expression. She hoped she was right, that he merely felt bad because he loved Arwen and couldn't give Gemlytha what she wanted.

He said something softly in Elven.

Gemlytha nodded and said a couple of words in kind before finishing telepathically so that Arwen could hear. *I knew without a doubt when you chose to levitate her out of the chasm first.*

Azerdash's eyebrows drew together. *That was merely a logical choice. She doesn't have the ability to levitate herself.*

Arwen, remembering Gemlytha lying dazed and bleeding on that narrow ledge, doubted *she'd* had the power to levitate then either, but she didn't say anything.

Logical. Yes, of course. Gemlytha smiled sadly. With... acceptance?

Had his choice made her decide not to fight for Azerdash after all?

Maybe Arwen should have felt triumphant, but she experienced some of Azerdash's regret that Gemlytha had to be disappointed, that she wouldn't get the man she'd loved for so long.

Azerdash's expression hinted of sadness, but he squeezed

Arwen's hands and managed a smile for her. She gripped him back, relieved that he wanted a baker instead of a warrior. Not that she wasn't some of both. She just couldn't singlehandedly snap people in half. Nor would she wish to. The thought of recovering from the battles by spending time in the kitchen peeling apples and making everything Amber had requested sounded so soothing she could have wept.

You peel the fruits called apples by hand? Azerdash asked her silently.

Are you reading my mind again?

To ensure you are not distraught or mentally damaged—I glimpsed your mother pressing that device to your head. Had the demon not had me pinned at that particular moment, I would have sprung free to assist you sooner. His expression turned to one of anguish and guilt that he hadn't been able to do that.

I'm fine. Thank you. And I have a special kitchen tool for removing apple skins. Arwen envisioned her beloved Oxo peeler.

Azerdash scoffed. *A tedious and lengthy task when done by hand. I have schematics for a gnomish device capable of peeling the rinds of fruits and vegetables. Square 74.*

That's not necessary.

To facilitate the speedy production of the baked goods the daughter of the Ruin Bringer described, I would enjoy building the tool. Maybe he had been reading Amber's mind too and salivated at the thought of streusel.

Gemlytha turned, squinting toward the sky as Zavryd finished looking for lingering enemies before gliding in to land on the rooftop. She tensed. So did Azerdash. They exchanged a long look, one that had nothing to do with their feelings for each other.

Would they flee if Zavryd attacked? Or fight back?

In a battle, Val would stand at her mate's side. And Arwen would stand at Azerdash's side, but the idea of having to fight against Val made her sick. She'd already had far more fighting than she wanted for the night.

Zavryd had landed facing Val, but his gaze soon swung toward the half-dragons.

Arwen tightened her clasp on Azerdash's hand, reminded that her problem might have been solved, but Azerdash was about to start a war with the dragons. Or had it *already* started? From what he'd been saying, it might be underway on Veleshna Var.

You have declared yourself an enemy of dragons, Zavryd announced to everyone, though his eyes were locked on Azerdash, *and my queen wishes you brought before the Dragon Council.*

Azerdash lifted his chin. *I am following my destiny to do what is right for the many intelligent species of the Cosmic Realms.*

Do not be impudent and interrupt when a greater being is speaking.

Val folded her arms over her chest and gave Zavryd a look that suggested he was being unpleasantly pompous, but she didn't say it out loud. Maybe she said it privately, because he gazed over at her before turning his focus back to the half-dragons.

Since you have battled with my mate against a foe to all, Zavryd said, *I will consider the rooftop of this building to be neutral territory and not strike at you.*

"Just the roof?" Val asked. "What if he jumps into the alley?"

Then I shall smite him, drag him through a portal, and deliver him to the queen's aerie.

"You're in a mood tonight. Did that demon singe your tail?"

My mate, you do not fully grasp the precarious position I am in.

Val sighed, lowered her arms, walked over, and leaned against his forelimb. "No, I get it. Thank you."

Her phone rang, the sound startling in the aftermath of the battle. In the distance, ambulance sirens sounded, and a handful of building lights were now visible from the rooftop. The power grid was still down everywhere, as far as Arwen could tell, but some places had to have generators.

"Hey, Willard," Val answered. After a pause to listen, she said, "The power is out all over the city? You don't say.... I don't know, but Arwen is here. Let me check." She raised her eyebrows. "I don't suppose you found the missing women while you were finding her." She pointed her chin at Gemlytha.

"We *totally* found them," Amber said.

Arwen nodded. "They're underground, accessible... via a hole in an alley by a restaurant near the water." Arwen realized she should have gotten the name.

"I can show you," Amber said.

"When we left, a device was oozing poisonous gas or the equivalent," Arwen said, "so we didn't remove the girls from their pods, but I think Amber figured out how to let them out."

"Yup," Amber said. "And if you have a half-dragon, you can blow the bad air away. A big industrial fan might also work."

"You hear that Willard? Amber can guide you, and maybe Gondo can find some high-powered fans."

"Gondo and Amber." Willard's mutter was audible. "Just the people I want to rely on to thwart dark-elven magic and save kidnap victims."

Amber scowled at Val's phone.

Arwen, reminded that Amber had wanted to prove herself, leaned close to the phone to say, "Amber was very helpful tonight. She was the one to figure out how to find the missing girls. And she kicked a half-orc over a railing and into the lake."

Val grinned and gripped Amber's shoulder. "That's my girl."

She'd either forgotten that she'd forbidden her daughter to meet with the kidnappers or would wait until later to ground her.

"All right," Willard said. "I'll come get you, and we'll retrieve the girls. Was our werewolf operative with them?"

"Yes," Arwen said.

"Good, though she may decide to go back to working for the family winery after this."

"I would," Amber muttered.

Gemlytha looked at Azerdash. *We should leave. If I understand the situation, you are needed on Veleshna Var.*

We are needed on Veleshna Var, he replied. *Yendral is currently in charge of the army.*

That's a distressing thought.

He is a competent troop. He will not lead them astray.

No, but he may offend the king by trying to seduce his wife. The elven queen is quite beautiful.

But frosty and aloof. She would not be enticed by his advances.

You never know. Remember the troll princess?

Azerdash grimaced. *And the* ogre *chieftess, yes.*

His tastes are unique and varied. Gemlytha glanced again at Zavryd, then made a portal.

Arwen decided she was glad she'd never let herself be *enticed*, as Gemlytha had said, by Yendral. His touch hadn't been unappealing, but she'd had another in mind.

She smiled at Azerdash, disappointed that he had to leave. And a little worried. Even though he'd made his choice, and Gemlytha seemed to accept it, Arwen couldn't help but wonder if she might try to change his mind once they were alone together. Arwen trusted Azerdash, but they were so newly together, and hadn't, as Gemlytha had been quick to point out, mated in a physical sense. It might take some time for her insecurities to wane.

Aside from that, Azerdash would be putting himself in danger again. He hadn't had time to heal from the demon battle, and she caught herself resting a hand on his chest, concerned about his burns and gouges.

He caught her hand and held it, his lashes lowering as he gazed at her. *Would you like to come with us?*

Arwen blinked. *To Veleshna Var? To a war?*

Yes. I can protect you or create a portal to send you back if you'll be in danger.

I do have some more cookies and cakes at the house, she offered. *If you want to stop by there, we could take them to your allies and troops. To motivate them.*

I was thinking more that, if there is time, I could prove *to you that I've made my choice.* Azerdash shifted so that his back was to Gemlytha and held Arwen's gaze. Maybe he'd caught her insecure thoughts? Did he want to join her for a tryst in an elven forest?

His eyes flared violet, making her think that was exactly what he wanted. A flutter of anticipation went through her.

That said, he continued, *if you're amenable to sharing your food with many, I am certain my troops* would *enjoy your desserts.*

I'm amenable to everything you suggest. It felt warm on the rooftop even though the flames had died down.

Everything? You'll let me build the device on Square 74 for you?

If such a project would make you happy, yes. I'll even let you add a sentience. Right after those words came out, Arwen wondered if that had been a little much. What if, like the robotic mower he'd altered, his sentient gnomish vegetable peeler went awry, shaving the fuzz off the couch fabric and the feathers off the chickens?

Not commenting on *that* imagery, Azerdash smiled contentedly. *That is why I love you.*

He kissed her again, this one less about relief that she'd lived and more about... a promise. She leaned into him, hoping they could finally have a night together to *claim* each other fully.

Yes, he whispered into her mind.

Val cleared her throat. At some point, she'd climbed onto Zavryd's back with Amber.

"We're off to find the girls, Arwen. Do you want to come?"

"Can you do it without me? Azerdash has invited me to go with him."

Gemlytha's eyebrows flew up, and she opened her mouth, as if she might object to bringing a *baker* to their war.

"To someplace romantic?" Val looked down.

Only then did Arwen realize Azerdash had been cupping her butt while he'd kissed her—and he was still doing so.

"Into battle," Arwen said.

Val nodded, as if that was a perfectly normal *someplace romantic* for girls like them. "We'll manage without you."

"Don't die," Amber said. "Not until you come back and make the caramel apples and apple betties. And cake. Oh, and can you make apple-cider donuts? I had those once. They're *amazing*. And yours would be even better."

You may need two *sentient gnomish peeling devices,* Azerdash remarked.

"Oh dear."

30

It was nighttime on Veleshna Var when Azerdash sailed out of a portal, Arwen on his back and Gemlytha flying ahead.

Arwen half-expected to come out in the middle of a battle with gouts of fire streaking above the treetops as elven archers weaved and dipped on their *evinya* mounts. But they arrived above a quiet forest, and Arwen couldn't sense any magical beings nearby, nor spot the lights of civilization.

I have camouflaged us so we won't be detected before we're ready, Azerdash told her.

Gemlytha had already disappeared to Arwen's eyes and senses.

Arwen patted the pack between her legs. In addition to her armored jumpsuit and a couple of changes of clothes, it held an assortment of cookies and pickled goods that she'd brought for the troops. Though she'd never met any of those troops, she wanted them to be content—as content as one could be on the eve of war—for Azerdash's sake. She supposed it was delusional to think that potential spies might enjoy oatmeal-raisin cookies so much that they would forgo plans of betrayal.

Azerdash! came a distant call. Yendral. *There you are. And you've brought Chef Arwen.*

Correction, Azerdash said dryly, *we won't be detected by* most. *Someone assiduously paying attention could have caught our arrival in the half second before we activated our camouflage.*

I was hoping you'd return with some of Chef Arwen's delightful desserts, Yendral said. *I did not expect you to bring her.*

Her dark-elf issue is resolved. Azerdash flapped his wings and headed over the dark forest in the direction of Yendral's telepathic voice.

The words brought to mind Gemlytha snapping Arwen's mother around the middle and Sarrlevi walking out with her brother's head. As garish as the memories were, and as guilty as she felt for being glad her kin were dead, they inspired fresh relief. It was true. She no longer had to worry about her father or any of her friends being kidnapped—or *worse*—by the dark elves.

That is most excellent news, Yendral said. *Our little camp here does not have an oven. There are cook fires. Can Chef Arwen prepare desserts with such limited resources? If you give me a list of ingredients she requires, I can speak with the supply sergeants and arrange their acquisition. You may recall that the elves have numerous types of nut flours.*

I did not bring her to bake *for you, Yendral.*

No? Was that not your reason for taking her to see world leaders?

Yes, but it is not why I brought her tonight. She is here to... fly into battle with us, to fight at our side. To fight at my side.

That wasn't exactly what he'd implied to Arwen when he'd invited her.

Azerdash glanced back at her with a gleam in his eyes and gave her an image of them entwined on a bed of ferns beside a moonlit pool, their clothes strewn among the fronds.

Her cheeks flushed. *You're not sharing that with Yendral, are you?*

No. Only you.

Will there be time for such activities tonight?

I am uncertain. I'm being told the dragons haven't yet attacked our forces here or on other worlds, but we believe it will be soon. If we can, we will strike preemptively. We are only waiting for the trolls and the dwarven army to arrive. Many dragons are perched around the elven capital. Whether all our forces are here or not, we may have to attack at dawn. I do not know if you wish to fly into battle with me, but I should warn you that any time my camouflage drops, they will target me.

I would have guessed that.

This could be our only night to... be together.

You'd better not die, if that's what you mean. Not when you finally — Arwen glanced to their left. She still couldn't see Gemlytha, but now and then she heard her soft wingbeats and knew she was flying close.

I will do my best to live.

You'd better. You promised me an apple peeler. You won't let yourself die before fulfilling that promise.

He snorted softly but didn't deny it.

If taking her into battle is what you intend, Yendral said, *I hope you will enchant her bow. Her weapon isn't strong enough as it is to harm dragons.*

Arwen wanted to object to that, since she'd punctured more than one dragon with an arrow, but that had always been after Azerdash temporarily infused her bow with his power.

I will do so, Azerdash said.

Good. This isn't going to be easy, Azerdash.

I am aware.

Gemlytha, Yendral said, *it is a delight to see you alive.*

I'm camouflaged, she replied. *You shouldn't see anything.*

I glimpsed your glorious albino form briefly as you came out of the portal. It has been far too long since we flew into battle together.

I was busy being dead.

I see you're still as warm and refreshingly outspoken as always.

My death didn't change me as much as you'd think.

As they bantered, sounding more like old enemies than old comrades, Arwen glimpsed the first signs of civilization. No, of a camp. Fires burned on ledges on a sole mountain rising above the forest. A dormant volcano? The top was lopsided, as if it had blown off at one point.

When they flew closer, Arwen sensed magical auras and weapons. Hundreds of both. No, *thousands.* A few dozen tents were pitched on the ledges, but legions of orcs, shifters, and more were camped in a valley that stretched beneath them.

"I didn't bring enough cookies," Arwen whispered. One of the orcs waved to them, and she recognized Brok standing with several of his mercenaries.

They can share, Azerdash told her.

She imagined a hundred orcs fighting over a single oatmeal-raisin cookie and the ones who came away with only a crumb being disgruntled.

Perhaps the squad leaders will give them out as rewards to those who do well in battle.

"I'm not sure my cookies can motivate men and women to fling themselves to their possible deaths."

You might be surprised. His telepathic tone turned grim. *Besides, there will be* flinging *regardless of cookies.*

Arwen was a little surprised the army wasn't camouflaged, but she did sense powerful defenses all around the camp. They came from a mixture of magical artifacts and mages standing guard.

As Azerdash soared toward a ledge overlooking the forest to one side and the valley behind, she picked out a few distant lights. Was that an elven city built into the treetops? Their capital?

It was too far away for her to sense if there were magical beings in that direction, but she spotted a telescope perched on the ledge near a tent. Yendral stood beside it in his elven form, his arms folded over his chest as he considered the distant lights.

Azerdash landed, levitated Arwen off his back, and shifted into his elven form. Gemlytha landed close enough that Arwen could see through her camouflage. She also shifted forms.

Yendral looked at them and smirked. *Azerdash and his women. Are you two getting along? Playing well together and sharing him?*

Arwen's jaw dropped. *Sharing?*

She couldn't tell from Yendral's smirk if he meant it as a joke or if he truly wondered if that was how they were resolving the issue. Arwen knew that such relationships sometimes existed, but she didn't even have experience with one lover. She wanted Azerdash, not other things.

You're a dolt, Yendral, Azerdash said as Gemlytha snorted.

I do not share my males, she said.

No? I thought you might be so eager to test the function of your female anatomy—in the aftermath of your death—that you would be game for almost anything. Yendral gave her a lazy smile as he looked her up and down. *I am, as always, available for testing, should you find yourself lonely tonight.*

Gemlytha snorted again. She *did* walk off with Yendral, but they headed toward the part of the ledge that overlooked the vast camp, so Arwen doubted romance—or testing—would ensue.

When they were alone, as alone as they could be near a camp with thousands, many of whom kept glancing toward Azerdash, he rested a hand on Arwen's shoulder.

"Thank you for coming. I am not certain bringing you was the logical choice, but..." He gazed at her. "I wanted you here."

"It's good to be wanted." Arwen leaned into his touch.

"Yes." He opened his mouth, as if to say more, but an elven male in magical silver armor engraved with leaves and vines strode up to him.

A full-blooded elf, he had a powerful aura and a deadly mien that reminded Arwen of Sarrlevi. He glanced uncertainly at her but didn't object to her presence. In a camp populated by a dozen different species, she couldn't be *that* strange.

He spoke to Azerdash in Elven.

How long has it been since they left? Azerdash answered telepathically, nodding to Arwen.

The elf glanced at her again, hesitating. Maybe he thought she was a spy? Or that someone with dark-elven blood could only be an enemy.

Arwen lowered her pack, opened it, withdrew a tin, and removed the lid. She offered a brown butter, sage, and orange cookie to him, figuring an elf would enjoy a sweet that incorporate fruit and herbs.

He stared in confusion and looked to Azerdash.

General Yasavar, this is Arwen Forester, a tracker and chef. Her human blood compels her to bake and grants her great power in the area of food preparation.

Human blood? The elf's haughty sneer brought Sarrlevi to mind even more. *I had not heard it conveyed any sort of power. It is considered...* He glanced at her. *Substandard.*

Arwen suspected an even more derogatory term had come to mind and that he'd edited it for his commander's sake.

Try a cookie. Azerdash made it sound more like an order than a suggestion.

Arwen opened her mouth to object—she didn't want people to be *forced* to eat her baked goods—but the elf obediently took one. He sniffed it and touched his tongue to it. Arwen barely resisted rolling her eyes. Nobody on Earth was ever so suspicious of her food.

Finally, the general took a bite. He chewed thoughtfully.

Even though Arwen had never met him, she watched, always hoping for a positive reaction. After all, Sarrlevi, despite his haughtiness, was a good ally. It never hurt to have elves on one's side.

In the distance, silver lights appeared in the sky. Her first thought was that they were a natural weather phenomenon here, but she realized with a sinking stomach that those were portals appearing over the forest. From this far away, she couldn't sense them, but they were above the treetops, so she had little doubt about which species was making them. Only dragons would arrive that high above the ground. A *lot* of dragons.

Neither the general nor Azerdash did more than glance at the portals. Maybe dragons had been arriving for some time.

How many would Azerdash's army face? Arwen hadn't had the impression that there were that many dragons in the Cosmic Realms, but their numbers might be much greater than she'd realized.

Finally, after his long, thoughtful chew, the general nodded. *Human blood. Interesting.*

Arwen was about to ask what that meant when the elf took another larger bite to finish off the cookie.

Sleveryn left with his strike force at dusk, the general said. *We chose a moment when many of the dragons were hunting in the forest, fueling their large bodies in preparation of the battle, and did not appear to be paying overmuch attention to our camp. Many were still arriving at the time, so even if the dragons had scouts watching us intently, the departure of some might not have drawn notice.*

Let us hope. Surprise is an important part of the plan.

What if it does not succeed?

Then we carry forward with a direct assault. We will have to do that regardless. The dragons have known from the beginning of my intent, so there will be no surprising them here.

Understood. We attack at dawn?

Yes. Tell the troops.

I will. The general regarded the tin Arwen was still holding and selected two more cookies. He started to turn away but rotated back to pluck up a few more. *For my troops.*

Of course. Arwen smiled at him and pushed the tin toward him. She had a feeling he would share and was a good person to distribute some.

He blinked, as if surprised she'd spoken—maybe random mongrels weren't supposed to address elven generals—but did accept the tin and even bowed to her, as well as Azerdash, before departing.

"How far until dawn?" Since it had been late on Earth when they'd left, Arwen feared it might be soon.

Nerves taunted her belly at the thought of flying into a huge battle, not merely a skirmish with a demon and a few dark elves. Would she and Azerdash survive the event? Had she been alone, she might have easily been ignored by enemies who would dismiss her, but the dragons would all be after Azerdash, and if she was on his back...

Do you wish to return home? Azerdash was watching her face— and her mind. *As much as I would like you here with me, this is not your war.*

Unless the dragons win and decide to send a ruler to take over Earth. She wished it were a joke, but more than one dragon *had* suggested that possibility within her hearing. Even her favorite most laid-back dragon, Zavryd's Uncle Ston, had said it would improve Earth. *My people would prefer that the dragons be derailed from thoughts of ruling the entire Cosmic Realms, including the wild worlds.*

Understandable, but it would likely be some time before they turned their eyes toward Earth. Your planet has little to offer.

She snorted at the dismissal of all that humankind could make, knowing he referred more to the paucity of natural magic in the ground there. *Except cookies?*

Except cookies. He nodded in agreement. *Also strawberry shortcakes.*

It's a shame strawberry season is about over. Before the kidnappings, she'd been picking the last of the ever-bearing varieties from the beds. There might be a few left when they returned, enough for a strawberry shortcake for Azerdash. *Harvest season is always a lot of work, but I like that it keeps me busy. Winter days are short and dreary in our area, and I miss growing things.*

As Admiral Hashyvar said, 'The spring has no meaning to one who never experienced winter.'

Yes, we have similar sayings. Arwen clasped his hands. *I will stay. Whether my people will ever know about it or not, I'll fight for their future and freedom. And for you.*

He returned the clasp and swallowed. Surprisingly, moisture gleamed in his eyes. Was he touched that she would stay with him? She squeezed his hands, glad that she meant that much to him.

Come with me. He withdrew one hand to point toward a tent pitched atop the ledge.

To take a nap before we go into battle? With one of their hands still clasped, she followed him.

A nap. He smiled at her, his eyes gleaming with a new emotion now. *Yes.*

As she realized what he had in mind, in a tent pitched next to others on a ledge not that far removed from thousands of troops, the term *stage fright* came to mind. The vision he'd shared had involved ferns and a pool and *privacy.*

I will ensure that we are not disturbed. Azerdash lifted the flap, holding it up for her, and nodded toward a nearby guard, a young elf in armor that wasn't as snazzy as that of his general.

Arwen hesitated before entering.

What if we, uh, disturb them? She well remembered crying out when they'd been together on the couch.

I can use magic to ensure that they do not hear us, but perhaps they would like knowing that their commander is having a pleasurable night and will be in a good mood in the morning when he leads them into battle.

I think they'd like cookies more. Arwen walked her pack over to the elven guard and handed the rest of the tins to him. *A gift from Azerdash. Please distribute them to some of the troops. Uh, maybe those camped close to this tent.*

Azerdash snorted softly and nodded when the elf looked uncertainly toward him.

Yes, ma'am, the guard said after getting his commander's approval.

He opened a lid, sniffing the contents as he picked his way down a path from the ledge, and called out to a mixture of troops camped below.

When Arwen returned to Azerdash, who still stood with the tent flap lifted for her, the nerves in her belly fluttered for a reason far different from the impending battle. But she gave him a shy smile and walked in with him.

31

When Arwen followed Azerdash into his tent, she didn't see a bed, cot, or even a blanket. Maps strewn over folding tables occupied most of the space inside. A lamp on a stack of books provided the only light, so it took her a moment to realize that one of the "tables" was lower, narrower, and longer than the others. That had to be a cot, though it was as covered with maps as the other surfaces. Where one might put a pillow, there was a model of a war machine, a cross between a catapult and a Gatling gun.

"Something you made?" Arwen smiled, sensing his magic about it.

"During a meeting, yes." Azerdash picked it up and looked around for a place to set it. When he didn't find an unoccupied surface, he instead held it up for her perusal. "I'm able to focus and think better if my hands are busy while my officers are briefing me."

She imagined his troops frowning as they delivered reports and wondering if their commander was listening to them. Though, since they were standing in his private tent, and he'd hinted of spending the night with her, her mind soon drifted to other imagery, of him shucking his clothes while pulling her down onto the maps.

She remembered them joking about sleeping with his sword and magical mechanical devices before and asked, "Do you tinker with things during sex too?"

Azerdash fumbled the war model, almost dropping it. "I, no." He hurried to set it on a map-strewn table. "I mean, not mechanical devices. More..." He reached toward her, hands gesturing vaguely in the air, before he jerked his arms down to his sides. Wondering if that had been too lewd?

She hadn't even been certain which body parts he'd been indicating he would tinker with.

"I'm not that experienced with this," she admitted. "Relations with men, I mean."

Sex.

"I know."

Of course. He'd read her thoughts many times.

Azerdash swept the maps off the cot and gestured toward it. "I'm actually not... an expert either," he admitted.

She raised her eyebrows. On the couch, and also when he'd levitated her into his arms in the rejuvenation pool, he'd known *exactly* what he was doing. Her body tingled with warmth as she remembered the way he'd used his touch and his magic to titillate and arouse.

"I'm not *inexperienced*," he hurried to add. Was that a hint of pink darkening his cheeks? The low-burning lamp made it hard to tell. "But I haven't been with as many women as Yendral."

"Has *anyone*?"

"I'm certain a few out there have known more." He smiled and looked around the tent.

It occurred to her that he might be nervous too. Their previous intimate moments had been spontaneous. This was more premeditated.

"If I'd often invited women into my command tent, I might have realized I should have romantic accoutrements in here." Azerdash knelt and peered under the cot.

"You don't think the miniature catapult is romantic?"

"Unless it puts you in the mood for a sexual encounter, probably not." He withdrew a folded blanket and pillow with a soft, "Ha."

"*You* put me in the mood for that." She meant it. There was something endearing about seeing someone with such a powerful aura, with such great magical ability, on his knees, looking for a pillow for her. She wondered if he would have bothered if he had been the only one sleeping in here tonight. He might have curled up on the maps and rested his head on the catapult.

"I'm glad," he murmured, gazing over his shoulder at her as he cleared off the cot and spread the blanket. "May I offer you a drink?"

"Something tasty that will act as an aphrodisiac?" Not that Arwen thought they needed such a beverage. Wine might have taken the edge off her nerves, but he'd already admitted he hadn't planned this out, so she wasn't surprised when he lifted a canteen.

"This was drawn from a pristine elven spring high in the Shydaresh Mountains."

"So... water?"

"Yes." Azerdash offered the canteen to her before sitting on the edge of the cot.

She joined him, her shoulder brushing his, and took a sip. It was good water with no taste of minerals or chemicals.

He watched her through his lashes, his eyelids drooping. Something about that attention and the intensity in his gaze made her feel sexy and alluring. Even though she was simply drinking and wiping her mouth. But he had a knack for making her feel desirable, despite her mongrel blood.

"You are *most* desirable," he murmured and brushed a leaf out of her hair.

Arwen stared, hardly believing she'd managed to stick her head in a tree during her crazy night in the city. How long had that been there?

He smiled. "I like that you always carry nature with you. You are most like an elf."

"I haven't noticed that they typically have twigs sticking out of their hair."

"You haven't met many yet. Once this is over, if we win... perhaps we can arrange a tour of their city for you."

"I would like that." Arwen leaned into his touch as his fingers drifted to her cheek, then traced her jaw.

"I believe you made a friend of Freysha with the lavender cookies." His eyes crinkled. "You've befriended *many* with your sweets."

"Some I didn't even want to."

"Yendral." He nodded, as if certain of his assessment.

She smiled. "Among others."

His face grew more serious as his fingers lingered under her jaw and he gazed into her eyes. "Every time I see you in danger, terror grips my heart like dragon talons. I want to change your world so that you're never in harm's way."

"You already have," she whispered, thinking of the dark elves, of how he'd kept showing up to help her, even when it had endangered him, when he should have stayed far away.

"I merely distracted a demon by letting it beat on me." A hint of magic trickled from his fingers, zinging along her nerves. It heightened her awareness of his touch, of his aura enveloping her. The power he emanated created an enticing sensation on her skin. "I *did* lop off a couple of its arms with my sword." He nodded to the sheathed blade he'd rested on a table. "Thorvald expressed her gratitude." He reconsidered the statement. "Grudgingly. After cursing me because it spattered demon ichor on her."

"She's a hard woman to please."

"I am relieved you are a more amenable soul." Azerdash brushed his thumb along her lips, and another zing of sensation rippled through her.

"Yeah." She caught herself scooting closer, reaching for his shoulders. "I hardly ever complain about ichor."

His eyes crinkled. "You would probably bake something with it."

"Few of my cookbooks mention demon bits and bobs." Arwen didn't know if *ichor* counted as either.

"Odd." His gaze fell to her lips, as if nothing had ever fascinated him more.

"Yes." She left them parted, wanting...

He kissed her, his fingers shifting to thread into her hair, rubbing gently at her scalp and sending the most delicious sensations through her. As she returned the kiss, she delighted in the taste of him and loved being close, inhaling his masculine scent. Even more, she delighted that he'd chosen her, that he'd had the opportunity to pick another, but his heart had called to hers.

She ran her hands from his shoulders down his arms, feeling the hard muscles beneath his tunic. She hoped her instincts guided her in this, that she would figure out what to do to make his time with her pleasurable. She didn't know how to entice him with magic but she stroked his body, moved her lips against his, and leaned into him, wanting him to touch all that she could offer him.

Azerdash growled like a wolf—no, a *dragon*. *I've wanted you for so long,* he whispered into her mind. *We've been interrupted so many times.*

Tell me about it.

Tonight, none will enter my tent or disturb us.

Even if the dragons attack?

I will mercilessly slay any dragon that dares interrupt us. His arm wrapped around her lower back, then shifted her into his lap, sliding her legs over his. She squirmed as close as possible and slid a hand under his shirt. Though she'd touched him before— not nearly as often as she would have liked—she felt brazen, maybe presumptuous, as she ran her hand over the ridges of his abdomen.

You are not presumptuous. You may touch anything you like. Everything you like. As I will. He smiled against her lips.

Presumptuously? Growing breathless, she was glad they had the ability to speak silently.

Yes. With a whisper from his magic, her shirt and bra loosened, and he cupped her breast. He stroked her, heated pleasure ricocheting through her.

She forgot all about words and kissed him harder, wanting him to know how much she longed for this. An ache built within her, and she shifted in his lap, aware of his hard body through their clothing. She pushed his shirt up, certain they had to be naked at some point. Besides, she wanted to see his lean, powerful form.

He let her tug his shirt over his head, forcing their kisses to pause for a moment, but he didn't stop touching her. His hand trailed lower, her excitement building as his fingers brushed over her stomach, then traveled between her legs.

Still wearing her jeans, she expected him to remove them, but his fingers lingered, brushing her along the seam, and she caught herself gasping at his touch so close to her hot core. A trickle of magic flowed from his hand, making her arch into him as she gripped his shoulders.

He continued, soft pulses of power touching her intimately through her clothing, making her hot and slick with need. Even though she wanted to make sure *he* was satisfied this time too, she couldn't help but selfishly enjoy his ministrations. All thoughts of undressing him fell out of her mind as she reacted to his touches, rocking in his lap, feeling a little silly as she ground against his hand, but she couldn't have stopped if she wanted to.

He watched her squirm intently, showing no humor at her antics. No, his eyes flared with desire as he sent increasingly delicious sensations through her.

Such great need built within her that she caught herself begging, whispering *please* aloud and into his mind. His every exquisite pulse rocked her body, made her arch into his hand. She needed him so badly.

With a perfectly placed brush of his magic, he brought her to her climax, and she couldn't keep from throwing her head back and crying out, the throbs in the aftermath crashing over her like waves on a stormy beach.

"Being with you is arousing," Azerdash whispered, his voice hoarse with his desire. He lowered his face to her throat, kissing her sweaty skin, breathing in her scent. "Amazingly arousing."

"Azerdash," she breathed, the throbs abating until he brushed her again with his magic. Right away, her body lit up, eager for more from him.

He smiled against her skin, his fingers finally moving to the button fastening her jeans. "I want to see you, *all* of you, the next time you come."

She nodded and helped him remove her jeans, though she wanted to see *him* as well. All of him. And she wanted to make sure he enjoyed himself as much as she enjoyed being with him.

"Good," he murmured, then shifted her shirt the rest of the way off her, lowering his head to her breasts, tracing her sensitive skin with his tongue. He sucked gently, and she gripped the back of his head, lifting her body so he could have better access. New sensations shot to her core as he nipped at her, teasing magic mingling with the pleasure evoked from his physical touch.

He shifted her aside, and she protested with a groan, not wanting to let him go. But he only rose so he could remove the rest of his clothing. With her body trembling again—or *still* trembling —she watched him as he revealed his muscled body and scars that hadn't fully healed. Her gaze descended to his erect cock, and his eyes flared with intensity again, as if he'd longed for nothing more than for her to look upon him.

Realizing she'd done nothing yet to bring *him* pleasure, Arwen reached for it. She grasped it lightly, stroking him, exploring the unfamiliar texture of his skin, the heat of his shaft. His body quivered under her explorations, and that excited her. A new desire formed within her. His touch through her jeans had been exquisite, but her instincts told her that she wanted this, wanted him inside of her.

Guided by those instincts, and what little she knew from books, she leaned forward and kissed him, then let her tongue trail over him.

His eyes flared even brighter until she lost sight of them, his head falling back and his fists clenching. His muscles were taut, the veins standing out. His aura was taut as well. Energy coiled within him, almost dangerous for its power, crackling in the air around her, but she knew he wouldn't hurt her. She trusted him with all her heart, and she wanted him to enjoy being with her, more than with anyone else he'd been with.

She explored further, doing more of the same whenever he gasped, his hips twitching toward her, as if he wanted to drive into her right there. She would let him if he wished. She wanted him to be satisfied, to love her the way she loved him.

Azerdash groaned, as if he would do just that, but instead, he touched her head and knelt. She opened her mouth to question if she'd done something wrong, but he brought his mouth to hers, kissing her with such hunger that she realized she was doing things right.

He pushed her back onto the cot, hands returning to her body, her nerves afire with his magical and physical touches. Soon, she couldn't think about pleasing him, could only react, grasping and panting as the need within her built again, even more intense than before.

Their bodies naked and gleaming with sweat, he shifted atop her. Between passionate, demanding kisses, they rubbed and pressed. She arched, aching to be filled, wanting him in her.

With a growl of desire, he obliged, bringing his hard shaft to her molten core as he caressed her with his fingers, stoking her fire to even greater heights. When he finally slid into her, she'd never been so ready for anything in her life. If it hurt at all, she didn't notice it, not with the pulses of need driving her to grip his shoulders and arch toward him. She wanted him harder, faster.

Growling, he complied, and they came together with frenzied need, synching themselves to each other as their hearts pounded, their breaths came in gasps. The cot creaked, and maps fluttered, falling off the tables.

For the second time that night, Azerdash brought her to the most exquisite climax. Waves of physical pleasure mingled with her emotional waves of love for him.

Right after, he came, pouring himself into her and roaring, the beast subsuming the elf for a time as he threw his head back, his entire body quivering with his release.

She gazed up at him, never having seen someone so beautiful. And she was so pleased that they'd finally had this moment that her soul ached. Was she greedy to hope they would have many more nights like this?

Azerdash lowered himself, shifting onto his side and drawing her over with him, a hand pleasantly cupping her ass. Or maybe possessively? Something about his expression seemed to say *Mine* as he nestled her close and gazed at her.

Good. She wanted to be his.

You will be. He kissed her. His hungry need had been sated, but his lips held a promise of the future. *Many more times.*

If that's going to happen, we had both better survive the battle.

We will. It has taken me far, far *too long to claim you. I will not lose you now.*

Arwen might have dozed, but the part of her mind that didn't want to miss any of her time with Azerdash, knowing the battle might be the end for one or both of them, roused her. With his arm wrapped around her, his hand on her waist, she wanted to enjoy being next to him—*with* him—before they had to get up.

She rested her hand on his bare chest and lifted her gaze, finding his eyes open. He smiled at her and stroked her back.

"I am glad you are here with me," he murmured.

"Me too."

"Though I have been contemplating sending you back before the battle begins. If I lost you after we finally came together..."

"I want to stay and fight with you."

"I know. I appreciate that."

He didn't argue further for sending her home, but she wondered if he would. She couldn't blame him for wanting to protect her and suspected he'd brought her because he'd been reasonably sure the dragons wouldn't attack during the night— and he wanted to have this time with her. The visions he'd shared the night before had suggested that.

As he gazed sleepily at her, his gentle fingers stroking her skin, Arwen thought of Gemlytha. During her time with Azerdash, she hadn't thought of the woman once, but now... she worried Gemlytha had seen them go into the tent together and would be hurt, not only that Azerdash had chosen Arwen but that he'd brought her *here* to have sex in the same camp where she was.

Should they have been more circumspect? It wasn't as if Azerdash could have abandoned his army hours before a battle and stayed at a Hilton with her.

But maybe Gemlytha had given him her blessing? Back at the Coffee Dragon, she'd seemed to accept his choice, even realizing he'd made it before he fully did.

"Azerdash?" she asked.

"Yes?"

"Are you... Is..." *Is Gemlytha all right?* was what Arwen wanted to ask, but she hesitated as it occurred to her that it might be uncouth to bring up another woman while in bed with a man. Maybe not as bad as bringing up another *man*, not that there were any of those, but... was this inappropriate? She was too inexperienced to know the rules. "Did you get any gnomish siege engines to use in the battle? I didn't sense any gnomes in your camp but know they promised to help."

What a thing to bring up in the aftermath of their joining. Arwen closed her eyes, feeling foolish.

When she opened them, she caught the knowing look in his eyes. Surely, when they were this close, he had no trouble reading her thoughts. But he answered the question she'd voiced and not the one she hadn't.

"Yes, there are quite a few gnomish machines in place under and on the platforms of the elven capital city. Large population centers that might see battle on the ogre, troll, orc, and shifter home worlds have also received them. The dwarves huffily said they could create their *own* defensive machines and didn't need gnomish magic or technology to protect them. Given how many of their cities are underground and already well-defended, that's not a statement of hubris." He smiled wryly. "I well remember how difficult it is to get into them and attack."

"That's good."

"For your edification, they are gnomish defensive engines rather than siege engines, since they are for protecting a city rather than attacking one's fortifications."

"One can't siege a dragon?"

"I suppose the definition allows that, but we prefer to simply attack them."

"I'm going to siege the ones we see with my bow." Arwen watched his face, wondering if he'd decided to send her back without saying so.

He hesitated. "If that is still your desire in the morning, I will do my best to add power to your bow."

"Thank you." She rested her cheek on his chest, the warmth of his skin and thump of his heartbeats pleasant. Comforting.

After a time, he said softly, "I believe Gemlytha is all right."

He *had* heard Arwen's unspoken question.

"She knew, better than I, my feelings," he continued. "It is always so with females."

"May I ask... I'm glad that I'm your choice, but, in some ways, she and I are very similar." Arwen didn't want to admit that in other ways Gemlytha was far her superior. She touched her chest. "Why me?"

He shrugged, as if it were a simple thing, and inexplicable emotions played no part. "You burble about your many passions, and you listen to me burble about mine. We are the same."

Smiling, he shared an image of himself working on his airplane project while noshing on her pickled watermelon rinds with her standing nearby and sharing trivia about the fruit with him.

"So, because we're both geeks?" Arwen could accept that. The idea that her dark-elfness might have nothing to do with his love amused her. More than that, it *pleased* her.

"Also, Gemlytha would *never* let me store my airplane project on her farm."

"Does she... have a farm?"

"She does not, but if she did, she would call that fascinating engineering construct a rusted hunk of metal unworthy of my time and likely incinerate it, given a chance."

"Goodness, I had no idea she was such a dreadful woman."

"She is not, but she does not understand my appreciation for..."

"Toilet-paper rolls full of gnomish notes?"

"Exactly." He paused. "I do wish... I regret that I cannot make her happy. After all we have been through, she deserves happiness." His arm tightened around Arwen. *As we've found,* the gesture seemed to say.

Arwen considered the strong woman she'd only spent a couple of hours with. "She seems the type to be able to find happiness independent of her relationship status. Or not to require a relationship to feel fulfilled."

"Perhaps." Azerdash fell silent, but his eyes remained open and unfocused.

Maybe Arwen shouldn't have brought up the subject, not if it left him feeling guilty or discontent. She wanted him to be happy too, not brooding and worrying about another. Or feeling that he'd failed Gemlytha.

Hoping to lighten his mood and bring him back to the moment —*their* moment—Arwen said, "You're meeting a lot of people as a commander amassing an army. Maybe you could set her up with a nice man who doesn't mind pale skin. *Very* pale skin."

"Hm." He touched his chin, then raised his finger, an idea sparking in his eyes.

"*Not* Yendral," Arwen said in case that was the idea.

"Oh." Azerdash lowered his hand.

"She should have someone faithful who's completely devoted to her. She deserves that."

Azerdash looked at her. Maybe he wondered how Arwen could be so sure after she'd known Gemlytha such a short time, but all he did was nod and smile, maybe glad of her assessment.

"I will consider your suggestion," he said.

Arwen didn't know if Gemlytha would want her commander to set her up on blind dates—probably not—but if she found a fulfilling relationship with another, Azerdash could set aside his guilt. Arwen would like that for him. Maybe *she* would try to set Gemlytha up with someone. Not that she knew that many available men. Or knew that many people at all. Before she'd met Val and Matti and started working for Willard, she'd barely left the woods and the farm. She thought of the available men she had met at the farmers markets, such as the horny shifters who hit on her, and shuddered.

"There are schematics for an ambulatory robot in combat armor on Square 102 of my gnomish notes," Azerdash said out of the blue.

Arwen stared at him.

"It is gnome sized, but creating a larger version would be possible. With the help of an enchanter, it could be given intelligence and the ability to offer conversation as well as physical companionship."

"Azerdash Starblade, Gemlytha needs a man, not a *robot*."

"Ah."

He fell silent, and Arwen thought the matter settled until he spoke again.

"It could be given a penis to make it sexually functional."

"*No*."

"Very well."

She kissed him to put all thoughts of *making* Gemlytha a boyfriend out of his mind. He returned the kiss, his body shifting and promising he was amenable to changing the topic of conversation.

There are a couple of hours until dawn, he said telepathically, his lips busy.

We should take advantage of that time.

Yes.

32

DESPITE THE INSULATING MAGIC AZERDASH HAD EMPLOYED ON THE tent the night before, when he and Arwen stepped out into the predawn light, a lot of eyes turned toward them. She supposed there weren't many doubts about what went on in a tent when a man and woman entered together. Her cheeks heated with warmth, but she didn't catch any scathing looks and told herself that what his troops thought didn't matter anyway.

As if to reaffirm the notion, Azerdash clasped her hand, brought it to his lips, and kissed it. She stepped close to him, wishing they could have spent longer in bed. They'd barely had time to sleep, not that she regretted that.

"After the battle, you will make me a strawberry shortcake, and I will build you the vegetable peeler diagrammed on Square 74. Then we will spend many more nights together."

"I look forward to that." Arwen liked that he was thinking optimistically and planned to survive.

He opened his mouth to say something else but must have sensed something odd, because he shifted to look in the direction of the elven capital. Arwen didn't see any new portals opening—

the dragons might all have arrived during the night—but that hadn't alarmed him, regardless. This had to be something else.

It was a moment before she could pick out five blue- or green-feathered *evinya* with riders flying toward them. A messenger with bodyguards? Arwen soon sensed the elves on the great birds' backs and was surprised to recognize one of the auras.

"Princess Freysha?" Arwen stared in surprise, especially when she sensed a powerful magical weapon balanced across Freysha's lap. A staff? No, a bow. There was also a quiver of magical arrows on her back.

Though Arwen hadn't spent much time with Val's half-sister, she hadn't gotten the impression that Freysha was a combatant in any way. Nor would she have thought the king and queen would allow their only daughter out of the city when it was surrounded by dragons. Hadn't their kind already mind-scoured her?

"She brings a message for me." Azerdash must have reached out telepathically to Freysha. "And a gift for you."

Before Arwen could ask for details, the *evinya* alighted on the ledge.

The guards—with armor, weapons, and grim faces, they did indeed look like bodyguards—slid off first. They scowled at anyone nearby before nodding for Freysha to dismount.

She smiled gently, as if she would have gotten down whether they approved or not, and slid off with the bow and quiver. Instead of going to Azerdash, she walked straight to Arwen.

"Good morning, Your Highness." Arwen bowed.

"Just Freysha, please. When I heard you were here with Azerdash, I was worried, *especially* when the general who was communicating with my father implied you would fly into battle with him." Freysha raised her eyebrows as if to ask for verification.

Arwen didn't think she'd said that within the general's hearing, but maybe Azerdash had shared it with his officer. She nodded. "Yes, but I'm a capable warrior. Not just a baker." She glanced around, but she hadn't seen Gemlytha since she'd walked off with Yendral.

"So I've heard." Freysha smiled again. "But dragons are mighty enemies, and Azerdash will be targeted."

"I know."

"When I told my father about you and that you were here, he said I could lend you this." Freysha held the bow horizontally in her open palms.

The beautiful weapon appeared to be made from silver wood, though Arwen was certain the strong magic imbuing it made it very sturdy if not indestructible. Elegant white elven runes glowed along the bow, and the string might have been made from spun gold. The fletchings on the arrows protruding from the quiver were also golden in coloring, though Arwen trusted nothing so heavy had been used in the crafting.

"It was the bow of a legendary elven archer, a distant ancestor of mine and... I suppose also yours." Freysha nodded toward Azerdash.

Val must have told her about the results from the heritage detector and how they were related.

"Yesarlalin the Just?" Azerdash asked.

"Yes. Sometimes known as Yesarlalin the Pointed, since he spoke his mind as he pierced his enemies with his arrows."

"I have read about him in the history books." Azerdash nodded. "He was a great combatant and leader of elves."

"You want *me* to wield his bow in battle?" Arwen reached toward the magnificent weapon but hesitated to touch it, feelings of not being worthy creeping into her. Worse, what if it was like Earth technology, and hissed and refused to work optimally because it was offended by her dark-elven blood?

"That will *not* happen," Azerdash murmured. "Elven magic isn't as temperamental as inferior Earth devices."

Freysha's keen ears caught the words. "It has its own quirks, but I am certain this bow will not object to you, Arwen. Yesarlalin the Just and Pointed was also Yesarlalin the half-elven."

"What was his other half?"

"He was also half dark-elven, which technically made him fully elven, but the people of the time sneered at him and refused to accept him as whole. He excelled in battle, regardless, and earned a place in the history books."

Azerdash must have known the story, because he only nodded.

"Ah." Arwen risked touching the bow.

A hum of magic coursed through it, and a tingle of warmth flowed into her. As if it were sensing her. Trying to get a feel for who she was as a person?

That was probably her imagination. It was a bow, not a colleague. At least the tingle wasn't painful or unpleasant in any way.

Hm.

Arwen blinked and looked around. Had... the bow made that sound in her mind?

You are young. Yes, that was the bow.

Freysha smiled as Arwen stood there with her hand on it. Did she know it talked? Like Val's Storm or Matti's Sorka? And that it would speak with *Arwen*?

I'm thirty, she replied.

A toddler.

"Really," Arwen murmured.

Freysha and Azerdash, apparently not privy to the bow's comments, arched their brows.

"It's, uhm, talking to me," Arwen said. "And it's haughty."

"Ah." Freysha nodded, as if she expected nothing less.

"Weapons imbued with intelligence tend to develop personalities," Azerdash said.

"Haughty ones?"

"If it's elven, yes. Dwarven weapons are usually snarky and

sarcastic." Azerdash drew his own galaxy blade, the white stars in the dark metal glowing. "Some have *all* of those personality traits."

Swords are unappealing, the bow said. *One's wielder must close to a dangerous distance to engage one's enemy.*

I agree, Arwen said.

Do you? Then you display uncommon intelligence for such a toddler.

Uhm, thanks. Do you... not mind my mongrel blood? Arwen couldn't imagine that an elven weapon would find either human *or* dark-elven blood appealing, but if the bow's former wielder had been part dark elven, it should at least be used to that.

It is not one's blood or origins that determine one's worth but one's actions.

I would agree with that.

Oh? Then why ask if your mongrelness matters?

I occasionally struggle with having belief in my self-worth. She rubbed her face. Why was she baring everything to a bow she'd just met?

We will slay many enemies together. You will get past that.

Many?

Many, the bow said firmly. *I have been a decoration on a wall in the royal palace for* ages. *My name is Eeshara ev Leheysa, which means Hailstorm of Havoc.*

That's pretty cool. Arwen didn't mention that it brought to mind heavy-metal bands.

Naturally.

"I'll be honored to wield the bow in battle," Arwen told Freysha. "Thank you, but it's such a great gift. Why... why me?" As she'd grown older, she felt like she'd grown better at accepting her self-worth, but it continued to be a struggle to get *others* to believe in her.

"You are most welcome, and it is because my father has felt... Well, he has not said as much, but I believe he has come to believe that the half-dragons were not treated well. Not when they were created and trained and not now. He would have preferred to offer them sanctuary when they asked—" Freysha gestured toward Azerdash, "—even if they didn't ask in the most tactful way."

"The *first* time we did," he murmured.

"My father had to consider the safety of all his people, and the dragons forbade any interaction with Commander Starblade and his brethren. He wasn't willing to defy them. Not until..." Freysha touched her temple and grimaced, reminding Arwen that she'd been caught by the dragons after their meeting on the goblin home world. Caught and mind-scoured.

Arwen touched Freysha's arm in sympathy, knowing how unpleasant that was.

"He is not pleased with them now," Freysha said. "And he wishes the half-dragons well in the battle. He might have also offered a great weapon to Commander Starblade, but since he already has a galaxy blade, I suggested that he might appreciate *you* being lent a bow capable of piercing dragon defenses."

"He *does* appreciate that," Azerdash said.

"Thank you," Arwen said again. "I'm surprised you were allowed out of the city to give it to me."

Especially if she'd recently been mind-scoured. The dragons clearly knew who she was and her importance to the elven king and queen.

"I was actually *ordered* to leave the city before dawn, when the dragons were resting. In case things don't go well." Freysha grimaced as she looked out over the forest toward her home. "My father and mother will stay for the battle, but they wanted me to find safety out here in the forest."

Azerdash nodded. "You and your guards will remain here when we leave the camp."

"Here or... around." Freysha waved vaguely, probably not

wanting anyone who might be captured and questioned to know her whereabouts.

Understandable, but Arwen hoped it didn't come to that. Though there wasn't much time to gain familiarity with the new bow, she was glad to have it. Maybe with these arrows, she could make a difference in the battle—and help ensure that Freysha could return home at the end of the day.

Freysha's grimace shifted to a smile as she met Arwen's eyes and whispered, "My mother enjoyed the cookies you sent back with me. If we all survive the day, and should you wish to visit our city when things settle, I believe she will allow it."

"We *will* all survive," Arwen said.

"Of course. Now that you have a decent weapon to use, I'm certain the day will favor us."

Decent! Havoc scoffed into Arwen's mind at the perceived insult.

She is also young, Arwen told the bow.

Yes, very much so.

"Did you say your mother?" Arwen asked, belatedly realizing the ramifications. "I'd heard she was..." A frosty bitch was the term Val had once used to describe her while Matti had nodded firmly. "I didn't realize she would enjoy cookies."

"She doesn't admit it, but she has a fondness for sweets."

"I wouldn't have guessed. I assume you'll want the bow back after the battle?" Arwen fought the urge to cradle it to her chest. She was glad her current bow wasn't intelligent and couldn't feel envy if she set it aside in favor of another. Already, she dreaded giving the elven bow back—even if it had called her a toddler.

"Well." Freysha scratched her cheek. "Hopefully not."

What did that mean?

"My father said for you to arrange to have it returned upon your death."

"Oh." If Arwen was fortunate enough to live a long life,

presumably on Earth, who would return it? She looked at Azerdash. Half-dragons presumably lived a long time, if they didn't die in battle—or under collapsed mountains. Maybe she could request that Azerdash or Yendral return it. Yendral, after all, had already been pressed into delivering Azerdash's airplane project if he died prematurely.

Azerdash must have been following her thoughts, because he said, "Should your death be in the distant future, your children might be able to return it."

"But I don't have children."

"Perhaps one day you will," he murmured, holding her gaze.

"Oh." Arwen bit her lip at the implication. Yes, she imagined the offspring of a half-dragon would grow up to be powerful enough to make portals.

Azerdash, Freysha, and her bodyguards all looked off into the distance, in the direction of the city.

"The dragons have realized that Princess Freysha left." Did Azerdash know? Or was he guessing? "They are heading this way."

Arwen couldn't yet see or sense them, but she didn't doubt him. Voices grew louder, and clanks and thumps sounded in the vast camp—troops grabbing their gear and getting ready for battle.

"I apologize," Freysha said. "I'd hoped I might deliver the weapon without their noticing."

"They intended to attack soon, regardless." Azerdash stepped back so that he could shift into his dragon form. He switched to telepathy and addressed everyone in the camp. *It is time, my troops. Let the battle begin.*

33

There hadn't been time for Arwen to take more than a few practice shots with the new bow before Azerdash levitated her onto his back, and they left the camp. She wore her armored jumpsuit and rested the elven weapon across her lap, trying and failing not to be nervous.

Azerdash, Gemlytha, and Yendral winged through the thick-trunked trees that towered hundreds of feet in the air while elven riders on *evinya* followed behind. The rest of the troops were levitated after them. Hundreds of powerful mages from the various intelligent species had come along with the thousands of warriors.

Arwen had expected the half-dragons and *evinya* to soar above the treetops, but as soon as she sensed dragons approaching, she guessed why Azerdash had chosen a lower elevation. His troops were less powerful than the dragons, but they were also smaller. They could navigate between the trees, dodging magical attacks, and ducking for cover when needed. The larger dragons would have a harder time flying around so many obstacles.

Distant screeches and *thwumps* of magical weapons firing

promised a battle had begun around the elven capital. The dragon forces must have split.

Battles have begun around important cities and strategic strong-holds on other worlds as well, Azerdash told her as they flew over one of the gnomish defensive machines that he'd mentioned, a huge glowing harpoon angled toward the sky. Most of the weapons had to be stationed around the city, but a few were poised in the forest with elves manning them. Those elves all lifted hands toward the half-dragons and their army as they passed overhead.

Arwen's nerves jittered as more and more enemies registered to her senses. She wiped one palm and then the other on her jumpsuit, hoping she could do the great elven bow justice when the armies met.

A red-scaled dragon descended through the canopy, the first of that color that Arwen had seen. She didn't recognize him, nor were there any familiar dragons among the others she sensed. For that, she was glad. If Zavryd and his uncle were a part of this battle —and she had to assume they would be—she didn't want to be forced to fight them.

The red dragon had emerald eyes that flared brightly when they focused on Azerdash. He wasn't flying camouflaged. None of his army was.

Be ready, Azerdash warned Arwen. *As I said, they know I lead and will target me.*

I'm ready. Arwen nocked one of the gold-feathered arrows.

As more of his allies descended into view, the red dragon tucked his wings to avoid the trees and streaked toward them. Gemlytha and Yendral flew upward to form a barrier to block access to Azerdash, but he roared, objecting to staying back while others protected him. His great wings flapping, Azerdash flew toward the red dragon.

Power swelled around him, enhanced by the galaxy blade that

was hidden when he shifted into this form but always remained close. He launched a coil of lightning-like energy that branched around trees to strike the red dragon's barrier. Magic flared white-blue around that barrier, crackling as it tried to get through.

Arwen aimed her bow, but she had to wait for a clear shot. Between the trees and Yendral and Gemlytha, who were also launching attacks at the red dragon, numerous obstacles threatened to get in the way. The last thing Arwen wanted was to hit an ally with a deadly magical arrow.

Finally, she loosed one. Azerdash must have been waiting, not wanting to ruin her shot, because he immediately banked.

A gout of fire streaked in from the side, startling Arwen. A dragon that had been camouflaged appeared, a silver-scaled beast that crouched on a thick limb.

Somehow, Azerdash had anticipated the attack, and the fire blazed through the spot where they'd been, its heat enough to warm the back of Arwen's neck. She hadn't gotten a chance to see if her first arrow had landed but shifted so she could target this new threat.

Azerdash sent a fiery attack of his own toward the silver dragon as her arrow streaked through it. Thanks to the flames, it disappeared, and she sensed rather than saw it pierce their enemy's barrier. The arrow thudded deep into a scaled flank.

The silver dragon screeched and sprang from the branch. Blue eyes the color of glacier ice glowed as their enemy flew straight for Azerdash.

He banked hard again. Arwen leaned forward, afraid she would fall off.

Always before, when she'd ridden on Azerdash's back, his magic had kept her steady, with no need for a saddle or anything to grip. But enemies were dropping through the canopy en masse now, and magical attacks of all kinds streaked through the forest. He might not be able to concentrate on keeping her astride.

Dragon screeches and roars mingled with cries of pain from elven, orc, and troll mouths. Azerdash's fast dodge changed Arwen's view, and she glimpsed a charred warrior falling through the air and a now-empty *evinya* flapping away with singed feathers. The reality of the situation crystalized in her as the elven body hit the ground.

The silver dragon chased Azerdash, leaving Arwen no time to dwell on mortality. She shifted to target those icy eyes and fired immediately, hesitant to hold her shots, aware of the pounding of her heart, the tremor of fear that could ruin her aim if she paused to think.

Azerdash flew around a tree, and, again, she didn't see if her arrow landed. He flapped his wings hard to gain altitude quickly.

Above, a green-scaled dragon—Arwen recognized that one as a Silverclaw she'd faced before—breathed fire at Gemlytha. She had a barrier up, but her wingbeats faltered under the great power, and her defenses wavered. That didn't keep her from hurling an attack back at the dragon, a blast of fire that engulfed his green scales. Unfortunately, the intense heat and power weren't enough to stop the Silverclaw.

Yendral roared and flew at the dragon from the side, slashing with his talons. The blows weren't sufficient to break through their enemy's barrier. Azerdash added an attack, a magical battering ram that snapped branches on its way to pounding into the Silverclaw from the opposite side.

Intent on trying to flambé Gemlytha, the dragon didn't react until Azerdash's magic, enhanced by his sword, pounded away his defenses. Arwen loosed another arrow, though it was a challenge to target their foe through all the fire and whirling magic. Briefly, a wind gusted, and the fire cleared enough for her to see her shot land in the dragon's neck, sinking deep.

The blow shocked him and sent him careening into a tree.

Gemlytha breathed more fire on him as he fell toward the forest floor far below.

Arrow delivery, Havoc spoke calmly into Arwen's mind.

"What?" she blurted.

With so much magic surrounding her, she didn't sense two of her arrows returning and was fortunate to spot them floating toward her. She snatched them from the air and jammed them into her quiver.

Thanks, she told the bow and was about to remark on how handy that power was when a telepathic shout came from Yendral.

Look out, Azerdash!

Arwen sensed three dragons coming up fast from below and behind them.

Heeding the warning, Azerdash spun away.

Arwen clenched her bow—and willed herself to stay molded to Azerdash's back—as he barrel-rolled through the sky, turning her upside-down, right-side-up, and upside-down again. Her stomach tried to climb into her throat.

Wave after wave of magical power slammed into Azerdash's magical barrier. Even with the galaxy blade assisting him, it was too much for him to defend against. His wingbeats grew frantic as he dodged through the trees, putting obstacles between him and his attackers.

But his pursuers were relentless. Trees burst into fire, and great trunks snapped and fell as the dragons chased him.

Arwen flattened a palm against Azerdash's scales, willing her power to aid him, to be enough to make a difference. Even with her help, his defenses fell, ripped away by magical talons.

Yendral, Gemlytha, and warriors on *evinya* launched attacks at the dragons chasing Azerdash, but Arwen feared it wouldn't be enough. With his defenses down, Azerdash could only fly erratically to avoid the magic blasting after him.

Azerdash dredged up enough power to form a portal ahead of them.

"Good idea," Arwen said, wind whipping her hair into her face.

If Azerdash fled, the dragons ought to be too busy defending against others to give chase. He could come back later in another spot.

Leap through, Arwen, Azerdash told her as a screech of pain came from behind them. That had sounded like Gemlytha. *It'll take you home.*

"What? You have to come too!"

Azerdash barrel-rolled again, barely avoiding a gout of fire blazing toward them. It singed his tail before he jerked it to the side. *I can't leave. Gemlytha is in trouble.*

"You're in trouble!" Arwen spun, loosing another arrow.

It was a wild shot and almost hit a tree. Through luck rather than skill, a dragon flew around the trunk at that second, and her arrow sank into its cheek.

Before she could feel any satisfaction, another flew into view right behind it, a red-eyed monster with Azerdash's death glowing in his eyes.

Levitation magic formed around Arwen, sweeping her toward the portal.

"Azerdash, no!" She tried to twist in the air to target the new dragon.

A thunderous snap of wood louder than a gunshot sounded, and a huge tree fell. Azerdash saw it coming and would have wheeled out of the way, but tremendous power came from his pursuers and wrapped around him. It halted him in mid-air. The tree smashed into him, knocking him flying, and the magic levitating Arwen toward the portal disappeared.

She couldn't keep from screaming as she plunged toward the forest floor far below.

34

ARWEN TWISTED IN THE AIR AS SHE FELL, TRYING TO POSITION herself to land in a way that wouldn't kill her, but there was no chance.

Until a whisper of power wrapped around her, slowing her fall. Azerdash.

She still landed hard, grunting as she rolled across roots and needles, her jumpsuit doing little to soften the pummeling. The bow almost flew from her hand, but she tightened her grip, not caring that she wrenched her elbow in the process. She wouldn't lose the precious gift.

Once she staggered to her feet, standing in the shadow of a great tree for cover, she peered up, hoping to spot Azerdash flying about. But she couldn't see him, not with all the flames streaking through the forest, lighting branches—and troops—on fire. Nor could she sense him. Only his assistance proved he'd survived having that tree fall onto him.

"You better not have used your dying breath to save me, Azerdash," Arwen whispered.

Shouts and cries and screeches from dozens if not hundreds of throats assured he wouldn't hear her, wherever he was. It was chaos up there. Booms and yells from the city promised it was still under assault. Arwen had no idea if their side was winning or losing.

Realizing she was vulnerable alone on the forest floor, Arwen reached for her multitool and its camouflaging power.

But she sensed an enemy right behind her and gasped in surprise, spinning and nocking her bow. It was the silver dragon she'd struck earlier. Her arrow was embedded in its flank, and one of its eyes had been damaged, dark gunk oozing from it as he glowered at her with the other.

She raised a barrier, but it wouldn't be enough against such a powerful foe.

Mate of the mongrel traitor, the dragon snarled, advancing and opening his maw. *Your death will wound him as much as a blade.*

Fire roiled from his open jaws.

Arwen loosed her arrow before she sprang behind the tree for cover. Flames struck it and her barrier, the sheer power almost dropping her to her knees. And it kept coming, the dragon's flames streaming as if from a hose. A *fire* hose.

The trunk offered some cover but not enough. Her barrier withered and died under the assault. Arwen sprinted away, angling toward another tree, hoping she could reach it in time to dive behind it.

A startling shriek came from the dragon.

Had her arrow struck it? If so, that was a delayed reaction. She made it to the tree and ducked behind it before peeking out on the far side.

You strike from behind while hidden? The dragon roared in fury. *You coward!*

Arwen couldn't see whoever he was facing, but she took advantage, raising her bow. From her position leaning out from behind the tree, she could only target his back half.

"No problem." It wouldn't be her first time aiming at a dragon's ass.

Even as she had the thought, she realized the powerful elven arrows might be able to slip through his barrier and crunch into his skull. She lifted her aim, but the dragon's head snapped toward the ground before she fired.

Shadows stirred as someone dodged the attack. Azerdash!

Blood streaked the side of his face and neck, and his clothing was charred, but he leaped over a giant root without hesitation and swung his galaxy blade toward his foe's face as the dragon snapped at him.

Afraid to aim at anything near Azerdash, Arwen lowered her aim. The ass it was.

Blade clanged against fang as Azerdash and the dragon came together.

Arwen fired, satisfied when the arrow sank deep into those scaled hindquarters. The dragon quivered but was too focused on Azerdash to look back. And for good reason. Even though he was in his elven form and more vulnerable, Azerdash gave the dragon hell. That blade blurred as it moved, sending streaks of starlight in all directions when it slashed through scale and into flesh.

A wave of pleasure rushed into Arwen as she nocked another arrow, both because Azerdash was still alive and fighting, and because she finally had a weapon capable of striking their powerful enemies.

Her next arrow pierced the back of the dragon's neck, eliciting a frustrated screech. Still not looking at her, he blasted Azerdash with a maelstrom of magic, but Azerdash's defenses were back up. The gale battered the trees but didn't reach him.

Another dragon sailed past overhead, roaring as it chased two elves riding *evinya*. It was catching up to them fast.

Arwen whipped her bow up and fired at its belly, aiming

between the scales for a vulnerable spot. Again, her arrow pierced the dragon's barrier and sank deep.

Their enemy had been about to snap into one of the riding birds, but her attack made it jerk so hard that it smashed into a tree. The elves had been in flight, but as the dazed dragon fought to recover, they turned their mounts and flew back in, casting spells and raising their weapons to charge.

Trusting they could handle it, Arwen turned back to Azerdash only to see him somersault through the air to land on the back of the silver dragon's neck. One of their foe's legs had crumpled, his shoulder tilted toward the ground and blood streaming down the forelimb.

As soon as Azerdash landed, he whirled, driving his sword into the dragon's skull. Like the elven arrows, the galaxy blade had no trouble piercing those scales. And the dragon's magical defenses had fallen, hacked apart by sword and arrow.

Not sure how much fight their enemy had left, Arwen raised her bow to help Azerdash, if needed. But he hacked again and again, and the rest of the dragon's legs buckled. He slumped to the ground, tail sprawling flat on the needle-carpeted forest floor.

Azerdash leaped off, landing lightly despite his injuries. He rushed to Arwen and hugged her.

She returned the embrace, though she also reached for her pocket, again thinking that activating camouflage would be a good idea.

The air had cleared, however, leaving no foes flying above, and the forest had fallen strangely quiet. The battle noises from the city had also faded.

Her senses told her the dragons were flying away. Retreating?

That surprised her since, despite the enemy she and Azerdash had managed to down, many dragons remained. They were so powerful—and so proud. Would they truly give up? Maybe they were regrouping.

Another dragon has arrived, Azerdash said.

What did one more matter when they'd been battling dozens?

In the distance, Arwen sensed dragons circling over a section of the forest. Azerdash stepped back, shifting into his scaled form and levitating her onto his back. He didn't mention sending her home again, instead flying above the canopy for a view of the dragons.

His troops found him and gathered in the sky around him. Azerdash gazed at the dragons in the distance and a couple still flying in that direction, their lopsided wingbeats indicating injury. Azerdash didn't order his troops to go after them. Arwen remembered when he'd let the assassin dragon, Saruknorath, go when he could have killed him.

A portal opened in the sky back over the camp on the volcano. Were more dragons arriving? To attack from behind?

Arwen nocked another arrow. But she recognized the aura of the half-dragon who flew out of the portal. That was Sleveryn.

Ah, Azerdash said.

Arwen didn't know how Sleveryn's arrival could have changed much until she remembered that he'd been away on a special mission.

A distant screech of ire came from the circling dragons.

I believe Sleveryn may have been successful. Azerdash sounded grim rather than pleased.

What was his mission? Arwen hadn't asked the night before.

Treacherous filthy beasts and mongrels, came a female dragon's telepathic cry. Was that the queen?

Arwen glimpsed Zondia's lilac scales in the distance, gleaming under the morning sun, and suspected Zavryd was in the area too. She was glad his family hadn't attacked Azerdash during the battle. Arwen would have hesitated to shoot Val's mate, even if he'd been arrowing toward them with the intent to kill.

You would steal our eggs? the queen cried. *Threaten our hatchlings? Those are the actions of a coward.*

Azerdash didn't respond, merely continuing to fly around, ready if the dragons came at them again.

That was Sleveryn's secret mission? Arwen asked.

Yes. Since the dragons were aware of my quest even before I took it on, we did not have the element of surprise. They are more powerful and had time to prepare for our insurrection. I knew we would have no advantage in dealing with them and would likely fail if we faced them head on.

Arwen wanted to say that they'd been holding their own and doing all right, but she did feel that the dragons had been whittling down their forces and that the end might have been inevitable.

We never wanted to kill them, regardless, just force them to leave the various worlds alone, letting the natives rule their own people. We knew we needed a bargaining chip to make that happen. I knew.

He used *I* not out of pride, Arwen could tell, but to take responsibility for the plan—and the blame for whatever repercussions it might bring. Sleveryn might have gone on the mission, but Azerdash had commanded him to do so.

I thought of how desperate the dark elves have been to ensure babies are born so that their species will continue, Azerdash said. *Dragons are also not fecund, usually capable of laying only one egg at a time, decades if not centuries apart. With the help of goblin spies, we were able to learn where the current Stormforge nests are. Sleveryn led a team to sneak in and capture the eggs. We will return them if the dragons agree to our terms.*

Arwen winced at the clan name. Why couldn't he have targeted those odious Silverclaws?

I believe Sleveryn got a couple of their eggs too.

Azerdash Starblade, the queen spoke again. She didn't call him a coward this time, but her telepathic voice quivered with barely restrained fury. *Are the eggs safe or have you destroyed them?*

Azerdash looked toward Sleveryn, who was flying toward their group, and must have confirmed with him.

They are safe, Azerdash told the queen, *and they will be returned to you if dragons leave the civilized worlds of the Cosmic Realms and allow—*

We know what you desire, she interrupted.

Then I await your response.

Arwen rubbed the back of her neck, the sweat growing cold now that she was sitting astride Azerdash's back instead of shooting arrows—and being terrified for her life. Long minutes passed without a response.

Sleveryn joined the group, tilting a wingtip toward Gemlytha.

They did the dragon equivalent of pacing until the queen spoke again.

Your vile ways have forced our hand, Starblade. You will *return our eggs and the future of our kind.* With defeat in her voice, the queen added, *We accept your terms.*

Arwen slumped down, pressing her face into Azerdash's cool scales.

It was over. They had won.

Very well, was all he replied to the queen. *Once a treaty is formalized and signed in blood by all parties, we will return the eggs unscathed.*

"Good job, Azerdash," she whispered to him.

It was a job that had to be done. He didn't sound pleased, perhaps because of the tactics he'd been forced to use.

Arwen thought they'd been perfectly logical. He and his allies had been the underdogs against the powerful dragons.

I will return you to your home. Azerdash didn't comment on her thoughts.

And come to visit me soon?

Yes. His tone was a little brighter when he glanced back and added, *We are mates now.*

Because we had sex?

Because all has been resolved, for a time, and we may enjoy each other's company without interruption.

Arwen wasn't sure they would be lucky enough to do nothing but enjoy uninterrupted company—she still worked for Willard, after all—but she smiled agreeably and pressed her cheek to his scales again. *I look forward to it. I love you.*

And I love you.

EPILOGUE

THE BACK SEAT OF VAL'S JEEP OFFERED MORE ROOM THAN THAT OF Amber's hatchback, but it wasn't exactly spacious. Arwen had enough room, but Azerdash was tall enough that his knees jutted against the back of the passenger seat, a fact the passenger didn't fail to note. Every time Azerdash shifted, Zavryd glowered over his shoulder at him.

As the Jeep sped along I-90, heading out of the Seattle area, Zavryd turned his glower on Val. "I fail to see the point of this assemblage and journey."

"We're going on a double date with Arwen and Azerdash." Val winked in the rearview mirror at Arwen. "They've claimed each other and are a couple now."

"Something that has been apparent since the half-dragon built for his mate a *yavasheva*. I am aware. But he is an enemy of dragons, and I have no desire to be in the same metropolis with him and certainly not in the same conveyance."

"We're going on a double date," Val said again. Firmly. "It makes sense to share a ride."

"A double date." Zavryd, who'd already known that,

harrumphed. "When we pursue such activities with Puletasi and Sarrlevi, we visit ice battles and meat repositories."

Arwen arched her eyebrows.

"Hockey and the Brazilian steakhouse," Val translated.

"I thought he usually dueled Sarrlevi when you went out together."

"Yes, that's often in the mix. Ideally *not* while we're at the rink or the restaurant, but when tempers flare, you never know where they'll end up springing around, hurling fireballs, and leaving craters."

"Are you allowed to visit the same rinks and restaurants twice?" Arwen asked.

"Sometimes, yes." Val hesitated. "Rarely more than three times. Recently, we flew to a steakhouse in Portland and went to a junior ice hockey game there."

"Because you're not yet banned in Oregon?"

"That's right. We're not banned from today's activity either since we've never been." Val looked at Zavryd. "We're going to the railway museum in Snoqualmie to ride a historic train after touring the Train Shed Exhibit Hall."

Azerdash, who'd been holding Arwen's hand during the ride and completely indifferent to Zavryd's glowers, sighed with contentment.

Arwen liked to think it was because of their warm touches and her adoring smiles, but she knew he was thinking about trains. Either way, she was glad he could find that contentment. Despite Azerdash making it clear that he was enjoying being with her, he'd been disgruntled and regretful because of the tactics he'd employed against the dragons, and it had been hard to lighten his mood.

Zavryd curled a lip at the explanation of their destination.

Arwen felt guilty that he was being dragged along. Originally, Arwen had planned to ask her father for a ride, but she'd thought it might be uncomfortable if the trains put Azerdash in a romantic mood, and he started stealing kisses on the way back. Even though her father approved of Azerdash—Arwen doubted she could have found a more appealing-to-her-father boyfriend if she'd been able to select from a thousand men—he didn't want to watch his daughter smooching with a man.

"It's not exactly *my* idea of an ideal date either," Val admitted, "but Arwen is paying, and there'll be drinks and snacks on the ride."

"Snacks of meat." Zavryd squinted at her. It didn't sound like a question so much as a threat. As in... there had *better* be meat. Or else.

"Don't worry." Val patted a pack in the seat well by Zavryd's feet. "I brought emergency rations just in case."

Arwen raised her eyebrows again. She'd brought some cookies to share with Val and Azerdash, and, being well aware that Zavryd would incinerate anything sweet, some lamb jerky for him. That should have been enough to tide him over until his next meal, surely.

"Just a few salamis," Val told her, then briefly steered with her knee so she could gesture to demonstrate a length of a foot and a half.

"That can double as clubs if a stranger gets frisky with you?" Arwen asked.

"Is that something I'll have to worry about in the train shed?" Val asked.

"Maybe. When I looked at photos on the internet, there were a lot of men in there." Arwen didn't think women were as inclined in general to be fascinated by trains. "Possibly single men."

Val snorted. "That sounds right."

"My mate is claimed," Zavryd stated. "Strangers will *not* get frisky with her."

Since he was in human form, it was only in Arwen's mind that smoke wafted from his nostrils.

Fortunately, Val took the exit for Snoqualmie, meaning the ride would come to an end soon. Arwen could have had Azerdash fly them here for a private date, but she hadn't been to the museum before and wouldn't have known how to direct him. Besides, she'd already had him give her a ride to Fremont that morning for a meeting with Val and Willard. Willard had handed over envelopes with their combat bonuses for defeating the dark elves and rescuing the kidnapped women, all while road crews worked out front, bringing in truckloads of dirt and rock to fill the chasm.

It was unfair to the neighborhood that every building *except* the Coffee Dragon, which had been at the center of the dark elves' ire, had been damaged. The shop had its powerful defenders and copious magical defenses to thank for that. It wasn't as if the dark elves hadn't *tried* to destroy it as they'd attempted to kill Val.

At least, thanks to the illusion that kept mundanes from sensing it, most of those who owned businesses on the street had no idea the coffee shop had escaped unscathed. Only the psychic, with her smidgen of magical blood, knew. She'd done enough glowering at it and its patrons to make up for everyone else in Fremont.

As far as Seattle at large went, the news had reported the series of earthquakes as inevitable, and various media outlets were debating if they counted as the oft-prophesied Big One. Neither Willard nor Val had been certain how the dark elves had activated the fault lines in the area, but Willard had people looking into it. It was possible it had been an accidental byproduct of their tunneling, something they'd undertaken when they realized their underground laboratory wasn't that far from the coffee shop of their loathed enemy, but Arwen suspected the quakes had been intentional. Maybe the first one, days earlier, had been an accident, but then they'd realized they could use them to knock out the lights and distract everyone.

When they parked, Arwen got out on the same side as Azerdash so they wouldn't have to unlink their hands.

I am pleased to be here with you, he told her telepathically, perhaps not wanting the nearby Zavryd to roll his eyes—or the dragon equivalent—at their mushy moments. *There were many times I wondered if the destinies that Fate chose for us would ever be sufficiently resolved for us to spend time together.*

I worried the dragons would kill you.

I worried the dark elves would kill you.

Valid concerns on both our parts, I believe, Arwen said.

Indeed. With luck, the dragons will accept that they were defeated without overmuch bitterness and the need to take revenge.

Is that likely?

I am uncertain. My decision to threaten their eggs was not... honorable. Not in the way I or the elves consider it, and I suspect the dragons feel the same way, but when one faces more powerful foes, guerrilla tactics may be required to achieve a victory.

A quote from a dead general?

No, those are my thoughts. The famous generals and admirals of the past were usually honorable, at least according to those who wrote about them and penned their words. Azerdash looked around wistfully, not even the presence of historical trains near the parking lot enough to brighten his face.

Arwen wished she hadn't brought up the topic of dragons. *I have a feeling all those old generals and admirals, in order to win their wars, sometimes had to use guerrilla tactics too. You're not considered a great commander if the way was easy and you went into battle with the odds stacked in your favor.*

It is possible.

I'm sure history will remember you as a legend. Arwen squeezed his hand and led him after Val and Zavryd. *Even if you didn't do it in a way that you would have preferred, you accomplished a great thing. You helped a dozen worlds gain their freedom. We have a saying on Earth that sometimes the end justifies the means.*

Hm. He didn't sound that mollified, but he did allow her to lead him away from the parking lot.

While Zavryd walked straight toward a blackboard that listed the departure times—*and* the menu that would be served—Azerdash veered toward a steam-powered locomotive, part of the frame cut away to reveal its engine, the parts labeled with signage.

"I see our mates are each exploring the passions that are of most interest to them." Val joined Arwen and handed her two tickets. "We've got fifteen minutes until boarding."

"Does Zavryd have any passions besides meat?" Arwen asked.

Val smirked smugly.

"And, uhm, *nest* activities?" Arwen added, guessing at the meaning behind her expression.

"His work for his mother keeps him busy, but he enjoys hunting, dueling, saunas, and occasionally races, but *not* with weakling dragons who get their tails nipped day and night and spend their lives fleeing from greater dragons. He says all that fleeing practice gives them an advantage in races."

"It's hard for me to imagine dragons fleeing from anything."

"As Xilneth will be quick to tell you, Starsingers are lovers, not fighters."

"Except for the assassin, Saruknorath?"

"He's a clan oddity, I understand. What we would call a black sheep."

A murmur of, "Inferior," from Azerdash wafted to them as he shook his head at some train part. Zavryd, still at the menu and probably oblivious to what Azerdash was doing or saying, murmured, "*Clearly* inferior," at whatever he was reading.

Arwen gave Val money for the tickets and was reminded that she owed Amber her percentage for her research. Also, Amber's willingness to risk going in person—whether Val and Arwen had wanted that or not—to find the dark-elf laboratory had to be rewarded.

Arwen counted out a batch of twenties. "Will you give this to Amber?"

"Yes, but I already paid her the agreed amount out of my combat bonus."

"For defying your wishes to help you?"

"She *was* instrumental in finding the girls. And getting our werewolf back. If we'd lost Winter, everyone in my neighborhood might have been banned from Wolf Winery."

"You don't drink wine, do you?" Arwen couldn't remember anyone in Val's circle mentioning a fondness for fermented grapes.

"No, but Matti likes their cheese, so she visits from time to time. And they feed Willard information on what the shifter community is up to, so we want to stay in their good graces."

"Well, I wouldn't want to renege on my deal with Amber. I'm sure she has clothes she needs to buy."

"Yes. She's grounded for the moment, but when that's over, she'll be ready to buy entire racks of clothes, I have no doubt. At least she's saving some money for college." Val accepted the bills. "The girl has a knack for getting paid twice for jobs."

"I noticed."

"She's talking about becoming a private investigator when she finishes school."

"She mentioned that," Arwen said, "though I think it was going to be on the side while she starts her own fashion business."

"Oh, naturally. It's easy to run two businesses at a time."

"She's young and ambitious." Arwen, who'd been juggling farm work, filling bakery orders, and battling dark elves all summer, looked forward to a vacation. Maybe not from the farm, since harvest season was in full gear, but Azerdash had promised to help with that by making more magical mechanical contraptions. He'd said they would allow her to do nothing more than soak in the elven rejuvenation pool and relax for the next week.

The evening before, Arwen had attempted to follow his suggestion to relax in there, but she'd been alarmed by a trio of large cubes with scissor attachments floating in the air over the water. For a moment, she'd been about to dive for the elven bow, thinking an enemy had sent artifacts past the recently repaired wards to assail her, but the contraptions had proceeded to the rows of artichokes beyond the pumpkin patch. They'd snipped off the buds and slurped them into the storage cubes with *ker-thuds*. She'd been impressed that Azerdash had programmed the devices to know to leave the lower stalk behind so that side shoots had time to produce buds for a second harvest. Her father must have instructed him on the ways of artichokes.

While the magical harvesting had been going on, he had been vrooming around the property on his souped-up tractor, startling chickens—and Arwen—as he yelled, "Yee-haw," as if he were the star of a rodeo movie. The evening hadn't been quite as restful as Arwen had envisioned. She was glad, however, that Father's mood had been much improved since she told him her mother would never threaten them again. A couple of nights earlier, he'd even cried with relief, something she'd never seen him do.

"Amber is indeed young and ambitious." Val nodded as Zavryd headed toward them, probably engaged in two conversations at once. "And feeling quite pleased with herself for not being kidnapped or mesmerized by an artifact while saving a bunch of women from lives of mindless breeding. Her words."

Accurate words. Arwen still shivered when she thought about how close those women must have been to being impregnated. What would have happened if she and Amber had found a way into the laboratory a few days later?

"Duck confit is a poultry dish, correct?" Zavryd asked.

"It is," Val said.

"Excellent." He eyed her pack, probably wondering how well duck paired with salamis long and stout enough to beat up ogres.

Noticing that Azerdash had climbed *onto* the engine, and someone in a uniform was frowning and walking in his direction, Arwen hurried over.

"I think we'll be boarding in a few minutes," she called up to him.

A steam whistle blew, perhaps announcing the same thing.

Though they were close enough to it that it was on the deafening side, Azerdash smiled with pleasure. "Is that a gnomish *gegorportel*?"

"I'm sure," Arwen said.

Azerdash hopped down, and the uniformed man who'd been heading their way stopped, shrugged, and walked away.

"I am most pleased to go on this journey with you." Azerdash clasped her hands. "I found a diagram explaining the various cars of the train and which ones will go on the adventure with us."

"It's only a two-hour tour past some scenic forests." Arwen hoped that wouldn't turn into an adventure. Azerdash wasn't as quick to insult Zavryd as Sarrlevi was, so she didn't *think* they would end up atop the train with swords out as they hurled fireballs at each other. It was, however, probably a good thing that she hadn't invited Matti and Sarrlevi along to make it a *triple* date.

"There is something called a sleeper car." Azerdash waggled his eyebrows and waved toward a sign. "It has numerous beds inside. Will you allow me to show you?"

"That depends on whether you think we should make use of those beds."

"They would not be there if they were not meant to be used."

"I think they're there for historic accuracy."

"Yes. Because they were historically used." Azerdash took her hand and led her to one of the train's open doors.

Another uniformed man stood there, probably to insist on

seeing tickets and keep people from boarding until it was time, but his eyes grew glazed as they approached, and Azerdash guided her up the steps without trouble.

"Dating a half-dragon is going to be interesting, isn't it?" Arwen supposed she should be glad he wanted to visit the sleeper car with her and not get randy on top of an engine.

"Most interesting," he agreed. "But far more agreeable, overall, than seeing a *dragon*, I am certain."

Arwen glanced out a window and spotted Zavryd arguing with someone carrying trays of food while Val stood behind him with her face in her hand.

"That may be true," she said.

THE END

BONUS: A GOBLIN CHRISTMAS

Originally published online in December 2023, this story takes place after the events in the Tracking Trouble *series.*

Gizsla of the Steamwrench Clan gripped a blue US postal mailbox taller than she was and peered across the street at the Coffee Dragon. Any second, she would muster the nerve to go in and ask for a job. Another goblin was employed there, and *dozens* of goblins gamed and guzzled espresso in the loft. The owners didn't mind their kind, and Gizsla was a hard worker. She could do this.

A huge black wolf loped out the front door and leaped onto a food truck parked at the curb. He lifted his snout toward the wintry gray sky and roared, his bushy tail swishing several times. Appearing quite full of himself, he roared again.

Gizsla wiped her damp palms on her thin dress. Maybe she *couldn't* do this.

Even though she'd been to the coffee shop a couple of times and knew the name of many of the powerful beings who visited there, she'd never *spoken* to any of them. They didn't know her from any other goblin, and most tall people considered her kind to be pests.

The door at the end of the food truck opened, and the half-dark-elven archer and baker Arwen Forester peered out. Despite her mixed blood, she appeared fully human, with an apron tied around her waist, flour dusting her clothes, and forks stuck into her blonde hair to keep her locks back. The last time Gizsla had seen her, she'd used sticks for the purpose.

The werewolf noticed Arwen—or perhaps sensed the aura of the other powerful being inside the truck—and leaped to the sidewalk and loped away from the food truck.

"Did we offend him somehow?" Arwen asked. "Or was that just his response to trying the dark, *dark* roast for the first time?"

"The goblin-fuel coffee beverage is quite stimulating." The half-dragon, Azerdash Starblade, leaned through the doorway, his shoulder brushing Arwen's.

"I'm glad he didn't pee on Nin's truck," she said. "It's a pain when the shifters get territorial."

"Had he done anything so disrespectful while we were inside, I would have incinerated him." Starblade had a predatory aspect even when he wasn't shape-shifted into his dragon form. With these words, his violet eyes glowed menacingly.

A chill went down Gizsla's spine, and she second-guessed herself. She badly needed a job, but working in an establishment visited by such powerful beings could be deadly to one as small and insignificant as she. People like that could accidentally slay a goblin with their magic without even trying. To make matters worse, Gizsla sensed the full-blooded dragon, Zavryd'nokquetal, inside. He had to be shape-shifted into human form to fit, but that didn't make him less deadly.

"Nin doesn't allow the incineration of her customers," Arwen said, "especially around the holidays. It's a time to have a generous spirit while cheerfully decorating our hearts, our homes, and select coniferous trees."

"Some might consider flaming werewolf fur to be cheerful."

"Not the wolf."

"Their kind are dour and without cheer."

"Especially when on fire."

Green-skinned fingers clasped Gizsla's arm. "I won't let you do it."

Gizsla frowned at her younger sister, Vareeka. "You're supposed to be at the park, watching my girls."

"They're with Hargok. Now that Mama has passed, it's my duty to look out for you."

"I'm the older sister, so it's my duty to look out for *you*. And that's why I'm here." Gizsla took a deep breath to steel herself. "I'm going to get a job in the human way and earn money. Work Leader Tinja said I can only move my family into the urban goblin sanctuary if I can earn five hundred Earth dollars to pay for our board and show her we're serious about succeeding as entrepreneurs."

"The park is free."

"And full of vandals, gangs, and shifters who like to *eat* goblins."

"That is true. It's scary at night. And sometimes during the day."

"It's not a safe place to raise children. I'm going to get my girls out of there. And you too." Gizsla waved to the coffee shop. "This is our way out. Once I have a job here, we'll be able to move to the safety of the sanctuary."

Vareeka folded her arms over her chest. "It's as dangerous as the park in there. I'll go in with you."

Another frisky werewolf loped out and roared. It *had* to be the coffee. Maybe it had been spiked with a more potent substance for the human holiday season?

Vareeka dropped her arms, squeaked, and ran down the street.

This werewolf, like the other, soon left. Telling herself she had nothing to fear from patrons high on caffeine and holiday snacks, Gizsla strode toward the front door. All she had to fear was failure.

Before Gizsla reached the coffee shop, the door to the food truck opened again. Arwen stepped out with a tray of brown gingerbread cookies in the shape of pinecones, the tips of their scales dusted with powdered sugar to look like snow.

"Are you going inside?" Arwen asked.

Gizsla, not certain the half-dark-elf was addressing her, looked around before touching her chest.

"Yes." Arwen smiled. "Sorry, I'm Arwen. And I'm a little..." She glanced toward the coffee shop as a half-orc female walked out, the roar of laughter and dozens of conversations escaping with her. "I get a little nervous in there when it's so crowded." She lowered her voice. "And also when it's not."

Gizsla blinked. The deadly archer with powerful dark-elven magic got *nervous*? And not from enemies trying to kill her but people sitting and chatting and drinking? Arwen wasn't a three-and-a-half-foot-tall goblin who had to worry about being stepped on. How strange.

"If you're going into the shop," Arwen said, "would you mind letting everyone know that the latest batch of cookies has cooled and is ready to purchase? I didn't realize the first three hundred would go so quickly this morning."

"I can tell them." Gizsla didn't know if the patrons would listen to her, but she would attempt to deliver the message.

"Thank you. Here. Please try a couple." Arwen held the tray at goblin nose level.

The delightful scents of ginger and molasses and spices Gizsla couldn't name tickled her nostrils, instantly prompting her to salivate. She took two cookies and chomped into one.

"I grow the ginger and some of the other spices on our farm, even those that can be difficult in this climate. I use... a few tricks."

Magic. That was why the cookies were so good. "They're delicious. Even though they're missing some key goblin ingredients."

"Such as lard collected from roadkill?"

"Oh, you're familiar with the culinary traditions of our people." Gizsla beamed a smile at her. So few with human blood bothered to learn about goblins and their culture.

"A little bit. I've had a lot of feedback from the goblin customers since I started selling my baked goods here once a week." Arwen's own smile was rueful. "I also get feedback from Val's mate."

"Val? Do you refer to the *Ruin Bringer*?" Gizsla whispered. "And her *dragon*? Lord Zavryd'nokquetal?" Gizsla glanced toward the front window, though the shape-shifted dragon wasn't visible to her. From the sidewalk at her height, she could see little but the ceiling beams and lamps.

"I call him Zavryd, and yes. He'll only eat meat, meat without a marinade or sauce, and certainly not *gravy* containing sugar of any kind. I've heard he does enjoy beef and lamb seasoned with Mediterranean seasonings, so I've made special gyro cookies to tempt his palate. Well, Nin said to call them *meaties*, since they don't qualify as cookies, and she doesn't want false advertising. I haven't tried them on Zavryd yet, but the shifters like them. They're more likely to have a sweet tooth—a sweet *fang*—so I put berries in theirs."

Gizsla nodded. She didn't know what Mediterranean seasonings were, but her people also enjoyed those meats.

After finishing the pinecone cookies, Gizsla headed inside to look for Nin, the quarter-gnome Earth native in charge of daily operations of the coffee shop, including hiring people.

Reminded of Arwen's request, Gizsla called, "There are fresh cookies ready to be purchased outside."

She wasn't sure her small voice would carry over all the conversations, but numerous sets of ears turned, and nostrils twitched in the direction of the open door. Someone from almost every table rushed out to the food truck, and Gizsla scrambled to get out of the way.

Laughter flowed down from the gaming loft, and a die the size of her fist bounced off a wall and down the stairs before sailing toward a table. A placid orc sitting there moved his coffee mug before it could land in it. A goblin head peeked around the corner halfway up the stairs.

"Did it land?" a reedy voice asked from the loft above.

"No," the peeping goblin said. "He moved his cup."

"Drat. That's another zero."

"You're very bad at this game."

"Moving targets are hard to hit!"

"You see what I have to deal with?" a woman with blue pigtails asked, her voice just audible over the dozens of conversations taking place at tables throughout the shop.

Not a single seat was empty, and some patrons were standing in groups. The clientele included ogres with heads that brushed the rafters, shifters who appeared human except for fangs that flashed when they ate their cookies, and mixed bloods of all sorts with their hands wrapped bracingly around their mugs.

In a corner, four goblins were ignoring their gaming brethren upstairs to work on a hydraulic stand supporting what Gizsla had learned was called a Christmas tree. Brightly wrapped gifts were stacked all around it, more than would have fit if not for the stand jacking up the evergreen.

An elf with twin babies in a chest carrier made from green vines watched and shook his head remorsefully, perhaps disturbed that the tree had been slain for the holiday. A half-dwarf female was on her back under the evergreen, like a mechanic changing oil on a human conveyance, applying enchanting magic to the boughs and trunk.

Matti Puletasi, Gizsla decided, and the elf was Varlesh Sarrlevi. They were friends of the owners. She'd seen them in here once before.

"I can't kick out the goblins," the pigtailed woman continued. "They pay too well. Where do their kind get so much money, anyway?"

Belatedly, Gizsla realized that was the very woman she sought: Nin.

"They don't pay taxes or rent," a tall blonde woman next to her replied. That was the Ruin Bringer. Appropriate for someone of that name, she wore a great dwarven sword in a harness across her back, as well as a magical firearm in a thigh holster. She either expected trouble or always came prepared to defend the coffee shop.

"It must be nice to be a goblin," Nin said.

Gizsla sighed wistfully. If only. She did not know how to pay human taxes, but she would have to pay rent to move into the urban goblin sanctuary. But it would be worth it. She wouldn't have to worry about humans forcibly clearing out goblin encampments, theft from gangs or rival clans, or poor weather when the rains grew bad. The sanctuary would be a much better place for her children, and Gizsla would have an opportunity to learn from the founder, Work Leader Tinja, who thrived in the human world despite her green skin.

Nin hustled off to clean up spilled coffee at one table and collect empty mugs from another.

Another mixed-blood woman worked behind the counter, and a quarter-dwarf man was carefully wiping smears from display cases holding enchanted decorations, but Nin had to handle the busy room by herself. She looked frazzled. Matti and Sarrlevi's babies started crying, people kept asking Nin questions, and a human male—how had he seen through the enchantments that hid the Coffee Dragon from those without magical blood?—kept inviting her to join him at his table.

Nin held up a finger, promising him, "Soon."

Gizsla bit her lip. Nin needed help. She needed a capable and hard-working goblin employee. This was the opportunity Gizsla had been waiting for.

With her arms full, Nin almost ran her over when Gizsla approached. Exasperation flashed in her dark eyes before she smoothed her face and smiled. "Yes, may I help you?"

"I'm a very hard worker, and I am seeking employment," Gizsla said. "Do you need assistance?"

Nin's lips pressed together. "I am short-staffed because my *last* goblin employee pickpocketed patrons, spent half his time gaming with the customers, and stole the paper-towel dispenser for a project before fleeing back to his home world because a justice enforcer came seeking him."

Gizsla digested the excess information, then nodded. "So you *do* need assistance."

"Not from a goblin."

Gizsla nodded, having expected this—few of the taller races respected goblins, so they had to fight harder than most to earn positions in society. As she was about to offer her first argument about why she should be hired, a *thunk* sounded.

Another oversized die hurtled down the stairs, ricocheting off the wall, and bouncing onto a table and into a mug held by a shifter. Even though he was in human form, he shoved back his chair and roared, like the bear he could turn into. Slamming his cup down on the table, he faced the stairs, where the same goblin as before peered around the corner.

"I will rip your head off and use your bloody hair to polish the floorboards." The shifter was only two steps from the stairs when Nin, moving surprisingly quickly for an almost-mundane human, stepped in front of him with her hands raised.

"No ripping and polishing over the holidays, please." She plastered a smile to her face and pointed at his mug. "May I get you a refill? Complimentary, of course."

The shifter bared his teeth.

Nin faced him down and kept smiling. Meanwhile, the goblin on the stairs called, "Three points," up to the loft before disappearing. A cheer floated down from above.

"I will include a cookie," Nin said. "Or one of Chef Arwen's *meaties*."

"The kind with cranberries," the bear shifter said.

"Naturally." Still smiling, though it looked painful, Nin took his cup.

She almost tripped over Gizsla, who'd ensured she would be in Nin's path.

"You need assistance badly," Gizsla said.

"Not from goblins."

"As I said, I am hard-working with children to care for. I'm not like those immature goofspheres that only play games."

Nin mouthed, "Goofspheres," and Gizsla feared she had gotten the human term wrong.

"Nin," the man in the D&D T-shirt said, "maybe you could give her a trial day. You *could* use some help." He smiled lopsidedly. "Especially since you won't let me assist you, even though it would be a chance for us to work side-by-side and spend time together on the holiday. Romantically."

"You did not find it romantic when I let you wash dishes on Thanksgiving."

"That's because you were supposed to do the chore with me, you washing and me drying. I had it all worked out until your espresso machine broke down."

"I am sorry, Thad. Running a thriving but chaotic coffee shop is not romantic."

He looked wistfully at her and then even more wistfully at Gizsla.

Gizsla raised her eyebrows as Nin turned a more thoughtful gaze on her.

"You have experience?" Nin asked.

"I have been cleaning up after goblins for my entire life. And, as I said, I have children."

"That *is* the kind of experience that is useful here. Much more so than that of a software engineer."

"I heard that," the man said dryly.

"There is a Christmas story about three gifts delivered by wise men," Nin said. "If you can successfully deliver three gifts to the Coffee Dragon, I will hire you on a probationary period."

Gizsla nodded eagerly, though she couldn't imagine what kinds of *gifts* one would give to a building. Something better than having its floorboards washed with blood from a decapitated head, presumably.

"Goblins are handy and good at making gifts," Gizsla offered.

Nin rolled her eyes. "I do not want anything made out of recycled bathroom fixtures—especially *our* bathroom fixtures." She waved toward a hallway in the back. "Consider these to be more *tasks*. If you can complete them today, I will give you a job. If you are successful, it will indicate you are the type of employee we need."

Though slightly disappointed that reconstituting bathroom fixtures wasn't a project being offered, Gizsla nodded again. "I'm ready. I must earn five hundred Earth dollars."

"First, find a way to entertain Matti's babies so they don't cry tonight at the holiday party." Nin pointed to where Sarrlevi was cooing at the twins in an attempt to appease them. Matti had finished enchanting the tree—it now appeared to have snow on the boughs, and it glowed green—and leaned in close as they discussed whether someone needed to be changed and if the

Coffee Dragon's recently maimed bathroom fixtures had been repaired.

Gizsla scratched her jaw. She knew many goblin songs and nursery rhymes that had occasionally delighted her children when they'd been babies, but would those unique twins—her senses told her they were one-quarter human, one-quarter dwarven, and half-elven—be entertained by such?

"Second," Nin continued, "you will find a way to put a smile on Lord Zavryd's face. He has been complaining that human holidays are ridiculous, due to the lack of races and duels, and is also peeved because Sarrlevi is too busy with his fatherhood duties to go on a quest with him this year."

"A... smile?"

Would Gizsla have to *approach* the dragon for that? Even in his human form, the aloof Zavryd, with his arms folded across the chest of his black elven robe as he frowned around the shop, looked anything but approachable. Even a dragon in a good mood could kill a goblin with a flick of his talons.

"Yes," Nin said.

Gizsla had expected to clean up messes and deliver beverages to patrons, not have to make dragons—or babies—smile.

"And finally," Nin said, "my customers dearly need you to convince the goblins in the loft to stop hurling dice down here in an attempt to get them to land in people's drinks."

"Hear, hear," a half-orc at a nearby table muttered.

Though daunted by the first two tasks, Gizsla might be the ideal person to accomplish the third. She'd been putting rowdy young goblins in line since before she'd become a mother herself. Those fools in the loft might be older than *most* kids that needed to be disciplined, but she was accustomed to goblin males taking a while to mature. A *long* while.

"If I can do those things, I can have a job?" Gizsla asked. "I'm saving money to be able to move my family into the urban goblin sanctuary in Green Lake. It is much safer than living in the park."

"A worthy goal, but you might not want to mention it to Sarrlevi or Zavryd," Nin said. "They live on that street and already feel that house is overly populated by goblins."

Gizla had heard the sanctuary had powerful and dangerous neighbors, but she didn't mind. If anything, having such beings nearby ought to deter trouble.

"I'll start right now," Gizsla said.

While Nin refilled the bear shifter's mug with coffee, Gizsla headed for the Christmas tree where Sarrlevi remained with one baby. Matti had taken the other to the bathroom, a place Gizsla had learned was for relieving oneself. Strange that humans—and so many of the coffee shop patrons—did not use bushes outdoors. Would there be bathrooms at the urban goblin sanctuary? If so, Gizsla might have to teach her children to use the ceramic water-filled bowls, as humans did. Given how high they were, that would be a challenge, but Gizsla knew how to deal with challenges.

The baby in Sarrlevi's hands started crying again as Gizsla approached.

"Greetings, Lord Elf. I am Gizsla, a future employee here."

"I am uninterested in being served." For a male holding a squirming baby, the elf was as aloof as the dragon.

"Your child may wish something. Does she like goblin singing?"

"She's never *heard* goblin singing. Only cackling from the dice-hurling maniacs in the loft."

"Perhaps I could offer her a song?"

The baby lifted a grasping hand toward tree branches draped with silver tinsel and ornaments, many shaped like dragons.

"I believe our children are distressed by the hordes of people and sounds and smells in here," Sarrlevi said. "I would not stay, but Matti has promised to enchant people's gifts if requested, and she has also been invited to the human holiday party tonight. I am standing adjacent to this lone tree, in case the scent of pine appeals to our half-elven babies, but it's possible they're disturbed because they can detect that the tree has been slain for this festival."

Gizsla didn't think the babies were old enough to detect their own toes, but she smiled. "For elves, slain trees are most distressing."

"Yes. As are noisy and crowded establishments in cities built on the ground." The way Sarrlevi looked around suggested he was at least as distressed by his environment as the babies. The kid looked like she wanted one of the dragon ornaments. Like the rest of the tree, it was glowing green.

When it didn't float off the branches and into her grasp, the baby cried again.

"Does she need a change too?" Matti asked, returning to Sarrlevi's side, the second baby in her arms.

"I do not smell evidence of that," he said.

"Your elven nose is keen."

"All of my senses are keen. It is what attracted you to me."

"Yeah, the first time I met you, after you slew werewolves in my backyard, that's all I could think about. How hot your nose was."

"You thought *many* parts of me were an above-average temperature," Sarrlevi said smugly. Their eyes glinted as they flirted, and they might have kissed, but the baby let out another bawl.

"This is probably because they're starting to teethe," Matti said. "I forgot to bring the rings for them to chew on."

"May I try to help?" Gizsla hopped onto a table and grabbed the closest dragon ornament.

Sarrlevi lifted a hand, as if she might represent a threat, but Matti rested her own hand on his arm and smiled at Gizsla. "Go ahead."

She glanced toward Nin. Maybe she'd heard about the three tasks.

Gizsla dangled the dragon ornament above the baby. The grasping fingers stretched for it, grabbed it, and lowered it to chew on. Matti reached over to extract it, but the baby threw the ornament first. It sailed over Gizsla's head and landed on the floor, which prompted more crying.

"Considering our children have one-quarter dwarven blood, they can be a touch brutish," Sarrlevi said.

"Don't forget the human blood," Matti said. "It lends brute tendencies too."

"I *have* observed that in the native species on this world."

"Maybe she thought it was a cookie." Gizsla debated what else the baby might like.

"A child of yours would be more delighted by a piece of cheese, would she not?" Sarrlevi smiled at Matti.

"Equally delighted, maybe."

"Can she have hard foods?" Gizsla didn't know how old the child was—six months, perhaps?—or when human—or elven or dwarven—babies were old enough to consume more than milk.

"We've just started giving them a few things," Matti said, "mostly because they were gnawing on their crib rails."

Another cry sounded, this one echoed by the twin.

"Perhaps I will take them outside to walk among *living* trees," Sarrlevi said.

Gizsla held up a finger, then ran to the coffee counter, where numerous snacks could be purchased. She selected two individually wrapped slices of cheddar cheese.

"I'll pay for this once I'm hired," she promised the barista.

That prompted a scowl and a long look at Nin. Nin was watching Gizsla, her shoulder to the Ruin Bringer's elbow as they discussed who knew what, and waved her fingers at the barista.

Seeing that as permission to take the cheese, Gizsla found a plastic knife. A crude implement for what she had in mind, but she'd carved food into shapes to entertain her children when they'd been young, and she managed to make something dragon-like if not entirely accurate. Once she had carved both slices of cheese, Gizsla rushed back to Sarrlevi and Matti, not wanting them to leave before she could complete the first item on her quest.

"Is that a duck?" Matti eyed the shaped cheese.

"I believe a horned *tragraknorith*," Sarrlevi said.

"They're dragons." Gizsla climbed on the table again and held them above the fussy babies. They stopped crying long enough for their eyes to focus on the cheese. "Much tastier than ornaments, I'm certain."

"It's a decent cheddar," Matti said. "I insisted on quality when Nin was ordering."

"Inferior to *dokdok* cheese," Sarrlevi said.

"Most things are."

Matti wriggled her fingers, a few tendrils of magic wrapping around the cheese shapes, and they started glowing green, like the ornaments on the tree. The cheese also grew harder. Maybe the babies weren't ready to gnaw down chunks of cheddar yet, so Matti wanted them to be more like the teething rings she'd forgotten.

"I don't think that's going to..." Sarrlevi started to say, but both babies cooed and waved their fingers at the gifts, and he trailed off.

Gizsla lowered the cheese dragons for them. When they went into the babies' mouths, the cooing turned into contented sucking sounds.

"I guess we should have tried that sooner," Matti said sheepishly. "Cheese is even better than teething rings."

"I will acquire *dokdok* cheese soon."

"And shape it into a dragon?" Matti patted Gizsla on the shoulder.

"Those are clearly horned *tragraknoriths*," Sarrlevi said.

"Or ducks."

They shared smiles.

Gizsla didn't care if her carving wasn't that accurate. The babies had stopped crying. She looked toward Nin to make sure she'd seen and counted this as a task completed.

Nin, whose arms were full of empty dishes again, met her gaze and nodded back at her.

The Ruin Bringer, who must have heard about the quest, held up two fingers as she smirked toward Lord Zavryd. Why did Gizsla have a feeling she and many Coffee Dragon employees had previously tried to find a beverage that would suit his tastes?

Not to be deterred, Gizsla marched past his table, out the front door, and up to the food truck. Arwen was distributing cookies while Starblade loomed at her side, ready to incinerate any disrespectful patrons. Many of those who'd rushed outside when Gizsla had announced the fresh cookies had already been served, so she didn't have to wait long to reach the front of the line.

"I would like two *meaties*, please," she stated.

Arwen used tongs to slip flat hunks of pulverized and reformed meat into a bag. "That'll be four dollars."

Gizsla had already been reaching for them when she heard the amount. Of course, money would be required. And Nin wasn't in sight to nod that Gizsla was on a mission and would pay Arwen back.

"The cookies earlier were free samples," Arwen added, "but quality ingredients are pricy so I have to charge as a rule."

"They are for a drink for Lord Zavryd."

"I charge dragons too," Arwen said.

"*And* half-dragons," Starblade murmured.

"Yes, but you can pay in massages." Arwen tapped his shoulder.

"I am on a quest to seek employment at the Coffee Dragon,"

Gizsla said. "Should I be hired, I will have the funds to pay you back."

"What if you're not hired?" Arwen asked.

"I could give you a *goblin* massage."

"What does that involve?"

"More squeezing and groping than the human version, I believe, but no human has ever massaged me, so I'm not positive."

Arwen's lips rippled with what might have been distaste. She handed the bag to Gizsla. "Take them."

"Thank you." Gizsla hurried inside and grabbed a chair so that she could stand on it to see over the counter to the barista's work area. She pointed at a blender. "May I borrow that to make a drink for a dragon?"

The barista glanced at Nin, who nodded again. By now, a number of people were watching Gizsla's quest.

Though she felt self-conscious, she took the blender, delved into a container full of ice, and dumped some of it inside.

"Are you making a smoothie?" the barista asked. "Lord Zavryd won't drink such a thing. He abhors sweets and fruits."

"I've heard that." Gizsla tossed the meaties in after the ice.

That caused more lip rippling from those who watched, those who were mostly human anyway. A couple of the shifters observed with interest when Gizsla pushed the button to blend everything together, the machine crunching and whirring with great enthusiasm.

Before it had completed its task, Gizsla sensed the great aura of Lord Zavryd approaching. Startled, she almost fell off the chair.

His eyes cool, Zavryd flattened a hand to the top of the blender. Though he didn't press a button, magic flowed from him, and the blades stopped spinning.

"Goblin, you and your kind will stop the incessant noise you constantly make in this peaceful drinking establishment."

"I..." With the powerful aura of the dragon so close, fear

washed Gizsla's words from her mouth—every thought from her brain—and she struggled to respond.

"Val," Nin said, "I think your dragon broke my blender. There is smoke coming out the back."

"Sorry." The Ruin Bringer fished in her pocket, pulled out a twenty-dollar bill, and handed it to Nin.

"It is a Cuisinart. That will barely cover the lid."

The Ruin Bringer gave her a flat look and produced two more twenties.

"Do not forget about the rampant inflation that has been afflicting this nation of late."

After sighing, the Ruin Bringer handed the rest of her money to Nin. "Zav, don't be a bully, please."

"The goblin *plague* infesting this place is intolerable. Not ten minutes ago, one of their dice would have pelted me in the head had I not acted to protect myself."

"You incinerated it and the clothes off the goblin responsible," the Ruin Bringer said. "They've lost enough."

"They never learn." Zavryd's baleful gaze returned to Gizsla.

She wanted to throw her hands up and proclaim her innocence. Instead, remembering her mission, she gently took the blender from Zavryd, removed the lid, grabbed a mug, and poured a serving of the icy meat-colored concoction.

"I may throw up," the barista said, a hand to her stomach.

Zavryd's nostrils twitched.

"An offering for you, noble dragon." Gizsla bowed her head as she held out the mug toward him.

"Hmm." After eyeing her suspiciously for a moment, Zavryd took the mug and sniffed it. "Goblins and other lesser species *should* make offerings to dragons."

"Of course," Gizsla said, keeping her head down.

"Do not look in my direction when you say such things, dragon," Sarrlevi said from across the room.

"I merely wished to ensure you were observing what *proper* behavior is for a lesser species."

"I know you are not insinuating that an elf and a goblin are *similar*."

"When it comes to how they should serve dragons, they are."

"You are pompous and odious."

"Your insults may prompt me to challenge you to a duel." After sniffing the meatie smoothie again, Zavryd took a sip. And then a guzzle that drained half the mug. "Ah, yes. Finally, this establishment offers a beverage suitable to the dragon palate." With his eyelids drooping, Zavryd walked to the Ruin Bringer and linked arms with her. "Come, my mate. Let us celebrate this holiday in the nest."

"What about the party tonight?" the Ruin Bringer asked in amusement.

"We will have our *own* party." Zavryd smiled and winked at Val before leading her out the door.

Gizsla wiped sweat from her brow—having a dragon that close was terribly unnerving—and headed for the Christmas tree. She had one more task to complete.

Not one but *two* dice clattered down the stairs, one hitting a troll in the leg and one bouncing off one of the display cases the quarter-dwarf was cleaning. Fortunately, the magical glass wasn't damaged by the projectile.

"Zero points," the goblin referee called up to the loft.

The troll who'd been struck roared in irritation.

"Possibly negative points," the goblin corrected.

Another roar followed, and the troll grabbed his club.

"*Definitely* negative points." The goblin squeaked and disappeared from view.

Nin hurried to intercept the troll. "Why don't I get you a free drink?"

He growled, but his shaggy white brows perked at the words.

Nin held up a finger toward the barista. Meanwhile, Gizsla removed tinsel draped on the Christmas tree, finding enough of the material to braid and shape into a basket. Since Matti, who'd recently demonstrated her enchanting ability, was nearby, Gizsla asked for a favor. She was happy to help, and the haughty Sarrlevi even contributed some of his power.

After delivering a drink to the surly troll, Nin came over to see what Gizsla was doing. "This is about the time I go upstairs to yell at the goblins and tell them to behave, but if you have a plan... you might know better how to deal with your kind."

"I know *well* how to deal with my kind." Gizsla smiled and held up the basket she'd woven.

Nin eyed it dubiously.

Gizsla nodded confidently. "This will only take a moment, and then you will wish to employ me."

Nin looked to where Zavryd had been sitting and toward Matti and Sarrlevi's babies who were happily sucking on their cheese-flavored teething tools. "Carry on."

With the slightly enchanted tinsel basket in hand, Gizsla marched up the stairs toward the noisy goblins. Nin and several curious patrons trekked up after her.

Gizsla had never been in the loft, but she had an idea about what to expect and wasn't surprised. Two dozen goblins were split between gaming tables and couches and chairs in front of a television. The loft was covered in gizmos and contraptions that included everything from miniature catapults—those were probably how the goblins launched their dice—to an egg-shaped chair rolling around with an occupant inside to toy vehicles made from recycled traffic signs. What had once been a robotic vacuum had been dissected for parts, and the housing was upside-down and holding a pile of potato chips. There were coffee cups everywhere.

"I *just* cleaned up here," Nin muttered.

The goblins froze when she, Gizsla, and the other customers

appeared. Several had been in the act of loading the catapult, but they tucked their dice-filled hands behind their backs and smiled innocently. A goblin with a chalkboard on a stand flipped it over, so the score being tallied wasn't visible.

"A female," one whispered, nudging another and looking at Gizsla.

"She's pretty."

"They so rarely come up here."

"Because you play simple goblin games," Gizsla said, deciding to be flattered by their interest, though she didn't see any likely providers in the lot. "If you played a sophisticated elven game that showed off your more attractive abilities, then more females might seek you out."

"Seek *us* out?" One with a squeaky voice touched his chest. He lowered his voice. "That's never happened."

"Because you're a buffoon," another said.

"What *elven* games are you speaking about?" the chalkboard goblin asked. "We are too short for their sports. And tree climbing."

"I refer to a game that would prove your magical aptitude and *smarts*." Gizsla touched her temple, then walked to one of the tables and rested the tinsel basket in the center. "You must unravel this and free all the strands of tinsel using only your minds."

"What?" one blurted. "No tools?"

"The tool of your mind," Gizsla said. "As an elf would use."

"But we have wrenches!"

"And catapults." One goblin squinted at the tinsel basket as if he might put it in the siege engine and hurl it at the closest wall to unravel it.

"Are you afraid to use mental magic?" Gizsla asked. "Are you... incapable of performing in such a manner?"

She gave the one who'd called her pretty a considering look, hoping he would want to play this new game if she reminded him that female attention might result. Of course, Gizsla couldn't promise that female goblins would flock to them if they unraveled tinsel with their minds, but it might keep the rowdy gamers quiet for a couple of hours, and the enchantment Matti had put on the basket would ensure it wasn't an easy task—even if they cheated and used tools.

"I'm very capable!"

"We're all capable."

"We will try it, but we must have more coffee to fuel our brains."

"Oh, yes. More coffee."

Several fistfuls of dollars—not singles or fives but twenties—were thrust toward Nin. She accepted them and took orders.

"You see why I've struggled to kick them out," Nin murmured as they headed downstairs, leaving the curious patrons to watch the goblins quietly staring at the tinsel basket. "They buy a *lot* of coffee. But it stimulates them and makes them insane. I thought secluding them in the loft would help, but it hasn't been as useful as you'd..." Nin trailed off when they reached the bottom of the stairs.

Every patron in the coffee shop was looking at them. Not only at them but up the stairs, though nobody else had followed them down. Maybe they were noticing the lack of dice flying down from above.

"This is our new employee, Gizsla," Nin announced.

That earned a few grunts, but mostly, people kept looking up the stairs.

"She has convinced the goblins to be quiet and put away their dice for a while," Nin added.

That brought a much more enthusiastic response, a cheer that bounced off the walls even more loudly than goblin dice. Several people came over to thank Gizsla, and some even dug out money and handed it to her. As wrinkled dollars and fives and even tens were stuffed into her grip, Gizsla looked at Nin in confusion.

If this kept up, she would soon have enough to move herself and her children into the urban goblin sanctuary, but... "Why are they giving me money?"

"I think those are tips."

"I haven't served your patrons yet."

Nin patted her on the shoulder. "Yes, you have."

THE END

AFTERWORD

Thank you for reading my Tracking Trouble series. I hope you enjoyed the adventures! If you have time to leave reviews for any of the books, I would appreciate it.

If you want to get a note when I release new books and run sales, please sign up for my newsletter:

https://lindsayburoker.com/book-news/

For updates between projects, you can find me on Facebook and Twitter:

- https://www.facebook.com/LindsayBuroker/
- https://twitter.com/GoblinWriter

Happy reading!

Made in United States
Troutdale, OR
04/12/2024

19128775R00235